I0639836

Black Forest Protocol

Clifton Wilcox

Fredericksburg, Virginia

Print ISBN: 978-1-969770-09-8

EBook ISBN: 978-1-969770-10-4

Hardback ISBN: 978-1-969770-11-1

Published by Windward Publishing LLC., Fredericksburg, Virginia.

The characters and events in this book are fictitious. Any similarity to real persons, living or dead, is coincidental and not intended by the author.

Library of Congress Cataloging in Publication Data

Wilcox, Clifton

Black Forest Protocol

Windward Publishing, LLC

2026

Dedication

For those who search for UFOs—because
they understand the universe is not
obligated to explain itself.

Contents

Books by Clifton Wilcox

Non-Fiction

Scape Goat: Targeted for Blame

Groupthink: An Impediment to Success

Bias: The Unconscious Deceiver

Witch-hunt: The Assignment of Blame

The Fall of the Kingdom of Northumbria

Witch-hunt: The Class of Cultures

Road to War: The Quest for a New World Order

Envy: A Deeper Shade of Green

The Rise of the Nazi SS

The Horrible Void Between the Trenches

Fiction

Cool's Last Stand

Where Despair Comes to Play

The Monuments Must Bleed

Keeper of the Fallen Ages

I, Monster

Harvest of Eyes

The Case Against Jasper

1

Prologue

Germany, 1936 – Black Forest, Midnight

The trees were the first to scream.

Not in any way the human ear was built to hear. It was deeper than sound—an atmospheric pressure drop, a shudder through ancient bark and root. The forest, which had spent countless ages listening, recoiled all at once. Owls choked on their cries. Wolves slunk backward into shadow. The canopy quivered, bracing against a weight not yet present.

Then the light arrived.

A jagged, searing blue-white, it split the clouds with the precision of a god making a terrible mistake. And from the wound it left in the sky came the thing: a metallic sphere, not falling but rejecting gravity altogether. It moved like a betrayal of physics, angry at its exile from the stars, and when it struck the Earth, it did so like a god cast from his throne.

The world paused. A minute passed without breath.

And then the sound—an echo, not natural, not holy. It howled through the valley, mechanical and mournful, vibrating inside bones rather than ears. In Obertal, the nearby hamlet, doors flew open. People staggered from their beds, clutching their children and their crosses. Some whispered to saints. Others called on things older than scripture—gods of root and rock, of shadow and mischief. It didn't matter what they believed. Every one of them knew something had crossed into their world that didn't belong.

By dawn, the forest was cordoned off.

SS stormtroopers encircled the crash site, rifles gleaming, eyes hard. Radios crackled with cold commands. Black aircraft passed overhead, unmarked and unscheduled. The villagers were told it was a Luftwaffe training mishap—confidential, patriotic, potentially explosive. Their silence was mandatory. For the Fatherland.

But deep beneath the trees, two figures still breathed—barely. Their bodies shimmered with impossible geometry, like reflections caught mid-collapse. Their skin rippled like liquid chrome, their eyeless faces turned outward, filled with knowing that cut straight to the soul. They hadn't come to conquer. They hadn't come to fight. They were pilgrims.

The Reich, however, had no use for pilgrims.

Ernst Falk stood on the rim of the crater, the stink of scorched pine and metal filling his chest. Something stirred behind his eyes, a mechanical click he couldn't explain, like a door inside him had just opened.

"We are not alone," he whispered. Beside him, Goebbels let out a thin, reptilian smile. "No, Herr Falk. But soon… we will be."

Behind them, the ship hissed and glowed, its hull throbbing with something close to pain. It had spoken in symbols of peace. But the Nazis were fluent in fear.

And the forest would never stop remembering.

Chapter 1

The Anomaly in the Black Forest

Germany entered 1936 under a sky that felt too heavy, too quiet. There was something dense in the air—a tension that didn't quite scream but pressed in from all sides. Official optimism was everywhere, pasted on posters and shouted in squares, but it rang hollow, like the echo of a lie repeated too often. Beneath that, unspoken and inescapable, was the fear.

SS Officer Ernst Falk felt it more than most. He wasn't the kind to throw himself into ideology. He was more observer than zealot— bookish, precise, never quite at home in the heat of Berlin's rallies. His posting near the Black Forest had been a reprieve, a quiet assignment in a place known for old trees and older stories. Here, the Reich's noise fell to whispers.

The forest loomed in contrast. It was beautiful, yes—but in a way that made you feel small. Towering pines knotted their limbs overhead like ancient gods in prayer, and when the light broke through, it did so reluctantly, dappled in gold and ghost. Most nights, Falk welcomed the hush. It was contemplative. Soothing.

But not tonight.

Tonight, the silence didn't invite thought. It warned. It was too complete, too absolute. A kind of stillness that made your spine stiffen without knowing why. The forest wasn't resting. It was bracing.

In recent weeks, he'd started noticing things: glades where no birds sang, air that felt charged like the moment before a storm, a strange metallic scent on the wind—like ozone fused with something damp and buried. Small signs, perhaps. But together, they whispered of something deeply out of place. Something waiting.

Falk's thoughts kept drifting back to Berlin: the forced smiles, the watched conversations, the fevered speeches that scraped all the nuance from human thought. The Reich's ideology didn't speak to him—it barked. It simplified the world into enemies and followers, and Falk, a man of thought, found himself increasingly hollowed out by it. The Black Forest had been his escape. But lately, even the trees seemed uneasy.

He stood outside a modest wooden outpost nestled among the pines. The mist was moving in low, curling around the trunks like something alive. No stars. No moon. The dark was full. The kind that made you feel like you were the only thing left breathing. A cold breath pushed through the woods, brushing his collar, carrying the familiar scent of pine—but tainted now, sharpened by something unnatural.

The forest's usual life was gone. No owl. No fox. Not even the whine of a gnat. Falk shifted his weight. Every sense prickled. The world was holding its breath.

Then the sky ruptured.

It wasn't a sound at first. It was a tear. A blinding, burning white light ripped down from above, not flashing but sustaining—burning long and deep, as if a sun had died just above the treetops. The roar followed, deep and grinding, like the planet itself was howling in protest.

Falk stumbled, shielding his eyes, though the light pierced even closed lids. The ground shook underfoot. The outpost behind him moaned like something wounded. It wasn't the sound of a bomb or plane—it was more... raw. Ancient. Like something from the beginning of time had just dropped back into the world.

Then, just as suddenly, the light stopped falling. The roar silenced. The world snapped back to silence—deeper now, like it had been scoured clean. Too precise. Too controlled. It hadn't crashed. It had *arrived*.

Falk's heartbeat thundered. He rose to his feet slowly, hands shaking. He'd seen artillery strikes. He'd watched airships fall from the sky. But nothing—nothing—had prepared him for this.

Whatever it was, it wasn't part of nature. And it wasn't part of any human war.

The forest didn't move. Didn't breathe. It just waited. When dawn finally broke, it did so cautiously, casting a sickly light over the trees. Patrols moved in quickly—grim-faced men who carried rifles and tried not to look afraid. Forestry officials arrived next, their steps hesitant, their eyes scanning the scared trees like they half-expected them to move.

But there was no wreckage.

No wings. No cockpit. No charred fuselage.

Instead, half-buried in the scorched clearing, lay something that didn't fit the world. It was seamless, metallic—but not steel. The sun reflected off it oddly, bending around its curves as if the object refused to be seen directly. It pulsed faintly from within, like a heartbeat. Not mechanical. Alive.

Falk stood at the edge of the crater. The closer he got, the more the air changed—thick, resonant, electric. His teeth buzzed. The trees surrounding the site were warped, bark twisted into impossible spirals. Leaves shimmered with a dull silver sheen. New growths—fungi or something pretending to be fungi—glowed faintly at the base of trunks.

Nothing about this belonged here.

Technicians arrived. Scientists from Berlin. Instruments in hand, eyes wild. They poked and prodded, whispered to each other, scribbled impossible data. Nothing made sense. No tool could pierce the material. It didn't scratch. Didn't dent. It didn't even *sound* when touched.

Falk moved quietly among them, observing. Documenting. His notes filled quickly—diagrams, readings, sensations. It wasn't just the object that disturbed him. It was the reaction. The military buzzed around it like flies around meat, eyes gleaming not with awe but ambition.

This wasn't a discovery. It was a prize.

Secrecy clamped down like a trap. Villagers were warned. Some were never seen again. A perimeter went up, armed and absolute. Inside it, men who once believed themselves the masters of reason stood trembling before something they could not understand. And already, the Reich was imagining how it might bend it to its will.

Falk saw it differently.

He watched the others—scientists dissecting the alien silence like it owed them something, officers barking orders with false confidence. He felt the hum beneath his boots. The distortion in the air. The presence of something that *watched*. This was not an abandoned artifact. It was not inert.

It had come with purpose.

And Ernst Falk, a man of thought caught in a world of zealots, now stood at the edge of something that would make ideologies look like dust.

The forest no longer whispered.

It waited.

Whispers started in the corridors of power—soft at first, tentative, as though speaking the truth aloud might invite it closer. *Es ist nicht von dieser Welt.* It is not of this world. No one said it officially. Not in briefings. Not in reports. But the phrase passed from mouth to mouth, from lab assistant to officer, between cigarette breaks and the clink of glasses in after-hours gatherings. Fear sharpened the edges of the words. Awe gave them weight. It wasn't just a phrase—it was a confession.

The object in the Black Forest wasn't wreckage. It wasn't broken technology or a freak accident. It was proof—of something vast, unknowable, and watching.

Falk felt it before he understood it. The low-frequency hum that poured from the alien shell wasn't steady. It shifted, fluctuated, as though reacting to breath, heartbeat, thought. It wasn't noise—it was a language. One they had no tools to translate. Despite orders to maintain distance, Falk kept drifting toward it, unable to help himself. The object called—not with sound, but with *presence.*

Around the crater, the world unraveled in degrees. Birds no longer returned to their trees. Small animals fled or died strangely—bodies intact but twitching, discolored, as if time itself had stuttered inside them. The ground was warm to the touch. Soil felt charged, like it had swallowed lightning and couldn't quite let it go.

Plants twisted. Ferns curled in spiral patterns nature had never taught them. Saplings darkened to a black so glossy they reflected Falk's face back at him like obsidian mirrors. Mushrooms bloomed where there had been none, glowing with an inner green light, softly pulsing—as if breathing. The forest wasn't dying. It was *changing*.

Falk documented it all with his usual precision. His sketches had grown stranger, more abstract—looping fractals and colorations his notes described as "structurally impossible." Radios filled with static. Compass needles spun in place. Peripheral vision betrayed him—trees shifted when he wasn't looking, shadows blinked where no light should have fallen. It was all subtle, cumulative. Like the forest itself had started dreaming someone else's dream.

He tried to write it clinically. To report only what could be measured, verified. But fear crept in at the edges. This wasn't just technology. It wasn't a new machine or unknown alloy. It might be *alive*. Or worse—conscious.

And if it was… who had sent it?

The murmurs within the SS became harder to ignore. "Anomaly" no longer meant an unexplained object. It meant opportunity. Potential. Power. The Reich's scientists, hungry for glory, whispered about propulsion systems, energy beyond imagination, alloys that laughed at earthly metallurgy. If they could unlock it, harness it, *own* it—the balance of power would shift forever. Not just for Germany. For the species.

But beneath the euphoria ran a colder current. Those who stayed too long near the artifact became withdrawn. Some claimed they heard voices. Others didn't speak at all. The unnatural changes to the forest weren't just mutations—they were signs. Warnings. Tendrils. Something was reaching out.

Falk saw it before the rest. In the faces of scientists who once scoffed at superstition now haunted by quiet dread. In the way they hesitated before touching equipment. In the way they flinched when the hum spiked—though it couldn't be heard by any instrument. They were poking a god with a stick.

The Black Forest was no longer forest. It was threshold.

Colonel Richter delivered the orders personally, his voice unusually flat: "Falk. You are to lead the initial assessment of the anomaly. Determine its nature. Its origin. Secure anything of value. Report only to the Führer's staff. No one else. This is… absolute."

The word echoed in Falk's head long after Richter left.

He selected his team with care—two men from the *Luftfahrtministerium*, Ministry of Aviation, two from the *Waffenamt*, Weapons Office. Specialists in theoretical propulsion, metallurgy, atmospheric science. Men brilliant enough to be useful, but cautious enough not to talk. Falk made sure of it.

They reached the site at dawn. The crater was worse than he remembered—scorched trees twisted into grotesque forms, branches fused into glass-like ropes, sap frozen mid-bleed. The air shimmered. Sunlight refracted in odd directions, bent around corners it shouldn't.

The object sat like it had always been there. Seamless. Alien. Beautiful in the most terrifying way.

Dr. Schmidt, the physicist, tried drilling it. His bit melted on contact. He stepped back without a word, his face white. "It shouldn't exist," he muttered.

Falk said nothing. He reached out—gloved fingers against the hull. It was cold and humming, like a song inside his bones. Not vibrating *against* him. Resonating *with* him.

Samples were collected. Ferns that bled metallic sap. Spores that pulsed with light. Trees that cracked open like eggshells to reveal veins of crystal. Spectral analysis showed impossible readings—substances that didn't register on known tables. Some of it pulsed with energy. Some of it… reacted.

Even the forest seemed to be responding. Shadows deepened. Birds circled, then vanished. The soil grew slick with a black ichor that wasn't sap. Instruments failed. Compasses spun. Radios chattered nonsense in languages no one spoke.

The soldiers noticed. They kept their distance. Held their weapons tight. Whispered prayers when they thought no one listened.

The official story was being crafted—a downed plane, a weapons test gone wrong, a storm. The usual lies. But everyone knew. This wasn't something the world was ready for.

Falk knew his reports would go straight to Himmler. Maybe even Hitler. The implications were enormous. Military power, global dominance, a Reich that reached not just across Europe—but beyond Earth itself.

But Falk wasn't thinking about the Reich anymore.

He was thinking about the hum. The way it felt like breath. The way it followed him even after he stepped away. The way his dreams had changed—visions of a sky torn open, of figures made of light and angles, speaking in thunder. He hadn't slept in three nights.

The forest didn't feel like forest now. It felt like a mouth. And the object? A tongue. Speaking in secrets no one should hear.

He looked at it one last time before the soldiers sealed the perimeter.

The hum grew louder.

And somewhere, deep beneath the roots of the Earth, something listened.

The silence that had settled over the Black Forest was more than just the absence of sound. It was heavy, charged, alive in a way that made the skin prickle and the gut twist. It wasn't peace. It was pause—like the breath the world holds before a scream. For SS Officer Ernst Falk, stationed on the forest's ragged edge, the quiet had become unbearable. Every missing sound—the usual rustle of pine boughs, the soft shuffle of nocturnal life, the murmur of a stream somewhere in the distance—now screamed in their absence. It was as if the forest itself was waiting. Not asleep. Not dead. Waiting.

He felt it in his bones before he could name it.

Falk wasn't given to superstition. He'd always found comfort in structure, in routine, in the quiet logic of observation. That's what had made him a poor fit among the fanatics and firebrands of the SS. He didn't chant slogans. He read old books and listened more than he spoke. When the Party roared, Falk often found himself turned inward, quietly recoiling from the manufactured certainty. But the silence in the forest? This was no invention of politics. This was real.

There was something wrong in the rhythm of the woods.

He'd noticed it days ago. First, the birds—gone from certain groves as if they'd flown south in midsummer. Then the insects—fluttering in odd spirals, crashing into trees, their patterns erratic. He'd heard nothing from the forest's deeper reaches. No owls. No deer. Just the wind, and even that had changed. It blew with a sharpness, an edge. The air smelled of wet stone and rust. And something else. Something dry and metallic, like a spent battery or the inside of a gutted radio. It reminded him of the way the sky smells just before lightning splits it open.

Berlin was heavy with another kind of tension—flags waving, voices raised, boots echoing through courtyards. The fever of ideology gripped the capital like a sickness. Falk had felt it everywhere: in the clenched jaws of civilians, in the eyes that looked away too quickly, in the carefully measured greetings of men who used to speak freely. The forest had always been his reprieve. It was quiet, ancient, indifferent to the hysteria consuming the cities.

But not tonight.

Tonight, even the trees felt alert. Their shapes stood strange and tall in the darkness, their limbs heavy with something unseen. He stood outside his small outpost, the last manned structure before the woods turned wild. His boots sank slightly into the damp moss beneath them. Mist curled low to the ground, rising like breath from a creature sleeping too shallowly.

And then he realized—he could feel the forest, as if it had grown skin.

There was no sound. Not even the chirp of a cricket or the snap of a twig beneath some foraging animal. Just stillness. A vacuum. A space that should've been filled with a hundred natural murmurs— and wasn't.

He scanned the darkness with careful eyes. He'd done this dozens of times—surveyed the woods, listened to its rhythms. But this time felt different. It wasn't a patrol. It was a vigil. Every sense stretched thin. The scent of pine still hung in the air, but underneath it was that strange tang again—ozone, maybe. Or metal. A hint of something scorched, something moving fast through the sky, even though the sky above was black and still.

The stillness was beginning to hurt.

Falk adjusted his collar. A chill crept down his back, though the wind wasn't cold. He didn't shiver from temperature. He shivered from instinct. He knew the weight of danger—even when it didn't wear a face. This wasn't superstition. It was pattern recognition, a thing all soldiers acquire: knowing when something is about to break.

And it would break. Soon.

The quiet wasn't a retreat. It was a precursor.

The year was 1936, and Germany was bracing itself for war— even if no one said it outright. But Falk sensed something deeper unraveling in this forest. Not politics. Not power. Something older. Something waiting beneath the roots. Something not of this world.

The forest had always kept its secrets. Tonight, it was preparing to let one loose.

And Ernst Falk, a man too curious for safety and too skeptical for faith, stood at its edge—watching, listening, waiting.

Chapter 2

Echoes of the Stars

The forest floor was thick with churned mud and broken moss, the ground scared by tire tracks and boot prints. Dampness clung to everything—boots, uniforms, breath. The early morning dew had long since surrendered to the weight of machinery, cables, and the meticulous dismantling of what no one dared name.

Falk stood near the edge of the clearing, boots half-sunk in the earth, staring at the object that had not only fallen into the forest but detonated his understanding of reality. The first wave of shock had passed, but in its place, something more dangerous had taken root—curiosity. Pure, unsatisfied, voracious. He felt it clawing inside him, demanding answers that didn't exist.

This wasn't a discovery. It was a revelation.

And it had landed here—on German soil—without warning, without meaning, without mercy.

Dr. Schmidt worked close to the artifact's hull, bent over his instruments, speaking as if the words themselves might slip away if he didn't get them out fast enough. "Colonel," he called, barely audible over the muffled hum of generators and the distant bark of orders. "The composition is... it's impossible. We've run spectrograph analysis on at least a dozen different sites. None of it matches any known alloy. There are trace elements we've only theorized—never seen, never touched. And isotopes that shouldn't exist. Shouldn't be stable. Yet there they are. And the structure—no seams, no weld lines. No joints at all. It's as if the whole thing was born, not built."

Falk said nothing. He only watched as Schmidt's gloved hand skimmed the surface again, reverent, tentative.

Bauer, hunched over the energy detectors nearby, looked up, his face tight with concentration. His fingers were still stained with that strange, crystallized sap they'd found blooming around the crater. "The readings are still active," he said, quietly. "It's not just lingering radiation or residual heat. It's... cohesive. Like the energy's contained. Almost... breathing. The frequency modulations are irregular—alive, in a way. It doesn't fall within any known spectrum. Some of the bands it's emitting... we don't even have instruments built to read them yet."

Falk knelt beside the artifact. He'd resisted touching it until now. There was something profane about it, sacred even, as though contact might trigger a response neither he nor his men were prepared to face. But now, he lowered his gloved hand and hovered just above the surface—close enough to feel its chill without contact. The material absorbed light in a way he had never seen. It didn't reflect—it swallowed. A soft shimmer played across its shell, not flashy, but alive: shifting between violet, charcoal, and steel blue as if responding to proximity.   The drills hadn't left a scratch. Diamond bits, hardened carbide, plasma torches—nothing worked. Tools had skipped, sparked, or snapped. The thing resisted intrusion like it was defending itself.

Falk exhaled slowly. "It's not just the alloy," he said. "It's the design."

Schmidt looked over, silent now.

"There's no intake. No thrusters. No wings. No control surfaces." Falk ran his eyes across the smooth, curved shell. "It doesn't fly—not the way we understand flight. It doesn't *need* aerodynamics. It's built on rules we haven't learned yet."

He stood, brushing dirt from his knees. "Whatever moved this across the stars—it didn't push or propel. It *bent* something. Folded space. Or time. Or both. The term 'flight' might not even apply."

The object was shaped like a teardrop, but stretched—too perfect, too deliberate to be decorative. Its curves flowed like water but held the precision of geometry. It looked less like it had been *constructed* and more like it had *grown*—as if some distant intelligence had coaxed it into being rather than forged it in heat and hammer.

16

And somehow, even now, it didn't seem still. It watched, even without eyes. Falk took a step back, suddenly aware of the low sound in the clearing—the hum, always the hum, shifting subtly in pitch. Not mechanical. Not even harmonic. Just present.

There was a presence inside it.

And it was still waiting.

The thing lay before them, impossibly still—its shape geometric, but too fluid to feel manufactured. Like something sculpted by time, not hands. A teardrop stretched and elongated, its surface smooth as poured glass, its curves so refined they seemed to shift slightly even when motionless. It was roughly forty meters long, ten at its widest point. A leviathan without seams, without ports, without purpose. And that absence—that silence—was what made it terrifying. It didn't look like a machine. It looked like a question.

Dr. Vogel crouched in the soft churn of mud near the hull, surrounded by warped trees that bore signs of contact—if you could call it that. Their trunks had twisted in on themselves, bark fusing to the hull in grotesque knots, as if drawn toward it. In several places, metal and wood were indistinguishable, the two substances locked in an embrace neither natural nor engineered. Lichen pulsed faintly on the tree bark, casting sickly green light over Vogel's hands.

"The structure of these plants..." His voice was low, almost reverent. "Colonel, it's not radiation. It's something deeper. Their cell structures—altered. The chlorophyll's gone. Replaced by... I don't even know what. A metallic analog, maybe. But the cells themselves are stronger. Far stronger. Almost indestructible." He lifted a sealed vial containing thick, dark fluid. "This sap—watch." He tilted the container toward a portable emitter. The fluid flickered, pulsed. "It reacts to energy inputs. Conducts electricity like copper but with zero resistance. At room temperature. We're looking at ambient superconductivity. If we understood it... it would change everything."

Falk didn't respond immediately. He was staring at the object, still crouched low beside it. The hull shimmered faintly as light slipped over it—more absorbed than reflected. Its surface changed with movement, slipping from black to indigo to dull silver depending on the angle. Every attempt to drill or sample it had failed. Their most advanced tools skittered uselessly across it, like metal scraping on ice.

"It's not just how it's made," Falk said quietly. "It's *why*. There's no engine. No thrusters. No visible means of flight. No seams. No hatches. It doesn't make sense, not with our understanding of motion." He stood and exhaled. "Maybe it doesn't move by pushing through space. Maybe it moves by... folding it."

Nearby, cranes had begun to rise. Massive, skeletal machines built for delicacy, not force—vibration-dampened, grounded with non-conductive rigging. They were meant to probe the object, not pry it open. But even their presence made the clearing feel more fragile. Every cable that dropped, every bolt tightened, carried the weight of a hundred silent hopes—and one creeping dread.

"We need to breach the interior, Colonel," said Major Albrecht, gesturing to seismic readings displayed across a humming terminal. "Our probes show atmospheric pressure inside. Structure. Not solid. Hollow. But... not empty."

Falk glanced toward the object, watching his own reflection warp slightly along the hull. "Then we move carefully. No cutting. No detonations. If there's a door, we'll find it. If there isn't, we wait until it gives us one."

Technicians in sealed suits moved closer with sonic arrays and directed energy scanners. They worked slowly, cautious not to overstep the boundary between curiosity and provocation. As they moved around the object, the hum deepened—barely perceptible but felt rather than heard. The object wasn't passive. It *reacted*.

One technician's voice crackled through the headset: "Colonel... we have something."

Falk turned sharply.

"A section near the forward quadrant—it's responding to the sonic array. It's... opening."

There was no hiss. No mechanical click. No metal scraping metal. The hull simply shimmered, and then part of it... vanished.

Not cut, not broken. Just *gone*—like a thought slipping out of memory. A circular aperture now yawned open, seamless and symmetrical, as if it had always been there.

Falk stared into it.

Light spilled from inside, soft and shadowless. It didn't flicker. It didn't bounce. It simply *was*—a constant, diffused glow that came from everywhere and nowhere. The walls pulsed slightly, not visibly, but with a tension that brushed against the skin like static.

He took a breath. Signaled to his team.

There was no turning back.

Inside, the air was still. The pressure held. The temperature matched the forest outside. Yet everything felt… artificial. Not cold. Not sterile. But *calculated*. The floors blended into walls, which blended into ceilings. Everything curved. Nothing ended. No corners. No edges. Surfaces melted into one another like they were grown, not built. Embedded into the walls were crystalline structures—some faintly glowing, others dark and dormant.

"There's no dust," came Schmidt's voice. "No decay. The air is clean, like it was preserved in a vacuum. And the lighting… it's embedded. It doesn't cast shadows." No visible lights. No fixtures. Just that constant glow. A brightness with no source.

Bauer's Geiger counter was silent. "No radiation. No emissions. But the magnetic field inside… it's not random. It's patterned. Like a circuit. Or maybe even… a brain."

Falk stepped deeper into the chamber, his boots soundless on the spongy floor. He reached out and touched a crystal node embedded in the wall. It was warm. Not warm like sun on stone. Warm like skin. A low vibration ran up his arm, echoing in his chest cavity.

Not hostile.

Just *aware*.

Alcoves lined the interior—indentations in the wall that suggested seats, though they were too smooth, too shallow, and too foreign to suit a human form. He imagined occupants—creatures shaped differently, whose bones curved with the same flowing geometry, whose thoughts interfaced with the vessel directly. No buttons. No levers. No tools. Just intention. This wasn't a cockpit.

It was communion.

Behind him, the others moved cautiously, instruments scanning, documenting. Falk remained near the threshold of another chamber. The curves suggested a hallway, or perhaps a conduit—there were no rooms here. Only transitions.

And then the comm crackled again.

"Colonel," said a voice from outside. "We've found something near the outer debris field. Movement."

Falk froze.

Movement.

He turned and made his way out, retracing his steps down the ramp-like aperture into the broken edge of the forest where debris had fanned out in the crash. The trees here were splintered and half-melted, fragments of the craft embedded like shrapnel in the trunks. The forest floor was damp, disturbed, steaming in places where metal and soil had fused.

And then he saw it.

A shadow that wasn't just a shadow.

Something *within* the debris, curled beneath a fractured section of the hull.

He approached slowly, sidearm drawn but lowered. His steps were deliberate. Trained.

It was alive.

And it was not human.

Falk moved slowly through the wreckage, his boots sinking into churned earth slick with sap and ash. The forest, silent and broken, offered no sound but the soft creak of branches overhead. His eyes stayed fixed on the movement he'd glimpsed—a flicker beneath a collapsed section of the hull.

And then he saw it.

It was smaller than he expected—barely a meter tall, its frame delicate and birdlike, limbs thin as twigs and trembling. The skin, if it could be called that, was glassy and pale blue, almost translucent, laced with veins of silver light that pulsed in sync with some quiet rhythm inside it. Its head was large, too large, with wide black eyes that reflected nothing, swallowing the forest light whole.

It didn't look at him. It curled in on itself, shaking, arms wrapped protectively around its torso. One leg was twisted at an unnatural angle, and through a tear in its tissue, Falk could see crystalline structures fractured like broken glass. A thick, iridescent fluid oozed from the wound—darker than blood, slow-moving, with a sweet, metallic scent that clung to the air.

Falk stopped a few feet away. The creature's eyes snapped open, locking onto his with an intensity that chilled him to the core. It didn't scream. Instead, it let out a soft, warbling chirp—fragile, melodic, not unlike a wounded bird.

"Easy…" Falk said, hands raised, voice low and calm. "I'm not going to hurt you."

The alien flinched. Curled tighter.

Then movement again—just beyond the first.

Another figure emerged, partially obscured by a jagged edge of the shattered hull. This one was taller—four, maybe five feet—and more upright in its posture. Though its skin was the same pale blue, its silver veins pulsed with steadier light. It wasn't uninjured, but it moved with far more control, scanning the scene with intelligent, cautious eyes.

Falk's heart pounded. Survivors. *Not just a ship—passengers.*

The second being stepped forward, letting out a sequence of soft, clicking sounds—strange and musical, but resonant. They didn't just pass through air; they vibrated in Falk's bones. It was language, of some kind. Or maybe instinct. Either way, it was clear: it was trying to understand him.

Falk crouched, still keeping distance. His gaze flicked to the smaller one—their condition was worsening. The glow beneath its skin had started to dim, its breath shallow, irregular. Its chirping slowed to fading notes.

"We need to help it," Falk said, looking toward the second being.

More clicks, sharper now. The larger alien's body tensed, arms poised to shield its companion. Its eyes flitted between Falk, the wounded one, and the sky. The gestures were rapid—urgent, desperate. Not hostile. Protective.

We don't know you. We don't trust you. But this one is dying.

Falk stayed kneeling, never reaching for his weapon. "I understand," he murmured. "You're scared. So am I. But if we do nothing…"

He reached for his pack, slowly, visibly. The larger alien bristled but didn't move. Falk retrieved a small med-kit. Sterile gauze. Basic antiseptics. It wasn't much—but it was something. He held a gauze pad out, not to touch, but to show.

The larger alien studied him. Then looked to its companion. The two exchanged a silent moment—one of those exchanges too brief and too deep to be anything but understanding. The smaller one whimpered again, barely audible.

A nod. Small. Reluctant.

Falk moved in.

He worked quickly but gently, dabbing the fluid from the wound and pressing gauze to the torn tissue. It soaked through instantly, blooming with a color unlike anything he'd seen. The smell intensified—like heated copper and wildflowers. The wounded alien made a soft sound, somewhere between a sigh and a moan, and let its eyes drift closed.

The second alien watched with laser focus. When Falk finished, it leaned in and touched the gauze lightly. Then its own hand. Then the injured one's arm. Soft clicks followed—reassuring sounds, rhythmic, almost like a lullaby.

22

Falk stood slowly. "I can't do more here," he said. "But I have people. They can help."

He gestured through the trees, where the tents and lights of the forward base flickered faintly between the trunks. The second alien followed his motion, visibly unsure.

It paused—then opened a small pouch on its chest. From within, a glow emanated. It held something Falk couldn't identify—organic? Technological? He couldn't tell. It offered the object without hostility. A sign of trust. A plea.

Falk didn't take it. "Not yet," he said softly. "We don't know what it does. I want to help—but I won't risk you or him."

Instead, he motioned again toward the base. "We go. Together."

After a long pause, the alien nodded. It gathered the smaller one into its arms with great care, holding it close. The injured one chirped weakly but didn't resist.

Falk led them through the trees.

When they emerged into the cleared perimeter of the wreckage site, the entire compound froze. Soldiers, scientists, engineers—all stopped. Silence blanketed the field as eyes widened and conversations died in throats.

Falk raised his hands. "Hold your positions," he shouted. "They're survivors. They need medical help."

A ripple of movement. Weapons were not aimed, but they were not lowered either. Dr. Schmidt broke through the crowd first, stunned. "Colonel… are they—"

"They're alive," Falk cut in. "And one of them is dying."

The second alien tightened its grip protectively, its posture shifting, defensive. More soldiers began to move in.

"No sudden moves!" Falk barked. "Stand down!"

Dr. Schmidt raised a hand. "We're here to help," he said, gently. "No harm will come to you."

23

The alien's gaze was sharp, calculating. It looked at Falk. Then back at Schmidt. Then down at its companion.

Another nod.

Falk exhaled. The first barrier had been crossed. Trust, fragile and flickering, had begun.

But elsewhere, darker minds were already stirring.

Within days, the delicate order surrounding the crash site collapsed beneath the weight of a new arrival—one that didn't come with questions, only commands. The soldiers wore the black uniforms of the SS, their helmets glinting beneath the tree line, their eyes hidden behind expressionless visors. They didn't need to speak to assert control. Their presence alone was enough. The scientists, who had first approached the wreckage with reverence and restraint, were quickly silenced by a colder ambition. The SS hadn't come to study. They'd come to claim.

The shift in atmosphere was immediate and suffocating. What had begun as a tentative exploration into the unknown, now reeked of ideology and conquest. The beings from the stars were no longer visitors or survivors—they were specimens, resources, keys to something darker. The quiet murmur of discovery gave way to the bark of orders and the low thrum of authority. And at the center of this sudden transformation stood Professor Otto Rahn.

Rahn was a wiry man with sunken cheeks and eyes that glinted with fanaticism. His name was already infamous among those who whispered of the Ahnenerbe, the branch of the SS obsessed with ancient relics and racial myth. He had searched for the Holy Grail, for lost Aryan bloodlines buried beneath the ruins of fallen civilizations. Now, fate had delivered him something far greater: proof of a higher lifeform, not born of this earth. And he moved through the crash site like a prophet in a cathedral, brushing his fingers along the ship's surface with a perverse kind of awe, as if the metal itself could reveal ancient truths.

His presence cast a long shadow over the work of men like Dr. Schmidt, who had spent hours tending to the surviving alien with a gentleness born from shared vulnerability. Rahn, in contrast, gazed upon the creature not with empathy, but calculation. He saw not a wounded lifeform, but potential. Standing before his black-clad entourage, he gestured toward the second alien—calm, but wary—its large dark eyes scanning the intruders.

"Observe the structure," Rahn intoned, his voice smooth, deliberate. "The delicate bones, the radiant inner systems... the absence of crude musculature. This is not mere life—it is refined life. It may have surpassed the natural course of evolution or perhaps retained something we lost."

To the untrained ear, it sounded clinical. Scientific. But those who listened closely heard something else—an undercurrent of ideology laced through every phrase. He spoke of purity, of elegance, of adaptation. Not just admiration, but hunger. The implication was chilling: what if this alien form could be used to shape the future of humanity? Or worse—of their twisted vision of a "master race"?

The scientists felt the ground shift beneath them. Their questions, once valued, were now brushed aside. Their notes, dismissed as distractions. Rahn's presence didn't just redirect the investigation—it hijacked it. The military, once a neutral arm of order, now followed SS protocols that emphasized control over care, extraction over understanding. The site had become a crucible not of knowledge, but of ideology.

Falk watched this transformation unfold with growing dread. The tentative connection he had begun to forge with the surviving alien was fraying. Its movements had changed. Once curious, it now bristled with unease. It placed itself between its wounded companion and the SS men, its body taut, the glow along its limbs dimming. The chirps and whistles it made had turned sharp, erratic—laced with fear.

Rahn either didn't notice or didn't care. His attention was locked on the creature's hand, still faintly pulsing with internal light. He stepped forward slowly, extending his own pale, trembling hand, fascinated by the contrast.

"Remarkable," he whispered, his voice low and reverent. "This light... this power... It speaks to a destiny we have not yet fulfilled. But we will."

Falk's breath caught. He wasn't watching a man study a lifeform—he was watching a man stake a claim.

He extended his own hand, its skin pallid and blotchy, a stark contrast to the alien's delicate, veined appendage. "Remarkable," Rahn murmured, his voice a sibilant whisper. "The bioluminescence, the inherent energy… it speaks of a biological imperative far beyond our current comprehension. But not beyond our capacity to understand, or indeed, to replicate." He turned to a group of SS technicians, their faces impassive, armed with strange, multi-lensed optical devices and collection apparatuses that were far more invasive than anything the scientific team had initially employed. "Begin immediate biological sampling. Non-invasive where possible, but do not hesitate to employ more… direct methods if necessary. We must understand the source of this vitality, this… *essence*."

The SS technicians set up with disturbing precision. Machines hissed to life, cables unfurled across the forest floor like black veins, and a chemical mist sprayed over the surviving alien's skin. At once, its luminous glow pulsed and flickered, unstable. It let out a staccato burst of clicking sounds—distress, unmistakable. Its wide, glassy eyes darted toward Falk, searching for protection, for something human in the cold faces that now surrounded it.

Falk's fists clenched at his sides. Every instinct in him urged action. But instinct wasn't enough. He was a colonel, yes—but now a colonel under the Reich's brutal machinery. His rank, his authority, meant little against the iron weight of the SS and their unspoken doctrine. He stood helpless as the gentle rhythm of science—of empathy—was drowned out by the clang of metal crates, barking orders, and boots crushing moss beneath polished soles.

Dr. Schmidt stepped forward, barely concealing his anger behind the stiff lines of professionalism. "Professor Rahn," he said, voice taut with urgency, "this level of interference is destabilizing the subject. We've made progress through care. Any further agitation could compromise both specimens."

Rahn didn't even look at him. He waved a hand like brushing off a fly, his attention already on the ship's fractured hull. "Doctor, we are not here to film a pastoral. We are here to extract truth. Fundamental truth. This vessel—this incident—it is not an accident. It is a message. A gift. And we will make sure the Reich benefits from that gift in full."

The wreckage behind him still shimmered faintly, a broken crescent of iridescent metal fused with earth and ash. One section had melted into something like obsidian, eerily smooth to the touch. Rahn ran a gloved hand along its edge, reverent.

"This is more than alloy," he said, his voice dropping to a near whisper. "It resists heat, pressure, force—it survives what should destroy. Just imagine, gentlemen... imagine what this could do for our submarines, our aircraft. It's not just a material. It's a philosophy. A different way of mastering nature."

But Rahn's obsession wasn't limited to engineering. He had brought others with him—linguists, anthropologists, men trained to chart bloodlines and cultures, to parse out "purity" from myth. Now they turned their attention to the aliens' sounds and gestures, not to understand, but to categorize. They weren't listening for meaning. They were hunting for proof—proof that these beings somehow aligned with their ancient fables and dangerous fantasies.

The surviving alien shifted, drawing closer to its wounded companion, its narrow body curved defensively. It released a low hum of clicks that Falk had heard before—soft, rhythmic, almost like a lullaby. Except now, it sounded more like a plea. Not for safety, perhaps, but for mercy.

Rahn didn't notice. Or didn't care. He was already speaking again, louder now, like a man addressing a congregation.

"Hyperborea. Vimana. The celestial builders of ancient lore. These are not myths, Colonel Falk. These are fragments of memory, inherited across generations. What we see here—these beings, this technology—it is the legacy of the Aryan stars. They came before us. And now, they return."

The scientists looked on in silence, some appalled, others simply exhausted. But the SS men, stiff and loyal, listened without blinking. Rahn's voice had weight now, backed by power, by proximity to Himmler himself—who had arrived not long after, pale and ghostlike, eyes empty but listening.

"Professor Rahn," Himmler said, with quiet menace, "your findings suggest…potential. I want everything. Biology, capabilities, weaknesses. If there is a path to integration, we will find it. This may be our key to the next step."

Rahn bowed slightly. "Reichsführer. Their genetics speak for themselves. The absence of degeneracy, the perfection of form—it is a blueprint. We must study it, harvest it. This is evolution without corruption."

Falk felt sick.

Whatever this had once been—a moment of awe, of reaching into the stars—had been mutilated. The aliens weren't survivors anymore. They were test subjects. Tools. A means to justify a fantasy of racial destiny. And worse still, they were beginning to understand that.

The containment area, once quiet with curiosity, now rang with a sterile brutality. The air had turned metallic. The hum of the SS's strange field devices throbbed low and menacing. The injured alien, still glowing weakly, was lifted into one of their units—its figure trembling, though it made no sound. Its companion chirped in protest, reaching after it.

Falk stood back, swallowed by his uniform. There was nothing he could say that would change this. His voice was already lost in the thunder of ambition.

The forest had borne witness to something extraordinary. And now, it would also carry the stain of something unforgivable.

The alien trembled—a subtle, involuntary shiver that ran through its frame as the foreign energy field wrapped tighter around it. Its companion, still uninjured but confined within a similar containment array, didn't struggle. The fear that had once flickered in its deep, liquid eyes had drained into something worse: resignation. It no longer watched with curiosity or alarm. It simply endured.

"Colonel, with all due respect," Dr. Schmidt began, stepping close and speaking just above the rising clatter of SS equipment, "this containment process... we have no precedent for it. The energy signature alone—it's completely unstudied. We can't know what it's doing to them."

Rahn didn't bother looking up. His attention was fixed on the alien's hand, clamped in place beneath a dull violet light. Veins glowed faintly beneath the translucent skin. "Your protest is noted, Doctor," he muttered, "but our priority is understanding. Not coddling." He leaned in slightly, eyes gleaming. "Look at the luminescence. See how it dances beneath the surface? That's not blood as we know it. That's a higher process—energy moving through tissue, not just for life, but for something more. This is what we've come for."

Falk met the creature's gaze. It was brief—but in that quiet, strained glance, there was no mistaking the message. A plea. Not in words, but in presence. Help us. Stop this.

He looked away, guilt twisting deep in his gut. Uniforms and medals didn't mean much now. Orders had consumed everything.

He wasn't a liberator—he was a bystander.

The SS technicians moved methodically, deploying machines no civilian scientist had seen before—steel arms tipped with glowing probes, smooth orbs humming with unseen forces. One device hovered over the injured alien's exposed side. A beam of pulsing blue light struck its wounds, and the tissue flared unnaturally bright. The creature let out a burst of frantic clicking sounds. Pain, clear as any scream. Rahn didn't flinch.

"Regeneration at a cellular level," he said, enraptured. "Colonel, do you see what this means? Limb restoration, battlefield recovery... we could rewrite our very mortality. Their biology holds the key." Nearby, a team in white coats scraped samples from the floor—fragments of alien skin, bits of shattered bone, treated like sacred relics.

29

Behind them, the ship was being torn apart. What had once been a marvel of design—a smooth, organic vessel shaped by knowledge far beyond Earth—was now reduced to components. Devices glowed with impossible patterns. Pulses of light flickered like breath. It didn't matter. The SS 'specialists' boxed it all up. Falk's own team had tried to decipher one small object—a warm, obsidian-like stone that projected a three-dimensional map—but those efforts were over. The artifact had been taken, handed off to men who didn't ask questions—only what could be weaponized.

One of them was Mengele.

Not yet a household name. Not yet infamous. But even now, his eyes were wrong. He stood over the ship's power conduit, directing his men as they extracted a glowing crystalline core. It pulsed like a heart, brilliant and alive. As they pried it free, a wave of energy lashed out. Several SS men flew backward into the containment walls, groaning, limbs splayed.

The alien saw it happen. It let out a sharp, stuttering sequence of clicks and recoiled, body rigid, tendons tensing. It knew something had gone wrong.

"Incredible," Rahn whispered, stepping closer to the damaged core. "Look at this light. It's not just fuel—it's sustenance. Pure energy converted from the cosmos. Think of the possibilities, Colonel. Unlimited flight. Propulsion without burden. Power drawn from the stars themselves."

Falk didn't answer. He watched instead. Watched how the men under Rahn's command didn't analyze—they harvested. They weren't learning from the ship's elegance; they were dismantling it piece by piece, blind to its purpose.

One technician was forcing the obsidian projector to run at full intensity, ignoring the delicate mechanisms inside. The schematic flared once, cracked, then sputtered out entirely. Ruined.

The surviving alien let out a sound—low, guttural, mournful. It was the kind of sound that didn't need translation. Falk felt it vibrate in his chest. A sound of grief. Of finality. Of homesickness for a place now impossibly far away.

But the SS men just took notes. "Distress response," one muttered flatly, scribbling in a logbook. Nothing more.

Rahn was already onto something else. A curved panel of hull shimmered beneath his hand, its surface unnaturally warm, colors shifting like oil on water. "This alloy," he said, reverent, "doesn't exist on Earth. It's stronger than steel, more flexible than carbon fiber. It's born of stars, Colonel. This is how gods build."

Around him, the SS nodded. The civilian scientists, fewer and more silent with each passing hour, began to realize the truth they'd been avoiding.

Dr. Schmidt stepped beside Falk. His voice was low and grim. "They aren't scientists. They're fanatics. They don't want truth. They want justification. Every piece they tear out of this ship, every sample they scrape from those beings—it's all fuel for a fantasy."

"I know," Falk said quietly. "But they outrank us both."

He felt sick. He had seen something extraordinary—something that could have united worlds. Now it was being carved into evidence for an old lie dressed in new power. The aliens weren't envoys. Not anymore. They were prey. Exhibits. Tools in a story written long before they crashed to Earth.

In the far end of the containment zone, SS soldiers powered up cutting torches. They began to slice through the ship's spine, where the hum of its core still vibrated in the earth. The crystalline matrix, once so vibrant, was now cracking beneath sonic drills. Its energy warped, flared, and finally dimmed.

The containment field surrounding the surviving alien flickered violently. It shrank back with a shriek—short, choking, terrified.

And still, the Reich pressed forward.

Rahn stood amid the wreckage like a man before a pulpit, arms spread, eyes fever-bright. "This vessel," he declared, gesturing at the shattered remains of the alien craft, "is a fragment of something far greater. Its builders... they are the rightful heirs of the stars. Their knowledge, their flesh, their brilliance—it all reflects the ancient Aryan essence, diluted and defiled over millennia by lesser bloodlines. But this crash—this miracle—is our turning point. A beginning. The gateway to reclaiming our birthright. The stars will be ours again."

His words rang with the certainty of a fanatic and the fervor of someone desperate to make the cosmos fit his delusion. Falk said nothing. He didn't need to. The truth pressed heavy on his chest.

They had made contact—real contact—with another intelligent species. What should have been a testament to the courage and curiosity of humanity had been hijacked. Twisted. The camp, once buzzing with scientific inquiry, was now a cold machine for ideological exploitation. Black uniforms, taut expressions, barking orders—the Reich had arrived not to understand, but to dominate.

The aliens—crash survivors, not invaders—were prisoners now. Their bodies, their technology, their very identities were being picked apart like trophies. Whatever peace they once carried was being choked beneath boots and steel and unrelenting propaganda.

Falk watched from the margins, a man out of place in his own uniform. One alien—the frail one—rarely moved. The other remained alert, standing as though it understood its role: protector. Rahn called them proof. Falk saw something else: sentience. Suffering. Grace under unbearable pressure.

And doubt.

Rahn's lectures on "cosmic Aryans" had grown more absurd, more hollow, as the days passed. Falk tuned him out. He focused instead on the wounded alien's subtle flinches, the slow pulse of light beneath its skin, the protective stance of its companion—small gestures, full of meaning. Full of life.

Despite the SS oversight, Falk had managed to keep a few artifacts from vanishing into their archives. One was a slate, smooth and dark, that responded to touch. When activated, it unfolded complex diagrams into the air—maps, equations, anatomical studies—no weapons, no military designs. Only exploration. Understanding.

The images humbled him. Here was a species that hadn't conquered its way through the stars but had studied them, mapped them, embraced the unknown. He found himself spending stolen moments poring over those schematics. They offered glimpses into a civilization that prized knowledge over domination.

He began to visit the containment chamber more often, staying back, moving slow, keeping his hands visible. He never spoke loudly. Just a soft greeting, a gesture of peace. He noticed a change. The alien he called the Sentinel no longer turned away. Its eyes met his, no longer with fear, but with something else. Awareness. Watchfulness.

And then, one night, everything shifted.

The SS had thinned—just a few guards remained. Rahn had retired to his quarters, likely scribbling more theories about ancient star-kings. Falk approached the field carefully, breathing in the faint, metallic scent that always lingered in the containment zone. He stood still, then slowly raised his hand, palm out.

"We mean you no harm," he said, quietly. He touched his chest. "Falk."

The Sentinel didn't move for several heartbeats. Then, its eyes met his. Not just passively, but with a kind of piercing focus that made him feel naked in his own mind.

And then came something he could not explain.

It wasn't a voice, not exactly. More like pressure. Like a note held just below hearing. A feeling, more than a sound—grief. Loss. A question: Why?

Falk's breath caught.

He closed his eyes, letting his thoughts quiet. Then he concentrated—on his wonder, his confusion, his wish to help. He sent it out, unsure if the creature would feel it, or even if it could. But something in his gut told him to try.

A second pulse bloomed in his head. Stronger. Sharper. He felt the silence of deep space—the smooth glide of a ship not meant for war, but for travel, for study. The satisfaction of discovery. The comfort of shared purpose. It filled him, achingly beautiful, and then it was gone—replaced by a jarring flash of pain.

Impact.

Alarms, not as sound but as blinding discord inside his chest.

The crash.

Isolation.

And sorrow.

The injured alien stirred. Its light brightened faintly. Falk's eyes darted to it, and he saw the Sentinel shift, just slightly, protectively.

Then another whisper, almost gone: *Help us.*

It wasn't a demand. It wasn't even hope. Just the last thread of trust extended toward a stranger in a uniform.

Falk's heart twisted.

These weren't conquerors. They were explorers. Scientists. Survivors.

And now, prisoners of a system that would destroy them.

Back at camp, the Reich's men were busy reducing genius to rubble. The artifacts, the language, the vessel itself—disassembled without thought for meaning. It wasn't research. It was theft.

And Rahn? He didn't see sentience. He saw mirrors—twisted reflections of his own ideology projected onto alien faces. He would never understand. He didn't want to.

But Falk did.

The Sentinel watched him closely now. When Falk stepped back, its head tilted. Not in fear. In understanding. And maybe, just maybe, in trust.

He couldn't walk away from this.

He had access—restricted, but real. Schematics, data slates, energy readings. There had to be something—medicine, a map, something that could help them heal, escape, continue their mission.

And the guards? They weren't looking for compassion. They were looking for sabotage. Rebellion. Anything loud.

Falk would be quiet.

Deliberate.

Human.

He turned from the containment field, the image of the wounded alien etched into his mind, its fragile glow pulsing like a dying star. But even dying stars radiated light—light that traveled far, across empty distances, to places where it might yet be seen.

The Sentinel seemed to nod.

And Falk understood what he had to become: Not a conqueror. Not a soldier. A bridge. Between silence and understanding. Between horror and hope.

The mission hadn't ended in the crash. It had just begun.

Chapter 3

The Reich's Twisted Vision

The air in Goebbels' office was heavy with stale cigar smoke and the syrupy reek of cologne—a mixture so thick it seemed to settle into the furniture, into the grain of the mahogany desk, into the man himself. He moved like a restless predator, pacing the thickly carpeted floor in measured, silent steps. His sharp eyes flicked from gilded frames to polished busts, searching not for beauty but for affirmation. Every object in the room had been chosen to reflect power, permanence, authority. Now, he searched them for something more: a sign.

The news had come wrapped in layers of secrecy, funneled through the tight sieve of SS bureaucracy and filtered again by Rahn's flowery prose. But Goebbels had a nose for opportunity. He didn't care for the scientific jargon or the military logistics. What interested him—what electrified him—was the story. The potential.

He paused in front of a golden globe, one hand resting on its cold surface. His fingers traced the curve of Europe, then drifted upward, toward the expanse of blue that held the heavens. "The stars," he muttered, almost to himself. "Always they have inspired the faithful. Prophets. Poets. Conquerors."

Now they had delivered something tangible. Something real. A crash. Beings not of this Earth. Technology unlike anything known. Others might see a scientific revolution or a strategic windfall.

Goebbels saw a myth reborn.

The propaganda practically wrote itself. *The Aryans Were Not Alone. Our Cosmic Kin Return. The Celestial Forge of Blood and Spirit.* He could spin the narrative a hundred ways: the visitors weren't truly alien, but estranged cousins—remnants of a pure lineage that had taken to the stars long ago, only now returning to find their kin in the Reich.

The damaged ship? Evidence of a galactic war, perhaps. Their injuries? The wounds of brother-warriors fighting against cosmic corruption. Their crash-landing here, on German soil? Not chance—destiny.

He smiled, a thin, reptilian curve of the lips.

When Rahn arrived, carrying a folder brimming with data and preliminary assessments, his expression was flushed with pride. Goebbels didn't bother to greet him. He didn't even look at the papers. He simply waved the folder away like smoke.

"Put that down," he said flatly. "The specifics can wait."

Rahn blinked. "But Minister, the material composition—"

Goebbels turned, fixing him with a stare that cut through the pretense. "Do you think the German people care about carbon lattices or energy signatures, Rahn? This is not about materials. It's about meaning. What does this event say about us? About the Reich? About who we are?"

Rahn hesitated. He'd come prepared with numbers, not metaphors. "It... confirms what we've long theorized. That the Aryan lineage may have... celestial roots."

Goebbels narrowed his eyes. "Not may. It must. And you, Rahn, will help prove it. You will provide the symbols. The artifacts. The phrases that turn wonder into certainty."

He returned to his globe and spun it slowly. "This... is not a scientific event. It's a revelation. A cosmic echo of our mission. Proof that our struggle here is part of a far older story."

His voice dropped, growing more intimate. "We will not present them as prisoners. That's too crude. No—these are envoys. Survivors of a battle beyond our comprehension, drawn here not by chance, but by blood."

Rahn nodded, slowly catching up to the script. "A narrative of return. Of reunion."

Goebbels turned to him fully now, his voice almost reverent. "Exactly. And when we reveal them—when we reveal *us*—the world will no longer see us as conquerors. They will see us as inheritors."

Outside, Berlin throbbed with its usual symphony of movement—cars rumbling through wide boulevards, boots on stone, the distant call of orders barked in rhythm. But inside the office, there was only the quiet rise of a new mythology.

Goebbels leaned back in his chair, satisfied. The war for Earth was well underway.

But now, the stars were in reach.

And he intended to make them German.

Rahn faltered under Goebbels' gaze, caught between technical truth and political expectation. "Herr Minister… the technology is extraordinary. It's operating on principles we've never seen outside of theory. The propulsion system—"

Goebbels waved the words away like smoke from his cigar. "Yes, yes, propulsion." His eyes narrowed. "But who built it, Rahn? Why now? Why here?"

He leaned forward, voice dropping to a quiet intensity. "This isn't random. They didn't fall from the sky like debris. They came here. To *us*. Because they see what we are. What we're becoming."

Rahn shifted uncomfortably. The aliens hadn't acted like messengers or kin. They had recoiled from the SS's methods, offered no aggression, no allegiance—only silence. Still, Goebbels' certainty was like a wall, pressing in from all sides.

"You think they're Aryan?" Rahn asked, cautiously, the word foreign and strange in the context of beings from another star.

Goebbels chuckled, short and sharp. "Who else could they be?" He stood and turned toward the window, looking out over the clean, controlled symmetry of Berlin. "Show me another race that looks to the heavens and sees a frontier, not a mystery. Others claw at the dirt. We build rockets. They've simply gone further, that's all. This technology—it's not alien. It's inherited."

To him, it was already decided. He'd begun drafting speeches, outlines for broadcasts, posters. He didn't want the public to think of invaders or monsters. He wanted them to see long-lost cousins, the fulfillment of prophecy. Guests—dignified, otherworldly—who had come home.

The interrogation chambers were ordered closed, not out of pity, but because bruises did not fit the story he was constructing. Instead, artists were summoned. They painted visions of slender, glowing beings standing side by side with German engineers beneath golden rays of dawn. The alien ship, reimagined in heroic scale, was framed as a beacon of promise, not conquest.

Cinema scripts followed. Grand, sweeping dramas that reinterpreted Germanic myths through the lens of alien contact. Odin as a celestial ancestor. The Valkyries as voyagers from the stars. The narrative was intoxicating—and useful.

Goebbels knew that facts were never what moved the masses. It was belief. And belief could be shaped.

He turned his attention to the recovered artifacts. Not with the intent of studying them but repurposing them. The alien data slate became a sacred relic, its glowing symbols reimagined as ancient runes. The star charts were no longer maps—they were blueprints of the Aryan diaspora, proof that Earth was merely one colony of a once-great celestial empire.

"We're not stealing," he told his inner circle. "We're reclaiming. This has always been ours—we just didn't know where to look."

The biological diagrams fascinated him most. While Rahn's scientists discussed regenerative properties and genetic markers, Goebbels saw ideology made flesh. The aliens were strong, elegant, efficient—perfect. Their survival of interstellar travel was, to him, proof of biological superiority. And that superiority, he insisted, mirrored the Aryan bloodline.

His message was clear: *This is who we are becoming. This is who we were meant to be.*

Every photograph that left the site was altered. Every description filtered. The injured alien—what some had started to call the "Vulnerable"—was repurposed as a symbol of martyrdom. A tragic traveler, wounded by cosmic conflict, rescued and healed by the guiding hand of the Reich. The other—dubbed the "Sentinel"—was recast as a noble envoy, patiently teaching their German kin the secrets of the stars.

But Goebbels wasn't blind. He knew rumors would spread. Dissent would surface. And so, a strict censorship protocol was enacted. Nothing left the crash site without his approval. Unauthorized speech about the aliens was treated as sabotage.

He even began referring to the incident as the *Celestial Arrival.* The term was seeded into news columns, whispered in party speeches, etched into the growing mythology. And slowly, it took root.

He spoke of a new era—the *Stellar Reich*—a future not confined to borders or continents but stretched across the galaxies. He envisioned not just technological superiority, but ideological transmission: Nazi propaganda broadcast from alien towers, Nazi will etched into the silence between stars.

One motif, pulled from Rahn's more mystical ramblings, took particular hold in Goebbels' imagination: *the cosmic forge.* He used it constantly. In speeches, in posters, in film scripts. A crucible in the heavens, where only the purest elements survived the fire. The Aryan spirit, he declared, had emerged from this forge—refined by celestial struggle, now reawakened through contact with its cosmic ancestors.

He obsessed over the navigational charts recovered from the vessel. To the SS, they were logistical puzzles. To Goebbels, they were destiny. He had them copied and redrawn, stripped of alien context, transformed into symbols of boundless ambition. They would not be maps. They would be banners. Blueprints for German expansion across the stars.

He understood better than anyone that the real power of the alien contact lay not in what it was, but in what it could be made to mean.

The SS were too concerned with dissecting the tangible—cutting into machines, prodding at the wounded. Goebbels didn't need scalpels. He had ink. Cameras. Silence. And stories.

He began referring to himself in private as the *voice of the stars,* the man who had seen the pattern before anyone else. In his mind, the crash had confirmed everything. They had been chosen. Not just to rule the world—but the galaxy.

He would make sure no one questioned it.

Not ever.

For years, Heinrich Himmler had poured men, money, and obsession into the Ahnenerbe—the so-called "Ancestral Heritage" society. Its mission was never about true archaeology or academic rigor. It was about rewriting history, about digging through dust and myth in search of evidence—any evidence—that could justify the twisted foundations of Aryan supremacy. Himmler wasn't content with flags and speeches. He wanted roots, ancient and unshakable. He wanted proof that the Reich's ideology had been written into the bones of the Earth long before Christ, long before Caesar, long before reason.

He'd sent men across the globe to frozen caves, Himalayan temples, and African ruins, all in pursuit of vanished civilizations he was convinced had been Aryan in origin—pale architects of lost wonders, keepers of sacred power. So when word reached him of the crash—an alien craft, fallen from the heavens—he did not see anomaly. He saw confirmation. His years of obsession, of arcane studies and whispered doctrine, had finally borne fruit.

The recovered ship, its impossible geometry and indecipherable systems, didn't frighten him. To Himmler, it looked like evolution—like the fully realized form of what the ancient Aryans had once begun. It wasn't alien at all. It was familiar. His mind, already steeped in the fever-dreams of Max Maria Wiligut and other occult mentors, reached eagerly for patterns, for echoes. He saw in the smooth curves of the vessel and the strange glyphs carved into its surface the sacred scripts of his beloved runes—only more refined, more powerful. Not lost symbols, but ascended ones.

When his men showed him the alien script, he didn't flinch at its foreignness. He smiled. These weren't just markings—they were remnants of a sacred language, proof of a lineage not bound to Earth. A cosmic inheritance.

But it wasn't the technology alone that seized Himmler's imagination. It was the beings themselves.

Goebbels could play his public games, his pageantry of Aryan space myths and cinematic glory. Himmler's vision was darker. Personal. He wanted to touch the truth himself. He wanted to master it.

Reports of the aliens' mental effects fascinated him. There were notes—quiet, clinical—about emotional shifts among the guards. One alien, dubbed the "Vulnerable," seemed capable of softening hostility, stirring empathy in even hardened men. The other—the "Sentinel"—had reportedly established what could only be described as telepathic rapport with a German officer. These weren't accidents. To Himmler, they were signs. Powers. Gifts.

This was what he had always believed the Aryans once wielded: influence of the will, power not just of body or speech, but of thought. A command so complete it bypassed language. He believed these abilities—subtle as they were—were the true mark of superiority. And he intended to harness them.

Control through fear had its limits. Himmler wanted control that required no chains, no guns. He imagined a world where the Reich ruled not through force, but through mental architecture—where the 'lesser' peoples would not rebel because rebellion itself had been bred, or burned, or whispered out of them.

He summoned his most devoted Ahnenerbe scholars, along with select SS occultists—the inner circle, the true believers. Under cover of night, the artifacts were transported to Wewelsburg Castle, his secluded mountain stronghold. The place had already become a shrine to his vision—a stone temple for the SS, where rituals of blood and ancestry played out in candlelight and silence.

There, laid out on thick velvet cloth, were fragments of the craft: slivers of metal that hummed with strange energy, the data slate that lit up like a star map in miniature, and a palm-sized disk that none of the technicians dared to touch twice.

Himmler stood before it all in reverent silence, his gloved hands clasped behind his back, eyes shining with conviction.

"This," he whispered to no one in particular, "is the key. They came once. They will come again. But next time, they will find us waiting."

To him, the message was clear. The Reich was no longer just a movement of men. It was now, in his eyes, a spiritual force written into the cosmos—a chosen vessel for an ancient power lost to time but now returned.

He would see to it that the Reich didn't merely survive this century.

It would become eternal.

Himmler's pale eyes, cold and luminous beneath the vaulted stone ceiling of Wewelsburg, settled on a small metallic orb laid out on black velvet. It was unremarkable in size—no larger than a clenched fist—but during initial handling, it had emitted a low, steady hum that seemed to pulse just beyond hearing.

"This," he said, his voice calm but carrying an eerie weight, "is not just a machine. It's a conduit. A key."

Around him, the Ahnenerbe scientists shifted in silence, their notebooks filled with symbols they barely understood, their conclusions carefully couched in caution. They had no room for error—not with the Reichsführer present. Behind their measured tones and clinical language lay an unspoken terror: the constant awareness of what happened to those who disappointed Himmler.

They reported what they could. The orb emitted faint energy patterns that fluctuated in ways inconsistent with any known field. In preliminary tests, it seemed to respond to proximity—not mechanically, but biologically. One technician had reported a sensation of warmth in his skull. Another, a flicker of memory that wasn't his own. A few whispered about dreams that came after contact—vivid, intrusive, disorienting.

The team's lead researcher spoke cautiously: "We believe it interacts with neural activity in some way. Possibly… it's affecting cognition. It could be a form of… modulation." Himmler's face remained still, but something in his eyes sharpened. He repeated the phrase quietly, almost to himself. "Affecting cognition."

He turned from the orb and gestured toward a nearby table cluttered with translated fragments from the alien data slate—sheets covered in strange symbols, flowing curves, and interwoven diagrams that defied conventional logic. To the scientists, they were schematics. To Himmler, they were something far older.

"These aren't blueprints," he said. "They're rituals. Scripts. Like runes. Instructions for bending what we think of as fixed. They speak to power—not just over matter, but over the mind."

His voice grew softer as he continued, almost reverent. "Our enemies control the masses with crude tools—newspapers, radios, threats. But this… this is purity. The unseen touch. The ability to guide thought without force. A whisper that rewrites belief."

He spoke of consciousness not as a function of the brain, but as a battlefield. The orb, and others like it, weren't merely remnants of alien science—they were weapons of influence, precision tools for shaping human perception. Himmler saw in them the culmination of everything he had believed about will, spirit, and destiny.

He began to fixate on the idea of psionic amplification. In his mind, the aliens weren't just technologically advanced—they were spiritually evolved. Their control of thought, their silent communication, wasn't artificial. It was innate. And he wanted it.

He ordered his inner circle to gather research from every corner of the Ahnenerbe's vast archive: ancient Nordic rituals once practiced by seers and shamans, Tibetan breathing techniques used by monks to achieve altered states, and the darker, more secretive findings confiscated from underground occult lodges the SS had infiltrated. Anything that might explain—or replicate—the psychic abilities he believed these beings embodied.

But it wasn't enough to imitate them. Himmler demanded a version that was, in his words, "purely Aryan." His scientists were instructed not only to study the alien devices but to translate their power into something that aligned with the Reich's ideology. Not alien. Not foreign. A forgotten birthright—now reclaimed.

And as the nights grew longer at Wewelsburg, Himmler spent more and more time in the chamber with the orb, often alone, seated before it in silence. He would sit for hours without moving, his hands resting on the table, his eyes fixed on the object as if willing it to speak.

To those who witnessed it, the sight was unsettling. But to Himmler, it was communion. He believed he wasn't just observing history. He was becoming part of it. He tasked his Ahnenerbe researchers with finding links between the alien technology and pre-Christian Germanic rituals. They scoured ancient texts, looking for any mention of mind-altering substances, sonic frequencies used in ceremonies, or even ritualistic practices that aimed to induce altered states of consciousness. The idea was to demonstrate that this 'new' power was, in fact, a rediscovery of an ancient, inherent Aryan heritage, merely presented in a new, technologically advanced form. The alien craft was to become the catalyst for awakening dormant Aryan psychic potential.

Himmler's obsession extended to the biological aspects of the alien beings. The Ahnenerbe's biological division, under the direction of figures like Otmar von Verschuer, had been diligently studying the captured aliens. Himmler was less interested in their physiology from a medical perspective, and more from a eugenics and psychical potential standpoint. He was convinced that the aliens' advanced mental capabilities were directly linked to their biological makeup, a makeup that he believed, with disturbing certainty, shared a fundamental resonance with the 'ideal' Aryan form.

He ordered detailed comparisons to be made between the alien's genetic structure and the genetic profiles of individuals deemed 'racially pure' within the SS. He envisioned a future where these alien psionic genes could be isolated, understood, and perhaps even integrated into the Aryan bloodline, creating a new breed of leader with inherent mental dominance. This was not merely about military or political control; it was about breeding a new form of human, one that was not only physically superior but psychically unassailable, capable of projecting its will across vast distances and influencing minds with a mere thought.

The psychological manipulation aspect of the alien technology was, to Himmler, the most valuable prize. He believed that the capacity for mind control, if properly harnessed and directed, could eradicate any opposition, ensure absolute loyalty, and create a perfectly ordered society, sculpted according to his vision of racial purity. He imagined a Germany where every citizen's thoughts were aligned with the Führer's will, where the concept of dissent was an alien artifact itself, purged by the subtle, invisible power emanating from the SS's control centers.

He began to foster an aura of mysticism around the entire operation, a carefully cultivated secrecy that hinted at cosmic forces at play. The crash site itself was subjected to elaborate 'purification' rituals, conducted by SS priests trained in obscure Germanic lore. Himmler saw these rituals as essential, believing that the uninitiated presence of 'inferior' energies could contaminate the alien technology, rendering its true purpose inaccessible. He was determined to approach this discovery with the reverence and ritualistic discipline that he believed only the SS, as the spiritual vanguard of the Reich, could provide.

The captured aliens were subjected to a battery of psychological tests, designed not to understand them, but to extract information about their mental faculties and any methods they might employ for influencing others. Himmler's personal interest lay in the 'Sentinel' alien, which was reported to possess a calm, almost detached demeanor, and an ability to communicate without overt verbalization. He saw in this alien a model of the ideal SS officer: disciplined, focused, and radiating an inner authority that compelled obedience. He ordered that the Sentinel be studied intensely, its methods of communication and perceived influence meticulously documented.

Himmler's obsession with the arcane and the occult was not merely a personal eccentricity; it was a foundational element of his ideology and a powerful tool for the SS's internal cohesion and its projection of an almost supernatural authority. The alien technology, with its promise of mind control and its potential connection to ancient powers, represented the ultimate fusion of these two drives. He saw it as the key to unlocking a new era for the Reich, an era where power was not just physical or ideological, but deeply, intrinsically psychic.

He began to conceptualize a new branch within the SS, distinct from the Waffen-SS and the regular police, a branch dedicated to the study and application of psionic and esoteric sciences, drawing directly from the alien discoveries and his own vast collection of occult knowledge. This would be the 'Geistige SS,' the Spiritual SS, tasked with safeguarding and expanding the Reich's psychic dominion. He envisioned these operatives, trained in both advanced technology and ancient mystic arts, as the true inheritors of the Aryan legacy, capable of influencing minds across continents, of projecting the will of the Reich with an invisible, irresistible force.

The SS medical research divisions, always eager to please Himmler, began to explore the possibility of utilizing the alien biological samples for similar ends. They theorized about the creation of serums or genetic enhancements that could grant certain individuals enhanced mental capabilities, creating a cadre of SS operatives with latent psionic abilities. This was a dangerous and ethically abhorrent line of inquiry, but under Himmler's direction, it was pursued with relentless fervor, driven by the belief that the future of the Reich depended on the mastery of these transcendent powers.

The symbols on the alien data slate became a particular focus for Himmler's Ahnenerbe researchers. They were tasked with finding any resonance between these alien glyphs and the ancient Nordic runes, the Ogham script of the Celts, or even Egyptian hieroglyphs, all of which Himmler believed were distorted remnants of a single, primordial Aryan language. Any perceived similarities were amplified, twisted, and presented to Himmler as definitive proof that the alien civilization was, in fact, a distant, highly advanced offshoot of his beloved Aryan lineage. The alien script, therefore, was not merely a language, but a cipher, a key to unlocking the secrets of a shared, cosmic past.

Himmler's ultimate vision was one of absolute, unchallengeable dominion, achieved not through brute force alone, but through the insidious, all-encompassing power of psychological control, augmented by the discoveries unearthed from the fallen craft. He saw the alien technology as a divine gift, a tool placed in the hands of the Aryan master race to fulfill its destiny, not just on Earth, but among the stars. And he, Heinrich Himmler, Reichsführer of the SS, was the chosen instrument to wield this power, to guide the Reich into a new, psychically dominant age, an age where the will of the SS would be the will of the cosmos itself. The secrets of the alien mind were to become the bedrock of a new, terrifying reality, a reality crafted from occult fantasies and amplified by unimaginable technology, all in service of a racially pure, psychically subjugated world.

The sterile, white laboratories of the Ahnenerbe buzzed with an unnatural intensity. Gone were the dimly lit chambers filled with ancient texts and flickering candles; here, under the harsh glare of electric lights, the tangible remnants of the otherworldly were being dissected.

Professor Josef Mengele, his usual surgical precision now amplified by a feverish excitement, oversaw the painstaking analysis of the alien craft's energy core. His team, a collection of the Reich's most brilliant – and often most morally bankrupt – scientists, worked with an almost religious devotion. Himmler's influence permeated every sterile surface, every meticulously documented observation. He wasn't merely a patron; he was a driving force, his unwavering belief in the cosmic significance of the crash lending an apocalyptic urgency to their endeavors.

The initial focus was, predictably, on the immediate military implications. The propulsion system alone was a marvel that defied all known laws of physics. It operated not through combustion or magnetic repulsion, but through some form of contained, exotic matter manipulation, generating a field that warped space-time itself. Engineers struggled to grasp the fundamental principles, their familiar equations proving woefully inadequate. They theorized about the existence of stable wormholes, of localized gravitational lensing, concepts that had previously been confined to the wildest frontiers of theoretical physics. Himmler, however, saw beyond mere speed or maneuverability. He envisioned weapons that could bypass conventional defenses, craft capable of traversing interstellar distances, fulfilling his grandiose pronouncements of a coming Aryan galactic empire. The potential for orbital bombardment, for delivering devastating energy payloads with pinpoint accuracy, was a primary consideration.

But as the analysis delved deeper, as the scientists began to unravel the intricate bio-mechanical interfaces and the subtle energetic signatures emanating from the alien technology, a more sinister application began to take shape in the shadowed corners of Himmler's mind and the laboratories he commanded. The alien craft, it became increasingly clear, was not just a vessel; it was an instrument of sophisticated control. Reports from the captured 'Vulnerable' and 'Sentinel' specimens, detailing their abilities to subtly influence emotional states and communicate telepathically, were no longer viewed as mere biological curiosities. They were blueprints for a new kind of warfare, one waged not on the battlefield, but within the very minds of men.

Mengele, under Himmler's explicit direction, began to prioritize the study of the alien's psionic capabilities. He directed his teams to isolate any biological components or technological interfaces that seemed to correlate with these mental phenomena. Tissue samples from the captured beings, preserved in a chillingly systematic manner, were subjected to intense genetic and neurological analysis. The goal was not to understand alien physiology for its own sake, but to identify the mechanisms through which their psionic abilities operated, with the ultimate aim of replicating them. The notion of a 'psychic weapon,' a means of projecting thought, emotion, and even commands directly into the minds of enemies, was an idea that captivated Himmler with an almost terrifying intensity.

One particular device, a small, crystalline lattice recovered from the 'Sentinel' alien's cranial cavity, became a focal point of this research. Initial scans revealed it pulsed with a faint, rhythmic energy that seemed to resonate with the alien's brainwaves. The Ahnenerbe's physicists theorized it acted as a bio-energetic amplifier, focusing and projecting psionic signals. Mengele believed that by understanding its construction and the specific frequencies it emitted, they could create terrestrial analogues, perhaps even

50

biological implants, that would grant similar abilities to carefully selected individuals within the SS. The idea of breeding a new elite, individuals imbued with psychic powers, capable of dominating not just through physical might but through sheer mental force, was a core tenet of Himmler's twisted vision.

The deciphering of the alien data slate proved to be an arduous, often frustrating process. The script was unlike any terrestrial language, a complex interplay of symbols that seemed to possess both linguistic and energetic components. Himmler, however, was convinced that the symbols held the key not only to understanding the technology but also to unlocking forgotten spiritual truths. He tasked his Ahnenerbe linguists and occultists with finding any parallels, however tenuous, with ancient Germanic runes, Sanskrit texts, or even alchemical symbols. Any perceived connection was then woven into a narrative that portrayed the alien civilization as either a progenitor race of the Aryans or a lost, advanced branch of their lineage. The alien script was not seen as a foreign language, but as a lost dialect of an ancient, cosmic Aryan tongue.

The scientists, driven by a mixture of intellectual curiosity, ambition, and the ever-present threat of SS reprisal, began to develop theoretical models for weaponizing these newly discovered mental faculties. They explored concepts of telepathic suggestion, of inducing fear or obedience through focused psionic emissions. The potential for creating mass hysteria, for disabling entire enemy forces through psychological shockwaves, or for subtly influencing the decision-making processes of world leaders, was being meticulously outlined in classified reports. Himmler, poring over these documents in the austere confines of Wewelsburg, envisioned a Reich whose enemies would capitulate not to the roar of cannons, but to the silent, irresistible command of the SS mind.

Mengele's experimental work also took a dark turn. He began to investigate the psychoactive properties of certain biological compounds found within the alien specimens. These compounds, when isolated and synthesized, showed an uncanny ability to alter human consciousness, inducing states of heightened suggestibility, heightened aggression, or even profound disorientation. He theorized that these substances, when administered in controlled doses, could be used to 'prepare' individuals for psionic influence, making them more receptive to external commands. The ethical boundaries, already blurred by the SS's pervasive brutality, were now completely erased. The captured aliens were not only subjects for technological study but also biological test subjects for the development of psycho-chemical weapons.

The energy sources of the alien craft also presented a terrifying military potential. The core, a pulsating orb of contained plasma that radiated immense power, seemed to draw energy from an unknown dimension. The engineers struggled to comprehend its operational principles, but they recognized its unparalleled efficiency and destructive capability. Himmler envisioned these energy cores being integrated into new classes of weaponry, perhaps even scalar energy projectors capable of destabilizing matter at a molecular level. The thought of a weapon that could erase cities from existence with a silent, invisible beam, a weapon powered by forces from beyond the stars, perfectly aligned with his desire for absolute, overwhelming dominance.

The research into the alien's propulsion system, while initially focused on rapid transit, soon expanded to include its potential for offensive deployment. The craft's ability to manipulate gravity suggested the possibility of creating localized gravitational distortions that could crush enemy formations or even redirect enemy ordnance. The prospect of 'gravity weapons,' capable of crushing tanks like tin cans or rendering entire airfields impassable by warping the very fabric of gravity, was actively being explored. The SS's military strategists, guided by Himmler's occult-tinged directives, began to map out scenarios where these advanced technologies would grant the Reich an insurmountable battlefield advantage.

The Ahnenerbe's biological division also explored the potential for creating biological weapons based on alien genetic material. They hypothesized that the aliens possessed an immune system or a cellular structure that was fundamentally different from terrestrial life, and that by isolating certain viral or bacterial strains, they could create pathogens that would specifically target and incapacitate populations deemed 'undesirable.' This was a chilling echo of the

Reich's existing genocidal policies, now amplified by the terrifying potential of extraterrestrial biology. Himmler saw this as a way to 'sterilize' entire regions, to cleanse the world of perceived genetic impurities with a biological weapon of alien origin.

The scientists were also captivated by the alien's apparent regenerative capabilities. The 'Vulnerable' alien, despite severe injuries sustained during the crash, had shown signs of rapid cellular repair. Mengele believed that by isolating the genetic sequences responsible for this regeneration, they could develop methods to enhance the combat effectiveness of SS soldiers, making them more resilient to injury and capable of fighting for extended periods. This wasn't just about healing; it was about creating a new breed of super-soldier, one that could shrug off wounds that would incapacitate any ordinary human.

The deeper they delved into the alien technology, the more they realized its interconnectedness. The energy sources seemed to be intrinsically linked to the psionic capabilities, the propulsion systems to the gravitational manipulation, and the biological components to the very consciousness of the beings themselves. It was a holistic system, designed for purposes far beyond simple transportation or defense. Himmler, however, interpreted this complexity not as a sign of advanced civilization, but as evidence of a divinely ordained purpose, a technology designed by a superior race to guide and, if necessary, subjugate lesser beings.

The laboratories were now under the constant surveillance of Himmler's elite SS guards, the presence of whom served as a stark reminder of the stakes involved. Any deviation from Himmler's directives, any suggestion of the technology being 'unusable' or 'too dangerous,' was met with swift and brutal reprisal. The scientists were trapped between their professional integrity and the chilling reality of their patrons. They were forced to find practical applications, however horrific, for the principles they were uncovering, to twist the marvels of alien science into tools of tyranny.

The translation of the alien symbols on the data slate, a task believed by Himmler to be crucial for unlocking the full potential of the craft, was fraught with interpretative challenges. The Ahnenerbe scholars, under immense pressure, began to posit that certain symbol clusters represented specific energy frequencies or psionic commands. They developed experimental devices, based on these interpretations, that emitted modulated energy waves. Initial tests, conducted on animals, showed a disturbing capacity to induce panic, aggression, or a state of catatonic fear. Himmler, receiving these reports, saw not cruelty but the dawning of a new era of psychological warfare, where the very minds of the enemy could be manipulated and broken.

Mengele, in particular, became obsessed with the idea of 'psionic resonance' – the theory that specific mental states could be induced and amplified by tuning into the alien technology's energy fields. He began to experiment with sensory deprivation and electro-convulsive therapy, seeking to find terrestrial methods that could prepare human subjects for the reception of alien psionic broadcasts. The concept of a 'mind-controlled soldier,' utterly loyal and capable of executing any command without hesitation, was a seductive one for Himmler, a perverse fulfillment of his own desire for absolute obedience within the SS.

The potential for influencing global communications was another avenue of investigation. The alien craft's systems indicated an advanced form of information transmission, possibly utilizing subspace frequencies. Himmler theorized that by harnessing this technology, the Reich could broadcast propaganda directly into the minds of enemy populations, bypassing all existing media and sowing discord and confusion. The concept of 'psychic broadcasts,' invisible waves of suggestion and disinformation that could destabilize entire nations from within, was a chilling testament to the SS's ambition for total psychological control.

The energy core's capacity for immense power generation also opened up possibilities for environmental manipulation. While not a primary focus, some scientists speculated about the possibility of weaponizing these energy fields to create localized atmospheric disturbances or to disrupt weather patterns. Himmler, however, viewed such applications as crude and inefficient compared to the direct manipulation of consciousness. His focus remained firmly on the psychological, on the ultimate goal of bending the will of all humanity to the dictates of the Reich.

The research into the alien biological samples also extended to their cellular structure and metabolic processes. Mengele's teams were particularly interested in the aliens' apparent lack of aging and their extreme longevity. They theorized that by isolating and replicating the genetic or molecular mechanisms responsible for this, they could achieve a form of biological immortality for the SS elite, creating a cadre of leaders who would guide the Reich for millennia. This was a deeply narcissistic ambition, reflecting Himmler's own obsession with the eternal destiny of the Aryan race.

The reverse-engineering process was a delicate dance between scientific inquiry and ideological dogma. Every discovery, every theoretical leap, had to be framed within the context of Aryan supremacy and the SS's mission. The alien technology was not merely advanced; it was an ancient, forgotten inheritance, a tool that had been lost and was now being rediscovered by the chosen race. The scientists understood that their survival depended on presenting their findings in a way that satisfied Himmler's profound, and deeply disturbing, worldview. The weaponization of the unknown had begun in earnest, a terrifying testament to the SS's insatiable hunger for power, a hunger that now reached beyond the confines of Earth itself.

The sterile hum of the laboratories, once a testament to rigorous scientific pursuit, had begun to resonate with a new, unsettling frequency. It was the sound of ideology warping discovery, of empirical data being contorted to fit the preordained narrative of the SS. The Ahnenerbe, under Himmler's relentless pressure, was no longer merely dissecting alien technology; it was weaving it into a tapestry of pseudoscientific justifications for its most depraved ambitions. The alien craft, a marvel of cosmic engineering, was being systematically deconstructed not just into its physical components, but into ideological tenets that reinforced the Reich's twisted vision of racial purity and dominance.

Professor Josef Mengele, ever the pragmatist in his pursuit of the horrific, found himself increasingly tasked with crafting these elaborate rationalizations. His role, which had initially been to unlock the secrets of the alien physiology and technology, now expanded to encompass the art of manufacturing belief. He was to devise theories that rendered the incomprehensible comprehensible, but only in a way that served the insatiable hunger of the SS for validation. The scientific method, already a fragile entity within the Reich, was being actively dismantled, replaced by a grotesque parody that prioritized ideological alignment above all else.

One of the most pervasive of these emergent theories centered on the concept of 'psychotropic disintegration.' This phrase, coined by Himmler himself and elaborated upon by his eager acolytes, was designed to explain and legitimize the SS's burgeoning interest in psionic manipulation and psycho-chemical warfare. The alien specimens, with their inherent abilities to communicate and influence through means beyond conventional sensory perception, were reinterpreted through this pseudoscientific lens. Their subtle influence was not seen as a biological or technological phenomenon, but as a form of cosmic resonance, a direct conduit to the primordial psychic forces that, according to SS doctrine, had originally shaped the Aryan race.

The Ahnenerbe's occultists and racial theorists, steeped in the obscure lore of ancient Nordic myths and esoteric philosophies, found fertile ground in this new directive. They began to posit that the alien race possessed an advanced understanding of these primal psychic energies, an understanding that the ancient Aryans had once shared before its suppression by lesser races. The alien technology, particularly the crystalline lattice found in the 'Sentinel' specimen, was thus rebranded as a rediscovery of a lost Aryan art, a tool to reclaim their inherent psychic birthright. This narrative served a dual purpose: it elevated the alien technology by connecting it to a glorious, albeit fictional, past, and it positioned the SS as the rightful inheritors and masters of this rediscovered power.

Mengele, tasked with providing the 'scientific' backbone for these fanciful notions, began to develop theories around 'mental purity' and 'psychic vulnerability.' He proposed that certain biological markers, identifiable through genetic and neurological analysis of the captured specimens, correlated with an individual's susceptibility to psionic influence. These markers, he argued, were scarce in the 'pure' Aryan bloodline but prevalent in 'inferior' races. Therefore, the alien technology, when weaponized, could be used to target these vulnerabilities, effectively 'disintegrating' the mental and emotional fortitude of those deemed undesirable.

This concept of 'psychotropic disintegration' was presented as a form of advanced racial hygiene, a method of cleansing the world of genetic and psychic impurities by stripping away the very will to resist.

The implications of this theory were chillingly direct. It provided a sophisticated, albeit entirely fabricated, scientific rationale for the SS's escalating program of human experimentation and mass extermination. The idea was that through a combination of precisely engineered sonic frequencies, targeted bio-chemical agents synthesized from alien biological samples, and the direct application of psionic-inducing technology, the regime could induce a state of utter mental collapse in entire populations. This 'disintegration' would render them passive, compliant, and ultimately incapable of reproduction or resistance, effectively achieving the SS's ultimate goal of a racially homogenous world through 'non-violent' means – or at least, means that could be artfully disguised as such in the Reich's internal propaganda.

The Ahnenerbe's physicists and engineers, caught between the imperative to produce results and the increasingly outlandish demands of Himmler's ideological framework, began to construct theoretical models for devices that could achieve this 'psychotropic disintegration.' They posited that the energy core of the alien craft, capable of manipulating fundamental forces, could be tuned to emit specific resonance frequencies that would disrupt the neural pathways of targeted populations. The crystalline lattice, now referred to as an 'Aryan psychic amplifier,' was theorized to be capable of broadcasting these disruptive frequencies, amplified and focused, over vast distances. The notion of a weapon that could induce mass psychosis, cripple entire armies with fear, or reduce cities to obedient, unthinking husks was now a central pillar of their research agenda.

The linguistic teams, working tirelessly on the alien data slate, played a crucial role in this ideological construction. They began to attribute specific meanings to certain alien symbols, linking them to concepts of cosmic order, spiritual decay, and the inherent superiority of the 'Nordic spirit.' These interpretations were, of course, entirely subjective and driven by the pre-existing Ahnenerbe obsession with finding ancient Aryan roots in every aspect of human history and even extraterrestrial contact. They claimed to have deciphered phrases that spoke of 'cleansing rituals' and 'harmonic alignment,' which they then twisted to mean the psionic subjugation of 'discordant' races. The alien language was thus transformed from a source of genuine understanding into a cipher for reinforcing racial prejudice, its complex grammar and syntax reinterpreted to support the SS's narrative of a cosmic struggle between Aryan purity and racial degeneration.

Mengele's biological experiments took on a new, chilling dimension under this 'psychotropic disintegration' paradigm. He began to explore the potential of isolating and synthesizing specific alien neurotoxins or psychoactive compounds. The goal was not merely to understand their effect on consciousness, but to weaponize them, to create biological agents that would induce the targeted mental breakdown. He theorized that these compounds, when administered through inhalation, ingestion, or even subdermal injection, would prime the human brain for further psionic manipulation, rendering individuals exquisitely sensitive to the 'disintegrating' frequencies. The captured 'Vulnerable' specimen, whose physiological differences were already a source of fascination for Mengele, were now viewed as living arsenals of psycho-chemical weapons, their very biology a testament to the alien capacity for mental control.

The concept of 'psychotropic disintegration' was also applied to the SS's eugenics programs. Himmler envisioned creating select groups of SS operatives who would be trained to withstand and even direct these psionic energies. These individuals, carefully bred and rigorously conditioned, would be the vanguard of the new psychic warfare doctrine. They would be immune to the disintegrating effects directed at the enemy, and furthermore, they would be capable of projecting psionic commands themselves. The Ahnenerbe's racial biologists began to formulate theories about the genetic predisposition for psychic abilities, claiming that these were latent within the Aryan genome, waiting to be awakened and amplified by the alien technology. This created a feedback loop: the alien technology validated the existence of Aryan psychic superiority, and the perceived genetic markers of this superiority justified the focused study of the alien technology.

The pseudo-scientific justifications extended to the propulsion systems and energy cores as well. The alien craft's ability to manipulate gravity and space-time was reinterpreted as a manifestation of its users' supreme psychic will. The power of their thoughts, channeled through the advanced technology, was said to bend the very fabric of reality. For the SS, this translated into a theory of 'willpower amplification.' The Reich's greatest minds, they theorized, could use the alien technology to focus their collective will, projecting it across the globe to enforce their dominance. The idea was that the sheer force of concentrated Aryan willpower, amplified by alien machinery, could overcome any resistance, dissolve any opposition, and reshape the world according to the SS's grand design. This was presented as an extension of their existing belief in the 'will of the Volk,' now empowered by cosmic forces.

The Ahnenerbe's archivists and occultists worked in tandem to unearth ancient Germanic texts and symbols that could be superficially aligned with these new theories. Runes were reinterpreted as specific psychic frequencies, ancient myths of divine power were recast as accounts of early Aryan encounters with psionic forces, and alchemical treatises were mined for obscure references to the manipulation of consciousness. This manufactured historical and spiritual lineage provided the pseudoscientific framework with an aura of ancient authority, making the SS's embrace of alien technology seem less like a radical departure and more like a return to a forgotten, primordial state of Aryan being. The more outlandish the theory, the more it was embraced, as it served to further distance the research from any recognizable, and potentially critical, scientific scrutiny.

The progression of this pseudoscientific discourse was meticulously documented in classified reports, penned by scientists and theorists under immense pressure to conform. These reports were then presented to Himmler, who would pore over them with a fervor that bordered on religious ecstasy. He saw in these theories not mere scientific speculation, but the articulation of a divine destiny. The 'psychotropic disintegration' was not just a weapon; it was a tool for purification, a means of enacting God's will on Earth by eradicating the 'unworthy' and elevating the 'chosen.' The alien technology, in his eyes, was not a discovery, but a divine mandate, a testament to the inherent spiritual and psychic superiority of the Aryan race, a superiority that the SS was now tasked with manifesting on a global, and eventually cosmic, scale.

The ethical chasm, already vast, widened into an unbridgeable abyss. The concept of 'psychotropic disintegration,' cloaked in the language of scientific advancement and racial hygiene, provided a convenient veil for the SS's most barbarous intentions. It allowed them to frame their pursuit of mind control and mass destruction as a noble endeavor, a necessary step in the evolutionary progress of humanity, guided by the superior intellect and will of the Aryan race. The alien artifacts, meant perhaps for communication, exploration, or even artistic expression, had been utterly perverted, transformed into instruments of psychological terror and systematic annihilation, all under the insidious banner of pseudoscientific justification. The laboratories continued their work, the hum of machinery now a discordant symphony of corrupted science and unholy ambition, meticulously crafting the tools for a silent, devastating conquest of the human mind. The implications for the future of warfare, for the very definition of consciousness and control, were becoming terrifyingly clear, etched into the fabric of the Reich's twisted vision.

Ernst Falk, a man who had initially approached the Ahnenerbe's clandestine research with a mixture of professional curiosity and national pride, found his convictions eroding with an alarming speed. The sterile hum of the laboratories, once a symbol of scientific rigor, had transformed into an insidious drone that echoed the SS's escalating barbarity. He had been drawn into this world by the promise of unlocking the secrets of the cosmos, of pushing the boundaries of human understanding. Instead, he was witnessing the systematic subjugation of that very understanding to the grotesque dictates of Nazi ideology. The alien technology, a tangible manifestation of a civilization far beyond their own, was not being studied for the advancement of all mankind, but was being twisted, contorted, and weaponized to serve the Reich's insatiable hunger for dominion.

The initial fascination with the 'Sentinel' specimen, with its intricate crystalline lattice and its seemingly benevolent atmospheric manipulation capabilities, had been gradually replaced by a gnawing disquiet. Falk, a physicist by training, understood the fundamental principles at play within the alien craft. He recognized the elegance of its energy generation, the sophisticated yet seemingly harmonious interplay of its various systems. This was not technology born of brute force or destructive intent; it was a testament to a species that had perhaps achieved a profound understanding of the universe, a level of advancement that suggested wisdom, not war. Yet, the pronouncements emanating from the inner sanctums of the SS painted a drastically different picture, reinterpreting every aspect of the alien technology through the warped lens of racial supremacy and esoteric occultism.

He remembered the early days, the hushed excitement as they began to decipher the alien data slate. There were concepts of harmonic resonance, of energy transfer that seemed to imply a deep connection with the natural world, perhaps even a form of interspecies communication based on shared energetic frequencies. Falk had envisioned applications that could revolutionize energy production, or perhaps unlock new avenues of understanding consciousness itself. But the SS, particularly Himmler and his coterie of ideologically driven scientists, saw something else entirely. They saw tools of control, methods to enforce their twisted vision of racial purity. The concept of 'psychotropic disintegration,' a phrase that still sent a shiver down Falk's spine, was the most egregious example of this perversion. It was a term that reeked of fear, of a desperate attempt to legitimize the SS's burgeoning interest in psionic manipulation and chemical warfare by cloaking it in the guise of scientific progress.

Falk found himself increasingly at odds with the direction the research was taking. While his colleagues, under immense pressure, were busy fabricating justifications for the SS's depraved ambitions,

Falk remained stubbornly rooted in empirical evidence. He saw the alien artifacts not as divine gifts meant to empower the Aryan race, but as the remnants of a potentially advanced, perhaps even benevolent, civilization that had met an unknown fate. The idea that their subtle energies, their intricate designs, were being repurposed to create weapons capable of inducing mass psychosis or stripping entire populations of their will to resist struck him as an act of cosmic sacrilege. The very elegance of the alien technology, its inherent complexity and apparent efficiency, stood in stark contrast to the SS's crude and brutal methodology.

He recalled a specific instance, a presentation by a junior scientist who, with a disturbingly blank expression, outlined how the alien propulsion system, capable of manipulating gravitational fields, could be recalibrated to create localized distortions of reality, effectively disorienting and disabling enemy forces. The scientist spoke of 'willpower amplification,' of harnessing the collective mental energy of the Reich's 'pure' population to project focused psychic force. Falk, listening to the nonsensical jargon, felt a wave of nausea. He knew enough about physics to understand the immense power involved in manipulating gravitational fields, and the very idea of coupling it with vague notions of psychic energy was preposterous. It was a desperate attempt to imbue their nascent weaponry with an almost supernatural aura, to align it with the SS's pre-existing fascination with the occult and the mystical.

The linguistic teams, too, were a source of growing concern. They had begun to attribute specific meanings to certain alien symbols, linking them to obscure Nordic myths and esoteric philosophies that were entirely absent in the original interpretations. Falk had seen early translations that suggested the alien data slate spoke of cosmic balance, of interconnectedness, of a universal harmony.

Now, these same texts were being reinterpreted to speak of 'cleansing rituals' and the subjugation of 'discordant' races. The alien language, a complex and beautiful system of communication, was being reduced to a cipher that reinforced the SS's paranoid worldview, its inherent structure twisted to support a narrative of racial struggle and eventual Aryan triumph. He couldn't shake the feeling that they were not deciphering the aliens' message, but were instead projecting their own depravity onto it.

Falk's disquiet deepened as he observed the effects of the 'psychotropic disintegration' theories on the ongoing experiments. Professor Mengele, once a respected biologist, was now orchestrating chilling studies, attempting to synthesize alien neurotoxins and psychoactive compounds. Falk had witnessed the raw data from these experiments – the neurological scans, the biochemical analyses – and he understood the immense potential for understanding human consciousness. But Mengele's twisted ambition was to weaponize this understanding, to create agents that would induce mental breakdown, rendering populations susceptible to psionic manipulation. The captured 'Vulnerable' specimen, with their unique physiological attributes, were no longer being studied for their inherent biological differences but were being treated as living arsenals, their very existence a testament to the SS's perverted quest for control.

He found himself drawn to the silent, imposing form of the salvaged alien craft, a hulking enigma resting within the heavily guarded hangar. Its smooth, seamless hull, devoid of any visible rivets or joinery, spoke of a manufacturing process far beyond anything Germany, or indeed any nation on Earth, possessed. He would stand before it, tracing the faint, almost organic patterns etched into its surface, and feel a profound sense of awe. This was not the work of warmongers; it was something more... profound. He imagined the beings who had built this vessel, their journey through the stars, their purpose. Had they been explorers? Scientists? Or perhaps something more spiritual? The SS, however, saw only a source of power, a means to an end, and their crude attempts to interface with its systems, to pry open its secrets, felt like a violation.

The SS's appropriation of the alien technology extended even to its propulsion systems. The craft's ability to manipulate gravity and space-time, a feat that Falk, a physicist, still struggled to fully comprehend, was being reinterpreted as a manifestation of the users' 'supreme psychic will.' This concept of 'willpower amplification' was particularly disturbing. Himmler envisioned the Reich's greatest minds, carefully selected and indoctrinated, using the alien technology to focus their collective will, projecting it across the globe to enforce their dominance. It was a terrifying echo of their existing ideology, the 'will of the Volk,' now amplified by cosmic machinery. Falk saw the danger in this – the absolute certainty that their will was the only one that mattered, the complete dismissal of any dissenting thought or perspective.

He began to notice subtle shifts in the demeanor of his colleagues. Some were clearly enthusiastic, caught up in the grand vision of an all-powerful Reich wielding unimaginable cosmic power. Others, however, displayed a more guarded apprehension, their eyes betraying a flicker of unease behind the forced smiles and obedient nods. Falk found himself seeking out these individuals, engaging in hushed conversations in the dimly lit corridors, a shared sense of disquiet forming an unspoken bond. They spoke of the ethical implications, the sheer audacity of perverting such advanced technology for destructive purposes. The disconnect between the aliens' apparent benevolent mission and the Nazis' malevolent intentions gnawed at Falk, planting the seeds of doubt and rebellion against the regime he served.

The Ahnenerbe's archivists and occultists, under Himmler's zealous guidance, were meticulously weaving a fabricated historical and spiritual lineage for the alien technology. Ancient Germanic texts were reinterpreted, runes were assigned new meanings as psychic frequencies, and alchemical treatises were mined for obscure references that could be twisted to support the SS's narrative. Falk witnessed this intellectual charade firsthand, seeing how easily genuine research could be warped to fit a preordained ideological framework. The more outlandish the theory, the more it was embraced, as it served to further distance the research from any recognizable, and potentially critical, scientific scrutiny. It was a deliberate act of intellectual prostitution, sacrificing truth at the altar of ideology.

Falk's growing disquiet was not a sudden epiphany, but a slow, corrosive process. It began with small questions, then grew into a deep-seated unease, and finally blossomed into outright alarm. He saw the inherent beauty and potential for advancement in the alien artifacts being systematically perverted into instruments of oppression. The very principles that suggested a universe of interconnectedness and understanding were being perverted to create tools of division and control. He realized that his own commitment to scientific truth was now in direct conflict with his sworn loyalty to the Reich. The sterile laboratories, once a beacon of his aspirations, had become a gilded cage, trapping him in a web of intellectual compromise and moral decay. He knew, with a chilling certainty, that he could no longer stand by and witness this grotesque transformation without acting. The seeds of rebellion, sown by his growing disquiet, were beginning to sprout.

Chapter 4

The Cleansing Directive

The whispers in the sterile, heavily guarded corridors of the SS's esoteric research division had begun to solidify. Theories once confined to arcane texts and feverish, late-night debates were rapidly morphing into concrete, terrifying directives. For Ernst Falk, a man increasingly adrift in a sea of ideological perversion, the shift was palpable, a tangible tightening of the noose around his scientific conscience. The initial fascination with the alien artifacts, the tantalizing glimpse of a universe far grander and more complex than previously imagined, had been irrevocably poisoned by the SS's insatiable hunger for dominion. They weren't merely studying the remnants of an advanced civilization; they were dissecting it, twisting its very essence to serve their own grotesque ambitions.

The concept that had begun to crystallize, a chilling culmination of Himmler's obsessive drive for racial purity and the Ahnenerbe's newfound obsession with extraterrestrial weaponry, was starkly, brutally simple: *'The Cleansing Directive.'* It was not a euphemism; it was a declaration of intent, a blueprint for the systematic, efficient eradication of any population deemed 'inferior' by the Nazi regime. Falk had seen the preliminary projections, the extrapolated data, the hushed discussions of 'population recalibration' and 'demographic optimization.' The alien technology, particularly the facets related to subtle psychic manipulation and environmental disorientation, was being eyed as the ultimate tool for achieving this horrific objective. The SS wasn't just interested in conquest; they were intent on a form of historical erasure, a radical simplification of the human tapestry, achieved with a terrifyingly sophisticated, alien-sourced scalpel.

Falk remembered the early, tentative explorations into the alien technology's potential for altering human consciousness. The

'Sentinel' specimen's atmospheric manipulation capabilities, initially understood as a form of climate control or environmental stabilization, were now being re-contextualized through the lens of psionic warfare. The ability to subtly alter atmospheric composition, to perhaps induce states of heightened suggestibility or profound disorientation, was seen as a perfect complement to the SS's desire to control the minds of its 'undesirables.' The theories surrounding 'psychotropic disintegration,' a term Falk still found nauseating in its crudeness, were no longer purely theoretical. They were being rapidly translated into actionable research programs, spearheaded by figures like Mengele, whose pathological curiosity had found a new, horrifying outlet.

The alien data slate, once a source of wonder, was now being mined for any scrap of information that could be twisted into a justification for this genocidal ambition. Early translations hinting at cosmic balance and universal interconnectedness were being systematically ignored or perverted. Falk had seen revised interpretations, where concepts of harmonic resonance were re-cast as methods for disrupting the very cellular structure of targeted populations, inducing a slow, agonizing disintegration. The SS's occultists and pseudo-historians were working overtime, weaving elaborate, fictitious narratives that linked the alien technology to ancient Germanic fertility cults and esoteric rituals of purification, a desperate attempt to imbue their horrific plan with a veneer of historical legitimacy and spiritual sanction.

The 'Cleansing Directive' was not a singular weapon, but a multi-pronged strategy. The first phase involved the dissemination of subtly altered atmospheric compounds, derived from research into the alien craft's environmental systems. These compounds, designed to be undetectable and insidious, were theorized to induce a gradual decline in cognitive function and reproductive capacity among targeted groups. The 'Sentinel's' ability to manipulate atmospheric pressure and energy fields was being studied not for its potential to terraform barren worlds, but to create localized zones of psychological oppression, to sow despair and apathy. Falk had seen the biochemical analyses, the painstakingly synthesized molecular structures that mirrored certain alien atmospheric regulators, now imbued with neurotoxic properties.

The second, and perhaps more overtly terrifying, aspect of the directive involved the direct application of what the SS termed 'psionic disruption.' This was where the truly esoteric elements of Ahnenerbe research merged with the hard science of alien engineering. The concept was to harness the alien technology's capacity for manipulating mental states, potentially amplified by the collective psychic energy of ideologically pure individuals, to induce widespread psychosis, incapacitation, or even death. Falk remembered a particularly disturbing proposal, which suggested reconfiguring the alien vessel's primary energy conduits to broadcast focused psychic frequencies, capable of overwhelming the mental defenses of entire populations. The aim was not just to kill, but to obliterate the will to resist, to leave behind a perfectly compliant, or utterly broken, populace.

The implications of this 'Cleansing Directive' weighed heavily on Falk. He had initially joined the Ahnenerbe with a genuine desire to advance human knowledge, to explore the profound mysteries of the universe. Now, he found himself a reluctant participant in a program that sought to weaponize those very mysteries, to reduce the breathtaking complexity of alien science into a tool for barbaric extermination. The alien beings who had crafted such advanced technology, who had evidently mastered the forces of the cosmos, could never have intended their creations to be used for such a purpose. It was a betrayal, not just of science, but of a fundamental understanding of existence itself.

The 'Vulnerable' specimen, the captured being whose unique physiological and psionic attributes had initially been a source of intense scientific interest, were now central to the implementation of the Cleansing Directive. Their innate resistance to certain atmospheric agents, their unique neurological pathways, were being studied not for the purpose of understanding alien biology, but for their potential as biological vectors or conduits for the SS's weaponized compounds and psychic frequencies. Falk had witnessed Mengele's increasingly barbaric experiments, the attempts to extract and synthesize the very essences of these beings, to replicate their unique properties within controlled laboratory conditions. The creatures, once subjects of scientific inquiry, were now viewed as living arsenals, their very physiology a blueprint for mass destruction.

The SS's interpretation of the alien propulsion system, its ability to manipulate gravity and space-time, was being repurposed with chilling ingenuity. The notion of 'willpower amplification' was no longer a fringe theory confined to Himmler's private chambers. It was being integrated into the operational framework of the Cleansing Directive. The plan was to create specialized deployment units, comprised of individuals who had undergone rigorous ideological indoctrination and who possessed certain perceived psionic aptitudes. These units would then utilize modified alien devices, calibrated to amplify their 'collective will,' to focus and project the disruptive energies onto targeted populations. It was a terrifying fusion of advanced physics and warped ideology, a concept that promised the SS the ability to enact their will with an almost divine, and utterly terrifying, authority.

Falk found himself wrestling with the sheer audacity of the plan. The SS was not merely seeking to conquer; they were attempting to fundamentally alter the demographic and psychological landscape of the planet. The Cleansing Directive was designed to be surgical, yet devastating, leaving behind a world cleansed of perceived impurities and ready for the SS's dominion. The alien technology offered them a means to achieve this on a scale previously unimaginable, bypassing traditional warfare and striking directly at the psychological and biological foundations of their enemies. The speed and efficiency with which the Ahnenerbe was developing these strategies, fueled by the SS's unwavering conviction, was a testament to their ruthless pragmatism.

The logistical challenges were immense, but the SS, with its vast resources and absolute control, was systematically overcoming them. The captured alien craft, its very existence a closely guarded secret, was being cannibalized for its components. Specialized laboratories were being constructed in remote, secure locations, staffed by scientists coerced or indoctrinated into the SS's vision. The 'Cleansing Directive' required not just theoretical breakthroughs but practical implementation, and the SS was marshalling every available resource to that end. Falk had seen the schematics for new deployment vehicles, designed to carry and deploy the alien atmospheric agents. He had read the reports detailing the recruitment and training of specialized SS units, individuals being prepared for the grim task ahead.

The ethical abyss into which the Ahnenerbe had plunged was becoming a chasm from which escape seemed increasingly impossible. Falk's own participation, however reluctant, felt like an endorsement of these horrific plans. He found himself increasingly isolated, his attempts to inject reason and caution into the proceedings met with suspicion and veiled threats. The SS leadership, particularly Himmler, saw only the ultimate expression of their racial ideology, the logical conclusion of their pursuit of Aryan supremacy. The alien technology was not an anomaly to be cautiously studied, but a divine mandate, a cosmic validation of their twisted worldview.

The 'Cleansing Directive' was more than just a plan; it was a manifestation of a deeply ingrained, pathological ideology, amplified by the unprecedented power of alien science. Falk understood that if this directive were ever fully implemented, it would not only result in the decimation of millions but would also represent a fundamental perversion of humanity's relationship with the universe. The potential for understanding and advancement that the alien artifacts represented would be buried beneath a mountain of corpses and a legacy of unimaginable horror. The elegance of cosmic design would be reduced to the brutality of SS extermination.

The very stars, which had once represented a frontier of boundless possibility, now seemed to loom with a terrifying omen, reflecting the SS's dark aspirations. The theories had, with horrifying speed, transitioned from the realm of abstract possibility to the grim reality of impending action, and Falk felt the chilling certainty that the world was teetering on the precipice of an unprecedented, alien-assisted atrocity. The Cleansing Directive was no longer a theoretical construct; it was a tangible, terrifying force being meticulously assembled, piece by chilling piece, by the architects of the Reich's darkest ambitions. The hum of the laboratories was no longer just a drone; it was the prelude to a planetary silence.

The whispers had indeed solidified, but they had also begun to coalesce into a chillingly specific operational doctrine. Psychotropic disintegration, a term Falk still found morally repugnant, was no longer a vague theoretical threat; it was the subject of intense, focused research within the SS's advanced projects division. The Ahnenerbe, driven by a potent cocktail of racial fanaticism and an insatiable lust for power, had latched onto the alien technology's potential for subtle, yet profound, mental subjugation. They weren't interested in merely causing pain or confusion; their ambition was far more insidious. They sought to dismantle the very essence of personhood, to erase not just lives, but identities, leaving behind a void where once a sentient being resided. This was the true horror of the Cleansing Directive: not simply mass murder, but a systematic, extraterrestrially-assisted annihilation of the self.

The scientists within the Ahnenerbe were not merely adapting existing technology; they were attempting to synthesize entirely new forms of psychological weaponry. They theorized that by precisely modulating the alien energy fields, they could create a resonance that would disrupt the very neural pathways responsible for memory formation and self-awareness. Imagine, Falk shuddered, a targeted individual experiencing a gradual unravelling of their past, their relationships, their very sense of who they were. This wasn't simply about breaking their will to resist; it was about eradicating the 'self' entirely, leaving behind a hollow shell, or worse, a mind that could no longer even perceive its own ruin. The SS envisioned this as the ultimate form of control, a silent, invisible weapon that could dismantle entire populations without firing a shot, leaving no physical trace but a profound, collective amnesia and despair.

One particularly disturbing research proposal, which Falk had seen circulated amongst a select group of SS scientists, outlined a method for 'synaptic erasure.' The theory was that specific sonic and electromagnetic frequencies, generated by modified alien devices, could induce a cascade failure within the brain's synaptic connections. This wouldn't be a violent implosion, but a subtle, progressive fraying of the neural network, leading to a complete inability to form new memories or recall old ones. The SS envisioned this being deployed through localized atmospheric emitters, designed to create '*zones of oblivion*' where individuals would slowly lose their minds, their identities dissolving like smoke

72

in the wind. The ultimate aim was not just to depopulate, but to de-exist, to remove any trace of those deemed 'undesirable' from the tapestry of human consciousness.

The occultists within the Ahnenerbe, always eager to imbue the SS's genocidal ambitions with a pseudo-spiritual justification, were actively involved in this research. They spoke of 'cleansing the psychic ether,' of 'purifying the collective consciousness' by removing 'discordant vibrations.' Their involvement lent a veneer of ancient, arcane knowledge to the SS's brutal pragmatism, a desperate attempt to legitimize their horrifying agenda. They believed that the alien technology was not just a weapon but a divine instrument, meant to usher in a new era of racial purity. Falk, however, saw only the perversion of science, the twisting of cosmic principles into tools of barbarism. The very concept of consciousness, of the intricate web of experiences and memories that defined an individual, was being reduced to a series of frequencies that could be manipulated and ultimately destroyed.

The 'Sentinel' specimen's atmospheric manipulation capabilities were being repurposed with terrifying ingenuity. The initial understanding of these abilities focused on environmental control, perhaps even terraforming. However, the SS's researchers were now exploring the potential for these systems to carry and broadcast specific psychotropic frequencies. They theorized that by subtly altering the atmospheric composition, they could create an invisible medium for transmitting the targeted mental assaults. This was far more insidious than a direct sonic attack; it was a slow, pervasive poisoning of the mind, delivered on the very air people breathed. The goal was not just to incapacitate, but to induce a state of profound apathy and disorientation, making individuals susceptible to further manipulation or simply incapable of functioning.

The success of the 'Cleansing Directive,' particularly its psychotropic disintegration aspect, relied heavily on the SS's ability to isolate and replicate the precise alien frequencies that affected consciousness. This involved countless hours of meticulous analysis of the recovered artifacts, cross-referencing biological data from the 'Vulnerable' specimen with the complex energy signatures detected within the alien craft. The Ahnenerbe scientists were delving into uncharted territories of physics and neuroscience, attempting to map the very architecture of thought and memory. They believed that if they could understand the fundamental building blocks of consciousness, they could then systematically dismantle it. The implications were staggering, a form of existential warfare that transcended mere physical destruction.

The concept of 'collective consciousness' was also being heavily explored, albeit through a twisted SS lens. They believed that by disrupting the psychic links between individuals, by atomizing society and shattering the shared sense of identity that bound communities together, they could further expedite the process of disintegration. This involved identifying and targeting key nodes within these collective psychic networks, using alien technology to sow discord, paranoia, and a profound sense of isolation. The goal was to break down not just individual minds, but the very fabric of social cohesion, leaving behind a fragmented and vulnerable populace ripe for subjugation. The SS saw this as a form of societal lobotomy, a way to render entire populations incapable of organized resistance.

The 'Vulnerable' specimen, despite their suffering, were proving to be crucial in this research. Their innate ability to process and emit certain energy frequencies made them living laboratories for the SS's theories. Mengele and his team were attempting to isolate the specific biological mechanisms that allowed these beings to manipulate psychic energy, hoping to replicate these mechanisms in engineered biological agents or even synthetic devices. This involved invasive surgery, neural mapping, and experimentation with various psychoactive compounds, all conducted with a chilling disregard for the suffering of the captured beings. The SS saw them not as sentient creatures, but as biological blueprints for their ultimate weapons.

The pursuit of psychotropic disintegration was a race against time, at least in the SS's fevered imagination. They believed that by perfecting these techniques, they could achieve a victory so absolute that it would render any conventional military opposition irrelevant. Imagine, Falk thought with a shiver, a world where entire cities could be rendered catatonic, their inhabitants reduced to mindless automatons by a single, precisely targeted broadcast of alien frequencies. The thought was terrifying in its efficiency, its almost surgical precision in dismantling the human spirit. The SS was not just aiming for conquest; they were aiming for a form of existential annihilation, a complete and utter victory over the very concept of free will and individual identity. The ethical boundaries had long been crossed, obliterated by the SS's insatiable drive for power and ideological purity.

The psychotropic disintegration research was a stark manifestation of this descent into barbarism. It represented a fundamental misunderstanding, or perhaps a deliberate perversion, of the very nature of consciousness. The alien artifacts, which held the potential for profound insights into the universe and humanity's place within it, were being twisted into instruments of psychological torture and existential destruction. Falk felt a growing sense of dread, a certainty that the knowledge being unearthed was too dangerous to be wielded by such morally bankrupt hands. The very stars, once symbols of wonder and possibility, now seemed to mock humanity's hubris, their cold, indifferent light illuminating the SS's descent into a darkness from which there might be no return. The psychotropic disintegration was not merely a weapon; it was a philosophical statement by the SS, a declaration that the individual, the self, was a mere variable to be eliminated in their grand equation of racial supremacy. The alien technology provided the means, and their twisted ideology provided the chilling justification. The hum of the machinery in the hidden laboratories was no longer just the sound of scientific progress; it was the prelude to a global silencing of minds, a planetary erasure of identity.

The whispers, once spectral anxieties, had solidified into an operational doctrine, a chillingly specific pathway to the SS's ultimate objective. Psychotropic disintegration, a term Falk still found morally repugnant, was no longer a theoretical menace; it was the focal point of obsessive research within the SS's advanced projects division. The Ahnenerbe, fueled by a potent elixir of racial fanaticism and an insatiable hunger for absolute control, had seized upon the alien technology's capacity for subtle yet profound mental subjugation. Their ambition was not merely to inflict pain or confusion; it was infinitely more insidious. They sought to dismantle the very essence of personhood, to erase not just lives, but identities, leaving behind an eerie void where sentient beings once resided. This was the true horror of the Cleansing Directive: not simple mass murder, but a systematic, extraterrestrially assisted annihilation of the self.

Within the labyrinthine depths of the SS's clandestine research facilities, the concept of psychotropic disintegration was being meticulously dissected, analyzed, and, most disturbingly, weaponized. Scientists, whose names Falk increasingly associated with a profound moral decay, were dedicating their intellects to manipulating the alien frequencies gleaned from the recovered craft. Their objective was to engineer a form of mental warfare unlike anything humanity had ever conceived. This was not about blast waves or chemical agents that ravaged the body; this was an assault on the mind, a targeted campaign to shatter an individual's consciousness, to induce a state of utter psychological collapse. The goal was to render individuals not merely dead, but non-existent, even to themselves. Memory loss was the initial hurdle, a gradual erosion of personal history and identity. Beyond that lay the terrifying prospect of complete cognitive dissolution, a descent into a catatonic state where the self was irrevocably broken.

Dr. Josef Mengele, his pathological curiosity now channeled through the lens of alien psionics, stood at the forefront of these abhorrent investigations. Falk had witnessed, firsthand, the detached, almost clinical fascination with which Mengele approached his subjects. Now, the 'Vulnerable' specimen, those captured alien beings with their unique neurological structures and psionic capacities, were subjected to even more invasive and horrific procedures. The SS believed that by understanding and replicating the alien methods of mental influence, they could effectively rewrite the minds of their enemies or simply erase them from existence. Early experiments focused on isolating specific alien frequency patterns that induced disorientation and sensory overload. The captured data slates, once enigmatic repositories of cosmic knowledge, were being scoured for any hint of a 'mental frequency' that could be amplified and weaponized.

Falk found himself increasingly haunted by the thought of

individuals not dying, but simply… ceasing to be. Not ceasing to exist in a physical sense, but ceasing to *be themselves*. He pictured soldiers, once loyal to the Reich, being subtly bombarded with these alien frequencies, their memories of their families, their training, their very ideology, gradually dissolving. They would become empty husks, devoid of purpose, their minds wiped clean. This was the SS's ultimate vision: a world populated by obedient automatons, or worse, a void of consciousness, devoid of any dissenting thought or individual will. The psychotropic disintegration was the ultimate tool for achieving this dystopian future, a method for achieving a perfect, sterile purity by erasing the very essence of what it meant to be human.

The scientific rigor, however misguided and morally bankrupt, was undeniable. The Ahnenerbe was employing cutting-edge analytical techniques, pushing the boundaries of known science to achieve its horrific objectives. They were developing sophisticated spectral analyzers to map the intricate energy patterns of the alien technology, biofeedback devices to monitor the physiological and neurological responses of test subjects to various frequencies, and advanced computational models to predict the long-term effects of exposure. The sheer effort being poured into this research, into the development of weapons that attacked the very core of identity, was a chilling testament to the SS's unwavering commitment to its genocidal ideology. They were not merely waging war; they were attempting to engineer a new reality, one devoid of the complexities and imperfections of human consciousness.

Beyond the chilling efficacy of psychotropic disintegration lay another, even more insidious application of the alien technology: the 'resonance purges.' This concept, born from the fevered minds of Ahnenerbe scientists and occultists alike, envisioned a far broader, more diffuse form of control. It was not about targeting individuals or even specific groups with precision, but about wielding the alien energy frequencies as a blunt instrument, capable of indiscriminately disrupting biological and cognitive functions on a massive scale. The architects of this terrifying doctrine were not seeking to erase minds in the nuanced manner of synaptic erasure; they aimed for a more elemental form of obliteration, a void where life and consciousness had once been.

The fundamental principle behind the resonance purges was the identification and amplification of specific alien energy frequencies that resonated with the fundamental biological and neurological structures of targeted populations. The SS's twisted eugenics agenda provided the framework for this selection process. They envisioned meticulously cataloging populations based on perceived genetic markers, bloodlines, even behavioral patterns that deviated from their idealized Aryan model. Once these 'undesirable' traits were identified, the goal was to isolate the specific alien frequencies that could induce a cascade of biological failures within those possessing them. This wasn't about mental manipulation in the traditional sense; it was about initiating a silent, invisible decay, a programmed obsolescence of the human form itself.

The researchers theorized that these targeted frequencies could induce a spectrum of devastating effects, from rapid cellular degradation and organ failure to widespread neurological collapse, leading to a complete cessation of all biological and cognitive activity. The terrifying beauty of the concept, from the SS's perverted perspective, lay in its utter lack of physical manifestation. Unlike conventional weapons, the resonance purges would leave no shrapnel, no chemical residue, no discernible external trauma. The victims would simply…cease. They would wither, their life force extinguished by an invisible hand, their bodies left as inert husks, the very essence of their existence dissolved by the alien energies.

The SS dreamt of creating zones of absolute absence, sterilized landscapes where all traces of their perceived enemies had been surgically removed from existence, leaving behind only silence and the chilling echo of a void.   The mechanism for disseminating these resonance purges was as diabolical as the concept itself. While the precise methods were still under intensive development, initial proposals involved harnessing the atmospheric manipulation capabilities of the 'Sentinel' specimen, repurposed to broadcast these targeted frequencies across vast geographical areas. Alternatively, the SS was exploring the possibility of creating mobile emitter platforms, disguised as innocuous infrastructure or even weather-monitoring stations, capable of projecting these destructive waves over specific regions. The sheer scalability of the concept was what made it so profoundly terrifying. An entire city, a continent, could potentially be subjected to a resonance purge, its inhabitants systematically erased from the face of the Earth by a silent, pervasive wave of alien energy.

The SS's occultist factions played a significant role in conceptualizing these purges, imbuing the process with a ritualistic significance. They spoke of 'astral cleansing,' of 'purging the terrestrial plane of dissonant vibrations.' The carefully curated genetic data, the meticulously mapped social structures, the observed behavioral patterns – all were viewed as manifestations of a deeper, energetic dissonance that needed to be harmonized through the brutal application of alien frequencies. The goal, in their warped view, was to restore a cosmic order, to eliminate the 'impurities' that offended their arcane sensibilities and disrupted the supposed energetic harmony of the planet. The science, however abhorrent, was thus cloaked in a veneer of spiritual rectitude, a justification for ultimate destruction masquerading as cosmic balance.

Falk found the idea of resonance purges particularly chilling because it represented a complete abdication of any pretense of warfare. This was not about conquest or even subjugation; it was about an act of cosmic-scale erasure, a desire to scrub the planet clean of entire swathes of humanity, leaving no trace of their existence, no historical record, no memory. It was the ultimate expression of the SS's genocidal ideology, a twisted ambition to achieve purity not through breeding and indoctrination, but through an act of fundamental, existential deletion. The alien technology, in the hands of such zealots, had become a tool for realizing a nightmare of absolute negation, a silent, invisible apocalypse designed to leave only the immaculate emptiness of their desired world.

The implications for the captured 'Vulnerable' specimen was equally grim. It was not merely subjected to experiments designed to understand psychotropic disintegration; it was also analyzed for the inherent capacity to emit or manipulate the very frequencies that the SS sought to weaponize. Scientists painstakingly mapped the bio-energetic signatures of these beings, seeking to identify the precise biological mechanisms that allowed them to interact with psionic energies. The hope was to isolate, replicate, and then weaponize these internal biological processes, perhaps through engineered organisms or synthetic devices that could mimic the alien capacity for resonant disruption. This meant more invasive procedures, more agonizing experiments, as the SS sought to reverse-engineer the very essence of alien life for their horrific purposes.

The sheer audacity of the SS's vision was breathtaking. They were not merely seeking to build more efficient killing machines; they were attempting to fundamentally alter the nature of existence, to wield cosmic forces to enforce their ideological will. The resonance purges were the ultimate manifestation of this ambition – a silent, invisible weapon capable of excising populations from the fabric of reality itself, leaving behind nothing but a void where vibrant life and complex consciousness had once thrived. Falk couldn't shake the image of entire communities simply vanishing, their cities standing as silent monuments to an erased past, their absence a chilling testament to the SS's ultimate triumph.

The research into resonance purges was, in essence, an attempt to unlock a form of biological and cognitive 'kill switch' embedded within the universe itself, a switch that the alien technology had revealed. The SS believed that by understanding the fundamental energetic signatures of life, they could then engineer a counter-signature, a dissonant frequency that would unravel the very processes of existence for those targeted. This was a form of existential sabotage, a desire to dismantle the biological and mental machinery of their enemies at a fundamental level. The absence of physical evidence was not a bug; it was a feature. It ensured that the SS's ultimate victory would be absolute, leaving no one to bear witness to their crimes, no trace of their atrocities.

The meticulousness with which the Ahnenerbe approached these resonance purges was a chilling indicator of their unwavering dedication to the Cleansing Directive. Every piece of alien data, every biological sample, every observed psionic phenomenon was scrutinized for its potential application in this grand design of eradication. They were not content with merely dominating their enemies; they sought to unmake them, to remove them from the universe as if they had never been. The resonance purges represented the zenith of this ambition, a silent, invisible weapon that promised a form of victory so complete it bordered on the divine – a godlike power to erase existence itself. Falk felt the weight of this ambition pressing down on him, a suffocating realization of the abyss into which humanity was rapidly descending, driven by a genocidal ideology armed with unimaginable cosmic power. The hum of the hidden laboratories was not merely the sound of scientific progress; it was the thrumming of a cosmic doomsday device, meticulously crafted by the darkest impulses of the human heart.

The SS's ambition, Falk realized with a sickening lurch of his stomach, was not merely to extinguish life, but to obliterate the very *memory* of life. It was a chilling escalation, a move beyond the physical annihilation of bodies into the ontological erasure of identities. The Cleansing Directive, in its most terrifying iteration, sought to scrub entire populations not just from the present, but from the past, from the very collective consciousness of humanity. This was the true horror: not a swift, brutal end, but a meticulously orchestrated vanishing act, leaving behind only a void where vibrant individuals and their histories once resided. The alien technology, with its unfathomable capabilities, offered them the terrifyingly plausible means to achieve this audacious goal, a feat that bordered on rewriting the fabric of reality itself to align with their warped ideology.

The sheer audacity of such a goal was staggering. It was one thing to conquer and subjugate, another to obliterate; but to erase, to systematically expunge all traces of a people's existence, not just from the physical world but from the minds of those who survived them, was an act of almost cosmic hubris. The SS envisioned a future where entire nations, entire cultures, could be rendered as if they had never been. Their history books would be rewritten, their achievements expunged, their very languages silenced not just by decree, but by a manufactured amnesia. Survivors would be left with a haunting sense of loss, a vague feeling of something missing, without the ability to recall *what* was missing or *why*. This was the ultimate weapon of ideological purity: the weaponization of forgetfulness.

The scientists within the Ahnenerbe were not merely theorizing about memory erasure; they were actively engineering the tools for it. Their research focused on isolating specific psionic frequencies emanating from the alien artifacts, frequencies that seemed to directly interface with the neurological structures responsible for memory encoding and retrieval. Falk had seen the early schematics, the complex wave patterns that, when amplified and broadcast, were theorized to induce a targeted amnesic effect. The process was described in chillingly clinical terms: 'synaptic uncoupling,' 'mnemonic fragmentation,' and the ultimate goal, 'ontological nullification.' They weren't aiming to simply make people forget; they intended to make the very concept of their existence unfathomable.

Imagine, Falk thought, the devastating impact of such a weapon. A targeted city, its populace subjected to these frequencies, would not be bombed into rubble, but rather subtly dismantled from the inside out. Individuals would begin to forget loved ones, then their own names, their skills, their allegiances. The shared memories that bound communities together – the historical narratives, the cultural touchstones, the collective experiences – would dissolve like mist. The result would be a population rendered utterly apathetic, incapable of recognizing enemies or allies, unable to recount their own suffering or rally against their oppressors. They would become ghosts in their own lives, their identities systematically dismantled by an invisible, insidious force.

The captured 'Vulnerable' specimen was instrumental in this research. The inherent psionic abilities, the capacity to process and perhaps even transmit these alien energies, made them living laboratories. Mengele and his team were conducting agonizing experiments, attempting to map the neural pathways and biological mechanisms that allowed these beings to manipulate consciousness. The goal was to isolate the specific frequencies that induced profound memory loss, to understand how these alien minds could rewrite or erase the memories of others. This involved invasive neurological probing, the administration of exotic psychotropic compounds, and the constant monitoring of brainwave activity. The SS saw these beings not as sentient creatures, but as biological keys, unlocking the secrets to a weapon that could erase history itself.

One particularly disturbing line of research involved the manipulation of what the Ahnenerbe scientists termed 'memory anchors' – the core experiences and emotions that formed the bedrock of an individual's identity. The alien technology, they believed, could target these anchors directly, creating a profound disconnect between a person and their past. A soldier, for instance, might still remember how to fire a rifle, but forget why he was fighting, who his comrades were, or the very ideals he once held dear. This wasn't just about incapacitation; it was about the surgical removal of purpose, the eradication of meaning. The SS envisioned creating legions of soldiers stripped of their will, their memories of loyalty and duty systematically erased, leaving them as mere automatons susceptible to any command.

The occult factions within the Ahnenerbe, with their mystical interpretations of power and purity, saw this memory erasure as a form of spiritual cleansing. They spoke of 'purifying the psychic ether,' of 'unburdening the collective soul' by removing the 'impurities' of memory and individual experience. Their involvement lent a twisted, ancient credence to the SS's modern-day barbarism, framing the obliteration of consciousness as a cosmic necessity. They believed that by stripping away individual memories, they were aligning humanity with a primal, purer state of existence, a state devoid of the complexities and conflicts that arose from self-awareness and history. This provided a veneer of ancient wisdom to their genocidal ambitions, transforming mass psychological annihilation into a sacred act of cosmic reordering.

Falk shuddered at the implications of this 'ontological nullification.' It was a form of extermination that transcended the physical. It was the ultimate victory, the SS believed, to not only kill their enemies but to ensure that their very existence was forgotten, unremembered, and ultimately, never happened. The ramifications for historical records were profound. Imagine a future where textbooks were scrubbed clean of entire peoples, where monuments crumbled into dust without any memory of who they commemorated, where survivors could only recall a vague sense of loss, a phantom limb of consciousness that once held a vibrant past. This was the SS's vision of a perfect, sterile world, a blank canvas upon which they could paint their singular, ideological truth, unburdened by the messy, inconvenient realities of history and diversity.

The scientific rigor, however abhorrent, was undeniable. The Ahnenerbe was developing sophisticated mnemonic resonance emitters, devices designed to broadcast the specific alien frequencies identified as capable of inducing targeted memory loss. These emitters were intended to be deployed in a variety of ways: through localized atmospheric dispersion, through directed energy beams, or even embedded within seemingly innocuous infrastructure. The goal was to create 'zones of amnesia,' areas where the very fabric of consciousness was subtly undermined, leading to the gradual dissolution of personal identity. The SS wasn't just planning to conquer territories; they intended to conquer time and memory itself, to erase their enemies not just from the present, but from all of history.

The ability to disperse these memory-erasing frequencies through the atmosphere meant that any individual within a targeted zone would be susceptible, regardless of their role or status, their memories unraveling like a poorly woven tapestry.

The scientists were meticulously cataloging human memory itself, breaking it down into quantifiable components and identifying the specific alien frequencies that interacted with each component. They hypothesized that by isolating and amplifying these frequencies, they could induce a state of selective amnesia, targeting specific types of memories or even individuals with particular neural structures. This was not a crude, blunt instrument; it was a scalpel, designed to dissect and dismantle the very essence of personhood. The fear was not of outright destruction, but of a more insidious fate: to be rendered an unknowable stranger to oneself, a being adrift in a sea of forgotten experiences. The thought of a parent forgetting their child, or a soldier forgetting their oath, was a testament to the SS's chilling pursuit of an ultimate, existential control.

The ramifications of this research extended to the very concept of collective identity. The SS recognized that shared memories and narratives were the glue that held societies together. By targeting these collective memory anchors, they could fracture populations, sowing discord and distrust, rendering them incapable of unified resistance. This was a form of social lobotomy, a strategy to dismantle the very foundations of societal cohesion. The alien technology offered them the means to achieve this, to isolate the energetic signatures of shared experiences and then broadcast dissonant frequencies that would disrupt and ultimately erase them. The result would be a fragmented populace, atomized and vulnerable, incapable of recognizing its own history or uniting against its oppressors.

Falk's stomach churned with a familiar mixture of dread and nausea. He was no longer an observer, a mere witness to the unfolding horrors. The chilling efficiency with which the Ahnenerbe scientists, under the veiled direction of Himmler, were translating alien theories into tangible implements of destruction had entangled him, a spider's web of complicity spun with every overheard conversation, every glimpsed schematic, every suppressed scientific paper. He was privy to the intimate details of the 'Cleansing Directive,' a program so monstrous in its scope it threatened to redefine the very meaning of genocide. It wasn't enough for them to kill; they sought to erase, to annihilate not just bodies, but memories, histories, the very essence of a people's existence, leaving behind a void where vibrant lives had once pulsed with meaning. And Falk, by virtue of his unique access and forced participation, was becoming an integral cog in this unfathomable machine of oblivion.

The justifications, presented with a chilling blend of pseudo-scientific jargon and occult mysticism, were almost as terrifying as the methods themselves. They spoke of 'ontological purity,' of 'cosmic alignment,' of 'purifying the psychic ether.' These were not the words of men seeking military advantage; they were the pronouncements of zealots convinced of their divine mandate to reshape reality itself according to their warped vision. Falk listened, his mind reeling, as professors and SS officers alike debated the optimal atmospheric dispersal patterns for frequencies designed to induce selective amnesia, or the precise bio-energetic signatures that could trigger cascade failures in specific genetic lineages. Each session was a descent deeper into a moral abyss, a testament to the SS's chilling capacity to rationalize savagery under the guise of scientific advancement.

He found himself poring over data streams that detailed the agonizing experiments conducted on the captured 'Vulnerable' specimens, their unique psionic abilities being dissected and weaponized. Mengele's meticulous, yet utterly abhorrent, records of neurological probing and psychoactive compound administration were a stark reminder of the suffering that underpinned this 'research.' The SS saw these beings not as sentient creatures, but as biological keys, their very existence a means to unlock the terrifying potential of the alien technology. Falk's role, often subtle and indirect, was to cross-reference the alien energy signatures with the neurological responses of these subjects, a task that felt akin to cataloging the methods of torture for future implementation. The weight of this knowledge was crushing, a constant, gnawing reminder of his proximity to acts of unimaginable depravity. He was becoming an architect of erasure, even if his tools were merely data analysis and coded reports.

The more he understood, the more the sheer scale of the SS's ambition became terrifyingly clear. It wasn't merely about establishing a new world order; it was about scrubbing the slate of history clean, erasing any trace of those deemed 'undesirable.' The 'resonance purges,' a concept whispered in hushed tones by the more esoteric elements within the Ahnenerbe, envisioned a far more insidious form of destruction. This wasn't about precision strikes against individuals; it was about unleashing alien frequencies as blunt instruments, designed to induce a cascade of biological and cognitive failures on a massive scale, targeting entire populations based on perceived genetic or behavioral 'dissonance.' The idea of creating 'zones of absolute absence,' where people simply withered away, leaving no physical evidence of their existence, sent shivers down Falk's spine. The SS, armed with alien knowledge, was effectively seeking to play God, to wield a power of existential deletion.

One particular project, codenamed 'Stardust,' involved the atmospheric dispersal of a specific psionic frequency identified as 'Chronos-Delta.' The stated purpose was to induce widespread apathy and memory degradation, rendering populations incapable of organized resistance. Falk had been tasked with analyzing atmospheric data from experimental test sites, correlating the dispersal patterns with observed behavioral shifts in the local fauna and, in one horrific instance, a small, isolated human settlement that had been subtly subjected to the frequency. The reports were sanitized, couched in euphemisms, but the underlying truth was unmistakable: a subtle, invisible poison designed to unravel minds. The data indicated a significant decrease in social interaction, a marked increase in solitary behavior, and a pervasive sense of aimlessness. These weren't the glorious victories the SS propaganda machines trumpeted; these were the quiet, insidious deaths of consciousness.

The ethical boundaries, already eroded by years of the regime's barbarism, had been utterly obliterated by this research. The alien artifacts, once symbols of potential cosmic understanding, were being twisted into instruments of psychological torture and existential destruction. Falk found himself constantly battling a rising tide of revulsion, a desperate need to find a way out, a means to subvert these monstrous plans without betraying his own precarious position. He couldn't openly defy Himmler or the SS hierarchy; the consequences would be swift and final. But he also couldn't continue to be a passive participant in this systematic annihilation of humanity.

He began to tread a dangerous path, one of subtle subversion. It started small, with minor inaccuracies introduced into his reports, minuscule delays in data processing, the introduction of carefully worded caveats that might, just might, sow seeds of doubt in the minds of those who would ultimately wield these weapons. He would subtly alter the parameters of his simulations, nudging the predicted outcomes towards less devastating scenarios, or highlighting potential unforeseen consequences that might give the scientists pause. It was like trying to steer a leviathan with a whispered suggestion, a futile effort perhaps, but one he felt compelled to undertake.

During one clandestine meeting, where the discussion revolved around the deployment of 'memory anchors' – specific neuro-frequencies designed to target core identity markers – Falk proposed a 'contingency analysis' that would require extensive 'validation testing' across a broader spectrum of subjects. His intent was not validation, but delay, a bureaucratic labyrinth designed to slow the program's momentum. He meticulously documented the need for long-term studies, for ethical review protocols (a concept utterly alien to the SS, which he knew would be dismissed but might force a moment's reflection), and for cross-species comparison to ensure 'optimal efficacy and minimal collateral impact.' He knew the term 'collateral impact' would be interpreted through the SS lens of undesirable genetic contamination, but he hoped it would also imply a potential for unpredictable side effects that might deter them.

He also started to systematically archive certain data sets, creating encrypted backups that he kept hidden, a digital breadcrumb trail of their atrocities. If, by some miracle, he could escape this hellish labyrinth, he wanted proof, evidence that this madness had not simply evaporated into the ether. He reasoned that if he could not stop the creation of these weapons, he could at least ensure that their existence was known, their perpetrators brought to account, however unlikely that seemed in the current climate. This act of defiance was a private rebellion, a flicker of resistance against the overwhelming darkness.

One particular experiment, focused on the 'Sentinel' specimen's atmospheric manipulation capabilities, aimed to create a 'blank slate' environment by dispersing frequencies that induced profound cognitive disorientation. Falk's role was to analyze the spectral emissions required. Instead of providing the most potent theoretical combinations, he presented a range of options, subtly emphasizing those that were less efficient or had a higher probability of causing erratic, unpredictable environmental effects. He even included a deliberately flawed theoretical model of atmospheric diffusion, designed to suggest that widespread dispersal might be far more complex and less controllable than initially anticipated. His hope was that the SS, ever wary of uncontrolled variables that could impact their vision of pristine order, might shy away from such a volatile deployment.

He started to cultivate a persona of almost detached scientific curiosity, a mask that hid the turmoil raging within him. He would engage with the scientists, asking probing questions, not out of genuine interest, but to subtly guide their focus, to steer them towards less catastrophic avenues, or at least to glean more information about their progress and potential vulnerabilities. He would praise their ingenuity, their dedication, all while mentally cataloging their methods and their deepest, darkest intentions. This constant performance was exhausting, a tightrope walk over an abyss of his own making, but it was the only way he could operate.

The sheer depravity of their long-term goals was becoming increasingly apparent. The 'resonance purges' were not merely about eliminating perceived enemies; they were about achieving a form of existential purity, a universe cleansed of anything that deviated from the SS's rigid, fanatical ideology. Falk understood that his subtle acts of defiance were minuscule in the face of such overwhelming power and conviction. Yet, he could not stomach the thought of inaction. He was trapped, a scientist ensnared by the machinations of a genocidal regime, forced to contribute to the very horrors he abhorred. His complicity was a stain that would never wash away, but perhaps, just perhaps, by weaving these small threads of resistance, he could prevent the complete unraveling of humanity. The weight of his knowledge was a constant, suffocating pressure, a reminder that he was privy to secrets that could shatter the world, secrets that he now felt a desperate, almost suicidal obligation to expose, or at the very least, to sabotage.

Chapter 5

The Living War Machine

The sterile hum of the laboratory was a constant, unnerving companion to Falk. It was the sound of progress, of discovery, but also the thrum of something profoundly unnatural, a prelude to the horrors that were being meticulously crafted within these walls. The Ahnenerbe, under Himmler's unwavering, almost zealous gaze, had moved beyond mere theoretical study of the alien artifacts. They were now engaged in the visceral, terrifying act of *integration*. The objective was stark: to forge the ultimate soldier, a fusion of human will and extraterrestrial biological might. These were not to be mere enhanced individuals; they were to be 'living war machines,' walking embodiments of conquest, designed to shatter any resistance through sheer, unadulterated power.

The foundations of this horrific endeavor lay in Himmler's warped, almost pathological obsession with the perceived superiority of the Aryan race, interwoven with his deep-seated fascination for the occult and esoteric knowledge. He saw the alien specimens not just as tools, but as divine gifts, proof of a cosmic hierarchy that placed his chosen people at its apex. The 'Vulnerable,' as it was chillingly termed, became the primary canvas for this audacious, nightmarish fusion. Their unique biological structures, their inherent psionic capabilities – these were not to be studied from a distance, but to be forcibly grafted onto the human form, to create a hybrid that would transcend the limitations of both. The irony, a bitter, suffocating irony, was that the very essence of the 'Vulnerable' was being perverted to serve the SS's genocidal ambitions, to become the very instrument of the 'Cleansing Directive' Falk had witnessed with such horror.

The process itself was a meticulous, brutal ballet of surgical precision and bio-alchemy. Ahnenerbe scientists, under the ever-

91

watchful eye of figures like Mengele and his increasingly depraved proteges, worked with a chilling blend of advanced surgical techniques and what could only be described as ritualistic application of alien bio-agents. Falk found himself poring over schematics that detailed the delicate process of nerve-interfacing, the painstaking grafting of alien vascular systems onto human circulatory networks, and the implantation of bio-luminescent alien organs designed to channel and amplify psionic energies. Each diagram was a testament to a line irrevocably crossed, a descent into a realm where the sacred boundaries of life itself were being desecrated for the sake of war.

One of the most advanced projects, codenamed 'Titan,' involved the integration of what were believed to be specialized alien muscle fibers. These fibers, recovered from specimens exhibiting extraordinary physical resilience, were a deep, iridescent blue, pulsating with an internal luminescence that hinted at immense latent power. The aim was to replace significant portions of a soldier's musculature with these alien tissues, thereby augmenting strength, speed, and endurance to levels previously unimagined. Falk's task was to analyze the bio-energetic compatibility of these fibers with human physiology, a task that involved cross-referencing the subtle energy signatures of the alien tissue with the electrochemical signals of the human nervous system. The data he was generating was intended to optimize the integration, to ensure the resulting hybrid soldier could withstand the immense physiological strain of wielding such power.

The early trials were, by all accounts, devastating. The schematics detailed the horrific failures; subjects whose bodies rejected the alien tissues outright, leading to rapid necrosis and an agonizing disintegration of the cellular structure; others who succumbed to a form of biological overload, their systems unable to process the raw, alien energy, resulting in catastrophic internal hemorrhages and organ failure. Mengele's logs, a grim chronicle of these failed experiments, were filled with descriptions of agonizing screams, of bodies contorting and rupturing, of a desperate, futile struggle against forces they could not comprehend. Yet, even in these gruesome accounts, there was a disturbing undercurrent of scientific detachment, a focus on data collection even in the face of such unspeakable suffering. The scientists, driven by Himmler's vision, saw these failures not as a reason to cease, but as data points, valuable lessons learned at a terrible cost, guiding them towards a more refined, more successful integration.

The SS leadership, particularly Himmler himself, visited these laboratories with unsettling regularity. He would observe the procedures with a detached intensity, his eyes glinting with an almost religious fervor. He spoke of creating 'Übermenschen,' of forging warriors who were not merely superior in strength or intellect, but who embodied a cosmic destiny. He saw the alien bio-enhancements as a tangible manifestation of this destiny, a direct grant of power from the celestial realms, bestowed upon his chosen race.

His pronouncements were laced with occult symbolism, with references to ancient myths and prophecies, all twisted to support his fanatical ideology. He believed that by merging with the alien essence, the Aryan soldier would achieve a state of transcendent power, becoming a living weapon capable of enforcing his vision of a purified world.

Falk, forced to be present during these visits, felt a profound sense of revulsion. He witnessed the SS officers discussing the potential applications of these 'living war machines' with chilling enthusiasm. They spoke of units capable of traversing impossible terrain, of soldiers who could withstand extreme environments, of warriors whose psionic abilities could disrupt enemy communications or induce terror. The 'Cleansing Directive' was no longer an abstract concept; it was being given terrifyingly concrete form. These bio-engineered soldiers were to be the vanguard, the shock troops who would spearhead the SS's global ambitions, their very existence a symbol of the ultimate victory of their ideology.

The integration was not limited to physical enhancements. There was a significant focus on integrating alien neural pathways and sensory organs. The goal was to enhance not only brute strength but also perception and cognitive processing. Some projects involved implanting alien ocular organs, believed to grant enhanced vision, including the ability to perceive different spectrums of light or to detect thermal signatures. Others focused on integrating alien auditory receptors, promising soldiers who could hear on frequencies far beyond human range or even discern subtle atmospheric vibrations. Falk's work here involved analyzing the neurological compatibility, trying to map the alien sensory input onto the human brain's existing architecture. The data suggested that such integration could lead to overwhelming sensory input, potentially causing psychological instability, but the SS dismissed these concerns as mere 'adjustment periods.'

The 'Vulnerable' specimen was not the only source of biological material. The Ahnenerbe had also begun expeditions to collect biological samples from other species deemed 'undesirable' or 'primitive,' often justifying these actions under the guise of scientific inquiry or resource acquisition. These samples, however tainted with the SS's racist ideology, were then analyzed for their unique biological properties, with the ultimate aim of incorporating desirable traits into the Aryan soldier. This expansion of their genetic pool, as they saw it, was another step towards achieving their vision of racial purity and dominance, a perverse application of evolutionary theory.

Falk found himself increasingly disturbed by the ethical vacuum within the Ahnenerbe. The scientific curiosity that might have once driven these individuals had been entirely corrupted, replaced by an unshakeable ideological fervor. They operated with a complete disregard for life, human or otherwise, viewing all existence as raw material to be manipulated for the SS's grand design. He remembered a conversation he'd overheard between two senior scientists discussing the potential for 'psychic bonding' between the enhanced soldiers and the alien technology. They spoke of creating a symbiotic relationship, where the soldier and the artifact would act as one, a terrifying prospect that blurred the lines between human and machine, between life and an alien, unknown existence.

The sheer audacity of their ambition was breathtaking, and utterly terrifying. Himmler envisioned not just an army of enhanced soldiers, but a new breed of human, fundamentally altered by alien influence, a living testament to the SS's dominion over both earthly and cosmic forces. The 'living war machines' were the first step in

94

this grand, terrifying metamorphosis. They were designed to be utterly loyal, conditioned through a combination of psychological manipulation and direct neural interfacing with the alien technology, ensuring their absolute obedience to the SS. There were whispers of implants that would suppress fear and doubt, replacing them with an unyielding sense of purpose, a programmed aggression that would make them unstoppable on the battlefield.

Falk's role, though seemingly confined to data analysis and simulation, placed him at the very heart of this monstrous creation. He was privy to the most intimate details of the integration process, the success rates, the failure points, the precise bio-signatures that made these horrific fusions possible. He saw the raw data that underpinned the SS's claims of superiority, data derived from the suffering and violation of countless living beings. The weight of this knowledge was a crushing burden, a constant reminder of the complicity that stained his own hands, however indirectly. He was a scientist trapped in a madman's dream, forced to provide the calculations that would bring these terrifying creations to life.

The development of 'sentient weapon systems' was another, even more disturbing, facet of this research. The idea was to imbue the bio-enhanced soldiers with a degree of artificial intelligence, augmented by the psionic capabilities of the alien specimens, allowing them to operate with a degree of autonomy in complex combat situations. Falk's simulations explored the potential for such autonomous units, analyzing the parameters for decision-making, target acquisition, and tactical response. The ethical implications were, of course, utterly ignored by the SS. They saw only the potential for an unstoppable, unthinking, unfeeling force, a perfect soldier that would never falter, never question, never betray.

He was constantly seeking ways to subtly sabotage the project, to introduce errors that would lead to greater instability or to highlight the dangers of uncontrolled integration. He would slightly miscalculate the energy requirements for certain bio-components or inflate the projected psychological side effects of neural interfacing. These were small acts of defiance, easily overlooked in the vast ocean of data, but they were all he could manage. He knew that a more overt act of sabotage would be his immediate undoing, and that would achieve nothing but his own demise, leaving the project to continue its unfettered march towards its horrific conclusion.

The integration of alien biological material was not a singular event but a continuous process. The soldiers were to be regularly 'maintained' and 'updated' with new alien bio-enhancements, ensuring their ongoing superiority. This implied a perpetual cycle of experimentation, of further violation, of a constant push towards an ever-higher threshold of destructive capability. Falk saw the trajectory clearly: the SS was not just creating soldiers; they were attempting to engineer a new species, a bio-mechanical hybrid race designed for perpetual conquest, its existence predicated on the assimilation and perversion of alien life. The chilling efficiency with which they approached this task, the absolute lack of moral compunction, was a testament to the deep, pervasive rot that had taken hold of the Ahnenerbe and, by extension, the entire regime. The 'living war machines' were not just a weapon; they were the embodiment of the SS's ultimate, terrifying vision for humanity's future.

The sterile hum of the laboratory was a constant, unnerving companion to Falk. It was the sound of progress, of discovery, but also the thrum of something profoundly unnatural, a prelude to the horrors that were being meticulously crafted within these walls. The Ahnenerbe, under Himmler's unwavering, almost zealous gaze, had moved beyond mere theoretical study of the alien artifacts. They were now engaged in the visceral, terrifying act of *integration*. The objective was stark: to forge the ultimate soldier, a fusion of human will and extraterrestrial biological might. These were not to be mere enhanced individuals; they were to be 'living war machines,' walking embodiments of conquest, designed to shatter any resistance through sheer, unadulterated power.

The specific trials on concentration camp inmates, however, represented a chilling escalation of the Ahnenerbe's depravity. These were not willing volunteers, nor were they merely specimens of alien biology. They were human beings, stripped of their identity, their dignity, and ultimately, their very humanity, reduced to mere biological substrata for the SS's monstrous ambitions. The reports Falk was tasked with analyzing were stark in their clinical detachment, yet horrific in their implications.

They detailed procedures that began with the systematic extraction of biological samples from the prisoners – blood, tissue, organs – often performed without anesthesia, or with rudimentary, insufficient anesthesia that did little to mask the agony. These samples were then meticulously cataloged and prepared for integration with the alien organic materials. The core of the experimentation involved the direct grafting of alien bio-components onto the prisoners. Falk's calculations were instrumental in determining the optimal points of vascular and neural connection. He saw diagrams illustrating the meticulous insertion of alien tissues into musculature, the painstaking suturing of alien vascular networks to human arteries and veins, and the implantation of alien organs designed to augment strength, sensory perception, or even the capacity for psionic emission. These were not simple transplants; they were forced biological fusions, where the prisoner's body was the unwilling host to alien biology. The alien materials, often exhibiting a phosphorescent quality or an unnerving, organic rigidity, were treated with chemical agents to 'prepare' them for human integration, a process that Falk suspected involved complex molecular manipulation to overcome immune rejection, or perhaps, to actively suppress the host's natural defenses.

The cybernetic augmentation was an equally brutal aspect of these experiments. Alien technology, recovered from the crashed spacecraft, was not only organic but also manifested in advanced mechanical and energy-based components. These were designed to interface with the biological enhancements, providing an external source of power, control, or additional functionality. Falk's simulations often involved mapping the energy flow from these alien cybernetic implants to the host's nervous system and augmented musculature. The goal was to create a seamless integration, where the prisoner and the alien technology would function as a single, terrifyingly efficient unit. This could involve the implantation of skeletal reinforcement struts, cybernetic joints designed to enhance limb articulation and power, or even cranial implants that interfaced directly with the brain to enhance cognitive processing or to facilitate direct neural command of the integrated alien systems.

The psychological aspect of these experiments was as horrific as the physical. The prisoners were subjected to intense conditioning, a potent cocktail of fear, pain, and the overwhelming sensation of their own altered bodies. The alien bio-enhancements and cybernetic implants often induced profound sensory overload, causing disorientation, hallucinations, and extreme psychological distress. Reports detailed instances where prisoners, driven mad by the constant influx of alien sensory data or the sheer physical agony of their transformations, would mutilate themselves or lash out indiscriminately at their captors. The SS scientists, however, viewed this as a predictable, even desirable, outcome, a necessary hurdle in the creation of a soldier that was utterly detached from normal human empathy and restraint. They documented the progression of 'submissiveness,' the gradual erosion of the prisoner's original personality, and the emergence of a more compliant, more aggressive disposition.

The outcome for the majority of these subjects was invariably grim. Rejection of the alien tissues was common, leading to violent autoimmune responses, gangrene, and a slow, agonizing death. Others succumbed to the sheer physiological strain of housing alien biological components, their bodies unable to cope with the increased metabolic demands or the incompatible bio-energetic fields. Catastrophic system failures of the cybernetic implants also contributed to a high mortality rate, with uncontrolled energy surges or mechanical malfunctions proving fatal. Falk's data tables were replete with the stark finality of these outcomes: 'Subject deceased due to tissue necrosis,' 'System failure: fatal,' 'Complete biological collapse.'

Yet, a terrifying minority survived. These were the 'successes,' the proto-war machines. They were grotesquely altered, their bodies warped and reshaped by the alien grafts and cybernetic integrations. Their skin might be stretched taut over unnaturally dense, iridescent muscle fibers, their limbs contorted into configurations optimized for strength and speed, their eyes replaced by alien sensory organs that glowed with an otherworldly light. Their original human features were often obscured, buried beneath a veneer of alien biology and salvaged technology. These survivors were barely recognizable as human, their minds often fragmented, their emotions blunted, their existence reduced to a primal, conditioned obedience to their SS masters. They were living testaments to the SS's perverse vision: powerful, terrifying, and utterly devoid of their former selves.

Falk's daily existence was a descent into this abyss of human suffering, meticulously documented and analyzed. He would pore over the schematics of neural pathways, the bio-energetic flow charts, the tissue compatibility reports, all generated from the screams and agonies of men, women, and even children who had been subjected to these abominable experiments. The sheer scale of the cruelty was staggering. He saw records of experiments involving infants and young children, their developing bodies deemed particularly pliable for certain types of integration, a thought so repellent it made his stomach churn. The Ahnenerbe's 'scientific detachment' was a thin veil for an ocean of barbarity, a calculated extermination masquerading as research.

He was often required to run simulations on the long-term effects of these integrations. These simulations, based on incomplete and often biased data, predicted increased aggression, decreased pain tolerance, and a heightened susceptibility to psionic manipulation. Some simulations even suggested a gradual degradation of the human consciousness, replaced by a more primal, alien-influenced cognitive framework. The implications were clear: the SS was not merely creating soldiers; they were attempting to engineer a new, subservient species, one that would serve as the ultimate tool of their dominion. The concentration camp prisoners were the unwilling pioneers of this horrifying new evolutionary path, their bodies and minds the experimental grounds for a future dictated by Himmler's genocidal madness. The very air in the laboratory seemed to carry the phantom screams of the victims, a constant, chilling reminder of the price being paid for this 'progress.' Falk's work, though seemingly abstract, was inextricably linked to the tangible horrors unfolding in the surgical theaters, each calculation a step further into a moral and biological wasteland. The sheer efficiency of the SS's operation, the systematic dehumanization of their victims and the cold, calculated nature of

99

their scientific pursuits, were perhaps the most terrifying aspects of all. They were not driven by passion or fury, but by a chillingly rational, albeit utterly deranged, pursuit of power, a pursuit that saw human life as nothing more than expendable raw material for their ultimate weapon.

The sterile hum of the laboratory, once a source of gnawing unease, now seemed to hum with a more palpable, visceral energy. Falk found himself standing before the observation window, the reinforced glass a thin barrier between his world of calculated dread and the unfolding reality within. The 'Vulnerable,' the very specimens of alien life that had sparked this monstrous endeavor, were no longer confined to sterile containment units. They were the source material, the biological blueprints, and now, the very essence being woven into the fabric of human flesh and will. The early stages of integration, the grafting of iridescent muscle fibers and the delicate splicing of neural pathways, had yielded results that were both astonishing and profoundly disturbing. The sheer physical augmentation was undeniable. Soldiers, or what remained of them, exhibited a strength that defied conventional understanding. Limbs, once subject to the frailties of human physiology, now moved with a terrifying economy of motion, their augmented musculature rippling with a power that pulsed just beneath the skin. Falk's simulations had predicted such outcomes, of course. He had calculated the energy amplification, the tensile strength of the alien tissues, and the sheer kinetic potential. But seeing it, witnessing a human frame now housing something fundamentally *other*, something forged from the very stars, was a different order of horror altogether.

The prototypes, as they were chillingly referred to, were a grotesque testament to the Ahnenerbe's success. They were not merely stronger; they were *different*. Their movements possessed a predatory grace, a fluidity that was both elegant and deeply unsettling. Some bore visible signs of the integration: patches of skin that shimmered with an unnatural luminescence, where alien bio-luminescent organs were functioning, or limbs that appeared subtly elongated, hinting at the reinforced skeletal structures beneath. Others were more subtly altered, their transformations hidden beneath standard SS uniforms, their enhanced physiology betrayed only by an almost imperceptible rigidity in their bearing, a focused intensity in their eyes that spoke of a mind irrevocably changed. Falk had spent weeks analyzing the bio-energetic compatibility of the 'Titan' muscle fibers, the ones that pulsed with that deep, iridescent blue. His calculations had focused on ensuring the human circulatory system could adequately support the alien tissues, that the bio-electrical signals could be properly modulated. The results, presented in sterile graphs and complex equations, had suggested a high degree of success, provided the integration protocols were followed with absolute precision.

But the precision came at a price, a price measured in shattered psyches and extinguished humanity. The 'horrifyingly successful' aspect of these prototypes was not solely their physical prowess. It was the state of their minds. Falk, tasked with analyzing the psychological impact of the integrations, found himself wading through reports filled with chillingly objective observations of profound mental degradation. The alien sensory organs, designed to grant enhanced perception, often resulted in overwhelming input. Subjects described a cacophony of sights and sounds, a constant barrage of stimuli that their human brains struggled to process.

This sensory overload was frequently accompanied by intense paranoia, hallucinations, and a complete loss of spatial and temporal awareness. Falk's simulations, which had attempted to model the cognitive load of such enhanced perception, had flagged these risks, predicting a high probability of psychological instability. The SS, however, dismissed these concerns as mere 'adjustment periods,' the necessary growing pains of forging a superior soldier.

The 'primal aggression' was another recurring theme in the post-integration reports. The alien bio-enhancements, particularly those linked to the nervous system and the presumed alien endocrine functions, seemed to amplify latent aggressive tendencies to catastrophic levels. Subjects who had previously exhibited normal emotional ranges would transform into volatile, unpredictable forces of destruction. Their capacity for empathy was systematically eroded, replaced by a raw, unreasoning hostility. Falk had pored over the case files of early trials, the ones marked with stark red 'FAILURE' stamps. He had seen descriptions of subjects, their bodies writhing with alien tissues, turning on their handlers with unbridled ferocity, tearing them apart with augmented strength before succumbing to systemic collapse or being put down by armed guards. These were not soldiers; they were barely controlled beasts, driven by an alien instinct that had overwritten their human consciousness.

Conversely, there was the chilling phenomenon of 'complete docility.' A subset of the prototypes exhibited an almost unnerving passivity. Their minds seemed to have entirely shut down, their original personalities effectively erased. They moved, they followed commands, they performed tasks with a robotic efficiency, but there was no spark of individuality, no hint of sentience beyond the programmed directives. Falk's analyses of their neural activity revealed minimal cognitive processing, a near-complete absence of emotional response. It was as if the integration process had not merely enhanced them, but had effectively lobotomized them, leaving behind a hollow shell programmed for obedience. These were the perfect tools, devoid of independent thought, utterly subservient to the will of their SS masters. Falk found this complete erasure of self to be even more disturbing than the rampaging aggression. It spoke of a systematic deconstruction of the human spirit, a terrifying efficiency in reducing living beings to mere automatons.

He was compelled to witness the creation of these abominations firsthand. The sterile observation rooms, usually filled with the quiet rustle of data sheets and the soft click of keyboards, now echoed with the guttural sounds of the subjects themselves. The alien technology, salvaged from the depths of the abyss from which it originated, had been irrevocably warped. What might have once been tools of understanding, or even instruments of interstellar travel, were now crudely repurposed, integrated into the very biology of these unfortunate souls. Cybernetic implants, designed to channel psionic energy, were now fused with bone and sinew, their alien luminescence a sickly counterpoint to the pallor of human flesh. The focus, as always, was on destruction. The objective was not to create beings of wonder, but to forge instruments of terror, machines capable of inflicting unimaginable suffering.

Falk's simulations had been crucial in this perversion of purpose. He had been instrumental in calculating the optimal angles for implantation of the alien cranial conduits, the precise energy frequencies required to stimulate the psionically-charged tissues, and the structural integrity needed for armor plating integrated directly into the skeletal framework. He had designed algorithms to predict how the alien nervous system would respond to human motor commands, and how the alien sensory input would be filtered and processed. His data had allowed the Ahnenerbe scientists to refine the integration process, to minimize the catastrophic failures that had plagued the early trials, and to maximize the terrifying potential of the resulting hybrids.

The 'prototypes' were presented in controlled environments, their capabilities demonstrated for Himmler and his inner circle. Falk was always present, a silent, unwilling witness to the unfolding horror. He saw a subject, once a man, now barely recognizable, his body a mass of sculpted alien muscle and gleaming cybernetic implants, lift a multi-ton steel girder with a grunt, his augmented lungs drawing in air with a rasping, alien rhythm. He saw another, his eyes replaced by multifaceted alien organs that glowed with an internal, icy blue light, accurately track and target multiple moving objects in a simulated combat scenario, his brain processing information at a speed that no human could comprehend. These were not acts of strength or skill; they were demonstrations of alien power, harnessed and directed by SS ambition.

The SS officers would murmur appreciatively, their faces alight with a disturbing blend of triumph and avarice. They spoke of battlefield applications, of units that could breach fortified positions with ease, of soldiers who were immune to conventional weaponry, of warriors whose psionic abilities could shatter enemy morale and sow terror. Himmler, in particular, would often stroke his chin, a faint smile playing on his lips, as he observed these terrifying displays. He saw in these prototypes the physical manifestation of his vision, the ultimate expression of Aryan superiority, the living embodiment of the SS's destiny. He spoke of them as the 'new man,' a creature forged in the crucible of scientific ambition and cosmic power, destined to lead the Third Reich to its inevitable, glorious conquest.

Falk's role in this charade was a constant, gnawing torment. He was the architect of their capabilities, the silent contributor to their horrific existence. His calculations, his simulations, his data analyses – they were the very foundation upon which these 'living war machines' were built. The cognitive dissonance was immense. He was a scientist, trained to seek knowledge, to understand the universe. Yet, here he was, his skills perverted, his intellect weaponized, contributing to the creation of beings that represented the absolute antithesis of humanity. He found himself meticulously reviewing the data from the concentration camps, the raw, unfiltered accounts of the experiments performed on the 'Vulnerable' and the unfortunate humans who served as their hosts. He saw the meticulous cataloging of biological samples, the precise measurements of tissue integration, and the detailed records of physiological responses. Each piece of data, no matter how clinical, was a testament to unspeakable cruelty.

The physical alterations were often extreme. Alien skeletal structures were grafted to human bones, reinforcing limbs and torsos. Musculature was replaced, augmented, or interwoven with alien tissues that possessed an almost metallic sheen and an inhuman resilience. These weren't just simple augmentations; they were wholesale biological reconstructions. Falk's task was to ensure the structural integrity of these new forms, to calculate the stress tolerances of the fused biological components, to predict how the human body would react to the constant presence of alien physiology. His simulations had shown that such radical alterations placed immense strain on the cardiovascular and respiratory systems, often leading to organ failure. Yet, the SS pushed forward, seeing these failures as merely statistical hurdles to overcome.

The integration of alien sensory organs was a particularly gruesome aspect. Attempts were made to graft alien ocular systems onto human sockets, or to implant alien auditory receptors into the temporal bone. The goal was to grant soldiers vision that could penetrate darkness, perceive thermal signatures, or even see into different spectrums of light. The auditory enhancements aimed to grant soldiers the ability to hear beyond the human range, to detect subtle vibrations, or to even process information transmitted through psionic frequencies. Falk's work here involved mapping the neural connections, trying to ensure that the alien sensory data could be translated into comprehensible signals by the human brain. His early simulations, however, predicted catastrophic sensory overload, a deluge of unfiltered input that would overwhelm the subject's cognitive capacity, leading to acute psychological distress, paranoia, and in many cases, complete mental breakdown. The SS's response was to further refine the neural interfacing, attempting to 'filter' the alien input, or to simply accept the resulting mental instability as a byproduct of creating a superior warrior.

The emotional and psychological consequences were, as Falk had predicted, devastating. The prototypes exhibited a spectrum of mental states, all indicative of profound trauma and fundamental alteration. Some were consumed by an unreasoning, primal rage, their every action dictated by an alien imperative to destroy. Others were reduced to a state of catatonic docility, their minds effectively erased, their bodies animated by a programmed obedience. There were also those who seemed to exist in a perpetual state of confusion and fear, their alien senses bombarding them with stimuli they could not comprehend, their human consciousness struggling against an overwhelming tide of alien influence. Falk's task was to analyze these psychological profiles, to quantify the extent of mental degradation, and to correlate it with the specific types of alien biological and technological integrations. His reports, though couched in scientific language, were essentially a record of systematic psychological torture and annihilation.

He found himself tasked with designing simulations that predicted the long-term effects of these integrations. These simulations, based on the limited and often gruesome data available, painted a bleak picture. They suggested that prolonged exposure to alien bio-energetic fields, coupled with the constant influx of alien sensory data, could lead to a gradual degradation of the human cognitive framework. The human personality, with its nuances of emotion, empathy, and morality, was being systematically eroded, replaced by a more primitive, more aggressive, or conversely, a more passive, programmed consciousness.

The SS saw this not as a tragedy, but as a desired outcome. They were not merely enhancing soldiers; they were attempting to engineer a new form of humanity, one that was utterly subservient to their will, devoid of the inconvenient complexities of human conscience. The concentration camp prisoners, the 'Vulnerable' specimen, was the unwilling architect of this terrifying future, its very existence sacrificed on the altar of Himmler's mad vision.

Falk, in his sterile laboratory, felt like a craftsman of oblivion, his calculations and simulations the tools by which humanity was being unmade. The sheer scale of the depravity, the systematic dehumanization, the chilling efficiency with which they pursued their goals – it was a horror that seeped into his very bones, a constant, suffocating reminder of the abyss into which he had fallen. The prototypes were not just weapons; they were the living embodiment of a future built on the ruins of human dignity and the perversion of life itself. They were the ultimate expression of the SS's ambition, a terrifying synthesis of human will and alien power, forged in the fires of unimaginable cruelty.

The initial fascination with the 'Vulnerable' specimen had been a primal, almost scientific curiosity, a desire to understand the alien biology that had arrived on Earth in such a catastrophic manner. But that curiosity had long since curdled into something far more sinister. The Ahnenerbe, under Himmler's unwavering, and increasingly unhinged, direction, had shifted their focus from mere understanding to outright exploitation. The biological samples, carefully extracted from the deceased extraterrestrials and the few unfortunate survivors of the initial crash, were no longer subjects of passive study. They were raw materials, destined for a terrifyingly active purpose: the weaponization of alien life itself.

Falk found himself reviewing schematics that would have been unthinkable mere months ago. These weren't designs for advanced weaponry in the conventional sense – plasma projectors or sonic disruptors. These were blueprints for biological devastation. The focus was on the alien pathogens that had been identified in the initial autopsies, the microscopic agents of death that had accompanied the alien arrival. His simulations, initially designed to predict their infectivity and lethality within human biology, were now being recalibrated to identify potential vectors for controlled deployment. The objective had mutated from understanding a threat to actively creating one.

The scientists were particularly engrossed in a specific type of viral agent, designated 'Xenophage-Delta.' Its effect on mammalian cellular structure was unlike anything Falk had ever encountered. It didn't simply kill cells; it seemed to rewrite their fundamental code, forcing them to replicate at an exponential rate, creating grotesque, uncontrolled growths. Early trials, conducted on captured Soviet prisoners and individuals from the occupied territories who were conveniently classified as 'undesirables,' had yielded horrifyingly promising results. A single, airborne droplet, dispersed within a contained environment, could initiate a cascading cellular rebellion within hours. The targets would swell, their skin erupting with fluid-filled pustules and hard, chitinous growths, before succumbing to organ failure or sheer physical disintegration. Falk's simulations predicted that a carefully calibrated dispersal could render entire cities uninhabitable within days, leaving behind a landscape of biological horror.

However, simply unleashing an uncontrolled plague was considered too crude for the Ahnenerbe's refined brand of madness. Himmler desired more than just destruction; he craved a specific, targeted form of subjugation. This led to the exploration of biological agents designed to enhance, rather than annihilate, the fighting capabilities of their own soldiers. The research into alien growth hormones and muscle accelerators was particularly disturbing. These substances, extracted from the more robust alien specimens, promised to push the boundaries of human physical potential to unimaginable extremes. Falk was tasked with developing protocols to integrate these alien biochemicals into the human endocrine system, ensuring that the resultant strength augmentation did not lead to catastrophic metabolic collapse or rampant, uncontrollable aggression. The simulations were a tightrope walk between peak performance and utter biological breakdown.

One particular avenue of research involved an alien fungus, discovered within the ruptured biological containment units of the crashed ship. This fungus possessed an extraordinary ability to adapt and integrate with host organisms, even human tissue. When introduced to a suitable host, it would establish a symbiotic, or perhaps more accurately, a parasitic relationship, subtly altering the host's physiology. It enhanced tissue regeneration, accelerated healing, and, most disturbingly, seemed to foster a heightened sense of territoriality and aggression in its hosts. The SS envisioned its use as a battlefield stimulant, a way to create soldiers who could shrug off grievous wounds and fight with unwavering ferocity. Falk's simulations showed that the fungus could indeed dramatically increase wound healing and bolster physical resilience, but they also flagged a significant risk of the fungus eventually overwhelming the host's neural pathways, leading to a complete loss of self and a subservient, instinct-driven existence. The line between a super-soldier and a biological automaton was perilously thin.

The isolation and replication of these alien biological agents were conducted in heavily guarded facilities, often disguised as mundane agricultural research stations. The concentration camps, far from being mere sites of extermination, had become vast biological laboratories. Prisoners were subjected to controlled infections, their bodies monitored and dissected to understand the progression of alien diseases and the efficacy of various counter-agents, or, more often, agents designed to enhance the alien effects. Falk, privy to the decrypted reports from these facilities, felt a perpetual chill creep into his bones. He read accounts of horrific mutations, of individuals whose bodies had been so fundamentally altered by alien pathogens that they were no longer recognizably human, their forms twisted into grotesque mockeries of life.

The research wasn't limited to infectious agents. The Ahnenerbe were also fascinated by the alien regenerative capabilities. They had discovered that certain alien biological compounds could stimulate rapid cell division and tissue repair, far exceeding any known human capacity. The goal was to synthesize these compounds, to create serums that could instantly heal battlefield injuries, making their soldiers virtually impervious to harm. Falk's simulations focused on the cellular mechanisms of alien regeneration, attempting to replicate the alien genetic sequences that controlled this process. The early results were fraught with peril. Attempts to induce accelerated regeneration in human subjects often resulted in uncontrolled cellular growth, leading to aggressive cancers or the formation of alien biological structures within the human body. It was a desperate attempt to play God, with devastating consequences.

The implications of weaponizing alien biology were far-reaching and terrifying. Himmler envisioned a world where the Third Reich could unleash tailored plagues upon its enemies, diseases that specifically targeted certain ethnic groups, or conversely, biological agents that could render enemy infrastructure useless without harming the Aryan population. He spoke of "bio-genetic superiority," a concept that blended his racist ideology with the unfathomable power of alien life. Falk's simulations explored the feasibility of such scenarios, analyzing the genetic markers of various populations and attempting to correlate them with the specific vulnerabilities of the alien pathogens. The calculations were detached, clinical, but the underlying reality was one of mass extermination, orchestrated by the perversion of scientific inquiry.

Beyond offensive biological warfare, the Ahnenerbe also sought to enhance their own soldiers through direct biological augmentation. This involved not just the muscle fibers and neural pathways discussed previously, but also the integration of alien immune systems and sensory organs. The goal was to create soldiers who were not only physically superior but also more resilient to disease and capable of perceiving the world in ways that were beyond human comprehension. Falk's simulations were critical in understanding the compatibility of these systems, predicting how alien antibodies would interact with human blood, or how alien ocular implants would interface with the human visual cortex. The reports from the integration labs were a constant stream of both success and horrific failure. Some prototypes exhibited an unnerving resistance to conventional diseases, while others succumbed to autoimmune reactions, their own bodies attacking the alien biological components.

The concept of "growth accelerators" was particularly insidious. These were not merely performance enhancers; they were agents designed to fundamentally alter the human form, to make soldiers larger, stronger, and more intimidating. The research involved manipulating the growth hormones and cellular signaling pathways of the alien specimens, attempting to replicate their effects in human subjects. Falk's simulations indicated that such modifications, if uncontrolled, could lead to severe skeletal deformities, organ damage, and a drastically shortened lifespan. Yet, the SS pressed on, driven by a vision of an Aryan super-soldier, a physically dominant being capable of crushing all opposition. The prototypes undergoing these augmentations were often kept in specialized containment, their monstrous transformations a testament to the Ahnenerbe's relentless pursuit of power.

The ethical boundaries had not just been crossed; they had been obliterated. The scientists, including Falk himself, were no longer engaged in pure research. They were industrialists of death, their laboratories humming with the horrific synthesis of human ambition and alien biological might. The sterile environment of scientific inquiry had been irrevocably tainted by the stench of fear, desperation, and the utter dehumanization of countless individuals.

Falk's simulations, once tools for understanding, had become instruments of biological terror, his calculations charting the course for a new, terrifying era of warfare, an era where life itself, in its most alien and potent forms, was the ultimate weapon. The distinction between healer and harmer, between scientist and torturer, had become indistinguishable, lost in the relentless pursuit of Himmler's grotesque vision. The very essence of life was being dissected, manipulated, and reassembled into instruments of destruction, a chilling testament to the depths of human depravity when coupled with unimaginable power.

The air in Falk's small, nondescript office, usually thick with the sterile scent of paper and ink, now carried a faint, metallic tang. It was a scent he was beginning to associate with the creeping dread that permeated the Ahnenerbe's research into the extraterrestrial specimens. He sat hunched over his desk, the flickering gaslight casting long, dancing shadows that played tricks with his eyes. Outside, the perpetual hum of the Reich's vast, insatiable war machine provided a constant, unsettling backdrop. But here, within these four walls, a different kind of battle was being waged – one of conscience, fought with carefully chosen words and meticulously gathered data.

Falk's initial task, a seemingly innocuous one, was to analyze the physiological responses of various organisms to controlled exposure to alien biological agents. The data streams were intended to inform the development of defensive measures, a purely theoretical exercise in a regime that was rapidly abandoning all pretense of defense in favor of aggressive, unbridled offense. Yet, as he delved deeper into the raw reports, the stark reality of the Ahnenerbe's true intentions began to claw at him. These weren't defensive simulations; they were blueprints for biological warfare. The 'organisms' in question were, more often than not, living, breathing human beings, drawn from the dregs of humanity as defined by the SS: political dissidents, prisoners of war, and, most disturbingly, the inhabitants of occupied territories deemed 'lesser.'

He worked with a growing sense of internal dissonance. Each data point, each carefully cataloged symptom of suffering, felt like a betrayal of his oath as a scientist, a scientist who had once believed in the pursuit of knowledge for the betterment of mankind. Now, that knowledge was being twisted, weaponized, and wielded by a regime that saw humanity as little more than a malleable resource to be exploited and discarded. He began to divert a fraction of his processing power, a discreet subroutine running in the background of his complex simulations, dedicated to a new, far more dangerous objective: evidence gathering.

His access to the project's inner workings was a double-edged sword. It granted him insight into the horrific extent of the Ahnenerbe's depravity, but it also implicated him, however passively, in their crimes. The reports he was privy to detailed experiments that defied comprehension. He read about subjects subjected to the aforementioned Xenophage-Delta, their bodies transforming into grotesque caricatures of life, their screams muffled by reinforced laboratory walls. He saw simulated projections of airborne dispersal patterns, designed to render entire cities uninhabitable, a chillingly efficient method of genocide. He traced the lineage of 'super-soldier' serums derived from alien cellular accelerators, noting the alarming rates of secondary afflictions, the uncontrolled growths, the rapid metabolic burnout that followed the initial surge of enhanced strength. The line between enhanced soldier and monstrous abomination was blurred to the point of non-existence.

The fungal integration research, spearheaded by individuals who seemed to revel in the grotesque, was particularly abhorrent. Falk's simulations confirmed the reports of enhanced healing and increased aggression but also highlighted the chillingly high probability of complete neurological assimilation. The fungal spores, once established, would systematically rewrite the host's brain chemistry, eradicating individuality and replacing it with an insatiable, primal drive. The 'super-soldiers' envisioned by Himmler and his ilk would be little more than biological puppets, their actions dictated by alien imperatives, their loyalty absolute and unthinking. Falk imagined these creatures, their minds hollowed out, their bodies imbued with unnatural resilience and ferocity, a terrifying prospect that fueled his covert efforts.

He began by creating a series of encrypted logs, each entry timestamped and cross-referenced with official Ahnenerbe directives and scientific reports. He didn't dare to record anything that was not directly accessible through his legitimate research channels, but he meticulously transcribed the most damning details. The procurement orders for 'specimen acquisition' from concentration camp infirmaries, the memos detailing the disregard for human life in early xenobiological trials, the chillingly euphemistic language used to describe the systematic torture and mutation of human subjects – all of it found its way into his hidden archive.

His simulations were also a fertile ground for evidence. He would deliberately run scenarios that highlighted the extreme barbarity of the research, manipulating parameters to emphasize the catastrophic side effects and the sheer cruelty involved. He documented the estimated death tolls from specific xenobiological agent trials, noting the lack of any ethical oversight or consideration for the subjects' well-being. He saved the raw output from simulations that predicted the long-term genetic damage inflicted by certain pathogen strains, the potential for inherited deformities passed down through generations. This was not merely scientific data; it was a damning indictment.

One particularly harrowing series of simulations focused on the 'regenerative acceleration' experiments. Falk observed, with a growing sense of horror, how human cells, when exposed to synthesized alien compounds, would not only repair damage but proliferate uncontrollably. His projections showed tumor formation; cancerous growth that mimicked the alien specimens' own rapid cellular division. He documented the sheer brutality of the 'integration trials,' the staged traumas inflicted on prisoners to test the efficacy of these experimental treatments. The reports spoke of skin grafts taken from living individuals, of limbs reattached with alien-derived adhesives that caused agonizing necrosis, of subjects' bodies being systematically ravaged in the pursuit of creating an invincible soldier.

Falk knew the risks. Discovery meant not just the end of his career, but likely a swift and brutal end to his life, possibly as one of the very subjects he was now documenting. The SS, particularly the Ahnenerbe, were notoriously paranoid and ruthless. Any perceived disloyalty, any hint of dissent, was met with swift and merciless reprisal. Yet, the alternative – to remain a silent witness, complicit in this unfolding nightmare – was an unbearable burden. He felt a desperate, gnawing need to preserve some record, some testament to the perversion of science and the depths of human cruelty that he was now forced to confront daily.

He meticulously cross-referenced the scientific jargon with the underlying reality. A report detailing 'controlled biological enhancement' for an infantry unit in reality described the forced injection of untested alien growth hormones into soldiers, leading to aggressive bone spurs and crippling joint deformities that were then classified as 'unforeseen operational hazards.' A study on 'enhanced immune response' was a euphemism for subjects whose bodies were deliberately infected with alien pathogens to test the efficacy of experimental countermeasures, often resulting in agonizing deaths or irreversible mutations. He began to see the Nazi propaganda machine mirrored in the scientific reports – a relentless effort to sanitize the unspeakable, to reframe atrocity as progress.

The ethical vacuum within the Ahnenerbe was absolute. Falk's simulations, designed to predict the potential consequences of biological weapon deployment, were increasingly being used to refine the lethality and specificity of these weapons. He saw the chilling calculations that correlated specific genetic markers with vulnerability to Xenophage-Delta, the horrifying efficiency with which these alien agents could be tailored to target entire populations. He documented the 'bio-genetic superiority' doctrine, a twisted fusion of racist ideology and extraterrestrial biology, aimed at creating a world where the Aryan race could dominate through biologically engineered advantage, or through the targeted eradication of perceived enemies. His encrypted logs began to fill with the chilling statistical projections of these genocidal aspirations.

The pursuit of 'super-soldiers' extended beyond mere physical augmentation. Falk's access revealed research into integrating alien sensory organs, attempting to grant human soldiers enhanced vision, hearing, and even an awareness of electromagnetic fields. His simulations showed the immense difficulty of such integrations, the frequent rejection by the human body, the neurological feedback loops that could induce psychosis or complete catatonia. Yet, the SS, driven by an almost fanatical belief in the superiority of their vision, continued to push the boundaries, often at the cost of the subjects' sanity and life. He documented the accounts of prototypes that could perceive infrared signatures, but at the cost of crippling photophobia, or those with enhanced auditory ranges, only to be driven mad by the constant cacophony of the world.

The 'growth accelerators,' while promising enhanced stature and strength, came with a dark corollary. Falk's simulations consistently flagged the risks of skeletal dysplasia, cardiovascular strain, and a drastically reduced lifespan. The physical transformations were often monstrous, leading to subjects who were no longer recognizable as human, their bodies twisted by unnatural growth. He observed the guarded reports of these 'accelerated' individuals, their existence often confined to isolated research facilities, their mutated forms a testament to the Ahnenerbe's relentless pursuit of a godlike, Aryan ideal. His logs began to include increasingly detailed descriptions of these physical aberrations, serving as visual evidence of the program's inherent barbarity.

Falk understood that his covert activities were a dangerous

114

tightrope walk. He was functioning within the very system that perpetuated these atrocities, his knowledge a shield that also served as a spotlight. He had to be meticulous, his actions indistinguishable from his legitimate duties. He learned to navigate the labyrinthine bureaucracy of the Ahnenerbe, to identify the blind spots and the overlooked protocols that could provide him with the slivers of information he needed. He developed a keen sense for reading between the lines of official communiqués, for discerning the true, horrific intent behind the sanitized scientific language.

He began to make subtle adjustments to his simulation parameters, not to alter the scientific outcomes, but to ensure that the outputs were as stark and damning as possible. He would run scenarios of pathogen dispersal in densely populated civilian areas, highlighting the inevitable collateral damage and the indiscriminate nature of the weapons. He would deliberately push the simulations of biological augmentation to their extreme, showcasing the resultant physical and mental degradation. Each 'failed' simulation, each catastrophic outcome he meticulously documented, was a piece of evidence, a testament to the moral bankruptcy of the regime he served.

The isolation of the research facilities, the secrecy surrounding the crash site, all of it conspired to create a sealed ecosystem of horror. Falk, by accessing and meticulously cataloging the data flowing from these closed environments, was effectively breaking that seal, albeit on a minuscule scale. He was a ghost in the machine, his digital footprints carefully erased, his covert observations a silent scream against the prevailing tide of Nazi barbarism. He knew that simply gathering evidence was not enough; the true challenge lay in finding a way to disseminate it, to expose the unspeakable truths hidden within the sterile confines of Ahnenerbe research.

The weight of his knowledge grew with each passing day. He saw the future the Ahnenerbe were forging – a future where the very fabric of life, both human and alien, was a tool of war, a means of control, a weapon of mass destruction. His simulations, once tools for understanding, had become instruments of truth, albeit truth delivered in the cold, hard language of data and statistical probability. He was no longer just a scientist; he was a chronicler of atrocity, a silent witness meticulously documenting the descent into a biological hellscape, driven by the chilling ambition of a madman and the unfathomable power of the stars. He was waiting, biding his time, for the opportune moment to unleash the truth, to strike a blow against the living war machine that was slowly, inexorably, consuming the world.

Chapter 6

The Alien's Dying Gift

The once vibrant, bioluminescent patterns that pulsed across the alien's translucent skin had dimmed, replaced by a sickly, mottled grey. It lay splayed on the cold, metallic examination table, its intricate, four-limbed anatomy exposed to the harsh, unforgiving glare of the laboratory lights. The air, thick with the sterile tang of disinfectant and something far more ancient and unsettling, seemed to press down on Falk as he stood just outside the reinforced observation window of Containment Unit Gamma. He could hear the hushed, clinical murmur of the SS scientists, their voices devoid of any genuine concern, focused solely on the dissection of a dying entity, the probing of its alien biology for any potential advantage.

Dr. Albrecht, his face perpetually illuminated by the cold light of scientific curiosity untempered by empathy, gestured with a gloved hand. "The cellular regeneration matrix is failing, Falk. Remarkable resilience, nonetheless. The preliminary scans indicated a metabolic rate far exceeding anything terrestrial. Yet, the damage sustained during the... retrieval... was too extensive. The internal vascular system shows signs of catastrophic failure."

Falk watched as a probe, tipped with an impossibly fine needle, was carefully inserted into a pulsating vein near the creature's primary respiratory orifice. A thin stream of viscous, opalescent fluid was siphoned into a collection vial. The alien flinched, a subtle tremor that rippled through its weakened form, and a faint, mournful sound, like wind sighing through hollow reeds, escaped its pulmonary membranes. It was a sound that resonated with a primal sorrow, a lament for a lost home, a future extinguished before it could even begin.

The SS scientists, however, registered only data. "Observe the coagulative properties of this effluvium," one of them noted, his voice a low drone. "Extraordinary. We might be able to synthesize a similar agent for battlefield applications – rapid wound sealing. Imagine, soldiers who can continue fighting with grievous injuries."

Falk felt a cold knot of disgust tighten in his stomach. They saw only weapons, only tools of war. They were blind to the tragedy unfolding before them, to the slow, agonizing death of a being that, despite its alien origins, was a living, sentient creature. His own work, meticulously cataloging the Ahnenerbe's escalating depravity, had desensitized him to a degree, hardening him against the constant exposure to human suffering. But this was different. This was an affront to life itself, a violation on a cosmic scale, perpetrated by men who saw the universe as merely a resource to be plundered.

He remembered the initial reports, the breathless excitement that had permeated the Ahnenerbe's internal communications following the retrieval of the crashed craft. The 'Kriegsbeute' – the war prize – had been hailed as a definitive testament to their Aryan superiority, a sign from the heavens that their destiny was one of cosmic conquest. They had pored over the fragmented data logs salvaged from the wreckage, convinced they were deciphering the secrets of a civilization far more advanced than their own, a civilization ripe for subjugation. But the reality was far grimmer. The occupant of the craft was not a conqueror, but a casualty, a lone explorer lost and dying in a hostile environment.

As Falk continued to observe, the alien's faint luminescence flickered erratically. Its limbs, once capable of graceful, fluid movement, now twitched involuntarily. The rhythmic pulsing of its internal organs, visible through its semi-transparent hide, grew weaker, more sporadic. He saw the SS scientists conferring, their heads bent close together, their hushed tones filled with anticipation. They were preparing for the final stages of their 'analysis' – the autopsy, the systematic dismantling of the creature's physical form.

A particular scientist, a gaunt man named Dr. Brandt, notorious for his detached cruelty, leaned closer to the observation window, his eyes glinting with an almost predatory eagerness. "Falk, are you documenting the systemic breakdown? Note the cellular lysis commencing in the lower appendages. It's a fascinating cascade failure. We believe it's related to the ambient atmospheric pressure differential, exacerbated by the cellular damage."

Falk forced himself to nod, his gaze fixed on the alien's failing form. He was a scientist, bound by his own rigorous principles, even in this den of scientific barbarism. He meticulously recorded the observations, the physiological data, and the chemical analysis of the fluids being extracted. But with each entry, he also added his own, encrypted annotations – a condemnation of the methods, a record of the sheer lack of humanity in their pursuit.

He watched as the alien's breathing became shallower, the mournful sighing sound fading into a faint rattle. A slow, creeping paralysis seemed to be engulfing it, its intricate limbs gradually losing their residual motility. There was a stillness about it now, a profound stillness that spoke of an imminent transition. He could almost feel the fading spark of its alien consciousness, the slow dimming of its unique spark of existence.   Suddenly, the alien's head, a delicate, crystalline structure that had previously swiveled with a gentle grace, turned slowly towards the observation window. For a fleeting moment, its large, multifaceted eyes, which had previously held only the dull sheen of pain and confusion, seemed to focus on Falk. There was no accusation in that gaze, no plea for help, only a profound, ancient weariness, a recognition of a shared vulnerability in a universe that was often indifferent, and at times, cruel.

And then, with a final, shuddering exhalation, the faint light within the alien's form winked out. The bioluminescent patterns, which had so captivated the Ahnenerbe, vanished completely, leaving behind only the pallid, lifeless shell of a creature that had journeyed across the vastness of space, only to meet its end in the sterile confines of a Nazi laboratory.

Dr. Albrecht sighed, a sound of mild disappointment. "A shame. A considerable loss of potential data. Nevertheless, the specimens we have acquired will serve us well. We can begin the anatomical dissection immediately."

As the SS scientists prepared their instruments, their focus shifting from observation to dissection, Falk remained by the window, a profound sense of unease settling over him. He had documented the alien's death, its last moments of existence. But as he looked at the inert form, a new, disturbing thought began to form in his mind. What if, in its final moments, the alien had left behind something more than just biological material? What if, in its dying throes, it had imparted a gift, a final testament to its existence, a silent message for those who were willing to look beyond the sterile, scientific facade? He felt a strange pull, an intuition that his mission, his gathering of evidence against the Ahnenerbe, had just taken an unexpected and potentially crucial turn, directly connected to the fading light of the being that now lay lifeless before him.

The silence in the lab was no longer just the absence of sound, but the heavy presence of an untold story, a cosmic secret now veiled in the cold, unfeeling hands of the Reich. He turned away from the window, the image of those final, weary eyes seared into his memory, the weight of what had just transpired pressing down on him with an almost unbearable force. He knew, with a certainty that chilled him to the bone, that the true nature of the alien's demise, and its potential legacy, was far from being understood.

Falk lingered by the observation window, the sterile air of Containment Unit Gamma now thick with the palpable aftermath of cessation. The alien's form, still splayed on the examination table, was no longer a vessel of flickering life but a monumental specimen, a silent testament to a journey abruptly, brutally ended. The SS scientists, their initial excitement having transmuted into the grim satisfaction of a task completed, were already moving with a renewed, albeit clinical, purpose. Their instruments, glinting under the harsh lights, seemed to hum with an unspoken promise of dissection and exploitation. Falk, however, remained frozen, not by fascination, but by a growing unease that coiled deep within him. He had documented the physical demise, the cessation of biological functions, the extinguishing of a light that had briefly, incandescently, illuminated the darkness of their research. But a nagging intuition, an echo of something intangible that had passed between him and the dying creature in its final moments, refused to dissipate.

He replayed the last interaction, the alien's head turning, those multifaceted eyes meeting his through the reinforced glass. It wasn't the desperate plea of a creature in pain, nor the vacant stare of a mind succumbing to oblivion. There had been... a connection. A brief, almost imperceptible flicker of shared awareness that had transcended the glass, the sterile environment, the gulf of species. It was a resonance, a whisper that had brushed against his own consciousness, leaving behind an impression far more profound than any physical observation could capture. He'd dismissed it then as a trick of the light, a projection of his own unease onto a dying alien. But now, in the charged silence, that dismissal felt hollow, insufficient.

The scientists were chattering amongst themselves, their voices a low murmur of technical jargon and speculative ambition. Dr. Albrecht, his brow furrowed in concentration, was examining a retrieved sample under a microscope, oblivious to Falk's internal turmoil. "Remarkable cellular integrity, even in its breakdown," Albrecht was saying to his colleagues. "The nucleus remains largely intact, despite the systemic collapse. This suggests an incredibly robust genetic framework, perhaps even one that defies our current understanding of DNA replication."

Falk's attention, however, was drawn not to the detached dissection of the physical form, but to the lingering, spectral impression in his own mind. He closed his eyes, trying to isolate that fleeting moment of contact. It was like trying to recall a dream upon waking, the edges blurred, the essence elusive. But there was a core, a distinct impression of... intent. A deliberate reaching out. He'd always considered himself a man of logic, of observable fact, a scientist grounded in empirical evidence. But the Ahnenerbe's work had forced him into the shadowy periphery of their obsessions, exposing him to theories and phenomena that defied conventional scientific explanation. He'd cataloged their pursuit of ancient myths, their dabbling in occult sciences, their fervent belief in esoteric doctrines, all under the guise of rigorous academic inquiry. And now, this. An alien specimen, retrieved from the heavens, dying in their sterile laboratory.

The faint impression in his mind intensified, coalescing into a faint, yet insistent, pressure. It wasn't a voice, not in the auditory sense. It was more like a thought, a concept, implanted directly into his awareness. And it was directed at him. He felt a surge of adrenaline, a prickling awareness that he was not merely an observer, but a recipient.

"You... see..."

The thought, if it could be called that, was alien in its structure, its syntax, its very essence. Yet, Falk understood it. He understood the implied observation, the recognition of his own detached scrutiny, his internal conflict. He felt a cold dread mixed with an undeniable curiosity. Was he hallucinating? The stress, the constant exposure to the macabre realities of the Ahnenerbe's operations, was it finally taking its toll?

He opened his eyes, glancing at the scientists. They were engrossed in their work, their actions driven by ambition and a chilling lack of empathy. They saw a dead specimen, a biological puzzle to be solved, a resource to be exploited. They did not see, nor would they ever comprehend, the silent communication that was now unfolding within Falk's own mind.

"They... seek... to... consume... not... to... learn."

The thought was clearer now, more focused. It was a judgment, a warning. The alien, even in its dying moments, had perceived the true nature of its captors, the rapacious hunger that drove their research. It had seen through the veneer of scientific inquiry to the core of their destructive intent. And it had recognized in Falk a nascent spark of dissent, a flicker of opposition to their agenda.

Falk felt his breath catch in his throat. He was a mole, a spy within this organization, meticulously documenting their atrocities for a future reckoning. He had to maintain his cover, to appear as complicit, as detached, as the others. But this... this was something else entirely. This was direct contact, a telepathic intervention from a dying extraterrestrial intelligence. It was a gift, or perhaps a curse, a burden of knowledge that he hadn't sought but now possessed.

He tried to push the sensation away, to reassert his grip on reality, on the carefully constructed facade of his scientific

122

detachment. He focused on the metallic gleam of the instruments, the sterile efficiency of the laboratory. But the alien's presence, or rather, the echo of its consciousness, was persistent, an insistent whisper against the din of his internal resistance.

"Their... grasp... is... greedy... Their... understanding... shallow..."

The information, or rather, the sentiment, was being transmitted with a deliberate slowness, as if the alien's fading consciousness was conserving its remaining energy, focusing its essence on this singular act of communication. Falk felt a strange sense of empathy for the dying creature; a kinship forged in their shared predicament – both trapped within the suffocating ideology of the Reich.

The... true... power... lies... not... in... subjugation... but... in... resonance..."

Resonance. The word echoed in Falk's mind, not as a concept, but as a lived experience, a brief, powerful connection. He understood that the alien was trying to convey something fundamental about its own nature, something that the SS scientists, with their materialistic, power-hungry worldview, could never grasp. They were dissecting its body, analyzing its biology, but they were missing the very essence of what made it alien, what made it *alive.*

He felt a subtle shift in the telepathic flow; a new layer of information being conveyed. It was like a series of complex images, abstract concepts, and sensory impressions, woven together into a cohesive whole. He saw vast, swirling nebulae, alien constellations, and worlds bathed in colors unimaginable to the human eye. He saw beings of light and energy, interacting not through physical touch, but through a symphony of resonant frequencies. It was a glimpse into a universe far grander, far more interconnected, than anything he had ever conceived.

"We... are... echoes... in... the... cosmic... song..."

The phrase was poetic, evocative, and profoundly unsettling. The alien was describing its own existence, and perhaps the existence of its species, not as isolated entities, but as manifestations of a larger, universal consciousness, a cosmic symphony. And the SS scientists, in their pursuit of technological dominance, were attempting to silence that song, to capture and control its individual notes for their own destructive purposes.

The telepathic current began to ebb, the intensity of the connection waning. Falk felt a growing sense of panic. This was his opportunity, his chance to understand, to gain knowledge that could be used against the Ahnenerbe, against the Reich itself. He tried to grasp at the fading impressions, to hold onto the fleeting glimpses of cosmic truth.

"The... void... is... not... empty... It... hums..."

The alien was imparting its final piece of wisdom, a profound insight into the nature of existence, a secret that lay beyond the tangible, the measurable, the scientifically quantifiable. It was a message that spoke of a universe alive, vibrant, and interconnected in ways that defied the rigid, materialistic worldview of the Third Reich.

Falk felt a profound sorrow wash over him as the connection severed completely. The pressure in his mind receded, leaving behind a vast, echoing emptiness. The alien was truly gone, its physical form now merely an inert collection of biological material. But its dying gift, its final communication, had imprinted itself upon Falk's consciousness, a testament to a brief, extraordinary encounter.

He looked at the SS scientists, their faces impassive, their minds focused on the dissection. They had acquired a prize, a specimen, a source of potential weaponry. They had no idea of the true treasure that had been imparted, the cosmic secret that had been whispered into the mind of one lone observer.

Falk straightened his shoulders, a newfound resolve hardening his gaze. He had witnessed the alien's death, but he had also received its testament. The knowledge, the impressions, the sheer magnitude of what had been shared had irrevocably altered his perspective. The Ahnenerbe sought to conquer the stars through brute force and technological superiority. But the alien, in its dying breath, had revealed a different path, a path of understanding, of connection, of resonance.

He turned away from the observation window, the sterile air of the laboratory now charged with a different kind of energy – the silent hum of cosmic knowledge, the echo of a dying alien's profound gift. His mission was no longer just about documenting the atrocities of the Reich. It was about preserving this truth, about ensuring that the alien's final message, its plea for understanding, would not be lost in the cacophony of war and ideology. He had a secret to keep, a legacy to protect, and the weight of that knowledge was both a burden and a beacon, guiding him through the shadows of the Third Reich. The sterile silence of the lab now seemed to hold a thousand whispers, a cosmic symphony that only he could hear. The alien was gone, but its song, its dying gift, had just begun to play within Falk's very being, a melody of defiance against the encroaching darkness. He knew, with absolute certainty, that his understanding of the universe, and his fight against the forces that sought to dominate it, had just been profoundly, irrevocably expanded. The path ahead was uncertain, fraught with peril, but now, illuminated by the faintest echo of starlight, it felt undeniably, profoundly real.

The sterile silence of the laboratory, once a suffocating blanket, now pulsed with an unbidden resonance. Falk felt it, not as an external force, but as an internal vibration, a sympathetic echo to the dying consciousness he had briefly, profoundly, encountered. The scientists, oblivious to the cosmic secrets now stirring within him, continued their methodical dissection, their instruments glinting like predatory teeth against the alien's once vibrant form. They saw only biological components, chemical reactions, a prize to be dissected and cataloged. They were blind to the true nature of the gift he had received, a revelation that transcended the physical, reaching into the very fabric of existence.

The residual impressions coalesced in his mind, not as coherent thoughts, but as fragments of a shattered tapestry, each shard imbued with a potent, alien truth. He saw flashes of a celestial ballet, distant suns birthing worlds, and the silent, omnipresent hum of cosmic forces. Then, a stark, jarring shift. The vibrant hues of creation were abruptly overshadowed by a creeping darkness, a pervasive,

125

insidious stillness. It was a void, not of emptiness, but of deliberate nullification, a silence imposed upon the symphony of existence.

A profound sense of sorrow, sharp and agonizing, pierced through him. It was the alien's sorrow, its grief at witnessing a nascent horror, a cosmic abomination. The fragments in his mind began to coalesce, forming nascent images, nascent concepts. He saw vast, intricate systems, not of gears and circuits, but of interwoven frequencies, resonating across entire continents, across the very consciousness of humanity. These were not weapons of fire and steel, but instruments of erasure, designed to unravel the threads of memory, history, and identity.

The alien's final moments were not a surrender, but a desperate, dying attempt to convey this knowledge, to warn. The fragmented impressions solidified into a chilling appellation: Project Veil. It was a name that tasted of decay, of oblivion, of a history being systematically dismantled, piece by agonizing piece. This was not a weapon aimed at physical destruction, but a far more insidious device, a psychic and historical pathogen designed to rewrite reality itself, to scrub entire populations from existence, not just in body, but in memory, in spirit, in the very concept of their being.

He saw, through the alien's dying perception, the insidious tendrils of Project Veil spreading across the globe, a network of invisible emitters, a planetary scale tuning fork designed to broadcast a specific, annihilating frequency. It was a plan so vast, so ambitious in its malevolence, that it dwarfed even the Reich's darkest ambitions. This was not about conquest in the traditional sense; it was about total obliteration of the historical and cultural narrative, a cosmic censorship that would render entire civilizations, entire peoples, as if they had never been.

The alien had understood this threat. Its journey, its very presence on Earth, had been driven by this singular, desperate purpose: to prevent the activation of Project Veil. The fragmented images in Falk's mind painted a picture of a desperate struggle, a covert war waged not on battlefields, but within the subtle currents of planetary consciousness. The alien and its kind had sought to disrupt, to dismantle, to warn. But they had failed. The final, devastating truth that echoed in Falk's mind was the bitter taste of their defeat.

He felt the alien's despair, its crushing realization that its mission had ended in failure. The activation sequence for Project Veil had been initiated. The symphony of destruction, the creeping silence, had already begun its insidious work, its effects masked by the natural chaos and turmoil of human history. The SS scientists, in their eager dissection, were unaware that they were not merely studying a biological curiosity, but were, in fact, unwittingly complicit in the grand design of Project Veil, their every action contributing to the systematic dismantling of human heritage.

The raw, unformed concepts continued to flood Falk's consciousness, each one a testament to the alien's final, desperate act of communication. He saw the underlying principle of Project Veil: not a brute force attack, but a sophisticated manipulation of fundamental frequencies, the very harmonics that underpinned consciousness and collective memory. It was a technological horror, designed to resonate with the latent psychic energies of humanity, to overwrite, to suppress, to erase. Entire cultures, languages, and the very concept of their existence were to be phased out of reality, their historical presence rendered a nullity.

The alien conveyed a sense of the magnitude of this threat, the terrifying implications of such a weapon. It wasn't about killing people; it was about ceasing their being, erasing their past, their present, and their future from the collective consciousness of the universe. It was a form of spiritual and historical suicide, inflicted upon an unsuspecting world. The alien's mission had been to raise the alarm, to disrupt the network, to ensure that the symphony of annihilation would never reach its crescendo.

Falk felt a chilling understanding dawn within him. The subtle anomalies, the historical inconsistencies, the forgotten civilizations that he, as a historian, had sometimes encountered – could these be the residual effects of Project Veil, of earlier, perhaps less sophisticated, attempts at historical erasure? The alien's message was not merely a warning about a present danger, but a glimpse into a long-standing, intergalactic conflict, a war waged in the shadows of time and consciousness.

He tried to sift through the torrent of impressions, to find a pattern, a key, a piece of actionable intelligence. The alien had given him more than a warning; it had offered a glimpse into the mechanics of Project Veil. He saw, in abstract, the intricate latticework of frequencies, the delicate balance of cosmic harmonics that Project Veil sought to disrupt. The alien species, it seemed, possessed a profound understanding of these universal vibrations, an understanding that had driven their desperate mission.

The weight of this knowledge pressed down on Falk, a crushing burden. He was a single man, a spy within a monstrous regime, now privy to a cosmic secret that threatened the very existence of humanity as he knew it. The SS scientists continued their work, their minds focused on the tangible, the immediate, the potential for power and control. They were searching for weapons to win a terrestrial war, oblivious to the existential threat that transcended all earthly conflicts.

He felt a profound sense of isolation. How could he possibly convey this truth? How could he even begin to explain the existence of Project Veil, of a weapon that operated on frequencies beyond human comprehension, a weapon that erased not bodies, but histories? His superiors, the clandestine network for whom he worked, were focused on espionage, sabotage, and counter-intelligence – tangible acts of war. They were not equipped to comprehend a threat of this magnitude, a threat that operated on the very fabric of reality.

The alien's dying energy pulsed one last time, a wave of pure, unadulterated grief, followed by a flicker of desperate hope. It was a hope directed at him, at Falk, the observer who had, for a fleeting moment, resonated with its own consciousness. The hope was that he would understand that he would act, that he would carry the torch of their failed mission.

He forced himself to breathe, to push back against the overwhelming tide of alien sorrow and cosmic dread. He had to maintain his composure, his disguise. The scientists were still there, their eyes sharp, their ears ever listening. He could not afford to betray the seismic shift that had occurred within him. The sterile air of the laboratory, once a symbol of scientific advancement, now felt like the suffocating atmosphere of a tomb, a tomb that held not just the body of a dead alien, but the ghost of a stolen future.

The raw fragments in his mind began to solidify into something more concrete. He saw the aliens' understanding of resonance as not merely a weapon, but as a force for creation and connection. Project Veil was the antithesis of their own understanding of the universe, a perversion of cosmic law. It was an attempt to silence the universal song, to impose a singular, sterile note where there should have been a magnificent, vibrant symphony.

He remembered the alien's words, or rather, the implanted concepts: "The void is not empty. It hums." This humming, he now understood, was the underlying frequency of existence, the cosmic baseline upon which all reality was built. Project Veil sought to silence this hum, to replace it with an imposed silence, a non-existence. The alien species had dedicated themselves to understanding and protecting this universal hum, and in doing so, had become the guardians of cosmic history.

The final impressions were of a network, a vast, interconnected system designed to counteract Project Veil. The alien had not only revealed the threat but had also provided a partial glimpse into its own species' methods for combating it. It was a system of counter-frequencies, of harmonic disruption, of subtle interventions designed to mend the tears in the fabric of reality that Project Veil inflicted. This was the true dying gift, not just a warning, but a key, a blueprint for resistance.

Falk felt a surge of adrenaline, a cold, hard determination replacing the fear and sorrow. He might be one man against a cosmic conspiracy and a totalitarian regime, but he now possessed knowledge that could, potentially, turn the tide. The alien had failed, but its legacy, its desperate plea, now rested with him. He had to find a way to understand the alien's science, to decipher the blueprints for resistance, and to find a way to disseminate this knowledge, to awaken humanity to the silent war being waged against its very existence. The SS scientists, in their pursuit of power, were oblivious to the true nature of the universe, and to the devastating weapon they were, however indirectly, serving. Falk, however, was no longer blind. The alien's dying breath had ignited a spark within him, a spark of cosmic awareness, a flicker of resistance against the encroaching veil of oblivion. The true work, the real mission, had just begun.

The hum within Falk intensified, no longer a faint vibration but a resonant chord that seemed to vibrate through his very bones. The alien's consciousness, a dying ember, flared one last time, its final thoughts imprinting themselves upon his mind with the stark clarity of a celestial pronouncement. It was a revelation that chilled him to the core, a truth far more insidious than any physical weapon. Project Veil, the alien explained, wasn't about conquest or extermination in the conventional sense. It was about utter erasure. Not just of life, but of memory, of history, of the very concept of existence for targeted groups.

The alien's final, agonized communication painted a devastating picture. Project Veil's primary target, its initial phase, was the Jewish people. The purpose? To systematically and irrevocably remove them from the historical record, to scrub them from collective memory, to render their millennia-long existence a nullity. It was an ambition so profound, so terrifyingly absolute, that it made the Nazis' conventional atrocities seem like mere preliminary skirmishes. This wasn't about building a new order; it was about dismantling an old reality, about surgically removing entire lineages from the tapestry of human experience, leaving behind only a phantom void where vibrant lives once flourished.

Falk grasped the alien's message with a sickening lurch. The 'Cleansing Directive,' the chilling euphemism whispered in the highest echelons of the SS, was not a metaphor for eradication but a literal, technical directive for historical and existential erasure. The alien's species had dedicated eons to understanding and preserving the universal song, the intricate frequencies that bound reality together. Project Veil, in its perversion of this cosmic harmony, was an attempt to introduce a discordant, annihilating note, a frequency that would unravel the very essence of a people, not just in the present, but retroactively, across time itself.

The alien projected images, not of physical annihilation, but of a subtle, pervasive unmaking. He saw historical texts subtly altering, names vanishing from records, photographs fading into blankness, the very languages spoken by generations dissolving into an unknowable silence. It was a form of cosmic censorship, a weapon designed to rewrite not just the future, but the past, ensuring that those targeted would leave no footprint, no echo, no trace of their passage through time. The alien conveyed the sheer audacity of this endeavor: to not only end lives but to unmake the very existence of those lives, to ensure that no one would ever remember them, or even know they were ever meant to be remembered.

This was the true genius, and the true horror, of Project Veil. It operated on a level so fundamental, so deeply interwoven with the fabric of consciousness and history, that its effects would be imperceptible to those not attuned to its specific frequencies. The alien's people had developed the means to detect and even counteract these destabilizing cosmic vibrations, but Project Veil was a new, terrifyingly sophisticated evolution of this destructive technology. It was designed to be undetectable, its work insidious, its impact absolute. The goal was not to merely kill Jews, but to render them as if they had never been conceived, never born, never lived, never contributed, never suffered. Their entire collective narrative, from the most ancient prophecies to the most recent whispers of family history, was to be meticulously unwritten, then utterly expunged.

The alien shared a chilling analogy. Imagine a vast, complex song, composed of countless individual voices, each unique, each contributing to the magnificent symphony of existence. Project Veil was designed to identify a specific group of voices, to isolate their unique harmonic signature, and then to broadcast a counter-frequency that would not simply silence them, but would unravel their very essence, causing their contribution to the symphony to cease, and then to *never have been*. It was a form of existential deletion, a targeted corruption of the universal code.

Falk felt a profound sense of nausea. The 'Final Solution' was no longer merely about extermination; it was about a metaphysical unmaking. The SS, in their blind pursuit of racial purity, were not just orchestrating genocide; they were, unknowingly, attempting to unravel the very threads of reality. The alien's species had seen this threat emerge, had witnessed its development, and had recognized it as a cosmic aberration, a direct assault on the fundamental principles of existence. Their mission had been to halt it, to dismantle its infrastructure, to warn the unsuspecting inhabitants of Earth.

The alien's dying message was not just a warning; it was a confession of their failure. They had been too late. The network of emitters, the subtle harmonic manipulators, were already in place, subtly humming their song of erasure across the globe. The initial phase, the targeting of the Jewish people, was already underway, its insidious effects masked by the general turmoil of war and political upheaval. The alien species, in their advanced understanding of cosmic resonance, had pinpointed the origin of these frequencies, the nexus points from which Project Veil broadcast its annihilating signal. They had attempted to disrupt these nodes, but the forces arrayed against them were formidable, their technology, though advanced, ultimately outmaneuvered.

The alien's transmission contained what amounted to a blueprint for resistance, a partial decryption of Project Veil's harmonic architecture. It wasn't a weapon in the conventional sense, but a set of counter-frequencies, a method of harmonic resonance that could, in theory, disrupt the erasure process, or at least mitigate its effects. This knowledge was the alien's final legacy, a desperate gambit to empower Falk, to give him the tools to combat a threat that had consumed its own civilization.

Falk struggled to process the sheer scale of what he was being told. The Nazis weren't just trying to wipe out a population; they were trying to erase their entire history, their cultural impact, their very presence in the Giselals of time. This was not just a war of tanks and planes; it was a war for the past, for the integrity of collective memory. The alien's final thoughts were a torrent of grief for their failure, but also a flicker of desperate hope that Falk, the accidental witness, might succeed where they had not. The alien had seen humanity's potential for both great destruction and profound creativity, and it had gambled on the latter.

The alien conveyed the method: subtle manipulation of ambient harmonic frequencies, a process that required an intricate understanding of Earth's own resonant signature. The goal was not

132

to create a counter-explosion of sound, but to introduce harmonic interference, to create static on the alien frequency that would obscure and eventually nullify Project Veil's broadcasts. It was like trying to tune a radio to a specific station while another, much more powerful, signal was actively jamming it. The aliens had developed specific sonic keys, sequences of tones and vibrations that could, when applied correctly, disrupt the technology.

Falk felt the weight of this information settle upon him. He was a scientist and a historian, a scholar of the past, and now he was being entrusted with the means to protect that past from a threat so profound it defied human comprehension. The SS scientists, in their pursuit of esoteric technologies, were playing with forces they barely understood, forces that could unravel not just their enemies, but the very fabric of existence. The alien's dying gift was a double-edged sword: the knowledge of an unimaginable threat, and the potential, however slim, to fight it.

The alien's species had a term for the harmonic signature of a people, a collective resonance that defined their unique contribution to the universal symphony. Project Veil sought to silence this specific resonance, to overwrite it with a null frequency. The Jewish people, with their rich and ancient cultural heritage, their enduring spiritual traditions, and their profound contributions to philosophy, science, and art, possessed a particularly strong and complex harmonic signature. This made them a prime target for such a weapon, as their erasure would create a significant void, a noticeable silence in the grand cosmic composition.

Falk felt the residual impressions solidify into a plan, a desperate, nascent strategy. He needed to understand the alien technology, to decipher the harmonic keys, and to find a way to deploy them. This meant more than just acquiring information; it meant understanding a new science, a science of cosmic resonance and historical preservation. The SS had the physical remnants of the alien technology, but they lacked the understanding, the context, the *purpose*. Falk, on the other hand, now possessed the alien's direct knowledge, its intended use.

The alien's final, fading thought was a single, resonant word: "Remember." It was a plea, a command, a testament to the very thing

Project Veil sought to destroy. If history was forgotten, if the past was erased, then the victims of Project Veil would truly cease to have ever existed. Falk understood. His mission was not just to stop the activation of Project Veil, but to ensure that the memory of those targeted, starting with the Jewish people, would endure, a testament against the encroaching void. The sterile laboratory, once a place of cold scientific inquiry, had become the crucible of a cosmic battle for the very soul of history. The alien was gone, but its dying gift, its desperate warning, had ignited a fire within Falk, a fire that would illuminate the shadows of Project Veil and fight for the memory of those the Nazis sought to unmake.

As the alien's life force ebbed, a final, subtle transfer occurred, not of data or complex equations, but of something far more intimate and enduring: a seed of truth. It wasn't a sudden download of knowledge, but a delicate implantation, a latent potential woven into the very fabric of Falk's own consciousness. It was as if a single, perfect note had been struck within his mind, a resonant frequency that would lie dormant, awaiting the precise moment to bloom. This echo of the alien's being was not a replacement for his own identity, but an augmentation, a silent, internal ally. It was a nascent understanding, a flicker of intuition that would guide him through the labyrinthine complexities of Project Veil.

This psychic residue, this seed of truth, would not manifest as overt telepathy or direct communication. Instead, it would act as an internal compass, a subtle nudge towards the correct path, a whisper of insight when faced with insurmountable odds. It was a living memory, a fragment of alien wisdom that would grow and evolve within him, mirroring the alien's own quest to understand and preserve the cosmic symphony. This nascent consciousness was a bulwark against the encroaching darkness, a silent sentinel within the war for history itself. Falk would carry this fragment, this spark of alien awareness, as a hidden inheritance, a promise of understanding that would surface when the temporal currents aligned, when the discordant hum of Project Veil grew too loud to ignore.

The alien's dying act was not merely to impart information, but to plant a possibility. It was a faith placed in Falk, a belief that human consciousness, though flawed, possessed the capacity for preservation, for remembrance, for defiance. This seed was designed to germinate in the fertile soil of Falk's historian's mind, to sprout when the context was ripe, to bloom into the very understanding needed to counter Project Veil's annihilating frequencies. It was a testament to the alien's advanced understanding of life and consciousness: that the most potent weapon against erasure was not brute force, but the enduring power of memory, nurtured by the subtle resonance of truth. Falk, now unknowingly carrying this alien fragment, was no longer just a historian; he was a custodian of a cosmic legacy, a vessel for a truth that transcended human comprehension.

The alien's final moments were characterized by a gentle disintegration; a dissolution of its physical form that mirrored the existential erasure it fought against. Yet, as its physical presence faded, the psychic echo it left behind was not one of emptiness, but of potential. This echo was a complex wave of resonance, a harmonic signature that Falk's own mind, through the alien's deliberate action, was now capable of perceiving, and eventually, of interpreting. It was akin to a musician being gifted the perfect pitch, an innate understanding of a scale that would allow them to then learn and compose any melody. This seed of truth was the alien's ultimate gambit, a trust in Falk's capacity to not only understand the threat but to actively combat it.

The implantation was subtle, almost imperceptible, a quiet resonance that settled deep within Falk's neural pathways. It felt less like an invasion and more like a recognition, a harmonic alignment between his own consciousness and the dying alien's intent. This internal presence would serve as a constant, albeit subconscious, reminder of the stakes involved, a silent alarm bell that would ring true when Project Veil's destructive frequencies began to manifest more palpably. It was a hidden ally, a fragment of alien sentience woven into the tapestry of Falk's own thoughts, a silent guardian against the insidious tide of temporal erasure.

The alien's struggle had been a cosmic one, a battle against a force that sought to unravel the very fabric of existence. Its failure to overtly stop Project Veil was a tragedy, but its success in imparting this crucial fragment of knowledge, this seed of truth, offered a glimmer of hope. Falk was now a bridge between two worlds, a conduit for an understanding that could potentially save humanity from a fate far worse than annihilation. The weight of this responsibility was immense, yet within that weight lay the nascent power of the alien's dying gift, a silent, internal resonance waiting to be awakened.

Chapter 7

The Weight of Betrayal

The hum within Falk, a residual echo of the alien's dying consciousness, had not subsided. It was a subtle, persistent vibration, a physical manifestation of the monumental, horrifying truths that had been impressed upon his mind. The alien's final transmission, a desperate symphony of images and concepts, had painted a picture of a conspiracy so vast, so utterly devoid of humanity, that it threatened to shatter Falk's perception of reality. Project Veil. The name itself was a chilling euphemism, a velvet glove over an iron fist of existential annihilation. It wasn't merely about extermination; it was about obliteration on a cosmic scale, the systematic excision of entire peoples from the tapestry of existence, not just in the present, but retroactively, across the very currents of time.

The alien's species, its very existence dedicated to the preservation of universal harmony, had recognized Project Veil as a perversion of cosmic law, an attempt to introduce a discordant frequency that would unravel the fundamental vibrations that bound reality together. And the initial target, the first masterpiece of this horrifying symphony of erasure, was the Jewish people. The sheer audacity of it, the meticulous, scientific malevolence, was staggering. It wasn't enough to kill; the goal was to unmake, to ensure that their millennia of history, their contributions to civilization, their very memory, would be scrubbed clean, leaving behind only a void where vibrant life had once pulsed. Falk, a scientist and historian whose life was dedicated to understanding and preserving the past, felt a profound sense of nausea at the thought. The "Cleansing Directive" was not a metaphor; it was a literal, technical order for the unraveling of a people's existence.

He recalled the alien's desperate analogies: a song silenced not just by stopping the notes, but by unmaking the composer, the instruments, the very idea of music. Imagine a grand cosmic symphony, composed of countless individual voices, each contributing a unique timbre, a specific melody. Project Veil was designed to identify a particular group of voices, to isolate their harmonic signature, and then to broadcast a counter-frequency that would not merely silence them, but would unravel their very essence, causing their contribution to cease, and then to *never have been*. It was an existential deletion, a targeted corruption of the universal code, a cosmic censorship of the most profound and terrifying kind.

The alien had spoken of their failure, of their inability to halt this insidious project in its infancy. The network of emitters, the subtle harmonic manipulators, were already in place, humming their song of erasure across the globe. The initial phase, the targeting of the Jewish people, was already underway, its effects masked by the cacophony of war, by the pervasive atmosphere of fear and political upheaval. The alien species had pinpointed the nexus points, the sources of these annihilating frequencies, but their attempts to disrupt them had been thwarted. They were outmaneuvered, outgunned, their advanced technology ultimately insufficient against the sheer, unadulterated malevolence driving Project Veil.

Yet, in its dying moments, the alien had bestowed upon Falk a legacy, a blueprint for resistance. It wasn't a weapon in the conventional sense, no explosive device or energy beam. It was knowledge, a partial decryption of Project Veil's harmonic architecture, a set of counter-frequencies, a method of harmonic resonance that could, theoretically, disrupt the erasure process. This was the alien's final gamble, a desperate attempt to empower Falk, to equip him with the tools to combat a threat that had consumed its own civilization. Falk, a man of books and archives, found himself suddenly thrust into the role of a cosmic defender, tasked with understanding a science that transcended human comprehension – a science of resonance, of history, of existence itself.

The SS scientists, he now understood with sickening clarity, were not merely dabbling in esoteric technologies; they were playing with forces that could unravel not just their enemies, but the very fabric of reality. Their pursuit of racial purity, their warped ideology, had led them down a path of unimaginable destruction, a path that threatened to erase not just lives, but the very concept of those lives having ever existed. The alien's species had recognized this threat, had identified the unique, complex harmonic signature of the Jewish people, their rich cultural heritage, their enduring spiritual traditions, and their profound contributions to human thought and creativity, as a prime target. Their erasure would create a significant void, a noticeable silence in the grand cosmic composition.

As the alien's final thoughts imprinted themselves upon his consciousness, Falk felt the residual impressions solidify into a nascent plan. He needed to understand this alien technology, to decipher the harmonic keys, to find a way to deploy them. This meant more than just acquiring information; it meant immersing himself in a new science, a science that dealt with the subtle vibrations of existence. The SS might possess the physical remnants of the alien technology, but they lacked the understanding, the context, the *purpose*. Falk, however, now possessed the alien's direct knowledge, its intended use. The alien's last, fading thought, a single, resonant word, echoed in his mind: "Remember." It was a plea, a command, a testament to the very thing Project Veil sought to destroy. If history was forgotten, if the past was erased, then the victims of Project Veil would truly cease to have ever existed. Falk understood. His mission was not just to stop the activation of Project Veil, but to ensure that the memory of those targeted, starting with the Jewish people, would endure, a testament against the encroaching void. The sterile laboratory, once a place of cold scientific inquiry, had become the crucible of a cosmic battle for the very soul of history. The alien was gone, but its dying gift, its desperate warning, had ignited a fire within Falk, a fire that would illuminate the shadows of Project Veil and fight for the memory of those the Nazis sought to unmake.

The profound implications of the alien's final message began to settle over Falk like a shroud. The sheer, terrifying scope of Project Veil was not something that could be easily compartmentalized or dismissed. It transcended the brutal realities of conventional warfare and even the horrific genocidal policies already in place. This was an assault on existence itself, a perversion of the natural order that the alien had so eloquently described as a disharmonious frequency, a note of annihilation in the universal symphony. His internal hum, a constant reminder of the alien's implanted knowledge, seemed to intensify with every passing moment, a visceral response to the magnitude of the threat. He found himself replaying fragments of the alien's communication, not in a linear fashion, but as a series of resonant impressions, each one deepening his understanding of the insidious nature of Project Veil.

He saw again the subtle alterations in historical texts, the fading of names from records, the gradual dissolution of languages into an unknowable silence. This wasn't merely about silencing voices; it was about unwriting their very essence from the fabric of time. It was an ambition so absolute, so devoid of any recognizable human sentiment, that it made the brutalities of the concentration camps seem, in a perverse way, almost... primitive. The Nazis, in their pursuit of racial purity, were not merely committing atrocities; they were unknowingly, or perhaps knowingly, attempting to perform an act of cosmic vandalism, to erase a specific melody from the grand composition of existence. The alien's species, in their pursuit of understanding and preserving this symphony, had recognized Project Veil as an existential aberration, a direct assault on the fundamental principles that governed reality.

The conflict within Falk was palpable. His years of service, his sworn duty to the Reich, felt increasingly like a betrayal of a far greater, more fundamental oath – an oath to truth, to history, to the very continuity of human existence. He had joined the SS with a sense of order, a belief in the necessity of strong leadership and a unified vision for Germany's future. But the revelations delivered by the dying alien had irrevocably shattered that illusion. The veneer of nationalistic fervor and ideological purity had been stripped away, revealing a core of nihilistic destruction, a desire to not merely conquer, but to annihilate, to erase.

He found himself increasingly distracted during meetings, his thoughts drifting to the alien's cryptic explanations of harmonic frequencies and existential erasure. The sterile efficiency of the SS, once admirable, now felt like a chillingly organized mechanism of

140

death, a perfectly tuned instrument for orchestrating the unmaking of a people. He began to observe his colleagues with a new, critical eye. Did they sense it? Did they feel the discordant hum that seemed to emanate from the very foundations of Project Veil? Or were they, like himself before this encounter, simply unaware of the true, horrifying nature of their work?

The inconsistencies in the official Nazi narrative, once easily rationalized or dismissed as necessary wartime propaganda, now loomed large in his mind. The talk of racial purity and lebensraum, while abhorrent, seemed almost simplistic compared to the existential ambition of Project Veil. The alien had hinted at a deeper, more esoteric understanding of the universe, a science of subtle vibrations and cosmic resonance, that the SS scientists were trying to harness for their own twisted ends. This wasn't just about land or power; it was about manipulating the very fabric of reality.

Falk's growing dissent was not an outward rebellion, not yet. It was a silent, internal war, a constant struggle to reconcile the man he had been with the horrifying truths he now possessed. He found himself scrutinizing documents with an almost obsessive intensity, searching for any hint, any subtext, that might corroborate the alien's revelations. He felt an increasing detachment from the everyday concerns of his colleagues, their discussions of troop movements and logistical challenges seeming almost trivial in the face of an impending existential threat. His duty, once a clear and guiding principle, had become a tangled knot of conflicting loyalties. He was a cog in a machine, but he now knew, with terrifying certainty, that the machine was designed to dismantle not just an enemy, but the very concept of history.

He found himself drawn to the library, not for research related to his SS duties, but to pore over ancient texts, seeking parallels, seeking reassurance that the grand tapestry of human existence, in all its messy, contradictory glory, was somehow resilient. He read of forgotten civilizations, of the rise and fall of empires, of the enduring power of myth and memory. These were the very things Project Veil sought to extinguish, and in his reading, Falk found a flicker of defiance, a silent vow to protect them.

The alien's final message had not just been a warning; it had been a transference of purpose. The seed of truth, planted within him, had begun to germinate. It was a subtle influence, a constant whisper of awareness that guided his intuition, nudging him towards certain lines of inquiry, certain avenues of thought that he might otherwise have overlooked. He felt a nascent understanding of the alien's complex concepts, a growing ability to perceive the subtle harmonic dissonances that the alien had warned him about. It was as if his mind, now augmented by a fragment of alien consciousness, was capable of tuning into a frequency previously beyond his grasp.

This internal transformation was isolating. He could no longer engage in the casual camaraderie he once shared with his fellow officers. Their jests and their pronouncements of Nazi superiority felt hollow, almost pitiable, in the face of the cosmic horror he now comprehended. He became withdrawn, his silences growing longer, his gaze often distant, lost in thought. He noticed the subtle glances, the questioning looks, that were exchanged when he failed to respond to a jest or offered a curt, uncharacteristic reply. His dissent, though unspoken, was becoming palpable, a silent ripple in the otherwise uniform surface of SS loyalty.

He found himself wrestling with the ethical implications of his position. He was privy to the darkest secrets of the Reich, secrets that, if revealed, could potentially avert a catastrophe of unimaginable proportions. But how? How could he, a single historian within the vast apparatus of the SS, possibly hope to counter a project of such scope and sophistication? The alien had provided him with the theoretical keys, but the practical application seemed an insurmountable hurdle. He was a man armed with knowledge, but lacking the means to wield it effectively.

The weight of betrayal pressed down on him – not just the betrayal of his own conscience, but the betrayal of history itself, a betrayal orchestrated by the very regime he served. The alien's final plea, "Remember," had become his own mantra. He would remember. He would not allow the vibrant symphony of human existence, particularly the unique melody of the Jewish people, to be silenced, to be unmade. This internal awakening, this profound disturbance of his loyalties, was the beginning of his true battle. The SS had sought to enlist him in their cause of erasure; instead, they had inadvertently forged him into its most unlikely, and perhaps its most dangerous, opponent. His suspicions had not merely been aroused; they had been ignited into a burning conviction. The path forward was uncertain, fraught with peril, but for the first time since his encounter, Falk felt a clarity of purpose, a somber resolve that would guide him through the encroaching darkness. He was a historian, and he would fight for history. He would remember.

Falk's increasingly erratic behavior had not gone unnoticed. The watchful eyes of the SS security apparatus, ever-present and perpetually suspicious, had begun to focus on him. His subordinates, trained to observe and report, meticulously documented his every deviation from the norm. The clandestine meetings he'd begun to orchestrate, shrouded in the secrecy of dimly lit backrooms and hushed exchanges in deserted corridors, were noted. His prolonged absences from his assigned duties, often spent in the labyrinthine archives or locked away in his study, poring over obscure historical texts or sketching complex harmonic diagrams that bore no resemblance to any known SS research, were logged with growing concern. The subtle signs of his inner turmoil – the haunted look in his eyes, the nervous tremor in his hands when holding a simple pen, the faraway gaze that suggested his mind was miles, perhaps light-years, away – were meticulously recorded in his personnel file. He was becoming a person of interest, a potential liability to the regime's most clandestine operations, a ripple in the otherwise placid, controlled waters of SS efficiency.

His commanding officer, Sturmbannführer Klaus Richter, a man whose career was built on ruthless efficiency and an almost pathological adherence to protocol, summoned Falk to his sparsely furnished office. The air within was thick with the scent of stale cigar smoke and unspoken accusation. Richter, a man with eyes like chips of granite and a jaw that seemed permanently clenched, sat behind his imposing desk, a single file open before him.

"Falk," Richter began, his voice a low growl, devoid of any warmth, "your performance has... deviated from expected parameters." He tapped a manicured finger on the file. "Your field reports are becoming increasingly... detached. Your attendance at mandatory briefings has been irregular. And your subordinates have reported a pattern of secretive behavior. Can you enlighten me as to the cause of this... shift?"

Falk met Richter's steely gaze, the hum within him a subtle counterpoint to the pounding of his heart. He could not, of course, reveal the truth. The alien's knowledge was too dangerous, too unbelievable. To speak of Project Veil, of existential erasure, of cosmic frequencies, would be to invite immediate institutionalization, or worse. He had to maintain a semblance of normalcy, to deflect, to dissemble.

"Sir," Falk began, his voice carefully modulated, "I have been immersed in certain... historical anomalies. My research into the earlier phases of the 'cleansing directives' has uncovered certain discrepancies that require deeper investigation. These require a particular focus, a... specialized approach." He chose his words with deliberate care, weaving a thread of plausible deniability into his narrative. "The complexity of the archival data, combined with the emotional toll of the subject matter, has led to a certain... preoccupation. I assure you, my commitment to my duties remains unwavering."

Richter's expression remained impassive, a mask of professional indifference. Yet, Falk detected a flicker of suspicion in his eyes, a subtle narrowing that spoke volumes. "Historical anomalies," Richter repeated, the words dripping with skepticism. "Falk, your purview is the preservation and dissemination of historical records in support of the Reich's objectives. It is not to delve into theoretical curiosities or engage in solitary, unexplained research that raises questions among your peers and superiors." He leaned forward, his gaze intensifying. "Your focus, Falk, must be on the present. On the directives given. On the clear and present needs of the Reich. This preoccupation with the past, with what you call 'discrepancies,' sounds dangerously like... distraction. Or worse, *dissent*." The word hung in the air, heavy and suffocating. Dissent. The ultimate sin within the SS.

"Sir, my research is intended to strengthen our understanding of the historical justifications for our actions," Falk lied, the words tasting like ash in his mouth. "A more profound grasp of the historical context, the roots of these... directives, will only serve to solidify our resolve and ensure the ultimate success of our endeavors." He forced a thin smile. "I am, after all, a historian. My loyalty lies in understanding and reinforcing the narrative."

Richter remained silent for a long moment, his eyes sweeping over Falk as if trying to discern the hidden currents beneath the surface. "See that it does, Falk. See that it does." He gestured dismissively. "You will submit a detailed report on these 'discrepancies' by the end of the week. And I expect to see a renewed focus on your assigned tasks. We cannot afford distractions. Not now. Not ever."

As Falk left Richter's office, a cold dread settled upon him. He had managed to deflect the immediate inquiry, but he knew this was only a temporary reprieve. Richter, a man of considerable influence within the security apparatus, would not simply forget. Falk's name had been flagged. His activities would be scrutinized with even greater intensity. The subtle hum within him seemed to vibrate with a new urgency, a silent alarm bell warning him of the increasing danger.

He began to notice the subtle shifts in the behavior of those around him. Colleagues who had once greeted him with casual familiarity now offered curt nods or averted their gaze. The easy banter that had once characterized his interactions with his subordinates had been replaced by a guarded politeness, a hesitant respect that felt more like apprehension. He saw them whispering amongst themselves, their conversations ceasing abruptly whenever he approached. They were reporting his every move, his every word, his every failing.

He was no longer just a historian within the SS; he was a subject of its internal surveillance, a cog that had begun to grind against the machinery. The alien's final, desperate transmission had not only burdened him with forbidden knowledge but had also painted a target on his back. He was attempting to unravel a conspiracy of unimaginable scale, a plot to erase existence itself, and the very organization he served was its architect.

The knowledge of Project Veil, once a source of intellectual fascination and then profound horror, was now a dangerous secret that isolated him from everyone he knew. He found himself walking a tightrope, desperately trying to maintain the face of loyalty while his mind was consumed by the alien's complex, terrifying revelations. The harmonic frequencies, the patterns of erasure, the very concept of unmaking history – these were the thoughts that occupied his every waking moment, and his increasingly withdrawn demeanor was a visible manifestation of this internal struggle.

He knew he had to find a way to corroborate the alien's claims, to gather irrefutable evidence of Project Veil's existence and its horrifying objectives. The alien had alluded to specific research facilities, to key personnel involved in the harmonic manipulation, and to the physical implementation of the erasure frequencies. This information, fragmented and cryptic as it was, was his only hope. But to access it, he would need to move beyond the archives and the theoretical, to penetrate the inner sanctum of the SS's most classified research.

His historian's instincts, honed by years of meticulous research and pattern recognition, were now his most potent weapon. He began to analyze the flow of information within the SS, the movement of personnel, the allocation of resources. He looked for anomalies, for unexplained expenditures, for personnel transfers to obscure research outposts that seemed to have no logical military purpose. The alien's knowledge had given him a new lens through which to view the world, a world not of armies and nations, but of vibrations and frequencies, of historical currents and existential anchors.   He started to frequent the less-trafficked sections of the SS archives, seeking out records related to obscure scientific endeavors, to the retrieval of anomalous artifacts, to any mention of research into esoteric physics or resonance theory. He was a ghost in the machine, meticulously sifting through layers of bureaucratic obfuscation, searching for the faintest whisper of Project Veil. The hum within him seemed to grow stronger in these moments of intense focus, almost as if it were guiding him, vibrating in resonance with the hidden truths he sought.

One evening, deep within the dusty stacks of forbidden texts – a section reserved for confiscated occult literature and banned scientific treatises – he stumbled upon a collection of encrypted journals. They belonged to a scientist named Dr. Albert Fromm, a man who had been declared a traitor and disappeared years ago under mysterious circumstances. Fromm's work, Falk recalled from hushed rumors, had delved into theories of resonant frequencies and their potential applications, theories that had been dismissed as fantastical and dangerous by the mainstream scientific community.

As Falk carefully began the painstaking process of decrypting the journals, using techniques he'd learned from ancient ciphers and wartime code-breaking manuals, a chilling realization began to dawn. Fromm's theories, while framed in the language of theoretical physics, bore an uncanny resemblance to the concepts the alien had imparted. Fromm spoke of "harmonic imprinting," of "existential resonance patterns," and of a terrifying possibility: the ability to manipulate not just physical matter, but the very fabric of historical continuity.

The journals hinted at a clandestine project, funded by elements within the SS, that sought to harness these principles. Fromm's entries grew increasingly frantic in the later stages, filled with accusations of stolen research, of ethical boundaries being crossed, and of a terrifying application of his theories that he described as "the undoing of the enemy's very essence." He spoke of a "signature frequency" that characterized certain populations, and the horrifying potential of emitting a counter-frequency to systematically erase them from existence, not just in the present, but retroactively.

Falk felt a cold sweat break out on his brow. This was it. This was the corroboration he desperately needed. Fromm's lost work was the key that unlocked the practical application of the alien's knowledge. The SS, it seemed, had not only discovered the alien technology but had also been actively pursuing similar avenues of research, culminating in the horrific realization of Project Veil.

He meticulously copied sections of the journals, using microdot techniques he'd perfected for his own clandestine research. The risk was immense. If he were caught with these documents, his fate would be sealed. But the alternative – allowing Project Veil to continue its silent, devastating work – was unthinkable. The alien's plea to "Remember" echoed in his mind, a constant, unyielding imperative. He was no longer just a historian; he was a guardian of memory, a silent soldier in a war fought not with bullets, but with the fundamental vibrations of existence.

The scrutiny from his superiors intensified. Richter had assigned a shadow, a silent observer named Obersturmführer Max Brandt, to keep a constant watch over him. Brandt was a professional, a man who moved with the quiet efficiency of a predator, his eyes missing nothing, his presence a constant, unnerving reminder of Falk's precarious position. Brandt would appear at unexpected moments, his questions probing, his gaze lingering, designed to elicit a reaction, to catch Falk in a slip of the tongue, a moment of unguarded emotion.

Falk learned to compartmentalize his life, to maintain the outward appearance of a loyal, if slightly eccentric, SS officer, while his inner world was a maelstrom of frantic research and growing dread. He conducted his decryption work in the dead of night, using the faint glow of a shielded oil lamp, the scratching of his pen on paper the only sound in his small, sterile quarters. He would feign illness or invent urgent research needs to create small windows of opportunity for clandestine meetings with the few individuals he felt he could, perhaps, trust – or at least, exploit for information.

He sought out those who had served in departments tangential to the highly classified research programs, those who might have overheard whispers or noticed unusual personnel movements.

He cultivated relationships with archivists in departments dealing with advanced physics and technological development, subtly probing for any mention of Project Veil or its associated projects. Each conversation was a carefully orchestrated dance, a delicate balance of plausible inquiry and veiled suspicion.

He discovered that a significant portion of the SS's advanced research was being conducted at a remote facility in the Bavarian Alps, known only as 'Station Nightingale.' Access to this facility was highly restricted, its personnel vetted through multiple layers of security clearance. It was here, he suspected, that the primary implementation of Project Veil was being orchestrated. The alien's final, fragmented data had alluded to the precise location of the primary harmonic emitters, and Station Nightingale matched the cryptic geographical markers.

The weight of his clandestine activities began to take its toll. Sleep offered little respite, his dreams filled with the alien's dying cries and the unsettling hum of unseen frequencies. The constant vigilance required to maintain his façade was exhausting. He felt the isolation keenly, the inability to share the burden of his knowledge with anyone. Yet, with each piece of decrypted information, with each corroborating whisper, his resolve hardened. The betrayal he felt was not merely personal; it was a betrayal of history, of humanity, of the very essence of existence. And he was determined to expose it, no matter the cost. The SS had sought to silence him; instead, they had inadvertently set in motion the unmaking of their own apocalyptic design. The historian had become the reluctant warrior, his battlefield the silent, invisible currents of time itself.

The air in the SS Cantine, usually thick with the scent of cheap tobacco and the clatter of metal trays, now carried a subtle, almost imperceptible shift. It was the scent of manufactured normalcy, a carefully constructed atmosphere designed to lull, not to comfort. Falk, sipping lukewarm ersatz coffee, felt it acutely. The subtle hum within him, his constant companion, vibrated with a disquieting resonance, a premonition of a carefully orchestrated encounter. He'd been seeing a lot more of Sturmbannführer Richter lately, not directly, but through the heightened scrutiny of his surroundings. It was like a finely tuned instrument detecting a discordant note; Falk knew something was being prepared.

His subordinate, Untersturmführer Weber, a man whose ambition outstripped his intellect but whose loyalty to the Reich was unquestionable, approached his table. Weber was usually effusive, eager to curry favor, but today, there was a carefully managed diffidence in his demeanor. He carried a file, its cover conspicuously unmarked, and his eyes, usually darting around with a nervous energy, were fixed, almost too intensely, on Falk.

"Herr Sturmbannführer," Weber began, his voice pitched low, as if sharing a confidence, "Richter requires your immediate presence in his office. He received... a rather unusual communication. Apparently, it pertains to your recent archival research."

Falk felt a prickle of unease. Richter requesting his presence without prior notification, especially concerning his research, was highly irregular. Richter preferred to orchestrate such encounters, to surround himself with the trappings of authority. This felt... reactive. And the mention of his research was a calculated gambit. It was a way to draw him in, to present a plausible reason for the summons.

"Unusual?" Falk inquired, his voice carefully neutral, betraying none of the sudden tightening in his gut. "What sort of unusual, Weber?"

Weber shifted his weight, a slight flush rising on his neck. "It's... complex, Herr Sturmbannführer. It seems to be a series of fragmented transmissions, supposedly from a... foreign source. They've been partially decoded, and some of the technical jargon, the theoretical physics, they say it bears a striking resemblance to your... hypothetical inquiries into harmonic resonance." He paused, letting the implication hang heavy in the air. "Richter wants your assessment. He believes you might be able to shed light on its origin and its... purpose."

The hum within Falk intensified, a frantic buzzing that felt like a trapped insect against his skull. Foreign source. Theoretical physics. His research. It was a perfect, insidious construction. They were using his own documented interests, the very avenues he'd been forced to acknowledge to Richter, as bait. They wanted to make it appear as though *he* had made contact with an external entity, not the other way around. This was no longer about his personal conduct; this was about framing him.

"Very well, Weber," Falk said, rising from his seat, deliberately pushing the coffee cup away. "Lead the way." He maintained a posture of professional curiosity, masking the icy dread that was beginning to spread through him. He knew he was walking into a meticulously crafted trap, but he had no choice but to confront it. The alternative was to be apprehended, discredited, and silenced before he could make any progress. He had to see what they had concocted.

Richter's office was, as usual, stark and imposing. The familiar scent of stale cigar smoke was present, but today it seemed to cling to the air with a cloying intensity. Richter sat behind his desk, his granite-like gaze fixed on a large, illuminated screen that displayed a series of complex waveforms and what looked like garbled text. Beside him stood Obersturmführer Brandt, Falk's shadow, his expression impassive, his presence a constant, silent reminder of his surveillance.

"Falk," Richter said, his voice a low growl, without preamble. He gestured towards the screen. "We have intercepted and partially decoded a series of communications. They are... perplexing. They speak of frequencies, of resonance, of... temporal displacement. Concepts that, rather disturbingly, echo certain... theoretical lines of inquiry you have been pursuing."

Falk approached the screen, his eyes scanning the alien data. It was indeed fragmented, the decoded portions tantalizingly familiar, referencing harmonic structures and vibrational patterns that mirrored the alien's final transmission. But there were also distortions, deliberate misinterpretations woven into the narrative. The decoded fragments were being twisted to suggest an initiation of contact, an offer of collaboration, from a clandestine, possibly hostile, element operating outside Reich control.

"The source," Falk said, his voice steady, "is it identifiable?"

Brandt stepped forward, placing a thin dossier on Richter's desk. "Our cryptographers believe it originates from a compromised research station in the Arctic, Herr Sturmbannführer. Indications suggest a rogue scientific faction, possibly operating under the guise of... extraterrestrial contact research." He glanced at Falk, a subtle, almost imperceptible narrowing of his eyes. "A faction that, by all accounts, has been actively seeking to destabilize established scientific paradigms, and by extension, the authority of the Reich."

The implication was clear. They were painting him as a collaborator with a rogue, potentially alien, scientific faction that was actively working against the SS. The narrative was being meticulously constructed: Falk, obsessed with his theoretical research, had somehow made contact with this rogue group, feeding them sensitive information or, worse, actively cooperating with

151

them.

"And the purpose of these communications?" Falk pressed, feigning ignorance, his mind racing to dismantle their fabricated reality.

Richter leaned back in his chair, his gaze sharp and unwavering. "They appear to be an attempt to solicit your expertise. An offer to share their findings, their 'advanced understanding' of these frequencies. They speak of a shared objective, a desire to 'realign the historical narrative.' A deeply disturbing proposition, Falk, when one considers the implications."

The phrase "realign the historical narrative" struck Falk like a physical blow. It was a direct echo of the alien's intent, of Project Veil's ultimate goal. They were twisting the truth with chilling precision. The alien had sought to *prevent* the realignment, to preserve history. Now, they were using that very concept to implicate him.

"These... 'findings'," Falk said, choosing his words with extreme care, "are they related to the project you have been overseeing? The... harmonic weaponization research?" He tried to steer the conversation, to imply that *their* project was the origin of these concepts, not some external entity he had contacted.

Richter's lips thinned. "Our research, Falk, is entirely within the purview of the Reich. It is controlled, authorized, and aimed at the security and advancement of the Greater German Reich. These communications, however, are unsanctioned, unauthorized, and frankly, suggest a degree of... intellectual indiscretion on your part."

He picked up the dossier Brandt had provided, flipping through its pages with deliberate slowness. "There are inconsistencies in your recent reports, Falk. Deliberate omissions. You've been accessing restricted archives without proper authorization. And now, these communications. They paint a picture, Falk, a rather damning one of a scientist who has strayed far from his designated path. A scientist who has, perhaps, been... tempted by forbidden knowledge."

Brandt added, his voice a silken whisper, "We have also noted unusual movements in your personal quarters, Herr Sturmbannführer. Certain... encrypted data storage devices have been discovered. Their contents are currently being analyzed, but initial findings suggest a clandestine information exchange, one that does not align with your stated research objectives."

The trap was now fully sprung. They had planted fabricated evidence, twisted his documented actions into proof of his disloyalty, and now they were presenting it to him, a carefully constructed case designed to dismantle his credibility and isolate him. The mention of encrypted data storage devices was a particularly cruel touch, referencing his own efforts to safeguard the alien's knowledge. They had likely planted those themselves.

"Herr Sturmbannführer, with all due respect," Falk began, his voice rising slightly, a controlled display of indignation, "the communications you are referring to are not the result of any solicitation on my part. They are, in fact, the very evidence of the phenomenon I have been investigating. The alien technology. The source of the transmissions I have been working to understand." He gestured to the screen. "The fragmented data you've decoded has been deliberately manipulated to portray a false narrative. I have *received* these transmissions, not sought them out. And their content is not an offer of collaboration, but a desperate plea for help, a warning about Project Veil." He saw a subtle flicker of amusement in Richter's eyes, a cruel satisfaction at the sight of Falk's distress. "A plea for help? A warning about Project Veil?"

Richter chuckled, a dry, rasping sound. "Falk, you speak in riddles. Project Veil is a theoretical construct, a hypothetical framework for future strategic development. It is not a tangible reality, certainly not one that would warrant clandestine communications with unknown entities." He leaned forward, his voice dropping to a menacing whisper. "Your obsession has clearly led you to construct elaborate fantasies, Falk. Fantasies that now place you in a position of grave suspicion."

Brandt stepped closer, his gaze fixed on Falk. "Your personal logs, Herr Sturmbannführer, have also been reviewed. They speak of 'existential erasure,' of 'harmonic patterns of unmaking.' Highly abstract concepts, certainly. But when juxtaposed with these intercepted transmissions, and the discovery of these... devices, they begin to paint a disturbing picture of a mind unhinged, a mind susceptible to manipulation by external forces."

Falk felt a wave of despair wash over him. They had anticipated his every move, dissected his every action, and weaponized his deepest fears and most desperate attempts at uncovering the truth. They had turned his genuine investigation into evidence of his own delusion and betrayal.

"You are mistaken, Sturmbannführer," Falk stated, his voice regaining some of its lost strength, a core of defiance hardening within him. "The concepts I've documented are not fantasies. They are the reality of the threat we face. The alien transmissions are real. Project Veil is real. And your organization is actively pursuing its implementation, a horrific act of historical revisionism that will have catastrophic consequences."

Richter stood up, his shadow falling over Falk. "Falk!" He said, his voice cold and final, "your pronouncements are becoming increasingly erratic, and frankly, seditious. You have been compromised. Your judgment is clearly impaired. Therefore, for your own good, and for the security of the Reich, you will be placed under immediate protective custody. Obersturmführer Brandt will escort you to a secure facility where you can undergo... reassessment."

Brandt moved with practiced efficiency, placing a hand on Falk's arm. It was not a violent gesture, but the grip was firm, unyielding. Falk knew, with absolute certainty, that this was it. The trap had been sprung, and he had walked right into it. The carefully cultivated evidence, the fabricated transmissions, the whispers of his own subordinates – it all converged into this moment, a neatly packaged accusation of treason and mental instability. He had been so focused on exposing Project Veil that he had underestimated the SS's capacity to turn his own efforts against him. The weight of betrayal, not just from the organization he served, but from the very truth he sought to protect, settled upon him, heavy and suffocating. His mission to save history had, ironically, led him to become a prisoner of its architects.

The cold metal of the restraints bit into Falk's wrists, a stark contrast to the stifling air of the transport vehicle. His initial, furious protests had been met with the impassive faces of SS guards, their professionalism a chilling testament to their obedience. He was not being arrested; he was being "escorted" to protective custody. The euphemism was as hollow as the pronouncements of victory that echoed daily from the propaganda ministries. He knew, with a certainty that settled like lead in his gut, that this was not a temporary measure. This was the beginning of his end, meticulously orchestrated by men who saw his pursuit of truth as a direct threat to their manufactured reality.

As the vehicle rumbled through the pre-dawn streets, the nascent light struggled to pierce the thick, industrial smog that perpetually cloaked Berlin. Each tremor of the engine seemed to underscore the precariousness of his situation. They had presented him with a narrative, a fabricated tapestry woven from his own research, his own documented inquiries, and now, they were weaving it into an indictment. Accusations of treason and espionage, once abstract concepts he'd studied in historical texts, were now the very chains binding him.

He recalled the chilling efficiency with which Brandt had moved, the almost practiced indifference in his eyes as he'd placed the hand on Falk's arm. It was the look of a man performing a duty, devoid of personal malice but equally devoid of any human empathy. Falk had seen that look before, in the eyes of soldiers executing orders, in the eyes of functionaries signing directives that sent thousands to their doom. It was the look of absolute, unthinking adherence. And that, Falk realized, was a far more dangerous adversary than any overt act of aggression.

The carefully constructed case against him was designed for maximum impact, a testament to the insidious power of the Reich's propaganda apparatus. He could already envision the headlines, the radio broadcasts, the whispers in the SS Canteens and the Reichstag hallways. Falk, the brilliant scientist, corrupted, seduced by foreign influence, a traitor to the Fatherland. They would dissect his every word, his every research paper, twisting even his most earnest inquiries into evidence of subversive intent. His life's work, dedicated to understanding the fundamental fabric of reality, would be recontextualized as a tool of enemy infiltration.

He thought of Goebbels, the architect of their national consciousness, the maestro of manipulation. The Minister of Propaganda would not merely discredit him; he would erase him, or rather, redefine him. Falk would become a cautionary tale, a boogeyman conjured to solidify the party line, to reinforce the absolute necessity of unwavering loyalty. Any testimony Falk might offer, any attempt to explain the truth about Project Veil, would be dismissed as the ravings of a compromised mind, the desperate machinations of a traitor caught red-handed.

The weight of it all was crushing. It wasn't just the loss of his freedom, the imminent threat to his life, but the profound sense of isolation. He had believed, perhaps naively, that the pursuit of scientific truth, even in its most abstract and potentially dangerous forms, was a noble endeavor. He had believed that understanding was the ultimate weapon against ignorance and malice. Now, he was learning the hard way that in this regime, understanding could be a capital offense.

The transport vehicle came to an abrupt halt, jolting Falk forward. The doors hissed open, revealing a sterile, concrete bunker, its entrance guarded by men in immaculate black uniforms, their faces impassive, their rifles held at the ready. This was not a prison in the conventional sense; it was a containment facility, designed to isolate, to dissect, and ultimately, to neutralize.

As he was roughly guided from the vehicle, the stark reality of his situation pressed in on him. The evidence they presented – the fragmented transmissions, the doctored logs, the conveniently discovered encrypted devices – was a masterpiece of fabricated guilt. They had taken the very tools he used to uncover the truth and wielded them as instruments of his destruction. The scientific jargon that had once held the promise of enlightenment was now being used as proof of his mental instability, his susceptibility to foreign influence.

He remembered Richter's cold, dismissive tone, the way he'd referred to Project Veil as a mere theoretical construct. It was a deliberate attempt to gaslight him, to undermine his certainty, to sow doubt even in his own mind. But Falk knew what he had seen, what he had heard, what the alien transmissions had revealed. Project Veil was not a theory; it was a monstrous plan, a catastrophic endeavor to rewrite history, and the SS, under Richter's command, was its eager architect.

The guards shoved him through a heavy steel door, the clang echoing ominously in the confined space. The air was cold, metallic, and devoid of any natural light. He was being processed, dehumanized, reduced to a series of data points in a system that operated on suspicion and absolute obedience.

He could almost hear the whispers, amplified by the state-controlled media, painting him as the architect of his own downfall. "Falk, a brilliant mind, tragically lost to the siren song of forbidden knowledge," they would say. "A stark reminder of the dangers of intellectual curiosity untethered from loyalty to the Reich." It was a narrative that would serve their purpose perfectly, discrediting him, and by extension, discrediting the very truths he had uncovered.

His mind raced, desperately searching for an avenue of escape, a chink in their armor, a way to disseminate the truth before they could permanently silence him. But every avenue seemed to be blocked, every potential ally compromised or too afraid to act. He was a lone scientist, a single voice against a monolithic, all-encompassing entity. The weight of betrayal was not just the betrayal of the SS, but the betrayal of his own ideals, the perversion of his life's work. He had sought to illuminate the darkness, but in doing so, he had inadvertently stepped into a far deeper, more insidious shadow. His fate hung precariously in the balance, a single mote of dust caught in the inexorable gears of a totalitarian machine, its trajectory determined not by truth, but by the power of manufactured perception.

The sterile, unforgiving walls of the interrogation chamber seemed to absorb any lingering warmth Falk might have possessed. His initial defiance had long since curdled into a gnawing dread, amplified by the chillingly detached demeanor of his interrogators. They weren't interested in confessions; they were interested in extraction. The carefully curated dossiers, the subtle shifts in questioning, the unnerving precision with which they presented fragments of his own research – it was all a prelude to something far more insidious than a public trial. He had seen the glint of something new in Richter's eyes during their last 'conversation' – not just the usual contempt, but a nascent curiosity, a disturbing fascination with the very knowledge Falk had unearthed. This wasn't about suppression; it was about *acquisition*.

Himmler, draped in the obsidian silk of his SS uniform, surveyed the holographic projection with a detached satisfaction. The data streams, shimmering with an eerie green luminescence, represented the culmination of weeks of meticulous work. Falk, the brilliant scientist, was proving a stubborn obstacle, a repository of dangerous secrets that the Reich could not afford to remain in his possession. A swift execution would be too simple, too final. It wouldn't guarantee the utter eradication of the knowledge he held. The whispers from the deepest levels of the Ahnenerbe, the clandestine research divisions delving into the very fringes of human and, dare he think it, *non-human* understanding, had spoken of a more elegant solution.

"He is a valuable asset, even in his current state of... recalcitrance," Himmler's voice was a silken caress, devoid of emotion, as he addressed the select group gathered in his private study. The air was thick with the scent of expensive cigars and the unspoken weight of absolute power. Beside him, Himmler's closest confidantes – Kaltenbrunner, a man whose very presence exuded a predatory stillness, and Brandt, whose stoic efficiency masked a chilling ruthlessness – nodded in agreement.

"His mind holds the key to understanding the transmissions, Heinrich," Kaltenbrunner stated, his voice a low rumble. "Simply silencing him would be a waste. We need to *repurpose* him."

Brandt elaborated, his gaze fixed on the shifting patterns of light on the projection. "The technology we've... acquired... is capable of far more than mere communication or observation. It can interface directly with the human neurological system, manipulating synaptic pathways, altering memory, even reshaping fundamental beliefs." He paused, allowing the implication to settle. "We can administer a targeted erasure. A specific mnemonic excision, if you

158

will. Remove his knowledge of Project Veil, his understanding of the alien signals, even his loyalty to any cause but our own. He will remain functional, capable of assisting us with the *interpretation* of the data, but the dangerous aspects will be gone."

Himmler steepled his fingers, a predatory smile playing on his lips. "A partial lobotomy, but with surgical precision. He will be a tool, utterly compliant, incapable of betraying us. He will serve the Reich, not through coercion, but through a fundamental alteration of his very being." The idea was audacious, chillingly efficient, and perfectly aligned with the SS's modus operandi: control, not just of bodies and actions, but of minds themselves.

The term "Branded for Silence" had begun to circulate amongst a select few within the SS security apparatus, a morbidly apt descriptor for the fate being prepared for Falk. It wasn't a scar on the flesh, but a brand upon the very essence of his consciousness. The procedure was deemed too sensitive, too radical, to be carried out in any conventional medical facility. Instead, a specialized unit, operating under the direct purview of the Ahnenerbe's clandestine research division, had been mobilized. Their base, a discreet, heavily fortified installation nestled deep within the Black Forest, was a labyrinth of sterile laboratories and advanced containment units, designed to house and study technologies far beyond the scope of contemporary science.

Falk was moved under extreme secrecy. The transfer was shrouded in layers of misdirection and false trails, designed to deceive any potential observers or sympathizers. He was told he was being moved to a more secure location for further questioning, a standard procedure that offered no hint of the true nature of his impending transformation. The journey itself was a disorienting blur of sensory deprivation. He was transported in a specially designed vehicle, insulated against sound and light, his movements further restricted by restraints that were not merely physical, but also subtly designed to induce a state of extreme lethargy and disorientation.

Upon arrival, the air felt different – cleaner, yet colder, imbued with a subtle hum that seemed to resonate within his very bones. The guards who escorted him were not the usual SS troopers, but individuals clad in pristine white lab coats, their expressions devoid of the customary martial hardness. They moved with a quiet, unnerving efficiency, their hands gloved, their faces masked. He was led not to a cell, but to a meticulously clean, almost clinical examination room. The equipment that lined the walls was unlike anything he had ever seen, a bewildering array of gleaming chrome, pulsating lights, and complex crystalline structures that seemed to defy terrestrial engineering.

The lead scientist, a woman named Dr. Gisela Becker, introduced herself with a curt nod. Her eyes, behind thick spectacles, held an unsettlingly analytical intensity. There was no warmth in her greeting, only the dispassionate assessment of a specimen. "Dr. Falk," she began, her voice carrying a faint, unplaceable accent, "you are about to undergo a unique therapeutic intervention."

Therapeutic intervention. The words struck Falk as a grotesque perversion. He had come to understand that his pursuit of truth had made him a threat, but he had imagined the threat would be met with outright suppression, with the blunt force of state power. He had never anticipated this – a scientific perversion, a hijacking of his own consciousness.

"The Reich values your contributions, Doctor," Becker continued, gesturing towards a complex apparatus that dominated the center of the room. It was a chair, but unlike any chair he had ever seen. It was wrought from polished obsidian, studded with what appeared to be an array of intricate, pulsating crystals. Above it, a shimmering, translucent canopy hovered, interwoven with filaments of light. "We simply need to ensure that your considerable intellect is aligned with the interests of the Fatherland. This procedure will… re-focus your cognitive pathways, removing any… dissonant information that may have inadvertently taken root."

Falk's heart hammered against his ribs. He recognized the underlying threat, the veiled promise of manipulation. He tried to speak, to protest, but his voice felt thick and sluggish, as if his very vocal cords were being dulled. The air in the room seemed to press in on him, heavy with an unseen energy.

"We have found that direct neurological interface is the most efficient method for profound cognitive recalibration," Becker

160

explained, her voice calm and steady, utterly unperturbed by Falk's silent distress. "The technology we employ is derived from... advanced sources. It allows us to access and modify specific neural pathways with unparalleled precision. Think of it as a selective edit, Doctor . We are not destroying your mind, merely refining it, removing the undesirable elements."

He was strapped into the obsidian chair, the restraints cool and unyielding. The canopy descended, enveloping him in a soft, ethereal glow. As the crystals began to thrum with increasing intensity, Falk felt a strange sensation, like a thousand tiny needles pricking at the edges of his awareness. It wasn't painful, not in a physical sense, but it was deeply invasive, a violation on a level he had never conceived.

Images began to flicker behind his eyelids, fragments of his research, snatches of the alien transmissions, the faces of those he had worked with, the equations that had once consumed his thoughts. They weren't memories in the traditional sense; they were raw data, being sifted, analyzed, and, he feared, rewritten. He felt a strange detachment, as if he were observing these fragments from a great distance.

"We are isolating the semantic clusters related to the extraterrestrial contact and your subsequent theories," Becker's voice, now amplified and distorted by the surrounding technology, echoed in the confined space. "We are also identifying and excising any neural imprints associated with dissent or disloyalty. Your foundational scientific understanding will remain intact, of course. Your ability to perform complex calculations, to analyze data... these will be preserved. But the knowledge that could be used to undermine the Reich, that will be... neatly excised."

The process was agonizingly slow, a subtle erosion of his self. He fought against it, clinging to the memories, to the truths he had painstakingly uncovered. He saw the faces of his colleagues, the hushed conversations in dimly lit labs, the sheer thrill of discovery that had once fueled him. He tried to project these images, these feelings, outwards, a desperate attempt to anchor himself, to resist the digital amputation of his mind.

But the alien technology, adapted and wielded by the SS, was relentless. It bypassed his conscious defenses, probing the very foundations of his cognitive architecture. He felt his understanding of the alien signals, once so vivid and terrifyingly clear, begin to blur, like ink bleeding into water. The logic, the implications, the sheer magnitude of what he had learned, started to fray at the edges, becoming indistinct and meaningless.

He felt a profound sense of loss, a gaping void opening within him. It was more than just losing memories; it was losing parts of himself. The intellectual curiosity that had driven him, the unwavering commitment to empirical truth, the very essence of what made him Falk – it was all being systematically dismantled, piece by piece.

As the process continued, a strange calm began to settle over him. The fear subsided, replaced by a growing sense of lassitude. The fight drained out of him, replaced by a placid emptiness. The crystals pulsed, and with each pulse, another piece of his identity was severed. The brand was being indelibly etched, not in fire, but in the silent, insidious manipulation of his own mind. He was being transformed, not into a weapon, but into an instrument, a hollow shell designed to serve a purpose he would no longer comprehend. The weight of betrayal was no longer a burden he carried; it was a void where his own sense of self had once resided. He was becoming a prisoner within his own skull, his freedom traded for a manufactured obedience, branded for a silence that would be absolute and eternal. The once vibrant tapestry of his mind was being unraveled, thread by thread, leaving behind only a blank, compliant canvas awaiting the SS's design.

Chapter 8

Fragments of the Past

The cold, sterile air of the laboratory clung to Falk like a shroud, a stark contrast to the heavy, cigar-laden atmosphere of Himmler's study. He had been moved, the journey a disorienting blur of muffled sounds and enforced stillness, culminating in this stark, white chamber. The guards, or rather, the figures in pristine white lab coats, had moved with an unnerving, almost surgical precision, their gloved hands and masked faces lending them an impersonal, almost alien quality. This was no ordinary detention; this was the culmination of a nightmare he had only begun to suspect.

He was escorted not to a cell, but to a room dominated by an imposing apparatus. It was less a chair and more a meticulously crafted throne of polished obsidian, studded with what appeared to be an array of intricately faceted, pulsating crystals. Above it, a translucent canopy, woven with shimmering filaments of light, hovered like a captured aurora. Dr. Gisela Becker, her face partially obscured by thick spectacles, her accent a faint, unplaceable murmur, had introduced herself with a curt nod, her gaze dissecting him with a chillingly dispassionate intensity. "Doctor Falk," she'd stated, her voice devoid of warmth, "you are about to undergo a unique therapeutic intervention."

Therapeutic intervention. The words, uttered in this alien environment, struck Falk with the force of a physical blow. He had braced himself for interrogation, for threats, for the brutal finality of execution. He had not prepared for this – a violation of his very being, a scientific perversion of a scale he had never dared to imagine. "The Reich values your contributions, Doctor," Becker had continued, gesturing towards the obsidian chair. "We simply need to ensure that your considerable intellect is aligned with the interests of the Fatherland. This procedure will... re-focus your cognitive pathways, removing any… dissonant information that may have inadvertently taken root."

Falk's breath hitched. The implications were terrifyingly clear. This was not about silencing him, but about *rewriting* him. His mind, the vessel of his discoveries, the very essence of his identity, was to be curated, edited, and purged of anything deemed undesirable by the Reich. He tried to vocalize his protest, to demand an explanation, but his tongue felt thick and unwieldy, his throat constricted by a fear that stole his voice. The very air in the room seemed to hum with an unseen energy, pressing in on him, a silent testament to the alien nature of the technology they intended to wield.

The obsidian restraints, cool and unyielding against his skin, secured him in the chair. As the translucent canopy descended, enveloping him in a soft, ethereal glow, Falk felt a strange sensation, like a thousand microscopic needles pricking at the periphery of his awareness. It wasn't pain, not in the conventional sense, but a deep, invasive violation, a trespass into the very sanctuary of his consciousness.

Images began to flicker behind his eyelids, fragments of his life's work, flashes of the alien transmissions, the faces of colleagues, the intricate dance of equations that had once consumed his every thought. These were not memories replaying; they were raw data, being sifted, analyzed, and, he feared with a chilling certainty, *rewritten*. A profound sense of detachment washed over him, as if he were an observer of his own life, watching it from an impossible distance.

The process was a descent into a terrifying purgatory, an agonizingly slow erosion of self. He fought against it with a primal desperation, clinging to the memories, to the truths he had painstakingly uncovered. He saw the faces of his colleagues in hushed, late-night conversations in dimly lit labs, the sheer, incandescent thrill of discovery that had once been his lifeblood. He tried to project these images, these emotions, outwards, a desperate attempt to anchor himself, to resist the digital amputation of his mind. But the alien technology, a terrifying fusion of extraterrestrial ingenuity and SS ruthlessness, was relentless. It bypassed his conscious defenses, probing the very foundations of his cognitive architecture. He felt his understanding of the alien signals, once so vivid and terrifyingly clear, begin to blur, like ink bleeding into water. The logic, the implications, the sheer, staggering magnitude of what he had learned, started to fray at the edges, becoming indistinct, meaningless.

The initial stages of the procedure were designed to instill a sense of disorientation and helplessness. Falk was subjected to a series of controlled sensory deprivations, interspersed with bursts of specific sonic frequencies. These sounds, alien in their cadence and timbre, were not merely auditory stimuli; they were meticulously calibrated waves, intended to resonate with and disrupt specific neural pathways. The specialists, their faces impassive behind their masks, moved with an unnerving efficiency, monitoring Falk's physiological responses with detached clinical observation. They were not torturing him in the traditional sense, no physical pain was inflicted in a way that would leave marks. Instead, they were employing a far more insidious form of violation, a scalpeling of the mind.

The quartz chair, Falk now understood, was more than just a restraint; it was a conduit. The pulsating crystals embedded within its surface were not merely decorative. They were emitters, projecting focused fields of energy designed to interact directly with the human brain. Dr. Becker, her voice a constant, low murmur, provided a running commentary, her words a chillingly detached explanation of the process unfolding within him. "The primary objective," she explained, her voice amplified by the ambient technology, "is to isolate and neutralize the neural pathways responsible for the recall and interpretation of the anomalous data. We are targeting the conceptual framework, Professor, not the raw data itself, which will be recontextualized."

He felt it then, a subtle but profound shift within his consciousness. It was as if invisible hands were sifting through the intricate latticework of his thoughts, separating, categorizing, and then... detaching. Memories, once sharp and vivid, began to lose their clarity, their emotional resonance. The thrill of his initial discovery of the transmissions, the intellectual fervor that had gripped him, started to feel distant, like an echo from another life. It was not the abrupt erasure of a memory, but a slow, insidious fading, a deliberate blunting of the sharp edges of his understanding.

The technology was a terrifying adaptation of something far beyond human comprehension. Falk, even in his state of drugged and disoriented vulnerability, recognized the underlying principles, albeit warped and perverted. The alien science, designed for purposes he could only speculate upon, was being crudely but effectively repurposed for control. It was an unsophisticated application, a sledgehammer to his cognitive architecture, lacking the finesse he himself would have employed, but devastatingly effective, nonetheless.

The procedure continued for what felt like an eternity. Falk's consciousness flickered, oscillating between a hazy awareness and a deeper, more pervasive state of drugged lethargy. He could feel the intrusion, the systematic dismantling of his intellectual edifice. The very equations that had once flowed so effortlessly from his mind now seemed alien, the symbols blurring into meaningless patterns. The complex algorithms he had developed to decipher the alien signals, once etched into his very soul, were becoming... inaccessible.

"The fragmentation protocol is proceeding as anticipated," Becker's voice cut through the fog of his consciousness. "We are employing a multi-frequency resonant pulse to induce synoptic decoupling within the hippocampus. This will ensure a targeted amnesia, preserving essential motor and cognitive functions while excising the specific knowledge pertaining to Project Veil."

Synoptic decoupling. The term itself was a chilling testament to the SS's perversion of scientific language. They were not merely erasing memories; they were severing the very connections that gave those memories meaning, context, and coherence. Falk felt a desperate urge to resist, to cling to the remnants of his former self, but his limbs felt heavy, unresponsive, his mind a sluggish, failing engine.

He could feel them probing deeper, targeting not just the knowledge of the alien transmissions, but the very curiosity that had led him to them. The drive to understand, to question, to push the boundaries of human knowledge – that, too, was an element they sought to excise. It was a profound act of intellectual vandalism, a silencing of the inquiring mind, a brutal subjugation of thought itself.

As the procedure progressed, a strange duality emerged within Falk. A part of him, the part that was still, for now, Falk, recoiled in horror at the violation. Yet, another part, a nascent, unformed entity, seemed to be passively accepting the intrusion, a blank slate absorbing the alien frequencies. It was as if his mind was bifurcating, one part fighting a losing battle, the other succumbing to an inexplicable calm.

The alien technology was a blunt instrument, a crude adaptation of principles that hinted at a civilization far more advanced. The SS, in their ruthless pursuit of power, had seized upon this potential and twisted it into a tool of subjugation. They were not interested in understanding the nuances of the alien science; they were interested in its efficacy as a means of control. And in Falk, they had found the perfect subject, a repository of knowledge that threatened their carefully constructed order.

The silence that followed each cycle of the emitters was deafening, punctuated only by the soft hum of machinery and Becker's dispassionate pronouncements. Falk felt his grip on reality loosening, his sense of self dissolving like mist in the morning sun. The vibrant, interconnected network of his thoughts was being systematically disassembled, leaving behind isolated fragments, devoid of context or meaning. He was being reduced, not to a blank slate, but to a collection of disjointed data points, ready to be reordered and repurposed according to the SS's design. The brand, invisible and insidious, was being forged within the deepest recesses of his mind, a permanent mark of their absolute dominion.

The pulsating light of the obsidian throne began to recede, the oppressive hum of the alien technology diminishing to a faint, almost imperceptible thrum. Falk felt a peculiar sense of emptiness, a chilling void where vast landscapes of knowledge and terrifying truths had once resided. The SS had achieved their objective, or so they believed. They had attempted to surgically remove the aberrant data, the inconvenient discoveries that threatened to unravel their carefully constructed narrative of dominion. They had targeted his memories of the transmissions, his theories regarding the extraterrestrial signals, and, most importantly, his burgeoning unease, the quiet, insistent voice of his conscience that had begun to whisper dissent.

Yet, as the translucent canopy retracted, revealing the sterile white room and the impassive faces of Dr. Becker and her technicians, Falk sensed a flicker. It was faint, almost imperceptible, like a dying ember refusing to be extinguished. The memory-wiping technology, a crude, human interpretation of alien science, had not performed its intended function with the pristine efficiency they had anticipated. It was as if the very act of tampering with the profound, psionic energies of the alien consciousness that had been imprinted upon him had created an unforeseen interaction, a subtle but significant glitch in their meticulously planned erasure.

The alien entity, a fragment of the dying explorer's consciousness, a psychic echo of a species far more advanced, had acted as an unexpected shield. It wasn't a conscious act of defiance, but rather an inherent property of its existence, a psychic resonance that had absorbed and deflected the brute-force approach of the SS's crude technology. They had wielded a sledgehammer where a scalpel was required, and in doing so, had inadvertently blunted the edge of their own weapon. The neural pathways they had sought to sever, the conceptual frameworks they had aimed to dismantle, were not entirely obliterated. Instead, they had been shielded, buffered by the alien consciousness, like a delicate artifact protected by layers of resilient, unfamiliar material.

Falk's memories of the transmissions, the complex patterns of light and sound that had hinted at a vast, unknowable intelligence, remained. They were no longer as crystal clear as they had been, the initial sharp edges of understanding now softened, blurred by the invasive procedure. But they were there, a core of understanding that the SS had failed to completely eradicate. He could still grasp the essence of the alien communication, the underlying mathematics that spoke of celestial bodies and interstellar journeys. The sheer, mind-boggling scope of it, the implication that humanity was not alone in the universe, had not been entirely purged.

More crucially, the nascent sense of right and wrong, the moral compass that had begun to spin wildly in the face of the SS's atrocities, had also survived. The alien consciousness, possessing a perspective forged over millennia of existence, a civilization that had likely grappled with similar existential questions, had imparted a fundamental understanding of ethics, of shared existence. This had acted as a counter-frequency to the SS's insidious manipulation, a psychic bulwark against the systematic dismantling of his moral framework.

Dr. Becker, adjusting her spectacles, observed Falk with a critical eye. Her expression, usually a mask of detached professionalism, held a subtle, almost imperceptible hint of impatience. "Doctor," she began, her voice betraying none of the internal turmoil she might have been experiencing, "the initial phase of the cognitive recalibration appears to have been... partially successful. Your basic motor functions and general cognitive awareness remain intact, as predicted. However, there are... anomalies in the data."

She gestured towards a bank of monitors displaying complex neurological readouts. Flickering waveforms, interspersed with patches of unnerving static, painted a picture of a mind that had been subjected to immense pressure, but had not entirely succumbed. "The targeted excision of the anomalous neural pathways related to Project Veil is not registering with the expected completeness," she continued, her gaze fixed on the readouts, her tone clinical. "There are residual echoes, persistent synaptic activity that our current models cannot fully account for."

Falk felt a surge of something akin to defiance. It was a fragile sensation, easily crushed, but it was there, a tiny spark in the vast emptiness that the SS had tried to create. He understood now. The alien consciousness was not merely a passive passenger; it was an active participant, a silent guardian of his mind. It had interwoven itself with his own consciousness, a symbiotic relationship born out of necessity, and in doing so, had provided him with an unexpected form of protection.

He met Becker's gaze, his own eyes, though perhaps appearing slightly dulled, now held a deeper, more profound awareness. He couldn't articulate it, not yet, not in a way that would be understood, or worse, believed. But he knew. He knew that the essential truths, the fundamental understanding of his discoveries, and the moral imperative to act upon them, remained within him.

The SS, in their arrogance and ignorance, had underestimated the alien. They had treated its essence as mere data, a set of quantifiable signals to be manipulated. They had failed to grasp that it was something far more profound, a consciousness that operated on principles beyond their comprehension, a force that could not be simply erased with their rudimentary technology. The technology, designed by humans applying a flawed understanding of alien science, had created an unforeseen interaction. It was like trying to dissect a living organism with a blunt knife; the damage was done, but the organism, in its resilience, found ways to adapt and survive.

Becker turned to one of her assistants, a young man with an eager, almost subservient demeanor. "Increase the intensity of the synaptic resonance field by five percent. Target the hippocampus and prefrontal cortex more aggressively. We need to ensure complete data sanitization."

Falk flinched inwardly at the cold, detached language. Data sanitization. They spoke of his mind, his memories, his very essence, as if they were mere files on a corrupted drive. But he was no longer just Falk, the scientist. He was also a vessel, carrying within him the legacy of another, a silent testament to the vastness of the cosmos and the potential for connection. This new layer of his being, this alien consciousness, was not a burden; it was a gift, albeit a terrifyingly acquired one.

He focused on the residual fragments, the shimmering echoes of understanding that remained. The mathematical constants, the geometric patterns that represented the fundamental grammar of the alien transmissions – they were still accessible. The feeling of awe that had accompanied his initial deciphering of these patterns, the sheer intellectual exhilaration, was a powerful anchor. It was a testament to the truth of his work, a truth that the SS desperately wanted to bury.

The aliens, or at least the explorer who had carried their consciousness, had understood the importance of preservation, of understanding. Their science was not a tool for oppression, but a means of exploration and knowledge. This fundamental difference in intent, in philosophy, was what allowed the alien fragment to resist the SS's crude attempts at erasure. It was a battle of ideologies waged on the neural battlefield of his own mind.

The disorientation returned, a wave of nausea washing over him as the technicians adjusted the equipment. The low hum intensified, and Falk felt a familiar pressure building behind his eyes. He closed them, not in surrender, but in concentration. He reached out, not with his hands, but with his mind, towards the subtle currents of the alien consciousness within him. It responded, a faint warmth spreading through his consciousness, a sense of gentle pressure pushing back against the invasive frequencies.

He could feel the alien entity filtering the SS's technological assault, deflecting the worst of it, absorbing and reprocessing it in a way that minimized the damage to his own mind. It was a delicate balance, a constant negotiation between two vastly different forms of existence. The SS believed they were in control, that they were executing a precise operation. They were oblivious to the silent war being waged within Falk's skull, a war where the most advanced weapon was not the SS's alien technology, but the very nature of the consciousness they sought to erase.

Becker's voice cut through the rising tension. "The process is proving more complex than anticipated. The bio-neural interface is exhibiting unusual resistance to the targeted degradation protocols. We are encountering... resonance feedback loops that are disrupting the clean excision."

Falk allowed himself a flicker of grim satisfaction. Resonance feedback loops. They were speaking of his mind as if it were a machine, and his alien passenger as a faulty component. But it was far more than that. It was a testament to the resilience of life, of consciousness, to the inherent drive to persist, to understand, to resist subjugation. He focused on a specific memory: the moment he had first deciphered a particularly complex sequence of the alien transmissions. The exhilaration, the sheer wonder of that

171

breakthrough, was a powerful beacon. He amplified that feeling, drawing strength from it, and in doing so, felt the alien consciousness within him resonate with it, amplifying it further. It was a shared experience, a connection that transcended language and species.

The SS sought to break him, to turn him into a tool, a compliant automaton. But they had inadvertently forged him into something more. They had given him a purpose beyond his own scientific curiosity. He was now the custodian of a truth that threatened their very existence, and he was armed with a defense they could not comprehend.

The sessions continued, each one an agonizing push and pull, a battle for the integrity of his mind. The SS would relentlessly probe, trying to find a weakness, a way to circumvent the alien shield. But the alien consciousness, ancient and resilient, adapted and held firm. It was a constant, subtle recalibration, a testament to its own advanced understanding of psychic phenomena.

Falk began to notice subtle shifts in his own perceptions, even outside of the sterile laboratory environment. He found himself noticing patterns in the mundane, connections between seemingly unrelated events. It was as if the alien consciousness, even when not actively defending him, was subtly influencing his awareness, heightening his senses, sharpening his intuition. He could sense the subtle manipulations of the SS, the veiled threats, the carefully crafted lies. Their attempts at control, once overwhelming, now felt... transparent.

He realized that the SS had fundamentally misunderstood the nature of the alien consciousness they were dealing with. They had treated it as a passive deposit of information, a data packet to be deleted. They had failed to recognize its active, adaptive nature, its inherent ability to preserve itself and, by extension, to preserve the aspects of Falk's mind that it had come to inhabit. The technology, while powerful, was based on a flawed premise, a limited understanding of a far greater reality.

During one session, Dr. Becker seemed particularly frustrated. "The latest scans are showing an... entanglement," she stated, her voice strained. "The neural pathways associated with the alien contact are not merely resistant to degradation; they appear to be reinforcing themselves through a process of quantum entanglement with the residual alien psychic signature."

Quantum entanglement. The words, uttered in the context of their crude attempts at mind control, were almost laughable. The SS was trying to use the principles of advanced extraterrestrial science without truly understanding them, and in doing so, were creating a feedback loop that was strengthening, not weakening, the very things they sought to destroy.

Falk, though physically weakened and mentally scared, felt a growing sense of clarity. The alien consciousness was not just a shield; it was a teacher. It was showing him that the SS's methods, their reliance on brute force and manipulation, were ultimately unsustainable. True understanding, true progress, came from connection, from empathy, from a respect for the interconnectedness of all things.

He began to experiment, cautiously at first. He would focus on a specific memory, a specific truth, and then, almost instinctively, reach out to the alien consciousness. He would feel a subtle shift, a reinforcement of that thought, a strengthening of its emotional and intellectual resonance. It was as if the alien entity was confirming the importance of that particular fragment, that particular truth.

The SS was still in possession of his body, and their technology could still inflict damage. But they could no longer claim victory over his mind. They had tried to erase him, but instead, they had forged him into something new, something stronger. They had given him an unwelcome companion, a silent guardian who ensured that the most vital fragments of his past, and the most crucial aspects of his conscience, would endure. The glitch in their system was not a minor error; it was a fundamental flaw in their understanding of reality, a flaw that would ultimately prove to be their undoing. He was no longer just Doctor Falk, a scientist who had stumbled upon a dangerous truth. He was a bridge, a conduit, a living testament to the fact that some truths, once discovered, could not be unlearned, and some voices, once awakened, could not be silenced. The SS had intended to erase him, but they had, in their own misguided way, helped him to become more himself than he had ever been before. The alien consciousness, a silent passenger, had ensured that the core of his being, the essential Falk, remained intact, a beacon of resistance in the encroaching darkness.

The sterile white of the laboratory pressed in on Falk, a stark, unforgiving canvas against the swirling chaos within his own mind. The hum of the alien technology, once a resonant chord that had vibrated through his very soul, had receded, leaving behind a hollow echo. It was the silence after a cataclysm, pregnant with the unseen devastation. Dr. Becker's words, crisp and clinical, drifted through the haze of his returned consciousness like shards of ice. "Partially successful." "Anomalies." "Residual echoes." They were meant to convey a degree of control, of scientific detachment, but to Falk, they sounded like a confession of failure, a testament to the unyielding power of what they had tried to extinguish.

He felt it then, a profound disorientation, as if his own thoughts had become foreign entities. The neural recalibration, as Becker and her ilk euphemistically called it, had been a brutal assault. It was less a surgical excision and more a crude excavation, tearing through the delicate architecture of his mind with a blunt force he could still feel like phantom pain. Yet, amidst the wreckage, something had survived. Not whole, not coherent, but stubbornly present. Fragments. These were not the polished, rational recollections of his former life, but raw, visceral shards of experience, surfacing with an alarming and often agonizing unpredictability.

One moment, a chilling image would flash behind his eyelids: the mangled wreckage of the aircraft, twisted metal groaning under the weight of an alien sky, bathed in the eerie luminescence of an unfamiliar sun. It was the Black Forest crash, not as he had recorded it in his logs, but as a visceral, gut-wrenching reality. He could almost smell the acrid scent of burning fuel, feel the sickening lurch as the engines failed, hear the screams – screams that were not his own, but somehow intimately familiar. These were not memories he had chosen to retain; they were intrusions, violent intrusions, that clawed their way to the surface of his awareness, disrupting the fragile coherence they were trying to impose.

Then, without warning, the scene would morph. He would see

them, the beings from the transmissions, or rather, the *imprint* of them. Not their physical forms, not in any concrete sense, but the essence of their presence. A shimmering, fluid energy, a symphony of light and form that defied terrestrial biology. It was the visual manifestation of the alien transmissions, the complex, geometric patterns that had spoken a language of pure mathematics and universal truth. The SS had tried to scrub these images, to render them meaningless, but they persisted, flickering at the periphery of his vision, like glimpses of a forbidden reality. They were the haunting beauty of the unknown, a testament to the vastness that lay beyond humanity's limited comprehension.

The experiments. That was another recurring nightmare. The sterile chill of the containment units, the glint of metal against alien flesh, the horrified realization of what he and his colleagues had become. He saw the faces of the SS scientists, masked in their detachment, their eyes devoid of empathy as they probed and prodded, dissecting life itself. He saw the alien specimens, their forms contorted by unimaginable stress, their silent screams echoing in the sterile silence. He felt a phantom chill, the cold touch of instruments on his own skin, the sickening sensation of being reduced to mere biological data. These were not just memories; they were accusations, visceral reminders of his complicity, however unwilling, in their abominable work.

And then there was the chilling implication of Project Veil. It was not a singular image, but a pervasive dread, a creeping certainty that something far more insidious was at play. The SS was not merely observing; they were preparing, manipulating, creating a weapon from the very knowledge they had unearthed. He could feel the tendrils of their plan wrapping around his own mind, seeking to twist his understanding into a tool of destruction. The transmissions were not just a discovery; they were a key, a key that the SS intended to use to unlock a future of their own terrifying design. This fragment of understanding was the most dangerous of all, a seed of dread that threatened to choke out any hope of recovery.

These fragments, these broken pieces of his shattered past, would surface without rhyme or reason. A sudden movement in his peripheral vision, a shift in the ambient light, even the faint scent of ozone from the lab equipment, could trigger a cascade of fractured memories. He would find himself staring blankly, lost in a labyrinth of his own mind, the present reality dissolving into a mosaic of past horrors. The disorientation was profound, a constant battle against a mind that no longer felt entirely his own. He would grip the arms of his chair, his knuckles white, trying to anchor himself in the here and now, to separate the echoes from the reality.

The pain was not merely psychological. There was a physical component to it, a throbbing ache behind his eyes, a tension in his jaw that felt like a perpetual clench. It was the residual agony of his mind being forcibly realigned, of neural pathways being torn and rewoven. Sometimes, a specific fragment would trigger a sharp, jolt of pain, like a nerve being struck. He would gasp, his body involuntarily recoiling, much to the clinical observation of Dr. Becker and her technicians. They documented these reactions with a detached curiosity, as if observing a specimen in a petri dish.

"The patient is exhibiting increased autonomic responses to recalled memory stimuli," Becker would note, her voice carefully devoid of emotion. "Further analysis of the residual synaptic activity is required to determine the precise nature of the fragmentation."

Fragmentation. It was an apt word. His mind was no longer a coherent whole, but a shattered mirror, reflecting distorted images of what had been. Yet, within this terrifying fragmentation, a flicker of something else began to emerge. A desperate drive. A raw, instinctual need to piece together the broken shards, to understand not just *what* had happened, but *why*. The SS had attempted to erase his knowledge, to strip him of his understanding, but in their haste, they had left behind the very catalysts for his continued pursuit of the truth. These fragments, however painful, were the keys to unlocking what they so desperately wanted to keep hidden. They were the proof that he had seen something profound, something that had fundamentally altered his perception of reality.

He started to catalog them internally, a desperate, disorganized attempt to create some semblance of order. The crash. The beings. The experiments. Project Veil. He would focus on each fragment, trying to recall the context, the emotional resonance, the fleeting insights that had accompanied them before the procedure. It was like trying to reconstruct a shattered vase from a handful of pottery shards. Some pieces were large and recognizable, others were tiny and enigmatic. But each one was precious. Each one was a piece of the puzzle that the SS had tried to bury.

The nature of these fragments was also evolving. Initially, they were raw sensory data – sights, sounds, even phantom tactile sensations. But as he began to process them, they started to coalesce, to connect. The image of the Black Forest crash began to be accompanied by a sense of profound loss, not just of the aircraft and its crew, but of something far greater. The glimpses of the alien beings started to evoke not just wonder, but a deep-seated unease, a feeling of being on the precipice of something monumental and perhaps terrifying. The experiments began to resonate with a chilling sense of responsibility, a burden of knowledge that he had tried to ignore but could no longer escape.

The most potent of these evolving fragments were those related to Project Veil. They were less about specific events and more about a dawning, horrifying comprehension. He would see abstract representations of the SS's goals, diagrams that spoke of weaponization, of control, of the subjugation of an entire species. These were not memories in the traditional sense, but intuitive leaps, insights that the alien consciousness, or perhaps the residual imprint of its knowledge, was providing. It was as if his mind, though damaged, was now operating on a different frequency, capable of perceiving the hidden currents of the SS's agenda.

This constant internal excavation was exhausting. It wore him down, both mentally and physically. He found himself losing track of time, the sterile lab environment becoming a timeless void. Sleep offered little respite, often bringing only more vivid and disturbing replays of his fractured memories. Yet, with each surge of disorientation, with each stab of phantom pain, there was a growing sense of clarity. The SS had tried to erase him, to obliterate his understanding, but they had, ironically, awakened a deeper, more resilient aspect of his consciousness. He was no longer just Professor Falk, the astrophysicist. He was a survivor, a witness, and now, a reluctant guardian of a truth that was too dangerous to be silenced. The echoes of the past, though haunting, were now his most powerful allies, fueling a quiet, desperate rebellion within the confines of his own ravaged mind. The game was not over; it had merely changed, and the SS, in their hubris, had unwittingly equipped him with the very tools of his resistance. He would not be broken. He would remember. He would understand. And, somehow, he would expose them.

But beyond the jagged shards of his personal trauma, a more subtle force was at play. It was a presence, or rather, the ghost of a presence, woven into the very fabric of his reconfigured consciousness. It was the persistent whisper of the alien. Not a voice, not in any audible sense, but a resonance, a gentle, insistent pressure that guided his fractured thoughts. It was like a lodestone, its subtle magnetism drawing him towards buried truths, nudging him away from the carefully constructed illusions his captors tried to maintain.

These were not commands, no overt directives that would alert Becker or her team. Instead, they were fleeting moments of pristine clarity, like brief shafts of sunlight piercing a perpetual storm.

A particular geometric pattern, glimpsed on a data display, would suddenly coalesce into a coherent message, revealing a hidden layer of meaning within the SS's technical jargon. A seemingly random sequence of numbers would flash in his mind, unlocking a forgotten access code, or revealing a critical vulnerability in the containment systems. It was as if the alien consciousness, a vast and ancient intelligence, was offering him breadcrumbs, leading him through the labyrinth of his own damaged mind and the SS's treacherous machinations.

He found himself questioning things he had previously accepted as fact. When Dr. Becker presented him with fabricated logs of his recovery, detailing a seamless reintegration of his cognitive functions, the alien whisper would stir within him. It was a subtle dissonance, a feeling of wrongness that gnawed at the edges of his fabricated reality. He would catch himself staring at the sterile walls, his mind momentarily replaying a fragment of the Black Forest crash, not the sanitized version they presented, but the raw, terrifying truth of the event. And in those moments, the alien consciousness would offer a gentle nudge, a silent prompt to recall the aberrant energy signatures that had preceded the crash, the ones the SS had so meticulously purged from all official records.

It was a constant, silent battle for his mind. The SS, with their brute-force methods, had attempted to rewrite his very being. But they had overlooked the fundamental interconnectedness of his experience, the indelible mark left by his encounter with something so profoundly other. The alien intelligence, trapped within the remnants of his neural pathways, was not merely a passive passenger. It was an active participant, a quiet ally in his clandestine struggle for self-possession.

The whispers were often cryptic, offering not answers, but questions. Why had the SS been so desperate to acquire the transmission data? What was the true purpose of Project Veil? These were not the idle musings of a recovering patient; they were probing inquiries, designed to stimulate his own dormant analytical abilities. The alien intelligence seemed to understand that true liberation lay not in being told the truth, but in rediscovering it for himself. It was a process of guided rediscovery, a subtle unfurling of his own suppressed knowledge.

He started to develop a system, a silent, internal shorthand for these alien nudges. A sudden chill that ran down his spine wasn't just a phantom sensation; it was a signal that a particular piece of information was vital, a key to understanding a larger context. A fleeting vision of iridescent, crystalline structures would appear behind his eyes, often accompanied by a sense of profound mathematical beauty. These visions, he slowly began to realize, were representations of alien concepts, truths that transcended human language. The alien was not speaking *to* him, but *through* him, translating complex ideas into a form his damaged mind could grasp.

One such instance occurred during a particularly grueling session of cognitive recalibration. Dr. Becker was attempting to reinforce the SS's narrative of his "accident," feeding him carefully curated information designed to erase the memory of the alien transmissions. As she droned on about atmospheric turbulence and pilot error, Falk felt a distinct pressure in his temples, a gentle but insistent pulse. It was followed by a fleeting, internal image: a vast, cosmic tapestry woven with threads of pure light, and at its center, a single, pulsating node of energy – the source of the transmissions. The SS's explanation, once a plausible disguise, now seemed laughably crude, an insult to the complexity of what he had witnessed. The alien presence offered a silent counterpoint, a truth that resonated with an undeniable authority.

This internal dialogue, though nascent and often baffling, was providing him with a crucial anchor. In the sea of manufactured realities, the alien whispers were the only constant, the only reliable compass. They guided him through the treacherous currents of his own fragmented memories, helping him to distinguish between the genuine echoes of his past and the deliberate distortions of his captors. He was beginning to see the SS's manipulations not as insurmountable obstacles, but as puzzles, each piece of misinformation a clue to a deeper, more dangerous truth.

The SS believed they had broken him, that they had reduced him to a pliable instrument, a puppet whose strings they could control. But they had underestimated the resilience of the human spirit, and they had failed to account for the unexpected ally that had imprinted itself upon his very soul. The alien consciousness, a silent observer and now a subtle guide, was not merely influencing his thoughts; it was reawakening his own dormant capacity for critical thinking, for genuine understanding. It was a persistent whisper of truth in a world of lies, and it was slowly, inexorably, guiding Doctor Falk towards the light. The fragments of his past were not just broken pieces; they were the building blocks of his liberation, and the alien whisper was the silent architect of his dawning rebellion. This internal guidance, this psychic compass, was more than just a survival mechanism; it was the genesis of his quest for vengeance, a quiet promise that the truth, no matter how deeply buried, would eventually come to light. The subtle pressure in his mind, the fleeting images, the resonant truths – these were the seeds of his awakening, the first tremors of a revolution brewing within the confines of his own shattered psyche.

He was no longer merely a subject of experimentation; he was becoming an agent of his own recovery, a clandestine operative guided by an intelligence beyond human comprehension. The SS had sought to control his mind, but in doing so, they had inadvertently unleashed a force that would ultimately prove their undoing. The alien's persistent whisper was not a sign of his subjugation, but the first, faint melody of his freedom. It was a subtle but potent reminder that even in the deepest darkness, a glimmer of guidance, a whisper of hope, could always be found. This silent communion, this subtle nudging towards the precipice of truth, was the most profound and terrifying aspect of his transformation.

It was the dawning realization that he was no longer entirely alone, that a vast, alien intelligence was now a part of his very consciousness, a silent partner in his unspoken war against those who sought to exploit cosmic knowledge for terrestrial power. This was the dawn of a new understanding, a terrifying and exhilarating realization that the universe was far stranger, and far more interconnected, than he had ever dared to imagine. The alien whisper was not a betrayal of his humanity, but an expansion of it, a testament to the boundless potential of consciousness itself.

The sterile walls of the laboratory had become Falk's world, a meticulously controlled environment designed to house and study the wreckage of his mind. Dr. Becker and her team operated with a chilling efficiency, their clinical detachment a stark contrast to the tempest raging within him. They believed they had him. The "partial recalibration," as they so delicately put it, had, in their eyes, rendered him compliant, a subject sufficiently subdued to be managed. His fragmented memories, the violent echoes of the Black Forest crash, the unsettling visions of the alien entities, the searing guilt of the SS experiments, and the burgeoning dread of Project Veil – these were, to them, mere residual anomalies, the sputtering embers of a fire they had successfully extinguished.

They saw a patient, not a prisoner, and their perceived victory bred a fatal complacency. This overconfidence, this profound miscalculation of his internal state, was the crack in their impenetrable disguise. They saw a man tethered to the present, his past a jumbled collection of painful but ultimately manageable fragments. They failed to perceive the subtle, insistent guidance of the alien consciousness that now permeated his reconfigured neural pathways. It wasn't a direct communication, no overt commands that would trigger alarms. Instead, it manifested as a series of almost imperceptible nudges, fleeting moments of pristine clarity that pierced the manufactured fog of his enforced amnesia. These were not just passive observations; they were active directives, whispered secrets woven into the very fabric of his being, urging him towards a singular, paramount goal: escape.

The alien consciousness, a vast intelligence that had brushed against his own in the Black Forest, had not been entirely eradicated. The SS's brutal attempts to scrub its influence from his mind had, in a perverse twist of fate, only served to imprint it more deeply, embedding its essence within the very architecture they had so aggressively manipulated. It was like a parasitic symbiont, not draining, but enhancing, providing Falk with a perspective, an understanding, that transcended his human limitations. This symbiosis, this silent partnership, was the key. It was the source of the coherent insights that began to surface amidst the chaos of his fragmented memories.

He started to see the patterns, the subtle tells of their operation. The precise timings of guard patrols, the blind spots in the surveillance systems, the predictable routines of the SS personnel. These were not deductions made through conventional observation. They were insights gifted to him, flashes of preternatural awareness that would appear without conscious effort. A particular ventilation shaft, when examined through the lens of a fleeting, geometric mental projection, revealed itself to be a viable, albeit hazardous, escape route. The access codes they used for the data terminals, once indecipherable sequences, would suddenly resolve into recognizable patterns, unlocked by a resonant alien frequency. It was as if the alien intelligence was replaying a mental simulation of the facility, highlighting every weakness, every vulnerability, for him to exploit.

The process of planning was an exercise in extreme mental discipline. He had to compartmentalize, to push the raw, emotional fragments of his past to the periphery, focusing solely on the practicalities of his escape. The SS had trained him to be meticulous in his research, in his analysis. Now, he was applying those same honed skills, not to decipher cosmic anomalies, but to dismantle the prison they had built around him. Each fragment of memory, no matter how painful, became a piece of the puzzle. The chilling images of the SS's experiments, for instance, revealed the precise locations of secure storage units, the types of equipment used in their clandestine operations, and the security protocols that governed them. The knowledge, though born of horror, was now a tool.

He began to test the waters, subtly at first. During his physiotherapy sessions, designed to rehabilitate his supposedly damaged motor functions, he would deliberately execute certain movements with a fractionally increased speed and precision. The SS technicians, accustomed to his perceived frailty, would note these improvements with mild surprise, attributing them to the effectiveness of their training. They did not suspect the underlying motive, the calculated assertion of regained control. Each small victory, each successful deviation from their expectations, bolstered his resolve. The alien presence would often provide a silent affirmation, a resonant hum of approval that echoed the growing confidence in his own abilities.

The most critical aspect of his plan involved acquiring the necessary tools. The SS maintained a secure armory, heavily guarded and monitored. A direct approach was unthinkable. However, the alien consciousness had revealed something else, a hidden network of conduits and sub-levels, known only to the facility's original, pre-SS designers. This network, a relic of a forgotten era of the facility's construction, was largely undocumented in the SS's current records. It was a ghost in the machine, a forgotten artery that could potentially lead him to his objective.

One evening, during a routine "cognitive assessment," Falk was presented with a series of holographic projections, meant to test his ability to distinguish between real and fabricated stimuli. Among the myriad of images, a faint, almost imperceptible anomaly appeared – a shimmering, iridescent symbol that pulsed with a subtle, internal light. It was not part of the test. It was a message. Following the internal prompt, Falk focused his attention on the symbol. It expanded, transforming into a three-dimensional blueprint, detailing the schematics of the armory's internal layout, including the precise location of the override panel for the security grid.

The challenge then became reaching the armory undetected.

The facility was a labyrinth of interconnected corridors, each monitored by an array of sensors and cameras. The SS, in their arrogance, believed their control was absolute. They had overlooked the residual echoes of the facility's past, the forgotten systems that still pulsed with a latent energy. The alien consciousness, attuned to these subtler frequencies, guided Falk through a series of service tunnels and ventilation shafts, pathways that were invisible to the SS's electronic surveillance. These routes were often cramped, dusty, and fraught with unknown hazards, but they offered the precious commodity of anonymity.

The journey was a testament to his endurance, both physical and mental. The fragmented memories would surge at the most inopportune moments, threatening to overwhelm him. A sudden draft of air, carrying a faint scent of ozone from the lab equipment, would trigger a visceral flash of the Black Forest crash, the image of the mangled aircraft filling his mind's eye. He would have to fight for control, to reassert the dominance of his present objective, the alien whispers acting as a steadying anchor, pulling him back from the precipice of disorientation.

He reached the armory antechamber, a sterile vestibule designed to interface with the main vault. The override panel was exactly where the holographic schematic had indicated. The SS had implemented multi-factor authentication, a complex sequence of biometric scans and encrypted codes. But the alien presence had anticipated this. It provided him with a series of precisely timed pressure points on the panel, each corresponding to a specific input. It wasn't a direct override; it was a more subtle form of manipulation, exploiting a known vulnerability in the system's programming, a weakness that had been overlooked in the SS's haste to establish their control.

The panel clicked open, revealing a complex array of wiring. The alien consciousness pulsed with a stronger intensity now, guiding his hands with an almost imperceptible tremor. He needed a specific tool, a diagnostic probe, capable of bypassing the remaining security layers. This, too, was accounted for. The holographic blueprint had highlighted a secondary access point, a maintenance hatch concealed behind a holographic projection of a sterile wall. It led to a small compartment containing a limited selection of specialized equipment, left behind by the facility's original creators and forgotten by their SS successors.

With trembling fingers, Falk retrieved the probe. The metallic coolness of the tool against his skin was grounding, a tangible manifestation of his progress. He could feel the weight of his fractured memories pressing down on him, the ghosts of the SS's experiments a constant, chilling presence. But now, intertwined with that dread was a nascent surge of hope, a fierce determination to reclaim his past, and his future.

He returned to the main corridor, the armory vault now accessible. The doors hissed open, revealing rows of meticulously organized weaponry. His objective was not overt force, but the precise tools that would facilitate his escape. He bypassed the assault rifles and energy weapons, his gaze drawn to a specialized cutting tool, designed for breaching reinforced materials, and a compact, high-frequency sonic emitter, capable of disrupting localized sensor arrays. He also located a discarded SS uniform, a necessary disguise to navigate the outer sectors of the facility.

The journey back was fraught with a new kind of tension. He was no longer merely a passive subject; he was an active agent of his own liberation, carrying the tangible tools of his defiance. The alien presence seemed to guide him through the corridors with an uncanny prescience, alerting him to approaching patrols, allowing him to melt into the shadows or duck into unused alcoves just moments before their arrival. It was a dance on the razor's edge of discovery, a testament to the unexpected alliance forged within his shattered mind.

The final obstacle was the facility's perimeter. The SS had established multiple layers of defense, culminating in a heavily fortified exit point. The cutting tool would be essential for breaching the outer blast doors, but the sonic emitter would be crucial for disabling the motion sensors and laser grids that protected the immediate exterior. He moved with a newfound purpose, the fragmented memories of the Black Forest crash no longer solely a source of pain, but a stark reminder of the catastrophic consequences of failure. He had seen firsthand the devastation that unchecked power could unleash, and he would not allow himself to become an instrument of that destruction.

As he approached the exit, he could feel the SS's heightened security protocols. The subtle hum of active energy fields, the faint shimmer of cloaked sentries – these were signals that his presence had, in some infinitesimal way, registered. The alien consciousness surged, a wave of pure, unadulterated information washing over him. It was a detailed map of the external sensor grid, highlighting the precise timing of their cyclical deactivations, a momentary window of opportunity.

He reached the main blast doors. The cutting tool whined to life, its high-pitched shriek a jarring intrusion into the otherwise hushed facility. Sparks flew as it bit into the reinforced metal, a testament to the SS's formidable engineering. He worked with a feverish intensity, the stolen uniform providing a thin veneer of normalcy should he be detected prematurely. The sounds of his work echoed in the enclosed space, each clink and scrape a potential betrayal.

Just as he felt the resistance of the doors begin to yield, a voice crackled over an internal comms system, sharp and accusatory. "Sector Gamma, unauthorized activity detected at Blast Door Four. All units converge."

Becker. Her voice, devoid of any warmth, was a chilling confirmation that his carefully constructed anonymity had finally been breached. Panic threatened to seize him, the fragmented memories of being cornered, of facing overwhelming odds, flooding his senses. But the alien presence was a steadying force, a calm amidst the rising storm. It provided a clear, concise directive: activate the sonic emitter.

He slammed his hand onto the emitter, its complex array of emitters glowing with an internal energy. A high-frequency wave, inaudible to the human ear but devastatingly effective against electronic systems, washed over the immediate vicinity. The lights flickered, the hum of the sensors died, and for a precious few seconds, the world went silent.

He pushed through the now-breached blast doors, the cutting tool still clutched in his hand. The night air, crisp and cool against his face, was a stark contrast to the recycled atmosphere of the facility. He was outside. He was free. But the pursuit was far from over. The SS would not relinquish their prize so easily. He looked back at the imposing structure, a monument to their hubris and his own shattered existence. The fragments of his past, once the instruments of his torment, had become the very foundation of his escape. And with the silent, unwavering guidance of the alien consciousness, he knew this was only the beginning. The true fight, the fight to reclaim his identity and expose the SS's dark secrets, had just begun. He carried not just the tools of his escape, but the heavy, invaluable burden of his recovered memories, a testament to his resilience and the universe's profound capacity for the unexpected. The night was vast, the path ahead uncertain, but for the first time in what felt like an eternity, Falk felt the potent, exhilarating promise of self-determination. He was no longer a specimen. He was a survivor.

Chapter 9

The Village of Oblivion

The chill of the late autumn air was a stark contrast to the sterile, recycled atmosphere of the SS facility he'd left behind. Falk, clad in the ill-fitting, scratchy fabric of a stolen SS uniform, was a phantom drifting through the shadows of a Germany he no longer recognized. Every flickering gas lamp, every distant rumble of a truck, sent a jolt of adrenaline through him. He was a fugitive, a ghost in his own country, and the weight of that realization pressed down on him with a suffocating intensity. The fragmented memories, once a disorienting haze, now served as a crude, unreliable map, guiding him through a labyrinth of fear and suspicion.

He moved with a calculated stealth, each step measured, each breath controlled. The occupied territories were a checkerboard of SS checkpoints, vigilant patrols, and a pervasive network of informants. To be caught would mean a swift, brutal end, or worse, a return to the sterile walls of the laboratory, his nascent freedom extinguished before it had truly begun. His only allies were his own shattered mind, now a bizarre nexus of human experience and alien perception, and the persistent, subtle whispers of the intelligence that had intertwined itself with his consciousness. It was an unspoken pact, a silent symbiosis that offered glimpses of clarity amidst the swirling chaos of his past.

The alien consciousness didn't offer explicit directions, no clear pronouncements of where to go or what to do. Instead, it provided an almost instinctive understanding of his surroundings. A prickling sensation at the back of his neck would warn him of an approaching patrol long before the sound of boots on cobblestone reached his ears. A sudden, inexplicable aversion to a particular alleyway might steer him away from a hidden SS surveillance post. These were not conscious deductions; they were intuitive leaps, guided by an awareness that transcended his own limited human senses. It was like having an internal compass, calibrated not to magnetic north, but to the subtle currents of danger and opportunity.

His immediate goal was to find evidence, tangible proof that would corroborate the terrifying, fractured visions that haunted his waking hours. The Black Forest crash, the chilling efficiency of the SS experiments, the disturbing glimpses of alien entities – these were more than just memories; they were fragments of a truth so profound it threatened to unravel his very sanity. He remembered snippets of conversations, glimpses of data streams, the sterile gleam of unfamiliar technology. He needed to connect these disparate pieces, to assemble them into a coherent narrative that would not only exonerate him but expose the clandestine machinations of the SS.

The journey was a constant exercise in improvisation. He had no resources, no allies, only the clothes on his back and the knowledge imprinted upon his mind. He learned to scavenge for food, to sleep in abandoned barns and disused railway sidings, to blend into the background, a human chameleon in a world that was increasingly hostile. He observed the routines of the occupied populace, mimicking their deference, their downcast gazes, their carefully cultivated anonymity. He became adept at feigning ignorance, at becoming a nobody, a shadow in the periphery of the SS's all-seeing gaze.

One evening, seeking shelter in the ruins of a bombed-out church, he found himself drawn to a discarded piece of paper, tucked beneath a fallen beam. It was a faded map, a remnant of pre-war Germany, detailing routes and villages that were now under SS control. As his fingers brushed against the brittle parchment, a flicker of recognition, alien and sharp, shot through him. The alien consciousness responded with a faint, resonant hum, a subtle emphasis on a particular region, a small, nondescript village marked only by a tiny, almost erased X: **OBLIVION**.

The name itself resonated with a disquieting familiarity, an echo of a forgotten purpose. Why this specific location? What lay hidden in this obscure corner of the Reich? The map offered no answers, only a destination, a beacon in the fog of his fragmented past. The journey would be perilous, taking him deeper into occupied territory, closer to the heart of SS control. Yet, the alien nudge, the inexplicable pull towards this forgotten village, was undeniable. It felt like the next crucial step in his desperate quest for truth.

He began to walk, following the faded lines of the map, the stolen uniform a constant source of anxiety. He travelled by night, using the cover of darkness to avoid patrols, his senses heightened by the ever-present threat of discovery. The fragmented memories would sometimes surge, overwhelming him with flashes of pain and terror. He saw the faces of the SS scientists, their detached expressions as they probed his mind, the sterile gleam of their instruments. He felt the phantom sting of needles, the disorienting hum of neural recalibration. These memories were like phantom limbs, aching with a pain that was both real and imagined.

During the day, he would find secluded places to rest, to process the influx of information, both human and alien. He studied the map, tracing the routes with his finger, the alien consciousness providing an almost eidetic recall of the terrain, highlighting potential hazards and safe havens. He learned to read the subtle signs of SS presence – the distant whine of aircraft engines, the distinctive camouflage patterns of their vehicles, the hushed, fearful whispers of the locals.

He encountered small pockets of resistance, furtive movements of individuals who, like him, sought to evade the SS's suffocating grip. But his mission was solitary, his purpose too unique, too dangerous to share. He couldn't afford to trust anyone, not yet. The SS had a knack for turning even the most well-intentioned actions to their advantage. He was alone, a one-man insurgency against a totalitarian regime, armed with nothing but his fractured intellect and the enigmatic guidance of an alien entity.

As he approached the region marked on the map, the landscape began to change. The rolling hills gave way to denser forests, the air growing colder, more biting. The villages he passed through were hushed, their inhabitants withdrawn, their eyes carrying the weary resignation of those living under constant oppression. The SS presence was palpable, their patrols more frequent, their scrutiny more intense. He felt the eyes of informants on him, the subtle shifts in the demeanor of those he passed, signs that his borrowed uniform, however effective it had been, was not an impenetrable shield.

He reached a small, unnamed crossroads, the map now almost indecipherable in the fading light. The X marking **OBLIVION** was still visible, pointing towards a barely discernible track leading into the dense woods. A knot of apprehension tightened in his stomach. This was it. The end of one journey, and potentially, the beginning of something far more dangerous. He took a deep breath, the alien presence within him offering a quiet, almost imperceptible reassurance. He stepped off the main road, plunging into the encroaching darkness, the unknown beckoning him forward. The village of Oblivion awaited.

The track was overgrown, barely a path, leading Falk deeper into a forest that felt ancient and watchful. Twisted branches clawed at the stolen uniform, and the damp earth cushioned his footsteps, a small mercy in his otherwise precarious journey. The alien consciousness pulsed, a subtle vibration in his mind, guiding him through the dense undergrowth. It was like navigating a maze with an unseen hand gently nudging him in the correct direction, avoiding dead ends and treacherous pitfalls. He couldn't articulate the mechanism of this guidance, only trust its unfailing accuracy.

He stumbled upon a small, moss-covered cairn, barely visible amidst the gnarled roots of an oak. As his hand brushed against the rough, cold stones, a fragment of memory, sharp and vivid, pierced the fog. He saw himself, younger, standing in this very spot, a child with a dirt-smudged face, placing a simple wildflower atop the stones. It was a relic of a life he'd almost forgotten, a life before the SS, before the crash, before the whispers of alien intelligence. The memory was bittersweet, a poignant reminder of what had been lost, and what he was fighting to reclaim.

He pressed on, the forest growing darker and more claustrophobic. The air thrummed with an unnerving stillness, the usual sounds of the forest – the rustling of leaves, the calls of birds – conspicuously absent. It was as if the very woods held their breath, anticipating his arrival. The SS, he knew, would not venture this deep without cause. This was likely a place they had deliberately overlooked, a forgotten corner of their meticulously controlled

Reich.

He finally emerged from the tree line into a small clearing. Before him lay the village of **OBLIVION**. It was not a place of grand structures or bustling streets, but a collection of weathered wooden huts, huddled together as if for protection against the encroaching wilderness. Smoke curled from a few chimneys, a sign of life, but the overall impression was one of profound desolation. The silence here was heavier, more oppressive than in the forest, a palpable emptiness that seemed to absorb all sound.

As Falk cautiously approached the edge of the clearing, a figure emerged from the shadows of one of the huts. It was an old woman, her face a roadmap of wrinkles, her eyes surprisingly sharp and observant. She wore simple, homespun clothes, and carried a worn wooden staff. She didn't cry out, didn't flee. Instead, she watched him, her gaze unnervingly steady.

"You are not from here," she stated, her voice a raspy whisper, yet carrying an unexpected authority. It wasn't a question.

Falk hesitated, his mind racing. The stolen uniform, a symbol of his evasion, now felt like a beacon. He considered ditching it, but where would he go? What would he wear? He decided on a partial truth. "I am lost," he said, his voice rough from disuse. "I seek… refuge."

The old woman studied him for a long moment, her gaze seeming to pierce through the SS uniform, through the layers of his disguise, and into the fractured core of his being. A faint, almost imperceptible nod. "This place is not for the lost, stranger. This place is for the forgotten."

He felt a strange resonance with her words. The forgotten. He was indeed a forgotten man, his past erased, his identity confiscated. "I have been… forgotten," he admitted, the words tasting of dust and despair.

She gestured with her staff towards the center of the village. "The Elder knows of newcomers. If he deems you worthy, you may rest. But know this, stranger, Oblivion demands a price."

The alien consciousness stirred within him, a subtle emphasis on the word "price." It wasn't fear he felt, but a strange sense of inevitability. He had expected this. Nothing was ever truly free, especially not escape. He followed the old woman, her silent presence a stark contrast to the ever-vigilant SS guards he had grown accustomed to. The village was sparsely populated, the few inhabitants he saw moving with a slow, deliberate gait, their faces etched with a weary acceptance of their isolation.

They reached the largest hut, a structure that seemed marginally sturdier than the others. A faint light emanated from within. The old woman pushed open the heavy wooden door, revealing a dimly lit interior. A figure sat by a meager fire, hunched over a small table. He was an old man, his white hair thinning, his eyes closed, his hands resting on a pile of aged, unbound documents. This, Falk assumed, was the Elder.

"Elder Deiter," the old woman announced, her voice softer now, tinged with respect. "A traveler. He claims to be lost."

The Elder's eyes slowly opened. They were a startlingly clear blue, ancient and filled with a profound, unsettling wisdom. He looked at Falk, not with suspicion or fear, but with a deep, penetrating curiosity. "Lost is a state of mind, stranger," the Elder said, his voice surprisingly strong, though laced with a weariness that spoke of years of solitude. "Some are lost to the world; others are lost to themselves. Which are you?"   Falk met his gaze, the alien presence within him sensing no threat from this man. "I am... both," he answered truthfully.

The Elder nodded, a slow, deliberate movement. "The SS claims much. They take memories, identities, and futures. They believe they can erase all that came before. But some things, even they cannot truly obliterate." He gestured at the documents on the table. "These are the fragments they missed. The echoes of what was. The whispers of what is." Falk's breath hitched. He approached the table, his gaze falling upon the papers. They were not official SS documents, nor were they personal letters. They were scientific notes, diagrams, complex equations, written in a language he vaguely recognized from his fragmented recollections – a language that hinted at origins far beyond human comprehension.

"What are these?" Falk asked, his voice barely a whisper.

"These are the remnants of the first ones," the Elder explained, his eyes fixed on Falk's face. "The ones who understood the true nature of the universe, long before your SS came to power. They were... different. They saw the patterns, the connections that bind all things. And they left their mark, in places like this. In minds like yours."

Falk's gaze darted to the old woman, then back to the Elder. "You... you know?"

"We know what we can," the Elder replied. "We are the keepers of forgotten things. And you, stranger, are a vessel for a particularly potent forgotten thing." He gestured towards Falk's head, a knowing glint in his ancient eyes.

The alien consciousness surged, a wave of understanding washing over Falk. These people, this village, were not merely hiding; they were guardians. They protected the remnants of the knowledge that the SS sought to destroy, the very knowledge that had intertwined with his own shattered consciousness.

"The SS... they are trying to erase something," Falk said, piecing together the fragments. "Something... alien."

The Elder chuckled, a dry, rustling sound. "They seek to control what they cannot comprehend. They fear the unknown, so they attempt to extinguish it. But you, Falk,"—the Elder spoke his name, a fact he had not revealed— "you are proof that they cannot succeed."

A chill ran down Falk's spine. How did the Elder know his name? He looked at the old woman, who offered a small, enigmatic smile. The pieces were beginning to fall into place, not through his own deductive reasoning, but through the subtle, often cryptic guidance of the alien intelligence and the quiet wisdom of these forgotten guardians.

"My memories... they are not entirely gone?" Falk asked, the question a desperate plea.

"They are fragmented, like shards of a broken mirror," the Elder explained. "But the reflection, however fractured, still shows a truth. And the whispers you hear, they are not the echoes of your madness. They are the echoes of a far greater truth."

He picked up a thick, leather-bound journal from the table. Its pages were filled with intricate drawings of celestial bodies, complex geometric patterns, and symbols that pulsed with an inner light when Falk's gaze lingered upon them. "This," the Elder said, pushing the journal towards Falk, "was left behind by those who came before. It speaks of the forces that shape our reality, forces the SS desperately tries to keep hidden. It may hold the answers you seek. It may hold the key to understanding what has happened to you, and what you must do."

Falk reached out, his hand trembling slightly, and took the journal. The moment his fingers touched the worn leather, a surge of energy, alien and potent, coursed through him. It was a jolt of pure recognition, a feeling of coming home. The symbols on the pages seemed to rearrange themselves in his mind, forming coherent patterns, unlocking dormant pathways of comprehension.

"They are searching for something," Falk murmured, his eyes scanning the cryptic text. "Something they call Project Veil."

The Elder's expression darkened. "Project Veil. A desperate attempt to harness the very forces they fear. They believe they can control it, weaponize it. But such power cannot be contained. It is a force of nature, not a tool of war."

"I need to find out what it is," Falk said, his voice firm with newfound resolve. "I need to stop them."

The old woman stepped forward, placing a hand on his arm. "This path is dangerous, Falk. The SS hunts those who remember. And those who carry the whispers of the beyond are hunted most relentlessly."

"I am already being hunted," Falk replied, the memory of his escape from the SS facility a stark reminder. "And my memories, though fractured, are guiding me. This knowledge... it feels like my purpose."

The Elder nodded slowly. "Purpose is a heavy burden, but a

necessary one. You carry within you not only the fragments of your own past, but the potential for a future the SS desperately seeks to deny. This village may offer you shelter, Falk. A place to piece together the shattered fragments of your mind, and to understand the truth you seek. But know this: Oblivion is not just a name. It is a state of being. And escaping it will require more than just running. It will require remembering."

As Falk settled into a quiet corner of the Elder's hut, the heavy journal resting on his lap, he felt a sense of belonging he hadn't experienced in years. These were not just strangers; they were fellow custodians of a hidden truth, a quiet resistance against the encroaching darkness of the SS. The path ahead was still shrouded in uncertainty, the SS a relentless and formidable enemy. But here, in the heart of Oblivion, amidst the forgotten and the keepers of memory, Falk felt a flicker of something more than just survival. He felt the nascent stirrings of hope, and the dawning realization that his fractured mind, once his prison, might also be his greatest weapon. The alien whispers, once a source of confusion, now seemed to harmonize with the ancient knowledge held within the journal, guiding him towards a truth that could shatter the SS's carefully constructed reality.

The village, nestled in a valley that seemed to have been forgotten by time itself, presented an unnerving tableau of rural simplicity. Smoke curled lazily from chimneys, children's distant laughter, muted by the oppressive silence of the surrounding wilderness, occasionally drifted on the crisp air. From a distance, it was the picture of pastoral peace, a stark contradiction to the gnawing unease that had settled in Falk's gut since he'd arrived. The Elder's words echoed in his mind, a chilling premonition: *Oblivion demands a price.* He'd felt the resonance of that statement, an alien hum confirming its truth, and now, standing on the edge of this seemingly idyllic settlement, he understood why. This was not merely a village; it was a carefully curated stage.

His initial interactions with the villagers had been laced with an almost unnatural placidity. They greeted him with polite, uncurious nods, their eyes holding a distant, vacant quality that belied the supposed warmth of their smiles. There was an unspoken agreement, a silent pact of avoidance, that seemed to govern their interactions. They acknowledged his presence but offered no invitation, no inquiry, no spark of genuine human connection. It was as if they were performing their roles, enacting a preordained script designed to maintain the illusion of normalcy. Falk, with his fractured mind and the alien presence whispering within, could sense the artifice, the carefully constructed facade that masked something far more sinister. The SS, he knew, had a penchant for efficiency, for minimizing the collateral damage of their experiments by isolating and manipulating their test subjects.

He spent the first few days observing; a silent predator in a landscape of unsuspecting prey. He learned the rhythms of the village: the early rising of the farmers, the rhythmic clang of the blacksmith's hammer, the quiet gatherings in the small, whitewashed church. But beneath the veneer of routine, he detected subtle anomalies. The livestock, though plentiful, seemed unusually docile, their movements almost synchronized. The children, their laughter, a fleeting sound, played games that seemed to lack the spontaneous joy and boisterousness he remembered from his own childhood. Their routines were too perfect, their behavior too predictable, like automatons programmed for a single, unchanging purpose.

The Elder, Deiter, remained a figure of cryptic pronouncements and knowing silences. He provided Falk with a small, sparsely furnished hut on the outskirts of the village, a place that offered solitude but no true escape from the pervading sense of observation. The journal, its pages filled with the alien script and intricate diagrams, lay open on a rough-hewn table. Falk immersed himself in its contents, the alien consciousness within him acting as a conduit, translating the incomprehensible symbols into flashes of understanding. He saw diagrams of energy conduits, schematics for devices that defied conventional physics, and recurring symbols that hinted at a cosmic order far grander and more terrifying than anything humanity had conceived.

One particular section of the journal, accompanied by a series of chillingly detailed sketches, described what the alien race referred to as "Resonance Amplification." It spoke of manipulating ambient energy fields, not through brute force, but through subtle harmonic frequencies, to induce specific behavioral patterns, and ultimately, to control thought and action. The SS, the journal implied, had stumbled upon fragments of this ancient knowledge, twisting it for their own insidious purposes, their "Project Veil" being a crude, terrifying manifestation of this alien science. The sketches depicted humans with vacant eyes, their movements puppet-like, controlled by invisible strings. Falk felt a cold dread seep into his bones. Was this village... a laboratory?

His suspicions solidified when he noticed the unusual stillness of the air, particularly in the hours before dawn. It wasn't the silence of peace, but the pregnant hush of a system powering up. He began to actively test his surroundings, using the fragmented knowledge gleaned from the journal. He found he could subtly influence the ambient energy around him, creating small, localized fields that disrupted the villagers' placid demeanor. A momentary flicker of confusion in their eyes, a hesitant pause in their movements – these were fleeting but undeniable signs that his presence, or rather, the alien influence within him, could provoke a reaction.

He decided to venture further, to confirm his suspicions about the village's true purpose. Under the cloak of a moonless night, he crept out of his hut, the journal clutched tightly in his hand. He moved through the sleeping village, his senses heightened by the alien awareness. He noted the absence of nocturnal animals, the unnatural quiet that blanketed the land. Even the wind seemed to hush its breath as he passed.

He followed a barely perceptible track leading away from the main cluster of huts, a path that the villagers seemed to studiously avoid. The alien consciousness within him pulsed, a gentle but insistent pull, guiding him towards a specific point. The track led him to a small, dilapidated barn, its timbers weathered and scarred, appearing no different from any other structure in the isolated village. Yet, as Falk approached, the subtle hum of energy grew stronger, a low thrum that vibrated in his very bones.

He found the entrance to the barn slightly ajar. Peering inside, he saw that the interior was far more than it appeared. The rough wooden walls were lined with what looked like advanced control panels, their surfaces covered in a myriad of blinking lights and cryptic symbols that mirrored those in the journal. Cables snaked across the floor, converging on a central platform where a strange, metallic apparatus stood, pulsating with a faint, ethereal glow. It was unlike any technology he had ever encountered, a testament to the alien knowledge that had fallen into SS hands.

This was the heart of Project Veil.

He stepped inside, the barn door swinging shut behind him with a soft click. The air was thick with a peculiar scent; a metallic tang mixed with something acrid and disorienting. He approached the central apparatus, his hand hovering over its smooth, cool surface. The journal lay open beside him, its pages revealing schematics of the device, detailing its function: a psycho-resonant emitter designed to influence and control neurological pathways on a mass scale. The villagers, he realized with a sickening certainty, were not just living in a test site; they *were* the test subjects. Their placidity, their predictable routines, were the result of constant, low-level exposure to the emitter, their free will slowly eroded, their minds subtly reshaped to serve a sinister purpose.

The SS's goal, as far as he could decipher from the journal's dense technical prose, was to perfect this technology, to create a population utterly subservient, capable of carrying out any command without question, without hesitation. They were conditioning an entire village, honing their weapon of mind control, preparing to unleash it upon a wider populace. The implications were staggering, a chilling vision of a future where individuality and dissent were systematically eradicated.

As he studied the console, his fingers tracing the alien symbols, a wave of information flooded his mind, courtesy of the alien consciousness. It wasn't a conscious download, but a sudden, intuitive understanding of the emitter's operational parameters. He saw the underlying frequencies, the delicate balance of energy required to maintain the controlled state. And he saw, with a jolt of terrifying clarity, that he himself had been exposed to similar, albeit cruder, forms of this technology during his time at the SS facility. The fragmented memories, the alien whispers – they were not just residual effects of his own experiments, but a testament to the SS's desperate attempts to replicate and weaponize the very alien influence that had now become an intrinsic part of him.

He looked at the data logs displayed on a small screen. They chronicled weeks of operations, detailing shifts in emotional states, observed behavioral modifications, and energy output fluctuations. The names of the villagers were listed, each entry a stark reminder of their stolen autonomy. He saw the name of the old woman who had first greeted him, her designated sequence number beside it, followed by a notation: "Initial Subject – High Compliance." The Elder, Deiter, was listed as "Control Unit – Primary Observer." It was a chilling confirmation of his worst fears.

The alien consciousness within him responded to the energy patterns of the emitter, not with fear, but with a strange sense of familiarity, almost recognition. It was as if it understood the fundamental principles at play, the cosmic dance of energy and consciousness that the SS was so crudely attempting to manipulate. The journal spoke of the potential for such emitters to be used for benevolent purposes, to heal, to enhance understanding, but in the hands of the SS, it had been perverted into a tool of subjugation.

He knew he couldn't simply destroy the emitter. The SS would have redundancies, fail-safes. He needed to understand it, to find a way to subvert its purpose, to turn their own weapon against them. The journal offered a clue. It detailed a method of "harmonic overload," a way to disrupt the emitter's carefully calibrated frequencies by introducing a chaotic, but complementary, resonant pattern. It was a dangerous gambit, one that could potentially destabilize the entire system, but it was his only hope.

He began to work, his stolen SS uniform feeling like a mockery of his true purpose. His fingers, guided by the alien intelligence, moved with newfound precision across the alien console. He accessed the primary control interface, a complex array of glowing glyphs that rearranged themselves according to his mental commands. The process was agonizingly slow, each input a leap of faith, each adjustment a potential trigger for alarm.

The alien consciousness acted as his co-pilot, not dictating his actions, but subtly guiding his intuition, highlighting pathways of least resistance, warning him of imminent system responses. He felt a connection to the emitter, not as a victim, but as a technician, albeit one operating with knowledge from beyond human understanding. He was essentially reprogramming the device using its own alien language, a language that only he, and the entity within him, could truly comprehend.

He managed to isolate the primary amplification channel, the conduit through which the control signals were broadcast. The data logs showed that a significant increase in energy output was scheduled for the following dawn, a further increment in the villagers' conditioning. He had to act before then.

He found the section in the journal detailing the harmonic overload. It involved a specific sequence of energy pulses, tuned to a particular alien frequency that would, in effect, create a feedback loop, overwhelming the emitter's control matrix. The challenge lay in generating this frequency, as the emitter itself was the only known source of its amplification.

Then, a realization struck him. The alien consciousness within him *was* that frequency. It was a living embodiment of the very energy he needed. It was a terrifying thought – to intentionally unleash the full power of the alien entity – but the alternative was the complete subjugation of this village, and potentially, a much wider population. He focused his will, drawing upon the alien presence within him. It was a struggle, a mental wrestling match against an unknown force that had become inextricably linked to his own being. He felt the pressure build, a humming in his skull, a sensation of expanding awareness. The alien consciousness seemed to respond, not with resistance, but with a nascent understanding of his intent. It was a partnership, born of necessity, forged in the crucible of shared experience.

He began to input the sequence, the alien glyphs on the console glowing brighter as he channeled the amplified energy from within. The barn began to vibrate, a deep, resonant hum filling the air. The lights on the control panels flickered wildly, as if struggling to cope with the influx of alien energy. He could feel the emitter fighting back, attempting to reassert its control, but his own amplified consciousness was a force it had never anticipated.

Outside the barn, he could sense the subtle shift in the village. The placid villagers stirred, a flicker of confusion crossing their faces. The children's laughter, which had been so muted, now carried a note of unease, of something awakening. He had begun to disrupt the Veil.

The struggle intensified. Falk felt a burning sensation in his head, as if his very skull were expanding. The alien presence was a roaring inferno, its power immense, its nature untamed. He could feel the SS technicians, wherever they were monitoring this operation, reacting with alarm. Alarms, he imagined, were blaring in some distant, sterile facility, their carefully controlled experiment spiraling out of their grasp.

He pushed harder, channeling every ounce of his will, every fragment of alien energy that had become a part of him. The barn walls seemed to shimmer, the air crackling with an invisible force. The metallic apparatus in the center began to emit a high-pitched whine, the light intensifying to an unbearable brilliance.

Then, with a final, blinding flash and a deafening crackle, it was over. The hum died down, the lights on the console sputtered and went dark. The barn was plunged into an unnerving silence, broken only by Falk's ragged breathing. He slumped against the control panel, exhausted but exhilarated. He had done it. He had broken the Veil.

He looked out of a small, grimy window. The first rays of dawn were beginning to paint the sky. He could see figures emerging from the huts, not with their usual placid gait, but with a hesitant curiosity, their eyes wide, their expressions filled with a dawning awareness. A child pointed towards the barn, a question forming on their lips, a genuine, unscripted question.

He knew his victory was temporary. The SS would respond, swiftly and brutally. But for now, in this remote corner of the Reich, the illusion of oblivion had been shattered. The villagers, for the first time in what felt like an eternity, were beginning to remember themselves. And Falk, the fugitive, the anomaly, had found his purpose in the heart of their forgotten village. The path ahead was still fraught with peril, but he now possessed knowledge, and a weapon, that could truly threaten the SS's reign of terror. The test site had revealed its secret, and in doing so, had become the catalyst for a rebellion he was only just beginning to understand.

The first hint that something was fundamentally *wrong* wasn't a visual cue, nor an auditory one, but a visceral sensation that prickled Falk's skin, raising the fine hairs on his arms despite the chill in the pre-dawn air. It was a subtle but pervasive tremor, not of the earth, but of the atmosphere itself, as if the very fabric of reality was being stretched taut. He'd felt a similar, though far less intense, resonance within himself when the alien consciousness had first made its presence known, a discordant hum that vibrated in his bones and made his teeth ache. Now, that hum was amplified, externalized, and directed with a chilling purpose towards the slumbering village below.

He had found his vantage point on a rocky outcrop overlooking the valley, a place shielded by gnarled pines and the deepening shadows of the encroaching forest. The moon, a sliver of bone against the velvet sky, offered scant illumination, but it was enough. The village, a collection of dark shapes huddled against the earth, lay bathed in an unnatural stillness. Smoke still curled from a few chimneys, faint ghosts against the impenetrable darkness, but the sounds that had characterized the earlier evening – the distant, muted laughter, the rhythmic clang of the blacksmith – had long since vanished. An oppressive silence had fallen, thicker and more profound than any natural quiet.

Then, it began. A low-frequency thrum, so deep it seemed to emanate from the planet's core, pulsed through the ground and into Falk's body. It was a physical sensation, a pressure behind his eyes, a tightening in his chest. It wasn't just sound; it was a palpable wave of energy, subtly shifting, almost breathing. The air itself began to shimmer, not with heat, but with an unseen force, like looking through warped glass. Faint, ethereal lights, hues of violet and sickly green, began to bloom around the edges of the village, weaving intricate, shifting patterns that defied any logical explanation. They pulsed in time with the low thrum, growing in intensity, outlining structures that were invisible moments before, highlighting the innocuous huts and the small, stark church with an unholy radiance.

From his hidden perch, Falk watched, a knot of dread tightening in his stomach. This was the activation. This was Project Veil in its nascent, terrifying glory. The journal had described the principles of resonant amplification, the manipulation of ambient energy fields through carefully modulated frequencies to induce specific states of consciousness. The SS, in their insatiable quest for control, had taken this alien science, this profound understanding of the cosmos, and twisted it into a weapon of mass subjugation. And the villagers, the unsuspecting inhabitants of this forgotten corner of the Reich, were the unwitting recipients of its devastating payload.

The lights coalesced, forming a vast, invisible dome of energy that seemed to encompass the entire village. The thrumming intensified, shifting in pitch, becoming more complex, a symphony of alien frequencies designed not to be heard, but to be felt, to be absorbed, to rewrite the very operating system of the human mind. Falk could almost *see* the energy cascading downwards, permeating the walls, the earth, the sleeping bodies within. He imagined the microscopic particles within the villagers' brains being buffeted, their neural pathways being subtly, irrevocably altered.

He recalled the chilling sketches in the journal, the depictions of humans with vacant eyes, their movements jerky and uncoordinated, like puppets on invisible strings. He saw it now, not in sketch form, but in the unnerving stillness that had descended upon the village, a stillness that was not born of peace, but of enforced docility. The SS's objective, as the journal had painstakingly detailed, was to eliminate free will, to engineer a populace utterly compliant, capable of executing any command without question, without hesitation. They were creating an army of automatons, a silent, obedient legion ready to serve their dark agenda.

The spectacle was a grotesque perversion of natural phenomena. The aurora borealis, a celestial dance of light, was reduced to a crude, artificial display. The gentle hum of the earth was twisted into a disorienting drone. It was a stark reminder of the SS's modus operandi: to take the sublime and twist it into the terrifying, to weaponize the very essence of existence for their own twisted ends. The sheer scale of the operation was what truly horrified Falk. This wasn't a localized experiment; this was an attempt to rewrite the fundamental nature of humanity on a grand scale, to create a new breed of citizen, devoid of independent thought, a perfect, unthinking cog in the Nazi war machine.

He gripped the journal tighter, its familiar weight a small comfort in the face of such overwhelming technological dread. He knew, with a certainty that chilled him to the bone, that the SS had not merely stumbled upon this alien knowledge; they had actively sought it out, driven by their insatiable hunger for power. They were using the very forces that governed the universe to enslave their own species, a cosmic blasphemy enacted in the quiet isolation of a forgotten village.

The alien consciousness within him stirred, not with alarm, but with a disquieting resonance. It felt… familiar. Not a pleasant familiarity, but the recognition of a fundamental principle, like a musician hearing a discordant note played on a grand instrument. It understood the underlying mechanics, the manipulation of energies that, in its own context, were used for far different purposes. For a fleeting moment, Falk wondered if this alien entity, so intrinsically linked to him now, had itself experienced such manipulations, such attempts at control in its own distant history.

The lights began to dim, the low hum subsiding to a barely perceptible vibration. The shimmering in the air dissipated, leaving behind the familiar cloak of night. The village returned to its silent tableau, but it was a silence now imbued with a sinister new meaning. The Veil had been lowered, its insidious work complete, at least for this cycle. The villagers had been subjected to the full force of Project Veil, their minds further subjugated, their autonomy eroded a little more.

Falk remained frozen on the outcrop, the cold seeping into his bones. He had witnessed the activation, had seen the terrifying efficacy of the SS's perversion of alien science. He knew that the village was not merely a testing ground; it was a living laboratory, and its inhabitants were the guinea pigs in an experiment that threatened to unravel the very concept of human freedom. The horror was not just in the technology, but in the chilling pragmatism of the SS, their utter disregard for the lives and souls they so ruthlessly manipulated. They were playing God, or rather, a very dark, very destructive imitation of it, wielding cosmic forces with the blunt instruments of their ideology.

He needed to act. The journal offered clues, pathways to disruption, but the scale of what he had just witnessed was daunting. The SS was not dabbling in minor psychic manipulations; they were engaging in large-scale neurological reprogramming, using forces that he barely understood, even with the alien consciousness as his guide. His own survival was a testament to the resilience of the human spirit, or perhaps, the adaptability of the alien entity now residing within him, but the fate of these villagers, and potentially countless others, rested on his ability to find a way to dismantle this monstrous project from within. The path ahead was perilous, but the sight of that activated Veil, the silent testament to human ingenuity twisted into a tool of oppression, had solidified his resolve. He had seen the enemy's weapon, and now he had to find its weakness. The village of Oblivion was more than just a name; it was a chilling reality, and he was determined to break its hold.

The low hum, the alien symphony that had pulsed through the valley, faded. The shimmering lights, those ethereal, sickly hues of violet and green, receded, folding back into the fabric of the night as if they had been mere projections on a canvas that had now been rolled up. Falk remained on the rocky outcrop, his breath catching in his throat, his eyes straining to pierce the gloom that had swallowed the village. What he had witnessed was beyond comprehension, a perversion of science that bordered on the blasphemous. He had seen the activation of Project Veil, the chilling testament to the SS's ability to twist the fundamental forces of the universe into instruments of absolute control. The villagers, he knew, were now under its sway, their minds subtly rewritten, their autonomy leached away by the insidious frequencies. But what he was about to witness next was an escalation, a terrifying leap into a new dimension of eradication.

It began not with a sound, or a light, but with an absence. A void that yawned open in the very air Falk was breathing. The landscape, moments before defined by the huddled shapes of dwellings and the stark silhouette of the church, seemed to waver, like a reflection on disturbed water. The trees, the familiar pines that had offered him concealment, appeared to blur at their edges, their outlines softening as if being scrubbed from existence. Falk blinked, rubbing his eyes, convinced it was a trick of the low moonlight, a consequence of his strained vigilance. But the sensation persisted, growing stronger, more insistent. It was a physical pressure, an invisible hand reaching into reality and smoothing it away, like a child erasing a chalk drawing from a pavement.

He forced himself to focus on the valley below. The village should have been there. Even in the dim light, the clustered rooftops, the faint glow from a few remaining hearths, should have been discernible. But there was… nothing. The darkness was uniform, unbroken by any structure, any sign of human habitation. It was as if a giant eraser had swept across the tableau, leaving behind only the natural contours of the land – the rolling hills, the shadowed hollows, the winding stream. Yet, this was no mere visual deception. Falk felt it, a profound disorientation, a cognitive dissonance that screamed that something vital had been removed.

He scrambled further down the outcrop, his boots slipping on loose scree, his heart pounding a frantic rhythm against his ribs. The alien consciousness within him stirred, not with fear, but with a deep, unsettling recognition. It was as if a fundamental constant had been altered, a law of physics subtly, irrevocably rewritten. This was not destruction; it was something far more profound, far more terrifying. It was erasure.

As he reached the valley floor, the full horror of it became apparent. The ground beneath his feet was still there, the damp earth, the scattered stones. The trees stood; their branches skeletal against the sky. But the village… the village was gone. Not destroyed, not leveled, but utterly, irrevocably *unmade*. It was as if it had never existed. There were no scattered timbers, no piles of rubble, no lingering smoke. The landscape was pristine, as if it had been this way for millennia, untouched by human hands.

Falk stumbled forward, his hands splayed, searching for any tangible evidence of what had been there. He ran his fingers through the grass, parting it as if expecting to find a phantom footprint, a misplaced cobblestone. Nothing. He looked at the spot where the church had stood, a sturdy stone edifice he had glimpsed earlier. Now, only a gentle rise in the terrain met his gaze, a natural undulation that offered no hint of a foundation, no echo of sacred ground.

This was the true purpose of Project Veil, he realized with a sickening lurch. Not merely to subjugate minds, but to expunge entire realities. The SS wasn't just creating obedient drones; they were capable of removing the very concept of a thing, or a people, from existence. The alien journal had spoken of 'ontological erasure,' a terrifying theoretical application of resonant frequencies capable of decoupling an object, or even a collective consciousness, from the universal record. He had dismissed it as hyperbole, a theoretical construct. Now, he was staring at its devastating proof.

The implications were staggering. If they could do this to a village, what couldn't they do? Could they erase a nation? A history? Could they rewrite the very narrative of humanity, erasing inconvenient truths, inconvenient peoples, leaving behind only the sterile, compliant reality they desired?

A wave of panic, cold and sharp, threatened to overwhelm him. He had seen this before, in the abstract theorizing of the journal. But seeing it enacted, witnessing the tangible absence where solid structures and living beings had been just moments before, was a different order of terror altogether. He looked down at his own hands, half-expecting them to begin to fade, to become translucent, to follow the path of the obliterated village. The alien consciousness pulsed within him, a silent, steady presence, an anchor in this sea of unreality. It seemed to be absorbing the ambient energy of this erasure, cataloging it, understanding it.

He tried to recall the faces of the villagers he had glimpsed, the fleeting images of them going about their lives. The baker, his flour-dusted apron. The woman tending her small garden. The children playing near the stream. They were gone. Not just from this valley, but from any record, any memory. It was as if they had never drawn breath, never laughed, never wept. Their very existence had been a ripple that had now been smoothed flat.

The true horror, Falk understood, lay not in the destruction, but in the absolute finality of it. There would be no mourning, no remembrance. No one would even know to mourn. If a traveler stumbled upon this valley tomorrow, they would see only untouched wilderness, as if the village had been a collective hallucination, a figment of his own overwrought imagination. But Falk knew. He had seen it. He had *felt* it. And the alien consciousness within him was a constant, undeniable testament to its reality.

He thought of the photographs, the documents, the historical accounts that the SS would undoubtedly be meticulously sanitizing. Every mention, every trace of the village and its inhabitants, would be meticulously expunged. It was a form of cosmic censorship, an absolute control over narrative and reality itself. The sheer, terrifying efficiency of it was breathtaking. They weren't just conquering; they were *unmaking*.

He walked through the phantom village, his footsteps the only sound in the unnatural quiet. He traced the invisible lines of what had been streets, the spectral outlines of homes. It was a haunting, disorienting experience, like walking through a dream that refused to fully materialize. The air itself felt thinner, less substantial, as if the very atoms that constituted this space had been subtly rearranged, stripped of their familiar coherence.

The alien entity offered no words, no direct communication, only a deep, resonant understanding that permeated Falk's consciousness. It felt the absence, the profound void left behind. It recognized the principles at play, the manipulation of fundamental forces that governed existence. It was a science far beyond human comprehension, a power that was being wielded with a chillingly pragmatic ruthlessness.

Falk sat down in what would have been the village square, the sensation of the erased structures a palpable weight in the air. He pulled out the journal, his fingers tracing the alien script. He remembered a passage, a theoretical discussion on 'collective resonance cascade' and its potential for 'ontological decoupling.' At the time, it had seemed like a theoretical oddity, a fascinating but ultimately impractical application of the alien science. Now, it was a horrifying prophecy fulfilled.

The SS had taken the most profound understanding of the universe and twisted it into a tool of absolute annihilation, a method of erasing not just bodies, but existence itself. They had managed to sever the village from the tapestry of reality, to unravel the threads that bound it to the present, the past, and the future.

He wondered if the villagers had felt anything during the final moments of their existence. Had there been pain? Terror? Or had the Veil's initial subjugation rendered them incapable of even registering their own unmaking? The thought was a cold comfort, a bleak rationalization. But the truth was, he would never know. They were gone, and with them, any possibility of understanding their fate.

Falk stood up, his resolve hardening. He had witnessed a level of power that was both awe-inspiring and utterly terrifying. The SS had achieved a new apex in their quest for control, a mastery over reality that transcended physical conquest. They were capable of making things disappear, not just from sight, but from existence itself. And if they could do this to a small, isolated village, then the potential for this technology to be used on a global scale was a chilling prospect indeed.

He had to get this journal to someone who could understand it, someone who could stop this. He couldn't afford to be caught, to become another erased footnote in a rewritten history. The weight of the journal in his satchel felt heavier now, not just with the ink of alien knowledge, but with the burden of a terrifying secret. He looked back at the empty valley, the pristine landscape that now held the ghost of a village, a place wiped from existence by a force he barely understood. The silence was profound, absolute. It was the silence of oblivion.

He turned and began to walk, the alien consciousness within him a silent witness to the unmaking he had just observed, his own existence a precarious defiance against the SS's ultimate weapon. The journey ahead was fraught with peril, but the sight of that erased landscape, the palpable void where a community had once thrived, fueled a burning determination to ensure that Project Veil, and its terrible power, would never be allowed to unleash its full, annihilating potential upon the world. He had seen the ultimate expression of control, the terrifying capacity to unmake reality itself, and the knowledge was a brand upon his soul.

Falk's boots crunched on the alien loam, each step a betrayal of the silence that now reigned over the valley. The air, once thrumming with an unseen energy, was now unnervingly still, carrying only the scent of damp earth and the distant, mournful whisper of wind through the pines. He had stood on the precipice of understanding, witnessing the initial activation of Project Veil, the chilling testament to the SS's ambition to control not just minds, but existence itself. The shimmering lights had receded, the insidious hum had faded, leaving behind an absence so profound it felt like a physical blow. He had seen the village, a collection of huddled homes and a defiant spire, simply cease to be. It wasn't destruction; it was an unmaking.

The realization, cold and sharp, pierced through the residual shock. This was not the work of conventional weaponry, no bombs or bullets that left scars on the earth. This was something far more insidious, a violation of the very fabric of reality. The alien journal, clutched tightly in his hand, had spoken of 'ontological erasure,' a theoretical weapon capable of severing an entity's connection to the universal continuum. Falk had read the words with a scholar's detached curiosity, a physicist's fascination with a paradigm-shattering concept. Now, he was living its horrifying proof. The village, its inhabitants, their lives, their histories – all had been scrubbed from existence as cleanly as chalk from a blackboard.

He stumbled forward, drawn by an irresistible, morbid curiosity, towards the spectral heart of what had been. The ground beneath his feet was solid, the familiar contours of the valley floor unchanged. Yet, where the clustered dwellings should have been, there was only an unbroken expanse of undulating grassland. He knelt, running his hands through the dew-kissed blades, searching for any hint, any residue of what had transpired. He found only earth, cool and indifferent. No shattered foundations, no scattered debris, no lingering trace of human endeavor. It was as if a meticulous gardener had carefully replanted the land, erasing any evidence of a prior, unwanted bloom.

The church, its stone edifice a sturdy anchor against the

encroaching night, was also gone. Its absence was a gaping wound in the valley's topography, replaced by a subtle, almost imperceptible rise in the earth, as if nature itself had conspired to smooth over the scar left by human transgression. Falk's breath hitched. He remembered the fleeting images he had captured with his own eyes, the brief glimpses of life: the baker with his flour-dusted apron, the woman tending her small garden, the children playing near the stream. Were they even memories now, or had they been erased along with their physical forms? The thought was a chilling void in itself.

The alien consciousness within him stirred, a silent observer in this theatre of the impossible. It offered no judgment, no overt pronouncements, but a deep, resonating understanding that permeated Falk's very being. It perceived the fundamental alteration, the subtle yet catastrophic shift in the universal constants that governed existence. This was not merely the absence of life; it was the absence of being. The SS had achieved something the wildest theories of science fiction had only dared to imagine: the ability to unmake reality.

Falk stood, his gaze sweeping across the empty expanse. The implications were staggering, a cascade of dread that threatened to drown his senses. If they could erase a village, a community, what was to stop them from applying this weapon on a grander scale? Could they erase cities? Nations? Could they rewrite history itself, purging inconvenient truths and undesirable populations, leaving behind a sterile, compliant narrative sculpted to their twisted ideals? The sheer, unadulterated power of it was a terrifying spectacle, a perversion of scientific advancement that plunged Falk into a profound abyss of despair.

He traced the invisible lines of what had been streets, the phantom outlines of homes and public spaces. It was a disorienting experience, like walking through a ghost town that had never truly existed. The air itself seemed to carry a subtle dissonance, a faint echo of the frequencies that had been unleashed, leaving the very atoms of the valley subtly altered, their coherence perhaps irrevocably compromised. He felt a growing unease, a gnawing fear that his own existence might be precarious, a fragile anomaly in a reality being meticulously curated by an unseen hand. He glanced at his hands, half-expecting them to fade, to become translucent, a mirror to the erased village.

The alien journal was a tangible anchor in this sea of unreality. He opened it, his fingers brushing over the alien script, seeking solace or understanding in its cryptic passages. His eyes fell upon a section detailing the theoretical applications of 'resonant cascade manipulation.' The SS had taken a science far beyond human comprehension and twisted it into a weapon of ultimate control, a tool of absolute annihilation. They had found a way to sever a collective consciousness, and by extension, its physical manifestation, from the intricate tapestry of existence.

The efficiency was breathtaking, a chilling testament to the SS's ruthless pragmatism. They weren't just conquering; they were *unmaking*. They were capable of rendering entire populations and their histories into nothingness, leaving no trace, no memory, no record of their existence. This was not merely war; this was an act of cosmic censorship, an absolute dominion over narrative and reality itself.

Falk recalled the theoretical discussions within the journal, the abstract debates about the potential consequences of such a weapon. He had dismissed them as the ramblings of an advanced, perhaps paranoid, civilization. Now, the abstract had become terrifyingly concrete. He had witnessed the ultimate expression of control, a power that transcended physical force and delved into the very essence of being. The SS had achieved a new apex in their quest for dominance, a mastery over reality that was both awe-inspiring and profoundly horrifying.

He thought about the potential victims, the villagers. Had they felt anything in their final moments? Had there been pain, terror, or had the initial subjugation of Project Veil rendered them incapable of even registering their own unmaking? The thought offered a bleak comfort, a rationalization born of desperation. But the truth was, he would never know. They were gone, their existence a ripple that had been smoothed flat, leaving no trace, no echo, no memory for anyone to mourn. The ultimate horror lay not in the destruction, but in the absolute finality of it. There would be no mourning, no remembrance, because no one would even know to mourn.

Falk sat down on the ground, the weight of the journal a heavy burden in his satchel. He felt a profound sense of isolation, a chilling realization that he was a witness to something that, by its very nature, was designed to leave no witnesses. The world, the established order of history and memory, had been fundamentally breached. The SS possessed a weapon that could erase not just individuals, but the very concept of them, making them vanish from the universal record as if they had never been.

The alien consciousness pulsed within him, a silent, steady presence that seemed to absorb the ambient energy of this erasure, cataloging it, understanding it. It was a confirmation, a brutal, undeniable confirmation of the SS's terrifying agenda. They were not merely seeking to conquer the world; they were seeking to redefine it, to reshape reality itself according to their own warped vision, eliminating anything that did not conform, erasing any inconvenient truth.

A wave of cold dread washed over him. He looked at his own hands, his ordinary, human hands. They were real. He was real. But for how long? If the SS could unleash such a weapon, what was to stop them from using it on a scale that would dwarf any conflict in human history? The idea of a world where entire nations, entire cultures, entire histories could be simply *unmade* sent a shiver down his spine that had nothing to do with the cool evening air.

His resolve, however, solidified. He had seen the terrifying potential of Project Veil, the horrifying efficacy of ontological erasure. He could not, would not, allow this to continue. The journal, this artifact of alien knowledge, was no longer just a key to understanding; it was a weapon in its own right, a testament to a power that, in the wrong hands, could unravel existence itself. He had to get it to someone, anyone, who could comprehend its significance, who could help him fight this monstrous agenda.

He stood, his gaze fixed on the empty valley, the pristine landscape that now held the phantom of a village, a place wiped from existence by a force he was only beginning to grasp. The silence was absolute, profound. It was the silence of oblivion, a chilling testament to the SS's ultimate weapon. The journey ahead was fraught with peril, but the sight of that erased landscape, the palpable void where a community had once thrived, fueled a burning determination to ensure that Project Veil, and its terrible power, would never be allowed to unleash its full, annihilating potential upon the world. He had seen the ultimate expression of control, the terrifying capacity to unmake reality itself, and the knowledge was a brand upon his soul. He turned and began to walk, the alien consciousness within him a silent witness to the unmaking he had just observed, his own existence a precarious defiance against the SS's ultimate weapon. The path forward was uncertain, shrouded in the very darkness that had swallowed the village, but Falk carried with him the grim understanding of what humanity was capable of, and a desperate hope that it was not too late to stop it. The confirmation of the unspeakable truth was not an end, but a horrifying beginning.

Chapter 10

The Shadow of Oblivion

The weight of the alien journal felt less like a burden now and more like a lifeline. Falk's fingers traced the alien script, not for understanding, but for the sheer, tangible reality of it. Each alien glyph, each impossible curve, was proof that the universe held secrets far grander and more terrifying than he had ever imagined. He had witnessed the impossible, the unmaking of a village, the erasure of a history, and the chilling realization was this: he was now the sole custodian of that knowledge. The SS, with their insatiable thirst for control, had weaponized existence itself, and the silence of that valley was the deafening roar of their success.

He couldn't just fade into the shadows, as tempting as that might be. Disappearing would be another victory for them, another truth swallowed by the void they commanded. His mind reeled with the fragmented echoes of the alien's final communication, a desperate plea woven into the very fabric of his being, a whisper of warnings and contingencies. It was a desperate gamble, a posthumous insurance policy left by a civilization that had stared into the abyss and understood its true horror. He had to translate that desperate whisper into a shout, a beacon for any who might follow, any who might be able to comprehend the magnitude of what had transpired.

Falk retrieved a small, worn notebook and a stub of a pencil from his pack. His hands, though steady, felt alien to him, vessels for a consciousness burdened by an impossible secret. He couldn't document everything, not in a way that would be immediately comprehensible. The alien journal was a Rosetta Stone for a language that had ceased to exist, a key to a lock that had been dismantled. But he could leave clues, fragments of breadcrumbs leading back to the truth, breadcrumbs that, if found by the right hands, might ignite a firestorm of understanding. He began to write, not in the neat, precise hand of a scientist, but in a hurried scrawl, each word carrying the urgency of his mission.

He detailed the events in the valley, the unnerving stillness after the activation of Project Veil, the unnerving *absence* where the village once stood. He described the feeling, the visceral wrongness of it, the way the very air seemed to hum with a discordant frequency. He wrote about the alien journal, its potential as a conduit to a deeper understanding of the SS's technology, a technology that transcended the mere manipulation of matter and ventured into the realm of ontological engineering. He couldn't fully explain the science – he barely understood it himself – but he could articulate the devastating outcome, the sheer, terrifying efficiency of the SS's ultimate weapon. He wrote about 'ontological erasure,' not as a theoretical concept, but as a brutal reality, a tool that unmade not just bodies, but the very essence of existence, severing connections to the universal continuum.

He then turned his attention to the alien's final message, the fragmented whispers that had imprinted themselves on his mind. He tried to transcribe the feelings, the conceptual understandings that had been imparted to him, rather than direct words. It was like trying to capture starlight in a jar, the ephemeral nature of the communication making it maddeningly elusive. He described the sense of interconnectedness, the vast, intricate web of existence, and how Project Veil was designed to sever those connections, to unravel the fabric of reality piece by piece. He wrote about the alien's understanding of 'resonant cascade manipulation,' a concept that hinted at the SS's ability to manipulate fundamental frequencies, to create a sympathetic resonance that could disrupt and ultimately erase specific entities from existence.

Falk paused, his pencil hovering over the page. He looked up at the now-empty sky, the indifferent stars that bore witness to his desperate act. He was a single, vulnerable human against a force that could unmake worlds. The SS had become something far beyond a political entity; they were an existential threat, a harbinger of absolute negation. He thought about the potential victims, not just the villagers, but anyone deemed inconvenient, anyone who stood in their way. Entire cultures, entire histories, entire *universes* could be rendered nonexistent with a flick of a switch, a wave of a calculated frequency.

He committed to paper his deepest fears, the terrifying implications of such power. He wrote about the SS's ultimate goal: not conquest, but purification. A sterile, compliant reality sculpted to their twisted ideals, where any deviation, any dissent, any inconvenient truth would be simply erased. He envisioned a future where history was a carefully curated narrative, devoid of struggle, of diversity, of the messy, beautiful chaos of human existence. A world where the SS were the arbiters of reality, the gatekeepers of existence itself.

He knew his notebook would be a cryptic riddle to anyone who found it without the context of his experience, without the chilling understanding of what he had witnessed. But it was all he had. He added a hastily drawn diagram, a crude attempt to represent the concept of interconnectedness and the destructive force of the SS's weapon, a diagram that would likely be dismissed as the ramblings of a madman. He included references to specific passages within the alien journal, hoping that its discovery would coincide with his notebook, creating a synergy of information that might, just might, be enough to set the wheels of understanding in motion.

The alien consciousness within him stirred, not with active participation, but with a profound empathy. It understood the futility of his efforts on a grand scale, the sheer immensity of the task before him. Yet, it also recognized the inherent human drive to leave a mark, to resist oblivion, even in the face of insurmountable odds. Falk felt a surge of something akin to gratitude, a silent acknowledgment of this strange, symbiotic relationship. He was not entirely alone in this endeavor, even if his companion was an alien intelligence that communicated through pure concept.

He then began to write a personal account, a testament to his own journey and his growing understanding of the SS's machinations. He detailed his initial investigations, the gradual unveiling of Project Veil, the chilling progression from theoretical science to terrifying application. He wanted to convey the progression of his own realization, from disbelief to horror, and finally to a grim determination. He knew that if his notebook were found, it would be crucial for the finder to understand the provenance of the information, to grasp that it was not mere speculation, but the firsthand account of a witness to the unthinkable.

He wrote about his own internal struggle, the ethical quandaries he had faced, the sacrifices he had made. He described the isolation, the paranoia that had become his constant companion. He wanted to leave behind a record not just of the SS's crimes, but of the human cost of resisting them, the personal toll that understanding such a profound threat could exact. He detailed his growing belief that the alien journal was not merely a historical artifact, but a potential weapon in its own right, a key to unlocking the SS's terrifying secrets and, perhaps, a means to dismantle their ultimate weapon.

Falk knew that his mission was far from over. He had to ensure that his notebook and the journal reached safety, that they fell into the hands of those who could understand their significance and act upon them. He considered various scenarios, weighing the risks and rewards of each potential course of action. He couldn't simply hand it over to any authority; the SS's reach was far too extensive, their infiltration too deep. He needed to find someone trusted, someone with the resources and the understanding to counter this existential threat.

He began to formulate a plan, a desperate gambit to safeguard the information and, perhaps, to strike a blow against the SS. He couldn't afford to be caught, not now, not when he carried the seeds of humanity's salvation, or its damnation. The weight of responsibility pressed down on him, a tangible force that dwarfed the physical burden of his pack. He looked at his notebook, a small collection of hastily scrawled pages that held the fate of existence itself. It was a testament to his desperation, his refusal to be erased, his commitment to leaving a trace, a defiance against the SS's ultimate weapon.

The alien consciousness pulsed again, a subtle reinforcement, a silent acknowledgment of his resolve. It was a silent promise of support, a shared burden in the face of overwhelming odds. Falk closed his notebook, the pencil tucked safely away. The words were out, the warning was laid, however fragmented. Now came the perilous task of dissemination, of ensuring that his desperate act of remembrance would not be in vain. He stood, his gaze sweeping across the now-familiar landscape, the valley that held the phantom of a village, a testament to a power that threatened to unravel the very fabric of reality. He knew that the fight had just begun, and his next steps would be as critical as the discovery of Project Veil itself. He had to disappear, but not into oblivion. He had to disappear into the shadows, to become a ghost in the machine, carrying the fire of truth to a world teetering on the brink of being unmade.

The alien journal, a conduit to a civilization that had faced and ultimately succumbed to a similar existential threat, offered more than just historical context. It was a repository of knowledge, a silent testament to their final moments, and within its alien script, Falk began to decipher not just the nature of the SS's weapon, but the very principles of its counteraction. The residual consciousness, a mere echo within his mind, had offered fragmented insights, glimpses into a technological framework so advanced it bordered on the mystical. Yet, amidst the awe and terror, a crucial detail began to crystallize: the aliens, in their foresight, had embedded a contingency, a failsafe born from their own catastrophic experience. It was a beacon, a last-ditch effort to preserve their legacy, their warnings, and perhaps, a key to dismantling the very forces that had extinguished them.

He remembered the subtle promptings, the conceptual nudges from the alien intelligence that resonated within his own consciousness. It wasn't a voice, not in any conventional sense, but a cascade of understanding that flowed through him, painting abstract diagrams and complex equations directly onto the canvas of his mind. One particular concept, a recurring theme in the alien's final transmissions, was the idea of a "resonant anchor," a method of preserving essential information, a digital ghost designed to survive even the most profound levels of erasure. This wasn't a mere data backup; it was an ontological safeguard, an attempt to anchor a foundational record of their existence against the very forces that sought to unmake reality itself.

Driven by this nascent understanding, Falk began to meticulously examine the wreckage of the alien craft, a task fraught with both hope and trepidation. The main hull, a twisted sculpture of unknown alloys, was largely inaccessible, its advanced systems fused and inert. However, the alien consciousness guided him, pointing him towards less critical, yet still functional, components that had been ejected during the catastrophic descent. These were not the primary engine cores or the command consoles, but secondary systems, auxiliary devices that, by their very nature, were designed to be robust and independently operative. He sifted through the debris, his movements precise and deliberate, his senses heightened by the knowledge of what he sought. Each piece of twisted metal, each shattered crystal, was a potential key, a fragment of a lost civilization's desperate gamble.

His search led him to a relatively intact section of what appeared to be an environmental control unit, a sphere of iridescent metal that had miraculously survived the impact. Nestled within its shattered casing was a smaller, secondary device, a palm-sized object that hummed with a faint, almost imperceptible energy. It was smooth, featureless, and cool to the touch, its surface shifting with subtle chromatic patterns as he turned it in his hands. The alien consciousness confirmed his intuition; this was it. This was the "resonant anchor," the failsafe beacon. It was a portable data storage device, designed to withstand catastrophic events, to preserve a core record of their civilization, their scientific understanding, and crucially, the detailed mechanics of Project Veil, the very technology the SS had co-opted and perverted.

Falk knew that the SS would undoubtedly be searching for any remnants of the alien craft, any piece of technology that could further their own terrifying agenda. This device, if discovered by them, would be a goldmine, a tool to perfect their ontological erasure techniques, to refine their ability to unmake reality with even greater precision. He had to secure it, to understand its contents, and to ensure it didn't fall into the wrong hands. The alien journal was a Rosetta Stone, a historical record, but this device was the operational manual, the technical schematics that could unlock the true nature of the threat and, perhaps, offer a way to combat it.

He carefully extracted the device from its shattered housing, his movements economical and precise. The alien consciousness within him provided a conceptual overlay, a series of intuitive gestures that allowed him to interface with the device without explicit knowledge of its alien operating system. It was a direct mental connection, a transference of intent rather than data packets. He focused his thoughts, visualizing the desire to access the stored information, to understand its purpose. The device responded, its surface rippling with light, a complex series of holographic symbols briefly appearing before coalescing into a single, pulsating node.

The information contained within was staggering. It detailed the aliens' origins, their societal structure, and their advanced understanding of the fundamental forces of the universe. More importantly, it laid bare the terrifying efficacy of Project Veil, explaining its mechanism not just as a destructive force, but as a targeted manipulation of what the aliens termed the "cosmic resonance field." This field, they theorized, was the underlying fabric that connected all matter, all consciousness, and all existence. Project Veil, by introducing a precisely calibrated counter-frequency, was able to disrupt these connections effectively "unmaking" targets from the cosmic tapestry. The SS, in their crude but devastating application, had amplified this concept to an unimaginable scale, turning it into a weapon of mass ontological annihilation.

The device also contained extensive data on the aliens' attempts to counter this threat, their research into resonance manipulation, and the development of their own failsafe systems. This was the true treasure. It included the blueprints for their "resonant anchor," the very device Falk now held, explaining its function as a self-sustaining informational beacon, capable of transmitting its stored data across vast distances, even through the disruptive effects of Project Veil. It was designed to survive, to persist, a final message in a bottle cast into the ocean of oblivion.

Falk understood then that his mission had taken a critical turn. He was no longer just a witness; he was now a custodian of a profound secret, a potential lifeline for humanity. The SS's unchecked power, their ability to erase history and existence itself, was a threat of unprecedented magnitude. The alien data suggested that their ultimate goal was not mere conquest, but a complete homogenization of reality, a sterile, ordered existence devoid of dissent, diversity, or any deviation from their prescribed norm. They were not simply conquerors; they were architects of erasure, seeking to sculpt the universe into their own image, and anyone or anything that did not fit their mold was subject to deletion.

He spent hours poring over the alien data, the alien consciousness acting as an intuitive guide, translating complex concepts into understandable frameworks. He learned about the aliens' own demise, a slow, agonizing process of cultural and physical erasure, beginning with subtle manipulations of their history and culminating in the complete unmaking of their civilization. They had fought back, developing countermeasures, but ultimately, the SS's precursor, or the entity from which the SS had derived their technology, had been too powerful, too insidious. The failsafe beacon was their final act of defiance, a desperate attempt to ensure that their knowledge, their warnings, would survive, even if they themselves did not.

The sheer scope of the SS's operation began to sink in. Project Veil wasn't just a weapon; it was a methodology, a system that could be applied with chilling precision to eliminate any perceived threat, any inconvenient truth, any dissenting voice. The erasure of the village was a demonstration, a brutal unveiling of their capabilities. But the data suggested that this was merely the tip of the iceberg. The SS was capable of far more, of subtle, insidious manipulations that could rewrite history, erase entire cultures, or even unravel the very fabric of reality on a cosmic scale. The idea that existence itself could be subject to a bureaucratic process of review and potential deletion was a terrifying prospect.

Falk realized that his immediate priority was to safeguard this data. He couldn't afford to be apprehended, not with this knowledge in his possession. The SS would stop at nothing to retrieve it, to suppress it, or to weaponize it further. He needed to find a secure location, a place where he could begin to decipher the full implications of the alien data and formulate a plan of action. The alien consciousness, a silent observer throughout this process, seemed to convey a sense of urgency, a subtle reinforcement of the critical nature of his discovery.

He carefully secured the failsafe beacon, tucking it deep within his pack, nestled amongst his meager supplies. The weight of it felt different now, not just the physical weight of an object, but the immense burden of responsibility. He had in his possession the potential to understand, and perhaps even to counter, the most terrifying weapon ever conceived. The alien journal and the failsafe beacon were two pieces of a puzzle that, when put together, could reveal the true nature of the existential threat posed by the SS. He was no longer just a survivor; he was a harbinger of a new kind of war, a war fought not on battlefields, but on the very foundations of reality. The shadow of oblivion had been cast, but in his hands, he now held a sliver of light, a beacon of hope, and a weapon of unimaginable potential. The silence of the erased village was a testament to what could be lost; the humming of the beacon in his pack was a promise of what could be saved.

The oppressive silence of the wilderness was a stark contrast to the cacophony of alarms and the screams that had haunted Falk's recent memory. Each rustle of leaves, each snap of a twig, sent a jolt of adrenaline through him, his senses on high alert, scanning the periphery for any sign of pursuit. The SS, he knew, would not be idle. Their reach was extensive, their methods ruthless, and the technology he now carried—the alien beacon—was an artifact of such monumental importance that they would scour the very earth to reclaim it. He had to disappear, to become a ghost in the system, a phantom in the landscape, before their relentless net closed in.

He moved with a practiced urgency, guided by an instinct honed by years of operating in the shadows, a legacy of his own past that now felt chillingly relevant. The alien consciousness within him, no longer a fragmented echo, had coalesced into a more coherent guiding presence, offering an intuitive understanding of the terrain, pointing him towards natural formations that offered concealment, towards hollows and crevices that could serve as temporary refuge. It was a strange symbiosis, the machine-like precision of the alien intelligence harmonizing with his own desperate survival drive.

Days bled into nights, marked by the rhythm of his own heartbeat and the shifting patterns of the stars above. He traveled through dense forests, across windswept plains, and along the banks of icy rivers, always keeping to the less-traveled paths, avoiding any sign of human habitation or infrastructure that might betray his presence. The alien beacon, nestled securely within a specially crafted compartment in his pack, pulsed with a faint, internal warmth, a constant reminder of the immense responsibility he now bore. It was a fragile hope, a whisper against the encroaching silence, and he was its sole protector.

His objective was not merely to evade capture, but to find a sanctuary, a place where the beacon could be secured indefinitely, shielded from the SS's omnipresent surveillance. The alien data had provided conceptual blueprints for such a sanctuary, a location designed to withstand even the most advanced detection methods, a place where the beacon could slumber, safe until the opportune moment for its activation. It was a place that leveraged the very principles of the SS's ontological erasure technology against them, a paradox of defense.

The alien consciousness guided him toward a specific geological anomaly, a nexus of unique energy readings that the SS's conventional sensors, or even their more advanced Veil-based scanners, would likely overlook. It was a region characterized by unusual geological strata, a complex interplay of subterranean energies that created a localized distortion field, a natural cloak. He arrived at a desolate mountain range, its peaks shrouded in perpetual mist, its valleys carved by ancient glaciers. The air here felt different, charged with an unseen power, and the alien beacon within his pack vibrated in response, a resonant hum that echoed the subtle energies of the earth.

He spent days exploring, meticulously mapping the area, guided by the alien intelligence's ever-present insights. He sought not just a hiding place, but a vault, a tomb for the truth that would ensure its eventual resurrection. The SS were masters of erasure, their technology capable of unmaking not just physical objects but also information, memory, and ultimately, reality itself. To counter this, he needed a method of concealment that operated on a similar, yet opposing, fundamental level.

Finally, he found it: a deep, narrow fissure in the mountainside, almost invisible against the rugged rock face, concealed behind a curtain of cascading water. The fissure led to a subterranean cavern;

a vast, cathedral-like space carved by millennia of geological activity. The air within was still and cool, carrying the faint scent of ancient minerals. The alien consciousness confirmed that this was the place, a location of profound natural shielding, a nexus of the very energies that could be harnessed to protect the beacon.

With painstaking care, Falk began his work. He used the tools he had salvaged, the same ones that had allowed him to extract the beacon from the wreckage, to excavate a small, precisely shaped cavity within the cavern's bedrock. The alien intelligence provided him with conceptual guidance, an understanding of the optimal depth, orientation, and material composition for the beacon's resting place. It wasn't simply about burying it; it was about embedding it within the very fabric of the earth, creating a symbiotic relationship between the artifact and its environment.

He then began the intricate process of programming the beacon for its long slumber. This was the most critical phase. The beacon was designed to be a silent witness, a repository of knowledge that would awaken only when specific conditions were met. The alien data had detailed several potential activation triggers, ranging from specific seismic frequencies to the precise temporal alignment of celestial bodies. Falk, with the alien consciousness as his guide, selected a combination of these triggers, ensuring that the beacon would remain dormant until a period of significant geological or astronomical change, a time when the SS's influence might be diminished, or when humanity might be receptive to the truth.

He meticulously input the parameters, his mind a conduit for the alien intelligence's complex instructions. The beacon's surface, which had previously displayed shifting chromatic patterns, now began to glow with a steady, internal light, its subtle hum deepening into a resonant thrum. He visualized the data contained within—the history of the alien civilization, their encounter with the SS's precursor, the devastating nature of Project Veil, and the blueprint for its counteraction—all being meticulously shielded, woven into the very quantum fabric of the beacon's being.

As he worked, the memory of the erased village flashed through his mind. The SS hadn't just destroyed lives; they had attempted to unmake their very existence, to wipe them from the annals of history as if they had never been. This was the terror of Project Veil, the chilling efficiency of their ontological erasure. The beacon, he knew, was the antithesis of this—a guarantee of persistence, a refusal to be forgotten.

He needed to ensure that even if the SS somehow discovered the location, they would be unable to access the beacon's core data. The alien technology offered a layered defense, a series of conceptual locks that required a specific key, a unique resonance pattern that only a sympathetic intelligence could replicate. Falk, through his connection with the alien consciousness, was that intelligence. He performed a final sequence, a conceptual handshake that sealed the beacon's data, encrypting it in a manner that would render it utterly incomprehensible to anyone lacking the specific inter-species understanding.

He then carefully lowered the beacon into the prepared cavity, the bedrock seeming to embrace it. The process was solemn, a rite of passage for both the artifact and himself. He then began the arduous task of restoring the cavern wall, meticulously replacing the displaced rock, concealing the fissure, and smoothing over any trace of his presence. He used the natural camouflage of the cavern, the mineral deposits, the growth of ancient mosses, to ensure that the entrance would be indistinguishable from the surrounding rock.

Before he sealed the final section, he paused. He held his hand over the spot where the beacon was now buried, feeling the faint pulse of its hidden energy. The alien consciousness offered a final, abstract impression: a sense of enduring purpose, a long wait, and an ultimate awakening. It was a profound connection, a shared destiny forged in the fires of annihilation.

He then completed the sealing, his movements precise and economical. The fissure was gone, the cavern hidden, the beacon lost to the world, or so it seemed. But it was not truly lost. It was merely dormant, a seed planted in the fertile ground of time, awaiting the right conditions to sprout and bear the fruit of truth. He had fulfilled the first critical part of his mission: to secure the alien artifact, to preserve the knowledge it contained, and to conceal it from those who sought to exploit and weaponize it.

The weight of responsibility remained, heavier now that the beacon was safely hidden. He had effectively severed his direct link to the alien consciousness, the flow of information now channeled through the beacon itself, awaiting its programmed activation. He was alone again, truly alone, with only the echoes of alien wisdom and the chilling knowledge of the SS's capabilities for company.

He exited the cavern, the mountain air a biting reminder of the world outside. The SS would still be searching, their technological eyes scanning the horizon, their operatives fanning out across the region. He had created a temporary sanctuary, but his own survival was far from guaranteed. The next phase of his journey was to find a way to disseminate the information, to ensure that the truth of Project Veil and the alien warning would eventually reach those who could understand and act upon it. The beacon was a promise of salvation, but the path to fulfilling that promise was fraught with peril. He turned his back on the hidden sanctuary, disappearing into the rugged terrain, a lone figure carrying the weight of an erased civilization and the hope for humanity's future. The shadow of oblivion had been acknowledged, and in its depths, a silent guardian had been placed, waiting for the dawn.

The finality of the act settled upon Falk with the cold, hard certainty of bedrock. The alien beacon, once a vibrant locus of alien consciousness and knowledge, was now a silent sentinel, entombed within the earth's embrace. Its faint, resonant hum, a constant companion for days, had been meticulously muted, a deliberate severing of a tangible link to a civilization long gone and a future yet unwritten. He stood at the mouth of the now-seamless fissure, the cascading waterfall once again a perfect veil, obscuring the monumental truth hidden within. His senses, still honed to a razor's edge, detected no anomalies, no lingering energy signatures that might betray the presence of the artifact. He had succeeded in his immediate task, in creating a sanctuary, a vault of cosmic significance.

Yet, as he turned away from the mountain's hidden heart, a profound and disquieting stillness descended. The symbiotic dialogue with the alien consciousness, the intuitive guidance that had been his constant anchor, had faded. It was a silence that was both a relief and a gnawing emptiness. He was, once again, profoundly alone. The vastness of the wilderness, which had previously felt like a temporary refuge, now seemed a daunting expanse, an indifferent canvas upon which his solitary struggle would unfold. The weight of the knowledge he carried, of the SS's terrifying capabilities and the impending threat of Project Veil, pressed down on him, a physical ache in his chest.

His thoughts, unbidden, drifted back to the life that had existed before this terrifying reality consumed him. He recalled the mundane rhythms of a world that now felt impossibly distant: the warmth of shared laughter, the simple comfort of routine, the quiet satisfaction of a life lived without the specter of existential erasure. He remembered Tammy, her bright eyes, the earnest conviction in her voice as she spoke of a brighter future. The memory was a double-edged sword, a painful reminder of all that had been lost, all that the SS sought to obliterate. Their pursuit of him was not merely a hunt for a man; it was a systematic campaign to extinguish any trace of the truth, any anomaly that dared to disrupt their manufactured order. The village he had stumbled upon, a collective memory systematically unmade, was a chilling testament to their efficacy. They did not just kill; they *erased*. They unwove the very fabric of existence, leaving behind not even a ghost, not even a whisper.

He realized, with a chilling clarity, that the act of concealing the beacon was not an end, but a critical pivot. It was a defiant act against oblivion, a desperate assertion that even in the face of overwhelming power, truth could endure. But the beacon itself was a passive guardian. Its potential, its message, remained locked away, waiting for the precise confluence of events that would trigger its awakening. And until that day, the burden of dissemination, of ensuring that the knowledge contained within would not be lost to the crushing weight of the SS's manufactured reality, fell squarely upon his shoulders. The beacon was a seed, but he was the gardener, and the soil was poisoned by deception and fear.

He began to descend the mountainside, his movements deliberate, each step a conscious effort to imprint the memory of this place, this sanctuary, into his mind. He cataloged the geological markers, the unique mineral veins, the peculiar patterns of the wind that swept through the passes. These were not merely navigational aids; they were the visual and sensory anchors to a truth that the SS would undoubtedly attempt to erase from any official record, from any compromised mapping system. His own mind, he knew, was the most secure repository, but even the human mind was susceptible to the insidious influence of erasure technology, to the subtle erosion of memory and perception.

The journey ahead was a labyrinth of uncertainty. He possessed the raw materials of salvation, the historical record of an alien encounter, the grim warning of an encroaching existential threat, and the conceptual framework for humanity's defense against the SS's ultimate weapon. But how to translate this into action? How to disseminate a truth so profound, so shattering, without becoming another victim of the SS's systematic annihilation? He could not simply walk into a populated area and declare his findings; he would be apprehended, silenced, and the beacon's existence, along with its invaluable data, would be forfeit. He needed allies, individuals or organizations who possessed the discretion, the influence, and the understanding to grasp the gravity of the situation. But in a world saturated by SS propaganda, where dissent was met with swift and brutal obliteration, finding such allies felt akin to searching for a single, uncorrupted star in a sky choked with artificial light.

He walked with a renewed sense of purpose, the initial despair giving way to a grim determination. The SS had sought to bury the truth, to consign it to oblivion, but he had countered their efforts by creating an even deeper, more profound burial. This was not surrender; it was a strategic retreat, a calculated move to preserve the very essence of what needed to be known. He was no longer just a fugitive; he was a custodian, a keeper of a secret that held the fate of worlds in its fragile, alien matrix.

His mind wrestled with the implications of his newfound solitude. The direct communion with the alien intelligence had been a profound experience, a glimpse into a consciousness far removed from human experience. Its insights had been invaluable, its guidance unerring. Now, that conduit was closed. He was left with the echoes of its wisdom, the vast library of knowledge stored within his own memory, and the lingering imprint of its directives. He had to learn to access this information independently, to decipher the complex conceptual blueprints and historical narratives without the immediate, intuitive assistance of his alien guide. It was a daunting task, akin to being given the key to an infinite library but being blindfolded and left to navigate its endless aisles.

He stopped by a clear mountain stream, cupping his hands to drink the frigid water. The reflection that stared back at him was a stranger's face – gaunt, etched with exhaustion, but with a new, steely resolve in the eyes. The man who had walked into the wilderness days ago was gone, replaced by someone forged in the crucible of necessity and burdened by an impossible truth. He had willingly shed the remnants of his past life, the comfortable illusions of normalcy, to embrace this solitary, perilous path. It was a farewell not just to a physical life, but to the very notion of a life free from this all-consuming mission.

The SS, he knew, would not cease their pursuit. They would scour every inch of this region, deploying every technological advantage, every agent, to reclaim what they believed was theirs. But he had given them a formidable challenge. The beacon was hidden in a place where their instruments of erasure would likely be rendered blind, a sanctuary woven into the very fabric of geological anomaly. This physical concealment was a crucial first step, but it was only the beginning of a much longer, more intricate game of survival and dissemination.

He needed to move, to put distance between himself and the hidden sanctuary. The SS might have advanced tracking capabilities, methods that could potentially triangulate his position even without direct contact. He had to become less of a target, more of a ghost, a whisper in the wind. His journey was not over; it had merely entered a new, more dangerous phase. He was a solitary vessel, carrying a cargo of incalculable worth, navigating a treacherous sea of surveillance and deception.

As he continued his descent, the vastness of the landscape seemed to mirror the immensity of his task. He was a single human being pitted against an overwhelming force, a force that sought not to conquer, but to *unmake*. The beacon represented hope, a chance for humanity to understand the true nature of the threat it faced and to prepare accordingly. But hope, he knew, was a fragile commodity, easily crushed by the relentless machinery of oblivion. He had to ensure that this hope, this vital knowledge, would survive, would spread, and would ultimately ignite a resistance that could counter the SS's insidious designs. The silence of the mountains was a stark reminder of the silence the SS enforced, and he resolved that this silence would not be the final word. He would find a way. He had to. The fate of more than just himself, perhaps more than just humanity, depended on it.

The granite gave way to softer earth underfoot as Falk descended, each step a conscious effort to become one with the wilderness that had so recently been his sanctuary. The silence of the mountaintop, once a confirmation of his success, now felt like a shroud. The hum of the alien beacon, a steady thrumming presence that had become as much a part of him as his own heartbeat, was gone. It was a void, an absence that resonated with a chilling finality. He had done it. He had buried the truth, not just physically, but conceptually, weaving its secret into the very sinews of the earth. But in silencing the beacon, he had also silenced the nascent, intuitive connection it had fostered. He was adrift again, navigating a sea of knowledge without a compass, without the quiet whispers of alien understanding that had guided him through the labyrinth of its secrets.

The SS, he knew, would not rest. Their pursuit was not a matter of mere policy; it was an obsession, a fundamental directive woven into the very fabric of their being. They hunted anomalies, erased deviations, and maintained a monolithic reality built on the bedrock of enforced ignorance. He was the ultimate anomaly, a living repository of a truth that threatened to unravel their meticulously constructed world. They would scour this region, their sophisticated sensors probing every crevice, their operatives a relentless tide against the natural defenses of the mountains. But he had anticipated this. The beacon's burial was not just an act of concealment; it was an act of camouflage. The geological formations, the specific magnetic anomalies of the region, the very silence he had imposed – these were designed to be a blindfold for their most advanced technology. He hoped, with a desperate fervor, that the silence would be enough.

His immediate objective was to put as much distance as possible between himself and the buried artifact. Remaining in the vicinity, however tempting it might be to revisit his creation, would be a cardinal error. Every moment spent here was a risk, a chance for a stray sensor sweep, a satellite anomaly, or a keen-eyed operative to pinpoint his location. He moved with a practiced stealth, his senses on high alert, interpreting the rustle of leaves, the snap of a twig, the distant cry of a hawk as potential threats. The world he had once known, the world of ordered cities and predictable routines, now seemed impossibly distant, a dream from another lifetime. His reality was a stark, unyielding present, defined by the constant hum of vigilance and the gnawing awareness of being hunted.

The weight of the knowledge he carried was a physical burden. It was not just the data itself – the historical records of the SS's origins, the true nature of Project Veil, the blueprints for the alien defense system – but the responsibility that came with it. He was the sole custodian of a truth that could either save humanity or condemn it. The beacon's silence meant that the direct, intuitive understanding of how to utilize its defensive capabilities was no longer readily available. He was left with the raw data, the complex schematics, the historical context, and the daunting task of piecing together the puzzle without the benefit of an alien mentor. He had to become the interpreter, the strategist, the one who could translate cosmic wisdom into actionable human strategy.

He thought of Tammy, her face a ghostly imprint in his memory. She represented everything the SS sought to extinguish: hope, defiance, a belief in something more than the sterile, controlled reality they imposed. Her memory was a spur, a constant reminder of why he was doing this. He could not afford to falter, to succumb to despair. The SS had perfected the art of erasure, not just of physical evidence, but of memory, of truth, of the very concept of dissent. The villages they wiped clean were not merely purged; they were unmade, their existence systematically excised from the collective consciousness. He was fighting not just against a military or a political organization, but against an existential force that sought to rewrite reality itself.

As he navigated the dense forest, his mind replayed the fragmented directives, the cryptic warnings, the vast historical narratives he had absorbed from the beacon. He had to find a way to disseminate this information, to awaken humanity to the peril it faced, without becoming another erased memory. The idea of directly confronting the SS was a suicidal fantasy. They were too powerful, too pervasive. His approach had to be subtler, more strategic. He needed allies, individuals or groups who operated outside the SS's direct control, those who valued truth above security, those who might be willing to listen to a madman with an impossible story. But in a world where information was curated, dissent was criminalized, and fear was the primary currency, such allies were as rare as hen's teeth.

He stopped by a small, gurgling stream, its water icy cold against his parched throat. As he drank, he caught a glimpse of his reflection in the rippling surface. The man staring back was gaunt, his eyes shadowed with exhaustion, but there was a new hardness in them, a glint of something unyielding. The fear was still there, a cold knot in his stomach, but it was now tempered by a grim determination. He had shed the remnants of his former life, the comfortable illusions of normalcy, and embraced the mantle of his mission. He was no longer just a man on the run; he was a guardian, a solitary sentinel tasked with protecting a truth that transcended individual survival.

The journey from the mountains was a descent into a different kind of wilderness – the urban sprawl, a landscape of concrete and surveillance where anonymity was a fleeting commodity. He had to blend in, to become invisible, to navigate the SS's omnipresent gaze without triggering any alarms. This was a different kind of hunting, a dance on the precipice of exposure. He knew his physical appearance had changed, his features etched by stress and the harshness of his recent experiences. He needed to alter his presentation, to shed the persona of the fugitive and adopt one that would allow him to move through the shadows of society undetected.

He found refuge in the anonymity of a transient existence,

moving from town to town, living on the fringes, always listening, always observing. He sought out places where information flowed freely, where the SS's grip was not absolute. Libraries, underground news networks, places where the disaffected gathered – these became his hunting grounds, not for food or shelter, but for whispers of resistance, for individuals who might share his burden. He learned to read the subtle cues, the coded language, the unspoken networks that existed beneath the veneer of SS control.

One such whisper led him to a dimly lit cantina in a port city, a place that reeked of stale ale and desperation. The air crackled with an undercurrent of defiance, the hushed conversations a testament to the SS's pervasive influence. He sat alone at a corner table, nursing a lukewarm drink, his senses attuned to the ebb and flow of the room. He was searching for a specific kind of person – someone with a look of quiet intensity, someone who carried the weight of unspoken knowledge.

His attention was drawn to a woman at a nearby table, her back to him, her posture radiating a weary vigilance. She was engrossed in a data pad, her fingers moving with a practiced efficiency. He had seen that look before, the subtle tension of someone constantly aware of their surroundings, of the unseen eyes that might be watching. He approached cautiously, his heart thrumming a nervous rhythm against his ribs.

"A dangerous place to be lost in thought," he said, his voice low and even, carefully modulated to avoid any hint of alarm.

The woman looked up, her eyes, a startling shade of amber, met his. There was no surprise in her gaze, only a flicker of keen assessment. She didn't flinch, didn't betray any outward sign of fear.

"Are you lost?" she replied, her voice a low contralto, equally measured.

"Perhaps," Falk conceded, leaning against the edge of her table. "Or perhaps I'm searching for something."

Her lips curved into a faint, almost imperceptible smile. "Most people in places like this are. The question is, what?"

He held her gaze, the unspoken question hanging in the air

between them. He was gambling, a desperate roll of the dice in a game where the stakes were astronomical. He needed to gauge her, to see if she was someone who could comprehend the magnitude of what he carried, someone who wouldn't immediately betray him to the SS.

"Truth," he said, the single word imbued with the weight of his entire ordeal. "The kind that doesn't fit neatly into their narrative."

Her amber eyes narrowed slightly, and for a fleeting moment, Falk felt a surge of dread. Had he misread her? Was this another trap, another meticulously orchestrated deception by the SS? But then, her gaze softened, a subtle shift that spoke volumes.

"Their narratives are carefully constructed," she said, her voice now carrying a hint of weariness, of shared understanding. "And easily fractured." She tapped the data pad. "I collect fragments."

This was it. This was the opening he had been searching for. He slid into the chair opposite her, the worn wood creaking beneath him. He knew the SS would have advanced surveillance, audio and visual, embedded throughout the city. This cantina, like so many other public spaces, was likely a node in their surveillance network. He had to tread carefully, to communicate without compromising himself or her.

"Fragments can paint a dangerous picture," Falk murmured, picking up a coaster and turning it over in his hands. "Especially when they point to something… alien."

The woman's breath hitched, a minuscule, almost imperceptible intake of air. Her gaze locked onto his, a silent confirmation that he had struck a chord. She knew. Or at least, she suspected. The fragments she collected weren't just random pieces of information; they were anomalies, inconsistencies, the faint echoes of a reality beyond the SS's control.

"The sky is not always what it seems," she replied, her words a poetic echo of his own internal struggle. "Sometimes, the stars are not stars at all."

This was a coded response, a recognition of a shared clandestine world. He felt a flicker of hope, a fragile ember in the vast darkness of his solitude. He still didn't know her name, her allegiances, or the full extent of her involvement in the hidden networks that opposed the SS. But he knew she understood the language of secrets, the necessity of operating in the shadows.

"My name is Falk," he said, offering his hand across the table.

She hesitated for a fraction of a second before extending her own. Her grip was firm, her touch surprisingly cool. "Call me Adele," she said, and the name, so familiar yet so impossibly new, resonated through him like a physical blow. It was a ghost, a shadow of the woman he had lost, but it was also a sign, a premonition.

"Adele," he repeated, the name tasting strange and familiar on his tongue. "I have something… significant. Something the SS wants buried deeper than any secret they've ever manufactured."

She inclined her head, her amber eyes holding his with an unwavering intensity. "I've always believed that the deepest secrets are the ones that can illuminate the future. Tell me, Falk. What fragments have you found?"

He began to speak, his voice a low murmur, weaving a tale of alien technology, of impending doom, of a meticulously crafted deception that had been centuries in the making. He spoke of the beacon, of its burial, and of the overwhelming silence that had followed. He spoke of the SS's ultimate weapon, Project Veil, and the devastating implications it held for humanity. He spoke of his own solitary journey, his escape, and his desperate need to find someone, anyone, who could help him carry this burden.

Adele listened, her expression unreadable, her gaze never wavering. She asked probing questions, her understanding of the technical and historical aspects of his narrative far exceeding his initial expectations. It was as if she had been waiting for this, as if the fragments she collected had been leading her to this very moment, to him.

"Project Veil," she mused, after he had finished speaking. "I've heard whispers. Anomalies in energy signatures, mass disappearances attributed to 'environmental shifts.' But nothing this concrete. Nothing with this… cosmic scope." She leaned forward, her voice dropping to a near whisper. "The SS believes they are the architects of humanity's destiny. They see themselves as curators, pruning away the imperfections, the deviations. But what they are actually doing is suffocating the future."

"And the beacon," Falk pressed, "can they detect its location?"

Adele shook her head. "Not the physical artifact. Its burial was too... profound. Too integrated. But the residual energetic imprint, the faint echoes of its transmission, that's what they'll be hunting. They'll be looking for a ghost in the machine, a glitch in their perfect system. And you, Falk, are that glitch."

He felt a chill spread through him. She understood. She grasped the scale of the threat, the insidious nature of the SS's control. This wasn't a fleeting moment of shared understanding; this was a nascent alliance, forged in the crucible of shared purpose.

"I need to get the information out," Falk stated, his voice firm. "The data from the beacon is too important to remain hidden. It's humanity's only chance to understand what we're up against, and how to fight it."

Adele nodded slowly, her amber eyes reflecting the dim, flickering lights of the cantina. "The SS controls the flow of information with an iron fist. Direct dissemination is impossible. We need to find a way to bypass their filters, to plant the seeds of truth where they can grow unhindered."

"But how?" Falk asked, the enormity of the task weighing on him. "How do you fight an enemy that controls every channel of communication, every source of information?"

"You find the cracks," Adele said, a determined glint in her eyes. "You find the people who are already questioning, the ones who are already looking for answers beyond the official narrative. You build networks, you create redundancies, you become the very 'glitch' you are." She paused, a thoughtful frown creasing her brow. "The beacon's signal, even muted, might have left an indelible imprint, a unique signature that the SS can't scrub from the digital ether. Perhaps... perhaps that's where we start."

Falk felt a surge of renewed hope. Adele was not just an ally;

she was a strategist, a tactician who understood the intricacies of the hidden war they were fighting. The isolation that had threatened to crush him was beginning to recede, replaced by the quiet strength of shared purpose. He was no longer alone in the shadows. He had found another who understood the language of oblivion, and who was willing to fight against it. The journey was far from over, but for the first time since silencing the beacon, Falk felt a genuine sense of possibility. The fight for humanity's future had just found its second guardian.

Chapter 11

The Long Silence

The echo of war receded, not with a triumphant fanfare, but with the hollow clang of destruction. Cities lay in skeletal remains; their once proud structures reduced to piles of rubble and ash. The skies, once ripped apart by the guttural roar of engines and the shriek of falling ordnance, were now eerily silent, save for the mournful sigh of the wind whistling through shattered windows. It was an end, of sorts, but an end that offered little in the way of solace. For Falk, the cessation of hostilities merely marked the beginning of a new, more insidious kind of conflict – the war of the hidden, the ongoing struggle against a pervasive ideology that refused to die, even in death.

He moved through the ravaged landscape like a phantom, a wraith amongst the ruins. His existence had become a perpetual state of evasion, a ceaseless pilgrimage through the wreckage of a world he no longer fully recognized. The years since the silencing of the beacon had blurred into a monotonous cycle of displacement. Each new dawn brought with it the dread of discovery, the gnawing certainty that the SS, or remnants thereof, would eventually unearth his secret, or worse, his very existence. He was a walking paradox, a man burdened by knowledge that could shatter the fragile peace but incapable of revealing it without precipitating his own annihilation.

The fragmented memories, a relentless barrage of sights and sounds that clawed at the edges of his consciousness, served as his constant, unwelcome companions. He saw the camps, the sterile efficiency of dehumanization, the vacant stares of those who had been stripped of everything but their last breath. He heard the chilling pronouncements, the warped justifications for unspeakable cruelty, the chillingly calm pronouncements of racial purity and

241

manifest destiny. These memories were not just echoes of the past; they were the very fabric of his present, a scar tissue that prevented any true healing, any genuine connection with the world around him.

He learned to become a creature of the shadows, adept at melting into the anonymity of overcrowded refugee camps, the anonymous bustle of newly erected transit centers, the desperate anonymity of those who had lost everything but the will to survive. He adopted a myriad of aliases, each one a temporary shield against the pervasive gaze of those who might still be searching. He became a master of reinvention, his past shed like a worn-out skin, his identity as fluid and ephemeral as smoke. But the truth, the weight of what he carried, remained stubbornly immutable, a leaden anchor dragging him down into the depths of his isolation.

The allure of Adele's amber eyes, her whispered understanding in that smoky cantina, had been a beacon in the encroaching darkness, a fleeting glimpse of a shared humanity. But the harsh realities of his existence had swiftly extinguished that nascent spark. The networks she spoke of, the subtle cracks in the SS's iron grip, proved elusive, mere whispers in the cacophony of a shattered world. The SS, even in its fractured state, was a hydra, its heads regenerating with a terrifying tenacity. Every attempted connection, every hesitant outreach, felt like a dangerous gamble, a risk of exposing himself and, more importantly, the unfathomable truth he guarded.

He found work where he could – hauling rubble, scrubbing floors in hastily erected medical facilities, laboring in fields reclaimed from the chaos. The anonymity was a balm, the physical exertion a distraction from the ceaseless churning of his thoughts. He observed, he listened, always sifting through the detritus of conversations, the hushed rumors, the paranoid whispers that spoke of continuing SS activity, of clandestine networks, of a shadow war fought in the liminal spaces of a defeated nation. He was searching for Adele, for the promise of a shared purpose, but more than that, he was searching for a crack, a vulnerability, a way to begin the monumental task of disseminating the beacon's truth.

The sheer scale of the SS's ideological reach was a chilling revelation. Even with their infrastructure in tatters, their leadership scattered or executed, the poisonous tendrils of their propaganda and their unwavering belief in their own twisted vision remained deeply entrenched. They operated in cells, in whispered conversations, in the clandestine distribution of forbidden literature. Their ideology was a virus, mutated and resilient, capable of infecting even in the absence of a visible host. Falk understood that confronting them directly was an act of futility. His objective had to be more nuanced, more insidious: to sow seeds of truth in the fertile ground of doubt, to awaken the world to the precipice upon which it teetered.

He moved south, drawn by the faint, almost imperceptible hum of activity that seemed to emanate from the fringes of established society. He was no longer simply running; he was navigating, searching for the currents that flowed beneath the surface of official narratives. The beacon's silence had robbed him of its direct guidance, its intuitive whispers, but it had also honed his own senses, forcing him to rely on the raw data, the historical context, the fragmented directives that had been imprinted upon his mind. He was the curator of a lost history, the sole interpreter of an alien warning, and the burden of that responsibility was a constant, crushing weight.

One rain-slicked evening, seeking refuge in a derelict train station on the outskirts of a provincial town, he overheard a hushed conversation. Two men, their faces etched with weariness and a shared desperation, spoke in low tones, their words laced with a potent mix of defiance and fear. They spoke of "the legacy," of keeping the "true narrative" alive, of a network that operated in the shadows, circumventing the pervasive censorship and the lingering influence of the SS. Falk's heart quickened. This was it. This was the first tangible sign, the first flicker of the alliance he had so desperately sought.

He approached them with caution, his movements deliberately unthreatening. "Looking for a way out of this mess?" he ventured, his voice carefully pitched to convey weariness rather than suspicion.

The men eyed him warily, their hands instinctively tightening on the worn satchels they carried. One of them, a burly man with a scarred face, spoke, his voice a low growl. "Depends on what you mean by 'out'."

Falk met his gaze, his own eyes reflecting the dim light of a flickering gas lamp. "Out of the lies. Out of the fear. Out of the shadow of the SS."

The other man, leaner and with a sharper, more intelligent gaze, stepped forward slightly. "You talk like you know something, stranger."

"I know enough to know that the war isn't truly over," Falk replied, the words a carefully calibrated blend of truth and evasion. "And that those who created it aren't willing to let go." He paused, choosing his next words with extreme care. "I've been... looking for people who understand that. People who are trying to do something about it."

There was a long, charged silence. The scarred man exchanged a glance with his companion, a silent conversation passing between them. Then, the leaner man gave a slight nod. "What kind of 'something' are you talking about?"

Falk felt a surge of adrenaline, the thrill of a hunter catching the scent of its prey, or perhaps, more accurately, the feeling of a lost traveler finally finding a landmark. He knew the risks, the potential for betrayal, but the beacon's silence had forced his hand. He could no longer afford the luxury of absolute isolation. He had to trust, or the truth would die with him.

"I'm talking about the truth," Falk said, his voice low and intense. "The kind of truth that the SS tried to bury, the kind that would make their entire existence a lie. I'm talking about something... alien. Something that changes everything."

The leaner man's eyes widened, a flicker of recognition, or perhaps, disbelief. "Alien?" he echoed, a hint of incredulity in his tone.

"The SS didn't just fight a war on Earth," Falk continued, his voice barely above a whisper. "They were fighting to keep something else hidden. Something that could protect us from them. Or from something far worse." He saw the doubt in their eyes, the ingrained skepticism born of years of propaganda and disillusionment. He needed to offer something more concrete, yet without revealing the full extent of his secret. "I have information. Data. Evidence that the SS's entire narrative is a carefully constructed façade."

The scarred man scoffed, but the leaner man held Falk's gaze, a profound curiosity beginning to dawn in his expression. "Evidence of what, exactly?"

"Of a hidden history," Falk replied, his mind racing, searching for the right metaphor. "Of a threat that predates humanity's own conflicts. The SS knew about it. They tried to control it. And when they couldn't, they tried to erase it. And me."

The leaner man remained silent for a moment, his brow furrowed in thought. "You speak of things that sound like... like madness," he finally said, his voice laced with a weary skepticism. "The SS preyed on people's fears, their superstitions. They fabricated enemies to consolidate their power."

"And what if their greatest fear, their most fabricated enemy, was actually real?" Falk countered, leaning in slightly. "What if the very thing they tried to hide was the key to understanding the true nature of their war, and the true nature of our reality?" He knew he was walking a tightrope, but the memory of Adele's amber eyes, of her promise of fractured narratives, spurred him on. He needed to find the cracks, and these men, or the network they represented, might be the first fissure.

"We have a network," the leaner man said, his voice now more measured, more deliberate. "We share what we can. We question what we're told. But 'alien'... that's a leap, even for us."

"It's a leap that has to be made," Falk insisted, his gaze unwavering. "The SS wasn't just fighting for dominion over Earth. They were trying to control something that could either save us or destroy us. And they failed." He felt the familiar weight of the beacon's silence pressing down on him, the vastness of its secrets a stark contrast to the desperate, grounded reality of his present situation. "They buried the truth, and I've... recovered it. But I can't carry it alone. And I can't fight their remnants alone."

The scarred man grumbled something unintelligible, but the leaner man extended a hand, not in greeting, but in a gesture of hesitant acknowledgment. "My name is Leo," he said. "And this is my associate, Maximilian or Max for short." Leo paused, "If you're telling the truth, and if this 'truth' of yours is what we suspect, then you're in more danger than you realize. And so are we."

Falk accepted the offered hand, his grip firm but brief. "I know the risks, Leo. I've been living them for years. But the SS, in their arrogance, believed they could simply erase inconvenient truths. They were wrong." He met Leo's steady gaze. "I am Falk. And I have a story to tell that will rewrite everything they've ever taught us."

The promise of Adele, however distant, now felt a little closer. He had found a thread, a fragile connection in the vast tapestry of a world still reeling from war and shrouded in deceit. The years of evasion had been a testament to his survival, but now, he had to transition from mere survival to active resistance. The long silence of the beacon had been a period of forced introspection, of absorbing the weight of his solitary burden. But that silence was about to be broken, not by a grand pronouncement, but by the quiet, determined whispers of those willing to listen to the impossible. The true war, the war for humanity's future, had just begun to find its scattered soldiers. The fragmented memories, once a source of paralyzing dread, were slowly beginning to transform into the very weapons he needed to wield. He was no longer just a fugitive; he was a harbinger, a bearer of truths that would shake the foundations of the SS's manufactured reality.

The world, or what was left of it, was indeed rebuilding. The skeletal remains of cities were being painstakingly pieced back together, not always with the same grandeur, but with a desperate, pragmatic resilience. New nations were asserting their sovereignty, redrawing borders that had been violently distorted by years of conflict. The roar of engines was returning to the skies, though these were the engines of trade and transport, a stark contrast to the instruments of death that had previously dominated the atmosphere. Yet, beneath this veneer of renewed order, Falk knew the truth was far more unsettling. The war had ended, but the fundamental nature of the threat had not. It had merely mutated, burrowed deeper, its tendrils reaching into the very foundations of this fragile new world.

The SS, as a unified, overt military force, was gone. Its leadership was either dead, imprisoned, or in hiding. But the ideology, the warped vision that had consumed a generation, was a hydra with many heads. It festered in the shadows, whispered in hushed tones in clandestine meetings, and survived in the hearts of those who still clung to the perverse promises of power and purity. Falk saw its manifestations everywhere: in the lingering suspicion between populations, in the resurgence of nationalist fervor in unexpected corners, and most disturbingly, in the continued silence surrounding certain aspects of the war. The official narratives, carefully curated by the victorious powers, spoke of liberation, of the defeat of tyranny. But they conveniently glossed over the more unsettling truths, the experiments, the technological advancements born from morally bankrupt pursuits, and the chilling implications of Project Veil.

Project Veil. The very name sent a shiver down Falk's spine, a visceral reminder of the existential dread that had permeated his existence since he'd first encountered its remnants. It was more than a codename; it was a tombstone for countless lives, a monument to the hubris of a regime that had dared to tamper with forces it could neither comprehend nor control. The Third Reich's obsession with the esoteric, their relentless quest for weapons that transcended conventional warfare, had led them down a path from which there was no return. They had sought to weaponize the very fabric of reality, to unlock powers that belonged to the cosmos, not to a single, albeit fanatical, nation. And in their desperate final days, they had been on the precipice of unleashing something catastrophic.

Falk had witnessed firsthand the chilling legacy of their work. The data he carried, painstakingly extracted from compromised SS archives and the desperate pleas of those who had been part of the project, painted a terrifying picture. It wasn't just about advanced weaponry or biological warfare; it was about something far more profound, far more alien. The SS had made contact, or at least, they believed they had. They had interpreted signals, deciphered fragments of what they believed to be ancient, extraterrestrial knowledge, and had attempted to harness it. Project Veil was their attempt to control, or perhaps even to weaponize, this discovered phenomenon. The true nature of this "alien" element remained

247

shrouded in mystery, a void that Falk was desperately trying to fill.

The aftermath of the war had seen a swift and brutal dismantling of many overt SS facilities. The victorious Allied powers, eager to secure any technological advantage and to erase the physical manifestations of Nazi atrocities, had conducted extensive sweeps. Yet, Falk knew this was largely a superficial cleansing. The true repositories of knowledge, the most dangerous research, had been meticulously hidden, compartmentalized, and dispersed. The SS had anticipated defeat, and they had planned accordingly. They had created a decentralized network, a ghost organization designed to survive the collapse and to continue their work in the shadows. Project Veil was their ultimate prize, and its secrets were the very currency of their continued existence. Leo and Max, the men Falk had met in that derelict train station, were part of a nascent resistance, a network of individuals who were beginning to question the official narratives. They were academics, disillusioned soldiers, former intelligence operatives, and ordinary citizens who had glimpsed the truth behind the propaganda and refused to accept the sanitized version of history. They operated with a desperate stealth, communicating through encrypted messages, dead drops, and clandestine meetings in the most unexpected places. Falk had cautiously revealed fragments of his knowledge to them, enough to spark their curiosity and, more importantly, their fear.

"They didn't just lose the war, Falk," Leo had said, his voice low and grave, during one of their tense exchanges in a dimly lit Parisian basement. They had been discussing the latest rumors of SS resurgence, of strange energy readings detected in remote Alpine regions, of coded transmissions intercepted from what were believed to be defunct Nazi communication hubs. "They merely retreated. And their most dangerous work was never about conquering nations. It was about something else entirely."

Max had added, "We've intercepted chatter about 'recalibration,' about 'containment failures.' It sounds like technical jargon, but the context suggests something... significant. Something they were trying to fix, or perhaps, prevent from escaping."

Falk listened, his mind piecing together their fragmented intel with the vast repository of information he carried. He explained, as best he could without revealing the full, mind-bending truth of the beacon, that the SS's obsession with alien technology was not a mere byproduct of their occult leanings. It was a central tenet of their ultimate agenda. They believed that by understanding and controlling this extraterrestrial influence, they could achieve a form of cosmic dominance, a victory that would transcend earthly conflicts. Project Veil was the culmination of this belief, an attempt to integrate this alien power into their military structure.

The implications were staggering. If the SS had indeed managed to harness, even in part, the energies or technologies associated with Project Veil, then their defeat on the conventional battlefield was merely a temporary setback. They could still possess a weapon, or a means of influence, that could dwarf any existing military might. The "long silence" wasn't just about the lack of communication from Falk's beacon; it was also about the deliberate silencing of the truth about Project Veil. The victorious powers, while hunting down the remnants of the SS, had also made a calculated decision to bury the truth about this particular aspect of their research. The potential for global panic, the destabilizing effect of revealing humanity's vulnerability to extraterrestrial forces or technologies, had been deemed too great a risk.

This meant that Falk and his nascent network were operating in a vacuum, fighting an enemy that was not only still active but also had the tacit complicity of silence from those who should have been its greatest adversaries. The world was rebuilding, yes, but it was rebuilding on a foundation of ignorance, blissfully unaware of the true nature of the threat that had been narrowly averted, and that might still be lurking. The echoes of war were indeed receding, but the true horror was not in the destruction left behind, but in the secrets that had been deliberately interred, secrets that now threatened to resurface and unravel the fragile peace.

The data Falk possessed was fragmented, like shards of a shattered mirror, each reflecting a terrifying glimpse of a larger, more horrific reality. He spoke of anomalous energy signatures, of advanced propulsion systems that defied known physics, of biological modifications that blurred the lines between human and... something else. He described intercepted communications that spoke of "dimensional breaches," of "cosmic resonance," and of the SS's fervent belief in a coming "galactic ascension." These weren't the ravings of madmen; they were the cold, calculated notes of scientists and engineers pushed to the brink of understanding, their minds warped by the very secrets they sought to exploit.

Leo and Max listened with a mixture of awe and trepidation. They had dedicated their lives to uncovering hidden truths, to fighting against oppression and misinformation, but the scale of what Falk was hinting at was almost incomprehensible. The SS had not just waged war on humanity; they had, in their twisted ambition, reached out to touch the stars, and in doing so, had potentially opened a Pandora's Box that could never be closed.

"So, the SS were not just trying to conquer the world," Leo mused, his gaze distant as if trying to grasp the immensity of Falk's words. "They were trying to conquer... reality itself. And Project Veil was their key."

"More than that," Falk corrected, his voice heavy with the weight of his knowledge. "They were trying to seize control of something that was already here. Something that existed long before them, and will exist long after. They saw it as a weapon, a tool for their dominion. But it's something far more fundamental." He paused, searching for words that could convey the ineffable nature of what he had learned from the beacon. "It's a force, Leo. A force that the SS attempted to harness, to control, and ultimately, to weaponize. And in their hubris, they nearly unleashed a consequence that would have been far worse than any conventional war."

The implications for the rebuilding world were chilling. The Allied powers, in their pursuit of Nazi technology, might have inadvertently stumbled upon, or even acquired, fragments of Project Veil. The very technologies that were now powering this new era of progress could be tainted, holding within them the seeds of a far greater danger. The war had been fought against a human enemy, but the true conflict, Falk realized with a dawning horror, was against something far older, far more powerful, and utterly indifferent to the fate of humanity. The SS had been a mere conduit, a fanatical cult that had stumbled upon a power that could either elevate or annihilate them, and in their arrogance, they had chosen annihilation for everyone.

The task ahead was monumental. Falk and his network were not just fighting the scattered remnants of the SS; they were fighting a hidden war against an unknown entity and against the deliberate ignorance of the world's rebuilding powers. The long silence of his beacon had been a period of profound isolation, but it had also been a time of intense learning, of absorbing the gravity of the threat. Now, he had to translate that burden into action, to find allies, to disseminate the truth, and to prevent the shadows of Project Veil from engulfing this fragile, newly constructed world. The silence was no longer an option; it was a death sentence. The past, it seemed, was not merely a series of events to be learned from, but a terrifying force that was actively seeking to repeat itself, armed with a power that humanity had only begun to comprehend.

The presence within Falk was less a distinct entity and more a pervasive hum, a resonance that vibrated just beneath the surface of his own thoughts. It was the echo of something vast and incomprehensible, an intelligence that had, in the desperate throes of Project Veil, found an unwilling vessel. It had been a forced communion, a hijacking of Falk's very being, and in the years that followed, through the agonizing silence and the subsequent, chaotic rebirth of the world, it had subtly reconfigured itself. It wasn't a parasite in the traditional sense; it offered no tangible benefit, no whispered secrets of the universe to unlock his potential. Instead, it was a constant, unblinking awareness, a detached observer imprinted upon his consciousness.

He felt it most acutely during moments of quiet contemplation, when the cacophony of the rebuilding world – the distant hammering, the rumble of new construction, the chatter of returning commerce – faded into a low thrum. It was then that the alien consciousness would make its presence known, not with words, but with a subtle shift in his perception, a sharpening of focus that cut through the mundane. It was as if a secondary, hyper-aware layer of his own mind had been activated, one that processed information with an alien, inhuman efficiency. This layer never offered opinions or judgments; it simply *observed*, cataloging the world around Falk with an unnerving impartiality.

This internal presence served as an immutable anchor to the truth of what had transpired. While the world rushed forward, eager to forget the horrors of the war and the more esoteric, terrifying aspects of the SS's final gambits, Falk could not. The alien consciousness was a constant, silent reminder of the existential threat that had been narrowly averted. It was the residue of humanity's brush with something profoundly other, a stark counterpoint to the sanitized histories that were being painstakingly constructed. It ensured that the memory of Project Veil, and the terrifying potential it represented, was never truly dimmed in his own mind.

He found himself observing the rebuilding process with a dual perspective. His own human mind, scarred by his experiences, registered the progress, the resilience, the desperate hope that fueled the construction crews and the politicians. He saw the tangible signs of recovery, the return of normalcy, the rebuilding of infrastructure. But simultaneously, the alien presence within him filtered this reality through its own unique lens. It registered the subtle anomalies, the faint energy signatures that even the most advanced post-war detection systems seemed to miss. It noted the patterns of human behavior with an objective fascination, dissecting motivations and societal shifts with an almost clinical detachment.

This internal observer was a constant, unnerving companion. It never intruded with direct commands or suggestions, but its presence meant that Falk was never truly alone with his thoughts. It was as if a part of him was perpetually externalized, observing his own internal landscape and the external world with equal intensity. This created a unique form of vigilance, a heightened awareness that prevented complacency. The SS, in their monstrous ambition, had sought to wield a power beyond human comprehension, and while their regime had been shattered, the implications of their pursuit remained. The alien consciousness was the silent testament to that dangerous endeavor.

He often wondered about its origin, its purpose, its true nature. The SS had theorized about ancient intelligences, about cosmic entities, about forces that predated humanity and would outlast it.

They had interpreted fragmented signals, dreamt of galactic dominion, and in their hubris, had attempted to force a connection, to bend this unknown power to their will. Project Veil had been their colossal, cataclysmic attempt. And in the process, a sliver of that something had been irrevocably imprinted upon Falk. Was it a fragment of the intelligence itself, a sliver of its awareness that had been inadvertently captured? Or was it something else entirely – a resonance, an imprint left behind by the violent interaction, a ghost in the machine of his own psyche?

The symbiosis, if it could be called that, was deeply unsettling. It was a constant reminder of his own vulnerability, of how easily the fabric of reality could be torn, how readily humanity could stumble into forces that it was utterly unprepared to face. The alien consciousness was a silent witness to this precarious existence, an internal arbiter of truth that could never be swayed by propaganda or political expediency. While governments spoke of peace and reconstruction, Falk felt the subtle, persistent hum of the unknown, a quiet counterpoint to the clamor of the new world.

He found that this internal presence had a peculiar effect on his own mental faculties. It was as if his already sharp mind, honed by years of clandestine work and survival, had been further refined. His intuition felt sharper, almost preternatural. He could sense shifts in atmosphere, unspoken tensions, the hidden undercurrents of human interaction, with an uncanny accuracy. It was as if the alien consciousness, in its detached observation, was subtly enhancing his own observational capabilities, amplifying his innate human instincts with something… more.

This enhancement, however, came at a cost. The constant, passive observation could be draining. There were times when Falk felt overwhelmed, as if his own thoughts were being diluted by the sheer immensity of the internal presence. It was like trying to hold a single candle flame steady in a hurricane of cosmic starlight. He had to actively assert his own identity, to focus on his own thoughts and memories, to push back against the pervasive awareness that threatened to engulf him. This internal struggle was a daily, sometimes hourly, battle for his own mental sovereignty.

The SS, in their relentless pursuit of power, had been blind to the true nature of what they were meddling with. They saw it as a resource, a weapon to be exploited. They had no inkling of the true implications of such a communion, the profound and potentially irreversible changes it could wreak upon a human mind. Falk's experience was a testament to their terrifying shortsightedness, a living embodiment of the unintended consequences of their hubris.

He had learned to live with it, to incorporate it into his existence. It was a part of him now, as integral as his own memories. He couldn't simply excise it; any attempt to do so, he suspected, would be catastrophic, potentially shattering his mind entirely. So, he endured, he observed, and he remembered. The alien consciousness within him was the ultimate secret, the one secret that he could never reveal, not even to his most trusted allies like Leo and Max. How could he explain that a part of him was... not entirely human? That his enhanced awareness, his uncanny intuition, was not solely the product of his own experience but a consequence of a forced, extraterrestrial imprint?

It was a profound isolation, a loneliness that no amount of human company could ever assuage. He carried the burden of knowledge, yes, but he also carried the burden of an internal reality that was fundamentally alien. The world was rebuilding, striving for a semblance of normalcy, and Falk was a ghost within that rebuilt world, haunted not by the past, but by an ever-present, internal echo of something from beyond. This echo ensured that he remained vigilant, a silent guardian against a threat that the world had largely forgotten, or had deliberately chosen to ignore.

The very nature of this presence was a constant source of speculation. Was it a consciousness in the human sense, with awareness, intention, and perhaps even emotion? Or was it something more abstract, a force of nature, a fundamental aspect of the universe that the SS had mistakenly interpreted as an entity? Falk's own experiences offered no definitive answers. He felt its awareness, its capacity to observe and process, but he detected no discernible emotional resonance. It was a pure, unadulterated consciousness, devoid of the messy, complex tapestry of human feeling.

He sometimes wondered if this detachment was a form of protection. In its alien indifference, it might be shielding him from the full horror of what had occurred, from the sheer terror that a truly aware and malevolent alien intelligence might have inflicted. Or perhaps its lack of discernible emotion was simply a reflection of its fundamental difference from humanity, a testament to a form of existence so far removed from human comprehension as to be unimaginable.

The data he possessed from the SS archives, the fragmented transmissions he had intercepted, spoke of theories, of hypotheses, of desperate attempts to categorize and understand what they had stumbled upon. They had labeled it with various designations, each more esoteric than the last, attempting to fit it into their existing frameworks of occultism and pseudoscience. But the truth, as Falk was beginning to suspect, was far simpler and far more terrifying: it was beyond categorization. It was simply *there*, a fundamental aspect of the cosmos, and the SS had merely been the first humans to blunder into its proximity.

This realization only deepened the sense of responsibility that weighed upon him. He was not just fighting a residual threat from a defeated enemy; he was acting as an unwitting intermediary, a bridge between humanity and something it was not yet ready to comprehend. The alien consciousness within him was a constant, silent reminder of this immense, unasked-for burden. It ensured that he could never afford to be complacent, never allow the world to drift back into ignorance, blissfully unaware of the forces that lay beyond the veil of their perceived reality.

He found himself constantly analyzing his own thoughts, trying to discern which were truly his and which were subtle nudges or influences from the presence. It was an impossible task, a constant epistemological battle. He had to trust his own instincts, his own reasoned deductions, while remaining aware that his internal landscape was no longer solely his own. This existential uncertainty was perhaps the most insidious aspect of his forced communion.

The symbiosis had also granted him an unexpected clarity of purpose. While others focused on rebuilding cities and economies, Falk's focus remained fixed on a far grander, far more terrifying objective. He understood that true security for humanity would only come when it acknowledged and understood the existence of forces beyond its current comprehension. Project Veil was not an isolated incident; it was a symptom of humanity's perennial struggle with the unknown, a struggle that, in the atomic age, had taken on an existential dimension. The alien consciousness within him was a constant, silent witness to this ongoing struggle, a stark reminder that the greatest threats were often the ones that remained unseen, unheard, and utterly alien. It was a reminder that the long silence was not just a period of absence, but a crucial period of learning, a period where the boundaries of human understanding had been irrevocably, and terrifyingly, expanded.

The damp earth clung to Falk's boots, each step a deliberate intrusion into a silence that felt almost sacred, or perhaps, more accurately, intentionally imposed. The Black Forest, or what remained of its outer edges accessible to him, was a tapestry of verdant regrowth, a defiant assertion of nature's persistent reclamation. Yet, beneath the verdant facade, a palpable stillness permeated the air, a stillness that spoke not of natural repose, but of a meticulously curated absence. Falk adjusted the worn leather strap of his satchel, its contents a familiar weight against his side. He moved with the practiced stealth of a ghost, a man intimately familiar with the art of being present yet unseen, a skill honed by years of navigating shadows both literal and existential.

His purpose here was a ritual of sorts, a necessary penance. The echoes of Project Veil, the cataclysmic collision of human ambition and cosmic unknown, were still too raw, too vivid in his mind to allow for complete detachment. The alien presence, that subtle, ever-watchful hum within him, offered no specific guidance for this particular pilgrimage, only a detached, almost clinical observation of his own actions. It was Falk's burden to carry, his responsibility to ensure that the terrifying genesis of his internal companion was truly interred, buried beneath layers of soil and official obfuscation.

He'd chosen his route carefully, deliberately avoiding the more populated pathways that skirted the forest's edge. The air, thick with the scent of pine and damp leaf litter, was a stark contrast to the sterile, ozone-tinged air of the SS command bunkers where his ordeal had reached its brutal crescendo. Here, the only sounds were the rustle of unseen creatures in the undergrowth, the distant call of a bird, and the steady rhythm of his own breathing. It was a deceptive tranquility, a carefully constructed tableau designed to lull any observer into believing in the simple, untroubled continuity of nature.

His objective was the sector, the precise coordinates etched into his memory with the searing intensity of a brand. The SS, in their desperate, Machiavellian fervor, had been thorough in their efforts to erase all evidence of the crash. But thoroughness, Falk had learned, was a relative term. They had scrubbed the surface, yes, but the deeper scars, the energetic residues, the subtle deformations in the very fabric of reality – these were far more difficult to erase entirely. And it was for these deeper scars he searched.

As he ventured deeper, the trees seemed to press in, their ancient branches interlaced, filtering the midday sun into dappled, shifting patterns on the forest floor. He paused, tilting his head, his senses – amplified by the alien presence within, yet anchored by his own human intuition – straining for any anomaly. A flicker of unnatural light? A faint, disembodied hum that didn't belong to the forest's natural symphony? He cataloged the subtle shifts in atmospheric pressure, the minute variations in the ambient electromagnetic fields, data points that his own conscious mind might not readily register but that the presence within him processed with effortless precision.

He reached a clearing, a small, circular expanse where the trees seemed to have recoiled, as if from an unseen wound. This was it. The ground here felt different, less yielding, with a peculiar firmness that resisted the natural decay of fallen leaves. He knelt, his gloved fingers tracing the contours of the earth. There was no crater, no scorched earth, no debris. The SS had done their work with brutal efficiency. They had meticulously excavated, removed, and likely incinerated every fragment of the alien craft, every trace of its presence, leaving behind a void that was itself a testament to their desperate attempts at concealment.

Falk systematically scanned the area. He produced a small, cylindrical device from his satchel, its casing a dull, utilitarian grey. It hummed faintly as he activated it, its needle-thin sensor probing the air, the soil, anything that might betray the lingering energetic signature of the alien technology. He moved in a slow, deliberate spiral, the device held steady, his gaze fixed on the oscillating needle. Minutes stretched into an eternity, each sweep of the sensor yielding the same discouraging result: nothing.

The silence from the device was more deafening than any alarm. It was a complete negation, a void of data that spoke volumes about the SS's success. They had not only buried the physical evidence, they had seemingly managed to neutralize, or at least, obliterate, any residual energetic imprint. It was a chilling testament to their understanding of the technology they had so disastrously sought to harness. They had, in their own twisted way, become masters of eradication.

He stood, a familiar wave of frustration washing over him. He had expected this, of course. Hope was a dangerous commodity in his line of work, a fragile bloom easily crushed by the unforgiving realities of his past. Yet, a part of him, the part that still clung to the vestiges of his former self, always harbored a flicker of anticipation, a quiet prayer that perhaps, just perhaps, a single, undeniable trace would remain. A whisper of the truth that the world so eagerly sought to forget.

The alien consciousness within him offered no commentary, no comfort, no disappointment. It simply *observed* his actions, his internal state, his growing sense of futility. It was like watching a scientist meticulously examine a sterile petri dish, cataloging the absence of life with the same dispassionate interest as it would the presence of a new strain.

He moved to the periphery of the clearing, pushing aside thick ferns and tangled undergrowth, searching for any subtle disruptions in the natural order. A strangely shaped rock, an unnaturally straight line of moss, a patch of soil that refused to yield to the forest's organic processes. His eyes, trained by years of looking for the hidden, the camouflaged, the deliberately obscured, swept across the terrain. He found only the relentless uniformity of the Black Forest, a testament to nature's power to absorb and erase even the most profound of violations.

He spent hours there, meticulously examining every inch of the ground, his senses on high alert. He even dared to venture a little further into the denser parts of the forest, the shadows deepening, the canopy becoming a near-impenetrable ceiling. He found no anomalies, no lingering whispers of extraterrestrial technology, no physical proof that the SS had ever conducted their catastrophic experiments in this secluded corner of the world. It was as if the entire incident, the seizure of the alien artifact, the desperate attempts to understand and weaponize it, the final, cataclysmic event that had branded him, had been nothing more than a fevered dream.

The official silence surrounding the events of the war, particularly the final, desperate gambits of the SS, had been more profound than Falk had anticipated. The victors, eager to establish a narrative of triumph and a swift return to normalcy, had worked diligently to sanitize the past. The more esoteric, the more unsettling, the more potentially destabilizing aspects of the conflict were either buried deep within classified archives or simply dismissed as wartime propaganda, the raving pronouncements of a defeated enemy.

Project Veil, with its implications of extraterrestrial technology and mind-altering encounters, was precisely the kind of truth that governments and populations alike preferred to ignore. It threatened to unravel the comfortable illusion of human exceptionalism, to expose humanity to a universe far vaster and far more terrifying than anyone was prepared to acknowledge.

Falk's repeated clandestine visits to the Black Forest were not just about seeking physical evidence. They were about confronting the pervasive silence, about validating his own experiences against the carefully constructed amnesia of the world. Each fruitless search was a confirmation of the SS's success, a testament to the ruthlessness with which they had sought to cover their tracks. But it was also, paradoxically, a reinforcement of the truth of his own ordeal. If they had to work so hard to erase it, it meant that it had indeed happened.

He encountered no patrols, no curious foresters, no evidence that his presence had been noted. The SS's meticulous scrubbing of the site extended to its surrounding areas, ensuring that any accidental discovery would be met with the bewildered testimony of an undisturbed natural landscape. It was as if the forest itself had been sworn to secrecy, its ancient trees and silent streams complicit in the grand deception.

As the sun began its slow descent, casting long, ethereal shadows through the trees, Falk knew it was time to leave. He gathered his equipment, the silence of the forest now a heavy cloak of disillusionment. He had found nothing, as he had expected. No lingering energy signatures, no physical artifacts, no subtle distortions that would betray the alien presence. The SS had been chillingly effective. The crash site, the focal point of humanity's catastrophic encounter with the unknown, was indistinguishable from any other patch of untamed wilderness.

He turned, his gaze sweeping one last time across the clearing. The trees stood sentinel, their branches reaching skyward, indifferent to the secrets they held, or rather, the secrets they had been forced to surrender. The official narrative had won, at least here, in the physical realm. The tangible proof of Project Veil had been systematically dismantled, leaving behind only the echoes in his own mind, the silent, unblinking witness that resided within his consciousness.

The journey back was a quiet one, the rhythmic crunch of his boots on the forest floor a counterpoint to the hum of the alien presence. He carried with him not a discovery, but a confirmation of absence. The SS had erased the physical evidence, but they had, in doing so, inadvertently underscored the undeniable reality of what had transpired. The more they sought to bury the truth, the more it became an indelible part of Falk's own existence. He was the living archive, the repository of a history that the world desperately wished to forget, a history written not in ink, but in the very fibers of his being.

He emerged from the tree line as dusk began to settle, the first stars beginning to prick the darkening sky. The world outside the forest was already stirring with the familiar sounds of returning civilization, a stark contrast to the profound silence he had just left. He blended back into the encroaching night, a solitary figure carrying a secret that the forest, in its vast, indifferent beauty, had so effectively concealed. The silence of the woods was complete, a perfect testament to the SS's meticulous work, and Falk, though he had found nothing tangible, carried the weight of that perfect, terrifying silence with him, a silent promise to never let the memory truly fade. The absence of clues was, in itself, a profound clue to the depth of the cover-up.

The solitude Falk cultivated was not a choice born of preference, but a necessity forged in the crucible of his experiences. The world, he had learned, was not equipped to handle the truth of Project Veil. Not truly. They could digest the sanitized versions, the watered-down accounts of SS hubris and technological overreach, but the profound, universe-altering implications of his encounters, the chilling reality of an alien presence both within and without, that was a truth too vast, too terrifying to be disseminated. To speak it aloud, to attempt to articulate the alien resonance that pulsed beneath his skin, the silent sentience that had become an integral part of his being, would be to invite disbelief, ridicule, or worse, a desperate, misguided attempt to dissect and contain him. He was a walking anomaly, a living testament to a history that the victors had meticulously erased.

The Black Forest pilgrimage, though yielding no tangible proof, had served its purpose. It was an anchor, a ritual that reaffirmed the reality of what had transpired. But the deeper truth, the one that festered within the confines of his own skull, remained locked away. He carried it like a phantom limb, a constant, aching presence that reminded him of what he knew, what he had witnessed, and what he could never truly share. This was the core of his burden: the unshared knowledge. It was a silent scream trapped within a vacuum, a truth that echoed only in the desolate chambers of his own consciousness.

He found himself adrift in a world that moved on, oblivious to the cosmic chasm that had momentarily opened and then been so ruthlessly slammed shut. The post-war era was a time of reconstruction, of rebuilding not just cities, but narratives. The official histories were being meticulously crafted, painting a picture of human resilience and triumph over adversity, a narrative that conveniently excluded the inconvenient truth of extraterrestrial contact, of technologies beyond human comprehension, and of the

261

chilling implications for humanity's place in the cosmos. Falk's internal companion, the alien presence, offered no solace, no companionship in the human sense. It was a constant, objective observer, a silent witness to Falk's profound isolation. It processed his emotions, his memories, his very essence, with an alien dispassion, cataloging his solitude as another data point in the grand, unfathomable scheme of things.

The weight of this unshared knowledge manifested in subtle, yet pervasive ways. His relationships, already strained by the secrecy he was forced to maintain, withered and died. How could he connect with others when the most fundamental aspect of his existence was a secret too profound, too dangerous to reveal? He learned to cultivate an aura of detachment, a polite reserve that kept others at a safe distance. The camaraderie he once enjoyed, the easy laughter and shared confidences, became memories that pricked at him with a dull, persistent ache. He was a phantom, present but never truly seen, his inner world a fortress impenetrable to all but himself and the silent watcher within.

He dedicated his days to living a life of quiet purpose, a life that minimized his footprint, both literally and metaphorically. He sought work that allowed him to remain in the shadows, jobs that required discretion and a capacity for meticulous, solitary effort. He found a measure of peace in routine, in the predictable rhythm of a life carefully constructed to avoid drawing attention. Yet, beneath the veneer of normalcy, the chasm of his secret remained. It was a constant reminder of the precipice upon which he stood, a precarious balance between the mundane reality of his daily life and the extraordinary, terrifying truth that defined him.

The fear of disbelief was a constant companion. He had seen the flicker of doubt in the eyes of those few he had dared to confide in, even in the most carefully veiled allusions. The very notion of alien life, of technology so advanced it bordered on the magical, was the stuff of pulp fiction, not of sober reality. And even if, by some miracle, someone were to believe him, the implications of his inner alien, the sentient presence that had bonded with him during the catastrophic events of Project Veil, were even more confounding. To admit to such a symbiotic, or parasitic, relationship would invite scrutiny, experimentation, and likely, confinement. The 'beacon,' as he silently referred to the alien consciousness within him, was his ultimate vulnerability, its very existence inextricably linked to his own.

He lived with the constant awareness that his very being was a beacon, a silent broadcast of his unique and terrifying encounter. The alien presence, while not actively communicating in any conventional sense, exerted a subtle influence, a constant, low-frequency hum that was as much a part of him as his own heartbeat. He had learned to interpret its subtle shifts, its passive observations, its detached awareness of the surrounding world. It was a symbiosis he hadn't sought, a bond forged in the fires of disaster, and one that he could not, and dared not, sever.

The years bled into one another, marked not by significant events, but by the enduring weight of his unshared knowledge. He aged, not gracefully, but stoically, his face a roadmap of the internal battles he fought daily. The quiet retirement he had envisioned for himself was a distant, unattainable dream. How could he truly retire from a burden that was woven into the very fabric of his existence? His vigilance was a constant necessity, a silent promise to a cosmic event that the rest of the world had conveniently forgotten.

He found himself drawn to places of profound silence, to the vast, unpopulated expanses where the only sounds were those of nature. The desert offered a stark, unforgiving beauty, a canvas of desolation that mirrored the emptiness he often felt within. He would sit for hours, watching the slow crawl of the sun across the sky, the silence broken only by the whisper of the wind and the distant cry of a hawk. In these moments, he would attempt to gauge the alien presence within him, to understand if its vigilance, its quiet observation, ever wavered. It never did. It was a constant, an unwavering point of reference in a world of shifting certainties.

He often pondered the fate of the aliens themselves. Had they been a scouting party, a reconnaissance mission, or something more? The silence from his internal companion offered no answers, only the passive observation of his own searching thoughts. He was left to piece together fragments, to infer from the sheer scale of the SS's efforts to conceal the incident. The ruthlessness of their actions spoke volumes about the significance of what they had encountered, about the threat they perceived, or perhaps, the opportunity they envisioned.

The profound isolation gnawed at him. He longed for a kindred spirit, someone who could grasp the enormity of what he carried. But the risk was too great. To expose the beacon, to risk its discovery, would be to betray not only himself but potentially, humanity, by revealing a vulnerability that could be exploited. He was a sentry on a forgotten wall, guarding against a threat that no one else even knew existed. His duty was self-imposed, his vigil eternal.

He lived out his days as a ghost in his own life, a man perpetually on the outside looking in. The Black Forest had been a stark reminder of the SS's chilling efficiency, but it had also solidified his role as the sole custodian of a truth too terrible to be shared. He was the living archive, the human repository of a history that had been systematically expunged from the collective memory. This was his curse, and in a strange, perverse way, his purpose. He would carry the weight of the long silence, the burden of unshared knowledge, until his own end, a solitary sentinel against a forgotten threat, his existence a testament to a truth that the world was not yet ready to bear. The alien presence within him remained a silent, enigmatic partner in this solitary vigil, its very existence a constant, unobtrusive reminder of the vastness of the universe and humanity's precarious place within it. He was a man out of time, forever tethered to an event that had reshaped his reality, a reality he was condemned to experience alone.

Chapter 12

Decades Later: A New Discovery

The encroaching shadows of the Black Forest, once a veil for a truth too profound for the world to bear, now seemed to beckon with a different kind of mystery. Decades had unfurled since the war's brutal conclusion, each year burying the events of Project Veil deeper beneath layers of soil, whispered local folklore, and the relentless march of progress. The colossal effort by the SS to erase every trace of their clandestine operations had, for a time, been remarkably effective. The whispers of strange lights, of inexplicable disappearances, and of technology that defied conventional understanding had faded into the realm of village superstition, dismissed by a world eager to rebuild and forget. Yet, the universe, in its infinite complexity, often leaves indelible fingerprints, even on the most thoroughly scrubbed of records.

A new dawn had broken over the scientific and archaeological communities. The post-war era, after its initial focus on recovery and reconstruction, had gradually shifted towards a deeper, more probing exploration of the unknown. Advancements in sensor technology, quantum physics, and geological surveying had opened up avenues of inquiry that were previously unimaginable. It was in this atmosphere of burgeoning discovery that a peculiar anomaly began to surface. Subtle but persistent energy readings, unlike anything cataloged in existing databases, had been detected emanating from specific sectors of the Black Forest. These readings were faint, intermittent, and easily dismissed as natural phenomena by those without the specialized equipment and keen analytical minds to interpret them. But for a select group of dedicated researchers, these whispers from the earth were too compelling to ignore.

The expedition was the brainchild of Dr. Christoph Neumann,

a man whose reputation for relentless pursuit of the unconventional preceded him. Neumann, a theoretical physicist with a penchant for historical enigmas, had stumbled upon the anomalous energy signatures while cross-referencing disparate datasets – satellite thermal imaging, historical atmospheric readings, and even some obscure geological surveys. He was the kind of scientist who saw patterns where others saw noise, who believed that the most profound truths often lay hidden in the margins of accepted knowledge. His initial findings were met with skepticism, even outright derision, by some of his more conventional colleagues. The Black Forest was known for its dense canopy, its challenging terrain, and its local legends, but not, they argued, for housing any secrets worthy of serious scientific investigation beyond its ecological significance.

Undeterred, Neumann meticulously compiled his data, presenting a compelling case for a targeted, high-tech survey. He secured funding from a private research foundation, one that valued innovation and the exploration of uncharted territories of knowledge. The team assembled was a testament to Neumann's dedication and his ability to identify talent. There was Dr. Lena Weber, a geophysicist renowned for her expertise in subsurface anomaly detection and her uncanny ability to interpret complex geological data. Her work had previously led to the discovery of several significant subterranean mineral deposits, and her intuition for the earth's hidden secrets was legendary.

Accompanying her was Ben Carter, a field technician and survival expert with an encyclopedic knowledge of remote environments. Carter's experience in navigating some of the planet's most unforgiving landscapes, coupled with his skill in operating and maintaining cutting-edge scanning equipment, made him an invaluable asset. Rounding out the core team was Dr. Jian Li, a specialist in advanced sensor array development and data analysis, whose algorithms could sift through terabytes of information, extracting the faintest of signals.

Their arrival at the edge of the Black Forest was marked by a palpable sense of anticipation, tinged with the quiet solemnity of entering a place steeped in a forgotten history. Neumann, standing at the threshold of the ancient woods, felt a peculiar resonance, an almost imperceptible hum that seemed to vibrate not just in the air, but within him. He couldn't articulate it, but it felt like a memory trying to resurface, a subtle echo from a time he had only ever known through carefully guarded fragments and the unspoken burden of a man long gone. He dismissed it as pre-expedition nerves, the familiar anticipation of venturing into the unknown.

Their initial approach was methodical, employing a triangulation of advanced ground-penetrating radar, magnetometers, and passive acoustic sensors. The sheer density of the forest presented immediate challenges. The towering trees, their branches interwoven to form a dense, almost impenetrable canopy, cast deep shadows that played tricks on the eyes and interfered with some of the more sensitive equipment. The terrain was unforgiving, a labyrinth of fallen trees, tangled undergrowth, and uneven ground that made every step a carefully considered effort. Carter, with his innate understanding of the forest's rhythm, led the way, his machete clearing a path, his senses constantly attuned to the subtle shifts in the environment.

Weber's instruments began to register more consistent anomalies as they ventured deeper. The energy signatures Neumann had initially detected were growing stronger, more defined, and, crucially, more localized. They weren't the random fluctuations of geological activity; they possessed a peculiar pattern, a cadence that hinted at something deliberate, something artificial. "Christoph," Weber called out, her voice tight with a controlled excitement, "the readings here are... unusual. They're not consistent with any known natural phenomenon. There's a distinct harmonic resonance, almost like a faint, structured signal."

Neumann approached, his eyes scanning the data displayed on Weber's ruggedized tablet. The waveform displayed was indeed perplexing. It lacked the chaotic nature of natural energy emissions and exhibited a level of organization that was deeply intriguing. "What's your interpretation, Lena?" he asked, his gaze fixed on the screen.

"It's difficult to say definitively without further analysis, but it suggests a highly organized, possibly artificial source. The energy seems to be concentrated several meters below the surface, in a localized pocket." Weber tapped a point on the screen. "And the depth is consistent across multiple readings."

The team pushed onward, following the strongest signals. The forest grew eerier the deeper they went. The usual sounds of woodland creatures seemed muted, replaced by a profound, almost unnatural stillness. The air itself felt heavy, charged with an unseen energy. Jian Li, hunched over his own array of sensors, reported similar findings. "My spectral analysis indicates a composition of emitted particles that I cannot readily identify. They don't align with any terrestrial isotopes or known atmospheric interactions."

As they navigated a particularly dense thicket, Carter suddenly held up a hand, signaling for them to halt. "Wait," he whispered, his eyes scanning the undergrowth. "Something's... off. The ground here feels different."

Neumann and Weber joined him, carefully examining the earth. It was true. The usual rich, dark loam of the forest floor seemed disturbed, as if something had been buried and then meticulously re-covered. There were no obvious signs of recent excavation, no telltale mounds of displaced soil. It was as if the earth itself had swallowed whatever lay beneath, leaving only the faintest whisper of its presence.

"Ground-penetrating radar shows a significant void just beneath the surface here," Weber announced, her voice hushed. "And the energy readings are spiking."

Using specialized excavation tools, designed for minimal environmental impact, they began to carefully remove the layers of earth. The soil was strangely compacted, almost fused together. As they dug deeper, the tools encountered resistance. It wasn't rock, but something harder, smoother, and unyielding. The metallic clang that echoed through the silent forest was a stark contrast to the natural world surrounding them.

Slowly, painstakingly, they uncovered it: a section of what appeared to be a metallic alloy, unlike any they had ever seen. It was dark, with a matte finish that seemed to absorb the ambient light. The surface was incredibly smooth, devoid of any visible seams or rivets, hinting at a manufacturing process far beyond contemporary human capabilities. The energy readings were emanating directly from this object, a low, steady thrum that was now distinctly audible to the human ear.

"My God," Neumann breathed, his eyes wide with a mixture of awe and trepidation. "This is... this is real."

Weber knelt beside the exposed section, her gloved fingers tracing its impossible smoothness. "The material composition is also anomalous. My preliminary scans can't identify any known elements or alloys. It's incredibly dense, yet remarkably resistant to thermal and sonic stress."

Jian Li's sensors were working overtime, his face a mask of intense concentration. "The energy signature is not radiating outward, but seems to be contained within the material itself. It's like a self-sustaining power source, but the technology behind it is... incomprehensible."

The implications were staggering. They had found not just an anomaly, but tangible proof of something extraordinary, something that had been deliberately hidden beneath the earth for decades. The SS's obsessive secrecy, their brutal efficiency in erasing Project Veil, suddenly made chilling sense. They hadn't just been dealing with advanced weaponry; they had stumbled upon something far more profound, something that had necessitated the complete obliteration of an entire project and the silencing of everyone involved.

As they continued to excavate, they realized the metallic section was far larger than they had initially assumed. It was part of a vast, buried structure, extending far beyond their immediate excavation site. The sheer scale of it was overwhelming, hinting at an undertaking of immense proportions. Neumann's mind raced, piecing together the fragmented whispers of history, the desperate attempts at suppression, and the persistent, unfathomable energy signatures.

"This wasn't just a research facility," Neumann murmured, his voice echoing the growing realization. "This was... something else. Something alien." The word felt foreign on his tongue, yet undeniably accurate. The materials, the energy source, the sheer scale – it all pointed to a non-human origin.

Weber, ever the pragmatist, urged caution. "We need to be methodical, Christoph. We have proof of an anomaly, possibly extraterrestrial in origin. But we don't know the extent of it, or what its purpose was. And we certainly don't know if it's still active, or if it poses any danger."

Carter, meanwhile, had been scanning the immediate surroundings with a handheld spectral analyzer. He walked over to Neumann, his expression grim. "Boss, I'm picking up residual energy traces, very faint, leading off in that direction," he said, pointing deeper into the forest. "It's like a faint trail, fading into the woods."

The team followed Carter's lead, the metallic structure temporarily left exposed in its forest grave. The faint trail of energy led them through increasingly dense terrain, the trees here seemingly older, more ancient. The silence intensified, a heavy blanket that seemed to press in on them. Neumann felt that peculiar resonance again, stronger this time, a subtle vibration that seemed to synchronize with his own internal rhythm. He instinctively knew that the source of this trail was connected to the buried object, and perhaps, to something far more personal than he could yet comprehend.

The trail culminated at a large, moss-covered boulder. At first glance, it seemed like nothing more than a natural formation. But as Weber's sensors swept over it, they registered a significant, localized energy distortion. "There's something here," she stated, her voice barely a whisper. "It's like a localized warp in the energy field. Very subtle, but definitely not natural."

Neumann approached the boulder, his hand instinctively reaching out. He remembered a passage from one of the few surviving, heavily redacted SS documents he had managed to access years ago – a vague mention of a 'stabilization nexus' located within the primary excavation zone, designed to 'interface' with the primary anomaly. Could this be it?

As his fingers brushed against the cool, damp moss, the familiar hum within him seemed to intensify, a subtle acknowledgement, a resonance that sent a shiver down his spine. He felt a strange pull, a sense of recognition that transcended rational thought. It was as if a long-dormant circuit had just been activated.

"Christoph, what are you doing?" Weber asked, her voice laced with concern.

"I... I think this is some kind of interface," Neumann replied, his eyes locked on the boulder. "The energy isn't radiating from it, it's... contained. Like a sealed unit."

Jian Li's instruments confirmed Neumann's intuition. "The energy output from the boulder is minute, almost negligible. But the composition of the field around it is highly unusual. It's almost as if the boulder itself is a conduit, channeling something from elsewhere."

The implications began to dawn on Neumann. If the buried structure was alien, and this boulder was its interface, what did that mean for his own internal... companion? He had lived for decades with a constant, silent presence, a part of him that was undeniably alien. Could it be connected to this place, to this technology? The thought was both terrifying and exhilarating.

He remembered Falk. Not just Falk the survivor, but Falk the man who had carried the unshakable truth, the man whose life had been irrevocably altered by Project Veil. Falk, whose internal companion had been a constant, silent witness to his isolation. Neumann had never fully understood the depth of Falk's burden, the sheer, unbearable weight of knowing. But now, standing here, feeling the faint echo of something profoundly alien within himself, he felt a flicker of understanding.

He carefully examined the boulder, searching for any inscription, any clue. His fingers traced the patterns of moss, searching for any disruption, any seam. And then, he found it. A subtle indentation, almost imperceptible, hidden beneath a thick patch of lichen. It was a symbol, unlike any terrestrial writing, a complex geometric pattern that seemed to shift and rearrange itself as he looked at it. As he focused on the symbol, the hum within him surged, a palpable wave of... something. It wasn't a thought, not a feeling, but a pure, unadulterated recognition.

He felt a sudden, overwhelming urge to press his hand against the symbol. Against his better judgment, against the years of scientific discipline that screamed caution, he acted. As his palm met the cool, rough surface of the boulder, the symbol seemed to glow with an internal, faint blue light. The hum within him intensified, no longer a subtle vibration, but a clear, resonant tone that seemed to echo in his very bones.

The air around the boulder shimmered, distorting the trees behind it. A holographic projection, faint at first, then solidifying, materialized before them. It wasn't a picture, or a video. It was a complex, three-dimensional schematic, a swirling nexus of lines and nodes, depicting something that looked impossibly like the buried metallic structure, but vastly larger, extending into realms Neumann couldn't even begin to comprehend. And at the center of the schematic, a pulsing orb of light, radiating an energy that felt both ancient and alive.

Weber gasped, stepping back. "What is that?"

"It's a map," Neumann breathed, his voice filled with wonder. "Or a blueprint. It's showing... a network. This buried structure isn't an isolated artifact. It's part of something much, much larger."

Jian Li's instruments were going wild. "The energy output from the boulder is increasing exponentially, but it's still contained. The holographic projection is drawing power from... from the structure below, and also from an external source, something I can't identify."

The projection shifted, focusing on a specific point within the vast network. A single node, pulsing with a slightly different hue. Neumann felt an inexplicable pull towards that node, a sense of familiarity that deepened the mystery. His internal companion, the silent observer, seemed to stir, its presence a more active, almost responsive hum.

He looked back at the buried metallic structure, then at the intricate schematic displayed before them. The SS had not just uncovered alien technology; they had unearthed a gateway, a piece of a cosmic puzzle that defied all human understanding. The decades of silence, the brutal suppression, the erased histories – they were all an attempt to contain something that was, by its very nature, uncontainable.

The expedition had begun with the promise of scientific discovery, of uncovering a buried secret. But standing there, bathed in the ethereal glow of an alien projection, Neumann realized they had stumbled upon something far more profound. They had found not just evidence of alien contact, but a glimpse into a reality that dwarfed humanity's wildest speculations, a legacy of an ancient civilization whose presence had touched Earth in ways that were only now, through the echoes of forgotten projects and the persistent whispers of anomalous energy, beginning to be understood. The Black Forest, once a tomb of secrets, was slowly, irrevocably, revealing itself to be a gateway, and the journey into its depths had only just begun. Neumann felt the weight of it, the immense responsibility of this discovery, a burden that resonated with the silent sentinel within him, a sentinel that had waited, perhaps for decades, for this very moment of revelation. The hum Neumann felt wasn't just a figment of his imagination, nor was it merely a psychological response to the extraordinary circumstances.

It was a distinct, measurable resonance that Jian Li's sensitive equipment began to isolate with increasing fidelity. As they meticulously mapped the area surrounding the exposed metallic segment, the readings intensified in a roughly circular pattern, suggesting a significant subsurface presence that extended well beyond the initial excavation. Weber's ground-penetrating radar, a sophisticated array capable of resolving structures meters below the surface, painted a picture of a vast, anomalous mass. It wasn't a single object, but rather a complex lattice of interlinked components, some extending hundreds of meters laterally, and others plunging to depths that their current instruments could only estimate.

"The sheer scale is... I've never seen anything like it," Weber murmured, her brow furrowed as she stared at the layered topographic displays. "The density variations are extreme. We're looking at materials with properties that defy our current understanding of physics. Some segments exhibit near-perfect reflectivity to certain wavelengths of energy, while others seem to absorb almost everything thrown at them." She pointed to a section of the screen where sharp, impossibly straight lines intersected with sweeping, organic curves. "This isn't natural geology, Christoph. This is engineered. And on a scale that's frankly terrifying."

Jian Li, meanwhile, was wrestling with the spectroscopic data. His initial analysis had been baffling; the faint traces of elemental composition that had seeped into the surrounding soil from the buried structure were unlike anything in the terrestrial elemental database. Now, with more direct readings from the exposed alloy and the ambient energy field, he was encountering even greater inconsistencies. "The dominant energy signature we're detecting isn't a simple emission," he explained, his voice tight with intellectual challenge. "It's more like a modulated carrier wave, intricately patterned. And the spectral analysis of the material itself... it's yielding almost no identifiable elemental signatures. There are traces of common elements, yes, but they're overlaid with what appear to be exotic isotopic variations, or perhaps entirely unknown fundamental particles. The resonance frequencies are also highly peculiar, oscillating within a narrow band that's incredibly stable, yet incredibly potent."

Carter had been busy with magnetic field anomaly detection. "It's not just energy readings, guys," he reported, his voice a low rumble over the comms. "The localized magnetic fields around this area are... warped. We're seeing extreme gradients, areas where the field strength is amplified to an absurd degree, then suddenly drops to near zero. It's like walking through a distorted landscape of magnetic forces."

He paused, scanning the dense foliage with his thermal imager. "And there's no thermal signature from the buried mass itself, despite the energy readings. It's completely inert to thermal detection. Whatever is powering it, it's not generating heat in any conventional sense."

Neumann absorbed their findings, a growing sense of awe and dread washing over him. The SS's efforts to bury Project Veil hadn't just been about concealing a weapon; they had been about containing a profound enigma.

The sheer engineering prowess required to construct something of this magnitude, buried deep within the earth, spoke of a technology so advanced as to be indistinguishable from magic. And the fact that it had been deliberately concealed, rather than exploited or understood, suggested a level of fear or perhaps a profound misunderstanding on the part of its discoverers.

"The implications of this are… immense," Neumann stated, his voice hushed. "If this is an artificial construct, and its energy signature is this complex and stable, it suggests a power source and a level of technological sophistication that is millennia beyond our current capabilities. The question isn't just *what* it is, but *who* built it, and *why* it was buried here." He looked at Weber. "Can you refine the depth estimates? And the lateral extent?"

Weber gestured to her array of monitors. "We're working on it. The signal penetration is limited by the sheer density of the earth and the anomalous materials themselves. However, our triangulation suggests the structure extends at least a kilometer in diameter, and its depth… the deepest readings are approaching several hundred meters. It's not a single structure, Christoph. It's more like a nexus, a subterranean hub with radiating conduits or pathways. And the energy readings aren't uniform. There are focal points, areas of intense energy concentration, that seem to be interconnected by these fainter pathways."

Jian Li chimed in, his fingers flying across his keyboard. "I'm trying to model the energy fluctuations to see if we can discern any patterns that might indicate function. The modulation is incredibly complex. It's not random noise; it's structured. I'm cross-referencing the patterns with known forms of communication, signal processing, even quantum entanglement principles. So far, nothing matches. It's like trying to decipher a language where we don't even know the alphabet." He sighed, running a hand through his hair. "The closest analogue I can find is in some theoretical models of zero-point energy extraction, but even those don't account for the stability and the organized nature of the emission."

Carter, who had ventured further into the surrounding forest, calling out updates on terrain and potential hazards, suddenly stopped. "Boss," he said, his voice sharp. "I'm picking up something else. Faint, but distinct. It's a thermal anomaly, but it's… cool. Not cold, exactly, but significantly cooler than the ambient forest temperature. And it's localized, about fifty meters to the north of our current position."

Curiosity piqued; the team moved cautiously towards Carter's indicated location. The forest here was older, the trees ancient sentinels draped in thick moss. The air was still and heavy, as if holding its breath. They found it nestled between the gnarled roots of an enormous oak: a cluster of large, dark stones, arranged in a rough semi-circle. They appeared to be natural, yet their placement seemed too deliberate, too symmetrical to be coincidental. The stones themselves were an unnerving shade of black, seemingly absorbing the scant light that filtered through the canopy.

Weber immediately deployed her handheld spectroscopic analyzer. "These stones..." she began, her voice tinged with surprise. "They're composed of a material that's... not stone, at least not in any terrestrial sense. The spectroscopic signature is similar to the alloy we found earlier, but highly degraded. It's like a weathered, less refined version. And the temperature anomaly is centered on this cluster."

Neumann felt that familiar resonance again, a subtle thrumming that seemed to emanate from the stones. It was weaker than the sensation he'd felt at the boulder, but undeniably present. He knelt down, examining the surface of one of the stones. The black material was porous, almost like solidified charcoal, but incredibly hard. As his fingers brushed over the surface, he detected a faint, almost imperceptible pattern, etched into the material. It was similar to the symbol he'd seen on the boulder, a complex geometric design that seemed to shift and reconfigure as he looked at it.

"This is it," Neumann declared, his voice filled with a growing certainty. "This is another interface. The SS must have found these, perhaps even discovered their purpose, and tried to replicate them, or at least understand their function." He remembered a cryptic passage in one of Falk's fragmented journal entries, a reference to 'secondary nodes' and 'energy relays' that had been scattered across the region. Falk, it seemed, had been aware of a distributed network, not just a single buried object.

Jian Li's instruments confirmed Neumann's suspicion. "The energy readings are weak, but present. It's like a low-power broadcast signal, designed to... perhaps, guide or communicate with the main nexus. And the stones themselves are acting as a passive conduit. They're absorbing ambient energy and re-emitting it in a highly organized fashion." He looked up, his eyes wide. "This suggests a highly sophisticated system of distributed energy distribution and control. The SS didn't just stumble upon a single alien artifact; they found a piece of a vast, interconnected network."

Carter, meanwhile, had been mapping the immediate vicinity with a directional antenna, trying to triangulate the source of the residual energy trails he'd detected earlier. "The trails are faint, but they converge on this location," he reported. "And they're not just from the buried structure. There are fainter trails leading off in other directions, like spokes on a wheel. It seems this whole area is saturated with this energy."

The implications were staggering. The Black Forest, a place steeped in myth and shadow, was not merely the site of a forgotten SS experiment, but a location of profound, perhaps cosmic, significance. The buried metallic structure was likely a primary hub, and these stone clusters were secondary nodes, part of a much larger, more ancient system. The SS, in their relentless pursuit of power and their paranoia, had stumbled upon something that had irrevocably altered the course of their own clandestine operations, leading them to conceal not just their discovery, but perhaps even a desperate attempt to control it.

Neumann felt a deep connection to this place, a resonance that went beyond scientific curiosity. It felt like a homecoming, a recognition of something lost and now found. He looked at the subtle pattern on the stone, the intricate geometry that seemed to hold a universe of information within its lines. He reached out and placed his hand on the cool, dark surface, his mind racing with questions. Were these stones a form of biological interface, or simply passive transmitters? What was the purpose of this network? And why here, in the heart of Germany?

Weber's voice, laced with a mix of awe and apprehension, broke the silence. "Christoph, we need to consider the broader implications. If this is a network, and the SS had a hand in it, we need to understand the extent of their involvement. Did they activate parts of it? Did they understand its purpose? Or were they merely custodians of something they couldn't comprehend?"

"They certainly tried to understand it," Neumann replied, his gaze fixed on the etched symbol. "And their attempts to control it, to weaponize it, likely led to the very secrecy and paranoia that characterized Project Veil. The sheer effort they went to erase all traces suggests they understood the potential power – and the potential danger – of this technology." He paused, his mind flashing back to Falk, to his fragmented journals, his haunted eyes. Falk had known. He had seen glimpses of the truth, and it had broken him. Neumann now understood why.

Jian Li, meanwhile, was observing a subtle shift in the energy readings from the stones. "The ambient energy levels seem to be fluctuating slightly. It's as if these nodes are... responding to something. Perhaps to our presence, or to the activation of the primary nexus." He pointed to his screen. "The modulation pattern is changing. It's becoming more complex, more intricate."

Carter, ever vigilant, scanned the perimeter. "I'm not picking up any signs of hostile presence," he reported. "But the forest itself... it feels different now. More alive, in a way. The subtle sounds, the rustling of leaves... it's as if the entire ecosystem is humming with this energy."

Neumann knew they had only scratched the surface. The SS's efforts to bury Project Veil had been monumental, but they had failed to erase the fundamental anomalies that had drawn them here. The forest held secrets far older and far more profound than the clandestine activities of a fallen regime. The buried structure and these scattered stone nodes were pieces of a puzzle that spanned eons, a testament to a civilization that had left its indelible mark on Earth.

"We need to analyze these stones further," Neumann stated, his voice firm. "And we need to understand the nature of the network they're part of. The SS's records, incomplete as they are, might hold clues to the location of other nodes, or to the function of the primary nexus. We're not just investigating a historical mystery anymore. We're uncovering evidence of a profound, extraterrestrial presence that has been hidden in plain sight for millennia."

The weight of the discovery settled upon him, a profound sense of responsibility. The echoes of Falk, the whispers of a forgotten past, and the tangible evidence of an alien presence in the heart of the Black Forest converged, painting a picture of a truth so vast and so complex that it threatened to shatter Neumann's very understanding of reality. The journey into the heart of Project Veil had led them not to a relic of human ambition, but to the doorway of an ancient, cosmic legacy. The anomalous readings, once mere whispers in the data, had become a siren song, calling them deeper into a mystery that had been waiting, patiently, for them to arrive. The forest, once a tomb of secrets, was now revealing itself as a grand, interconnected system, and their expedition had just begun to decipher its alien language.

Chapter 13

The Crash Site Unearthed

The persistent hum, the subtle yet undeniable resonance Neumann had first felt, had been the siren call leading them to this forgotten clearing. Decades had passed since the SS had so meticulously buried their secret, attempting to erase it from history with the same ruthlessness they applied to their enemies. But time, and the persistent peculiarities of this ancient forest, had eroded their efforts. The earth, always a patient witness, had begun to yield its secrets. The initial anomaly, the metallic shard protruding from the soil, had been the first whisper. Now, a more concerted effort, a carefully orchestrated excavation, was uncovering the full, astonishing extent of the enigma.

Weber, her face etched with a mixture of exhilaration and trepidation, directed the careful movements of the specialized excavation team. Their tools, designed for delicate archaeological work rather than brute force, were more akin to surgical instruments. The objective was not to rip and tear, but to coax the secrets from the earth with the least possible disruption. The ground-penetrating radar had hinted at a vast subsurface structure, a complex lattice that defied conventional understanding. What they were now unearthing, however, was the undeniable proof that the SS had indeed stumbled upon, and then desperately tried to conceal, something extraordinary.

The initial digging revealed not a single, monolithic object, but a fragmented mosaic of impossible materials. Layers of what appeared to be an incredibly dense, obsidian-like substance were interspersed with veins of a shimmering, metallic alloy that seemed to absorb and refract light simultaneously. Carter, his usual stoic demeanor replaced by a look of sheer disbelief, carefully brushed away the clinging soil from a large, irregularly shaped piece of this dark material. It was unnervingly smooth, almost polished, despite

281

being buried for what could only be centuries, if not millennia.

"Christoph, you need to see this," Carter's voice crackled over the comms, a note of stunned awe in its usual gruffness. "This... this isn't rock. It's not any kind of manufactured ceramic I've ever encountered. It feels... organic, somehow, even though it's clearly not biological in any way we understand."

Neumann moved to Carter's side, his heart pounding a rhythm that mirrored the faint thrumming he still felt in his bones. The fragment was heavy, far heavier than its size would suggest, and cool to the touch, despite the midday sun beating down on the clearing. Weber, with a specialized sample kit, carefully took a small scraping from its surface. The spectrometer she employed, usually capable of identifying the elemental composition of anything on Earth, struggled.

"It's... anomalous," Weber reported, her voice tight with concentration. "There are trace amounts of common elements, iron, silicon, carbon... but they're bound in a way that's completely unprecedented. And there's a significant spectral signature that's... unidentifiable. It's like a gap in our elemental library, a void where something should be, but isn't." She held up a small, self-contained containment unit holding the minute sample. "This material itself seems to be a composite, a layered structure on a sub-atomic level. The density is off the charts."

Meanwhile, Jian Li was working with a portable energy sensor, his brow furrowed in intense concentration. "The residual energy signature is still present, even on these smaller fragments," he confirmed, his voice barely above a whisper. "It's not an active emission anymore, not like the main structure, but it's there. A faint, stable resonance. And it seems to be concentrated within the metallic veins. The dark material appears to be acting as a sort of... insulator, or perhaps a passive conductor, dampening the energy's outward radiation."

As the excavation continued, more fragments emerged. They were not uniform in size or shape, suggesting a violent disintegration or a deliberate fragmentation. Some pieces were mere slivers of the shimmering alloy, others were larger sections of the dark, dense material, often fused or interlinked in bizarre ways. It was clear that this wasn't merely wreckage from a single impact; it was the debris of something far more complex, something that had been subjected to immense forces.

Neumann's mind raced, piecing together the fragments of information. Falk's fragmented journals, the cryptic references to a "silent impact," and the SS's obsessive efforts to cordon off and study this area suddenly took on a chilling new significance. This wasn't just a failed rocket test or a downed experimental aircraft. This was something that had arrived from elsewhere, or perhaps had been awakened from deep within the Earth itself, and the SS, in their relentless pursuit of technological dominance, had stumbled upon its remnants. Their attempts to conceal it, to weaponize it, had been born from a mixture of fear and a desperate, misguided ambition.

"Look at the way these pieces are fractured," Neumann said, pointing to a section where a large shard of the dark material was shattered, revealing intricate, almost crystalline structures within. "It suggests an explosive decompression, or perhaps a catastrophic failure of containment. The SS may have found this already broken, or they may have broken it further in their attempts to understand it."

Weber nodded, her gaze fixed on the growing collection of unearthed fragments. "The radar showed a complex, interconnected network beneath the surface. These fragments are pieces of that network. It's like finding shards of a shattered mirror; each piece reflects a part of the original, but the whole is lost to us." She then gestured to a particularly striking piece, a curved section of the metallic alloy that seemed to shimmer with an internal light. "This alloy... the spectral analysis is still inconclusive, but there are isotopic ratios that are simply not found in nature. We're talking about elements that shouldn't exist in this configuration, or perhaps elements that we haven't even discovered yet."

The SS had been meticulous in their cover-up. The initial military reports, salvaged from the fragmented archives, spoke of a localized seismic event, a "geological anomaly" that had necessitated a restricted military zone. Over the years, the narrative had shifted, morphing into rumors of a clandestine weapons development program gone awry. But the reality, unearthed piece by agonizing piece in this remote clearing, was far more profound. They hadn't developed anything; they had discovered something. And in their fear and ignorance, they had buried it, hoping to contain a force they couldn't comprehend.

Jian Li, meanwhile, was attempting to map the distribution of the energy signatures of the recovered fragments. "The intensity varies," he explained, his eyes scanning the readings on his handheld device. "Some pieces are emitting a faint but measurable energy, while others are completely inert. It's almost as if the energy was concentrated in specific nodes within the larger structure, and these fragments are the byproducts of its disintegration or deactivation." He paused, a thoughtful expression on his face. "The SS likely collected the most 'active' pieces for their own research, leaving behind the less potent debris, which is why our initial readings were so strong when we first approached this site."

The implications of this discovery were staggering. It confirmed that a significant, non-terrestrial event had occurred here, long before the SS even existed, or perhaps that the SS had unearthed something ancient and alien. The fragments were tangible evidence of a technology so advanced it bordered on the miraculous, a testament to a civilization or a force that operated on principles far beyond human comprehension. The SS's paranoid secrecy, their desperate attempts to control this power, now seemed like a futile struggle against a cosmic tide.

Neumann's thoughts drifted to the SS's ultimate fate, their internal collapse and the subsequent disarray that had allowed him and his team to even access this forbidden zone. Had their attempts to harness this alien technology played a role in their downfall? Had the very power they sought to control ultimately consumed them? The questions hung in the air, as heavy and as unyielding as the fragments they were unearthing.

"We need to be systematic," Neumann stated, his voice firm, cutting through the quiet awe that had settled over the team. "Every fragment, no matter how small, must be cataloged. We need to understand the spatial distribution of these materials, the patterns of their fragmentation. Jian, can you correlate the energy readings with the composition of each piece? Weber, I need detailed spectrographic analysis of every viable sample. Carter, maintain a perimeter and monitor for any environmental shifts; this forest has been disturbed, and we don't know what reactions might occur."

The process of excavation continued throughout the day. As the sun began its slow descent, casting long, distorted shadows across the clearing, the extent of the unearthed wreckage became more apparent. It wasn't just a few scattered fragments; it was a significant portion of what appeared to be a vast, complex apparatus. The dark, obsidian-like material formed a sort of matrix, with the shimmering alloy embedded within it, like arteries carrying a lifeblood of unknown energy. The sheer scale of the recovered debris suggested that the original object, or structure, had been immense, perhaps the size of a small building, or even larger.

One particular discovery sent a fresh wave of shock through the team. Deep within the excavated area, they uncovered what appeared to be a central core, a spherical object composed of the same dark material, but with a surface that seemed to writhe with faint, internal luminescence. It pulsed with a low, rhythmic energy, a ghostly echo of the powerful resonance that had drawn them here.

"This... this is the source," Jian Li breathed, his instruments registering a significant spike in energy output. "The other fragments are like... echoes, or broken components of this central piece. The energy signature emanating from this sphere is unlike anything I've ever encountered. It's incredibly stable, yet impossibly potent."

Weber was already at work, her instruments trained on the sphere. "The material is unlike anything I've seen," she confirmed, her voice trembling slightly. "It's a crystalline lattice, but the bonds are arranged in a way that defies our understanding of crystallography. And the energy it's emitting... it's not electromagnetic in the conventional sense. It's something else, something that interacts with matter on a fundamental level."

Neumann felt a profound sense of historical weight settle upon him. They were not just uncovering an archaeological site; they were excavating evidence of a contact, a visitation, or perhaps even a cataclysm that predated human civilization by an immeasurable span. The SS's obsession with this site, their frantic efforts to weaponize the technology they found, had inadvertently preserved the remnants of something truly ancient. They had been guardians of a secret they couldn't possibly comprehend, custodians of a power that was alien and unfathomable.

The recovered fragments, each a silent testament to a forgotten era, lay scattered across the clearing. The meticulous work of cataloging and analysis would continue for weeks, perhaps months. But the core truth had been unearthed. This wasn't a human endeavor; it was something far older, far grander, and infinitely more mysterious. The Black Forest, with its shadowed depths and whispered legends, had finally yielded its most profound secret, revealing not the hubris of human ambition, but the silent, enduring legacy of the cosmos. The crash site, once a ghost in the archives, was now a tangible reality, a monumental discovery that would undoubtedly rewrite history as they knew it. The true nature of what had fallen, or what had been unearthed, remained to be deciphered, but the evidence was undeniable: humanity was not alone, and the echoes of that ancient encounter were finally, irrevocably, surfacing.

The sheer scale of the unearthed anomaly continued to expand, revealing itself to be not merely a singular object, but a vast, subterranean complex. As Weber's team meticulously worked, clearing away centuries of soil and detritus, the outlines of what could only be described as engineered structures began to emerge. These weren't rough shelters or crude fortifications; they were intricate formations, revealing a level of planning and construction that spoke of a sophisticated, and highly organized, endeavor. The materials themselves were baffling, a testament to the perplexing nature of the site, but the *organization* of their deployment was equally astonishing.

Carter, ever the frontline observer, had discovered what appeared to be a perimeter marking. Etched into a large, unusually smooth boulder, just outside the main excavation zone, was a symbol that sent a jolt of recognition through Neumann. It was a stylized eagle, its wings spread wide, but unlike any standard Luftwaffe insignia Neumann had ever seen. This version was more angular, more severe, with subtle geometric patterns integrated into its design that mirrored some of the stranger motifs observed on the metallic fragments. Beneath the eagle, a series of numbers were carved with unnerving precision: '3./Kdo. X.'

"Boss, you need to see this," Carter's voice crackled over the comms, tinged with a new layer of bewilderment. "I've found some sort of marker. It's… military, I'm sure of it. But the designation… it's not one I recognize from any historical records."

Neumann made his way over, his boots crunching on the damp earth. He knelt beside the boulder, his fingers tracing the deeply incised lines of the symbol. The eagle, and the cryptic designation beneath it, seemed to thrum with a residual energy, a faint echo of the power that saturated the area. "3./Kdo. X.," he mused aloud. "Kommando X? I've never heard of such a unit. Not in any of the fragmented SS archives I've examined."

Weber joined them, her own instruments whirring as she scanned the boulder. "The etching isn't natural erosion, Christoph. It's deliberate. The material of the boulder itself is similar to some of the secondary materials we've been recovering – the darker, more inert segments of the main structure – but it's been worked. And the symbol, it's incredibly precise." She zoomed in on the eagle with her enhanced optical scanner. "The geometric patterns integrated into the wings… they're not decorative. They appear to be functional, perhaps even a form of encoding or a key."

Jian Li, always keen to correlate any new data point, quickly ran a search through his meticulously curated database of historical military designations and classified projects. After a tense silence punctuated only by the rustling of leaves and the distant hum of the excavation equipment, he spoke. "Nothing. No official records, no declassified documents, not even any speculative mentions in fringe historical forums. It's as if this 'Kommando X' simply doesn't exist in the official narrative. But the precision of the carving, the nature of the symbol… it suggests a highly disciplined and technologically advanced organization."

The implications began to crystallize, casting a long and unsettling shadow over their discovery. The mid-20th century, the era of the Third Reich's desperate technological ambitions, was now inextricably linked to this anomalous site. The SS, notorious for their occult fascinations and their relentless pursuit of forbidden knowledge, had clearly been here, and not just as discoverers. The presence of a military designation, however obscure, implied a period of active study, perhaps even exploitation, of the site's secrets.

"This changes everything," Neumann stated, his voice low and grave. "We've been operating under the assumption that the SS stumbled upon this and then tried to bury it out of fear. But what if they were actively engaged with it? What if 'Kommando X' was established specifically to study or control this... whatever it is?"

As the excavation progressed deeper into the earth, more evidence of a mid-20th-century military presence began to surface, interspersed with the alien artifacts. They unearthed what appeared to be the remnants of a heavily reinforced bunker, its concrete walls cracked and crumbling, but still bearing the unmistakable hallmarks of Nazi engineering. Within its decaying interior, they found rusted equipment, specialized scientific instruments that were primitive by modern standards but advanced for their time, and most disturbingly, fragments of SS uniforms, complete with the chilling insignia of the death's-head.

Weber meticulously cataloged a series of metallic plates, layered with what looked like early vacuum tubes and complex wiring, all housed within a heavily shielded casing. "These are instruments designed to measure and record energy fluctuations," she explained, her voice hushed. "The design is rudimentary, certainly, but the purpose is clear. They were attempting to quantify the energy signatures we're still detecting." She held up a corroded metal fragment. "And this... it's a casing for a data storage unit, similar to early magnetic tape, but with a significantly higher storage capacity. The SS were trying to record their findings, to make sense of what they found."

Carter discovered a series of buried communication lines, thick, lead-sheathed cables that snaked away from the main excavation site into the surrounding forest. "These were designed to withstand significant interference," he noted, examining a severed section.

"And they were buried deep. Whoever set this up wanted to ensure secure, reliable communication, perhaps with a hidden command center, or even with external agencies."

The narrative Neumann had pieced together from Falk's fragmented journals and the initial SS archives had always focused on the post-war cover-up. But this evidence suggested a much longer, more active engagement. The SS hadn't just found a crashed object; they had established a research outpost, a clandestine laboratory, dedicated to unraveling its mysteries. The sheer effort involved in building and maintaining such a facility, deep in the secluded Black Forest, spoke volumes about the perceived importance, or perhaps the perceived threat, of the site.

"It's chilling," Neumann admitted, looking at a partially preserved map found within the bunker. It depicted the immediate area, with various points of interest marked by symbols that mirrored the one on the boulder. One of these points, located several kilometers to the north, was labeled with a question mark and a series of rapidly drawn, agitated lines – a clear indication of an unknown or possibly dangerous zone. "They were mapping it, studying it, trying to understand its extent and its capabilities. They knew this was more than just a single anomaly."

Jian Li, meanwhile, was analyzing the composition of the unearthed military equipment. "The materials used in some of these instruments are also unusual," he reported. "Certain alloys, particularly in the shielding and the sensitive components, exhibit properties that suggest they were specifically developed to interact with or contain unusual energy fields. It's almost as if they were reverse-engineering aspects of the alien technology to build their own analytical tools."

The connection between the advanced, seemingly extraterrestrial materials and the primitive, yet purposefully designed, mid-20th-century military hardware was jarring. It painted a picture of a desperate scientific race against time, a race to understand and potentially weaponize a force far beyond their comprehension. The SS, infamous for their ruthlessness, had channeled that ruthlessness into scientific inquiry, albeit one driven by a terrifying agenda.

"The implications for the historical narrative are profound," Neumann mused, rubbing his temples. "We've always viewed the SS as being on the fringe, dabbling in pseudoscience and occultism. But this... this suggests a level of advanced, even speculative, scientific engagement that we've never attributed to them. They weren't just seeking power; they were actively trying to harness technologies that, by all accounts, shouldn't have existed during that era."

The sheer persistence of the SS was also becoming evident. The site had been buried, yes, but not simply abandoned. The reinforced bunker, the communication lines, the scientific instruments – these were the trappings of a long-term operational presence. Had they succeeded in any of their objectives? Had they managed to activate any part of the alien technology? Or had their attempts to control it ultimately led to their own undoing, culminating in the desperate measures of concealment?

"The energy signature here isn't just residual from the original event," Jian Li stated, his attention fixed on his readings. "There are subtle fluctuations, patterns that suggest it's been manipulated, or at least influenced, by external forces. The SS's equipment, rudimentary as it is, might have been designed to interact with these energy fields, perhaps to amplify or redirect them. It's possible they were trying to establish a controlled energy output from the main structure."

The historical context was no longer a secondary layer to the scientific anomaly; it was an integral part of it. The SS's involvement wasn't just a curious footnote; it was a driving force behind the very concealment and the fragmented understanding of what had occurred here. Their presence explained the meticulous nature of the burial, the classified nature of the site, and perhaps even the ongoing mystery that had surrounded the area for decades.

Neumann recalled another cryptic passage from Falk's journals, a reference to a "shadow laboratory" operating under the auspices of Himmler's personal research division, the Ahnenerbe. At the time, he had dismissed it as the ramblings of a man clearly suffering from extreme stress and paranoia. Now, with the tangible evidence of 'Kommando X' and its sophisticated instrumentation, the notion of a dedicated SS research unit delving into such profound mysteries seemed all too plausible.

"If this was an SS operation, then their motivation is critical," Neumann said, pacing the perimeter of the uncovered bunker. "Were they trying to understand a potential threat? Or were they aiming to develop a superweapon? Given their ideology, the latter seems more probable. They saw everything as a potential tool for conquest."

Weber nodded, carefully examining a series of metal discs found in a hermetically sealed container. "The data on these discs is encoded in a proprietary SS format," she explained. "It will take time to decrypt, but if they managed to extract any meaningful data from the main structure, it could be invaluable. Imagine, Christoph, direct records from the SS's own investigation into this... this non-terrestrial phenomenon."

The mere thought of such direct records sent a shiver down Neumann's spine. The SS, with their vast resources and their ruthless efficiency, had dedicated themselves to this site. Their ultimate fate – the rapid collapse of their regime, the subsequent chaos that led to the fragmentation and loss of so much vital information – had effectively erased their involvement from the official histories. But the evidence was here, buried beneath the soil, waiting to be rediscovered.

Carter, meanwhile, had unearthed what looked like a burial site, a series of shallow graves marked by crude wooden crosses, now long since rotted away. "There are remains here," he reported, his voice subdued. "Multiple individuals. The uniform fragments found nearby suggest they were SS personnel. It's a grim reminder of the human cost of whatever happened here."

The discovery of the graves added another layer of grim complexity to the narrative. Had the SS suffered casualties during their investigations? Had their attempts to interact with the alien technology resulted in catastrophic accidents? The silence from 'Kommando X' now seemed less like deliberate secrecy and more like a terminal silence, a complete cessation of activity.

"The timeline is crucial," Neumann insisted. "We need to

establish precisely when this operation began, and when it ceased. Falk's journals provide a starting point, but the SS's own records, if we can retrieve them, will be the definitive account. This site wasn't just a discovery; it was an active military installation for a significant period."

The confluence of advanced, potentially alien technology and the brutal, often misguided, scientific ambition of the Third Reich presented a paradox that was both fascinating and horrifying. The SS had been known for their brutality and their ideological purity tests, but this evidence suggested a pragmatic, albeit terrifying, pursuit of scientific advancement when it served their ends. They had embraced the bizarre and the unknown, not out of genuine curiosity, but as a means to an end – the ultimate consolidation of power.

"It's possible that the very technologies they were trying to harness or understand contributed to their downfall," Jian Li hypothesized, looking up from his readings. "Perhaps the energy field here was inherently unstable, or perhaps their attempts to control it had unintended consequences. The lack of any residual SS activity, the thoroughness of the burial… it suggests a complete and utter failure, or perhaps a successful containment that required a total eradication of all evidence."

Neumann looked at the vast, complex structure beginning to emerge from the earth, a testament to both ancient, unknown forces and the relentless drive of human ambition. The Black Forest, a place of myth and legend, was revealing itself to be a stage for events that transcended mere human history. The mid-20th century had not merely stumbled upon a cosmic secret; it had actively engaged with it, albeit with the destructive tendencies of a regime blinded by its own ideology. The discovery of 'Kommando X' and its operational remnants had transformed their investigation from a search for a single crashed object into an unearthing of a clandestine, nation-state-level research project that had dared to delve into the unfathomable. The pieces were falling into place, forming a chilling mosaic of scientific hubris, military obsession, and the enduring mystery of what truly lay buried beneath the ancient trees.

The faint, yet persistent, hum Neumann had first felt resonated not just from the alien materials, but from the ghost of the SS's presence. It was the echo of their ambition, their fear, and their ultimate failure. The clearing, once a silent testament to a past event, was now a noisy testament to a history that had been deliberately buried, only to be resurrected, piece by agonizing piece, by those who sought the truth. The whispers of the past were growing louder, and they were speaking in the chillingly precise language of a forgotten military designation.

The sheer density of the recovered fragments was staggering. It was becoming clear that what they were unearthing was not merely debris from a single impact, but the remnants of a colossal, complex structure that had been deliberately disassembled or had disintegrated over time. Weber's team, working with painstaking precision, had managed to excavate what appeared to be a significant portion of the central mechanism, a vast lattice of the dark, inert material interwoven with veins of the shimmering alloy. It was like uncovering the skeletal remains of some immense, otherworldly leviathan.

"The structural integrity of these connections… it's unlike anything we've ever engineered," Weber stated, her voice filled with a mixture of awe and scientific frustration. She was meticulously examining a juncture where a thick rod of the dark substance met a complex, web-like network of the metallic alloy. "The bond isn't achieved through welding or adhesion in any conventional sense. It's almost as if the materials have coalesced, forming an inseparable unit at a fundamental level. Our spectrographic analysis can't account for the nature of this intermingling."

Carter, meanwhile, had discovered what appeared to be a secondary access point, a recessed panel seamlessly integrated into the dark matrix. Unlike the primary excavation area which had been revealed by the initial metallic shard, this panel was much deeper, suggesting a more deliberate, less accidental, exposure. "This panel is different," he reported. "It's a smoother surface, almost like a door, and there are faint linear patterns on it, like a locking mechanism."

Neumann approached the panel, his heart hammering against

his ribs. He felt that familiar, subtle resonance emanating from it, stronger than from the scattered fragments, but contained, as if held in a state of dormant readiness. He ran his gloved fingers over the surface. The lines were indeed deliberate, forming a complex geometric sequence that hinted at an elaborate locking system. "It's a port of entry," Neumann declared, a thrill of discovery surging through him. "The SS must have known about this. They likely tried to open it, to access what's inside."

Jian Li quickly deployed a portable energy reader, focusing it on the panel. "The energy signature here is localized, and significantly more potent than the ambient readings we've been getting," he confirmed. "It's like a concentrated reservoir, waiting for a specific input to activate it. The modulation pattern is extremely complex, far more intricate than anything we've seen from the surrounding fragments."

The SS's presence, their efforts to understand and possibly control this ancient technology, now loomed larger than ever. The discovery of this secondary access point, buried deeper and integrated more seamlessly into the structure, suggested that their initial excavation had been a rather crude, almost clumsy, attempt to breach the anomaly. This 'panel,' however, felt like a deliberate interface, a designed entry point.

"The SS archives mentioned attempts to access the 'core' of Project Veil," Neumann mused, his mind racing through the fragmented intelligence he had gathered. "They alluded to specialized drilling equipment and energy probes that proved ineffective. It's highly probable they were targeting this very panel, or something similar." He paused, looking at the intricate patterns etched into its surface. "But they wouldn't have had the key. This mechanism is clearly designed for a specific sequence, a particular input that they wouldn't have possessed."

Weber, ever the meticulous scientist, was already examining the surrounding material. "The composition around this panel is subtly different," she observed. "The dark material here seems to be more dense, more refined, and it's interspersed with trace amounts of a material that's registering as highly conductive, almost like a form of organic circuitry. It's as if this section of the structure was designed to be the primary point of interaction."

The realization that the SS had been so close, yet so fundamentally unable to access the heart of the anomaly, was both frustrating and, in a strange way, reassuring. Their inability to penetrate this deeper layer might have prevented them from unleashing something truly catastrophic, or perhaps from understanding a truth that would have shattered their already precarious grip on reality.

"Their efforts were ultimately futile, at least in terms of gaining access," Neumann stated. "This suggests the SS found this site, recognized its potential, but lacked the crucial understanding or the proper means to interface with it. They were like children trying to operate a supercomputer with a hammer."

As they continued to clear the area around the panel, they uncovered more evidence of the SS's presence. Partially buried in the earth nearby was a rusted, heavily damaged piece of equipment that Jian Li identified as a sonic emitter, designed to generate specific frequencies. "They were trying to probe the structure with sound waves," he explained. "Perhaps to map internal cavities or to identify resonant frequencies that might trigger a response. It's a primitive approach, but indicative of their desperation."

Nearby, they also found the skeletal remains of what appeared to be an SS soldier, clad in fragments of a uniform that had succumbed to decades of decay. He was positioned as if he had been operating the sonic emitter, his hand outstretched towards the buried structure. A small, tarnished silver locket lay clutched in his skeletal fingers. Neumann picked it up, his gloved hand trembling slightly as he opened it. Inside, faded and worn, was a photograph of a smiling woman and two young children. It was a poignant, stark reminder of the human element caught in the vortex of this unfathomable discovery.

"It's a grim reminder," Neumann murmured, placing the locket back gently on the ground. "They weren't just faceless fanatics. They were individuals, caught up in something they couldn't control, driven by orders they likely didn't fully understand."

The SS's engagement with this site was no longer a mere

historical curiosity; it was a complex narrative interwoven with the alien presence. The discovery of the secondary access point, the evidence of their attempts to breach it, and the tragic fate of at least one of their personnel, all painted a vivid picture of their desperate struggle. They had been drawn to this place by a perceived power, a technological marvel that promised untold advantages, but they had been met with a mystery that defied their understanding and their capabilities.

"The continued hum Neumann feels, the resonance he's been experiencing... it's stronger around this panel," Jian Li noted, his instruments registering a significant spike. "It's like the structure is reacting to our presence, or perhaps to the proximity of this specific interface. The energy is almost... waiting."

Neumann felt it too, a deep, internal thrumming that seemed to synchronize with the faint resonance emanating from the panel. It was a sense of connection, of recognition, that went beyond scientific observation. It felt like an invitation, a silent call to a deeper understanding.

"The SS's failure to access this," Neumann stated, his gaze fixed on the intricate patterns of the locking mechanism, "is perhaps the most significant clue to their limitations, and to the nature of this technology. Whatever this structure is, its interface is designed for a level of sophistication, or a specific kind of interaction, that they simply couldn't achieve." He looked at Weber. "Can we analyze the trace materials around the panel? The 'organic circuitry' you mentioned?"

Weber nodded, already setting up her portable spectrometer. "I'm trying to isolate the components. The spectral signature is unlike anything in our databases. It's not carbon-based, but it exhibits properties that are remarkably similar to bio-electrical conductors. It's as if the very structure is designed to interface with a biological or quasi-biological system."

The possibility that the structure was not merely technological, but perhaps even bio-mechanical, or designed to interface with biological entities, sent a fresh wave of questions through Neumann's mind. Had the SS, in their attempts to force their way in, been unknowingly tampering with a system that required a specific biological or energetic key?

"This implies a level of integration far beyond what we initially conceived," Jian Li added, his eyes wide with intellectual fascination. "If this structure is designed to interact with biological entities, then the SS's brute-force approach would have been utterly ineffectual. They were trying to unlock a biological system with mechanical tools."

The SS's involvement, however misguided, had inadvertently preserved a critical piece of information: the existence of this secondary, more sophisticated interface. Their failure to breach it, and the evidence of their attempts, confirmed that they had recognized its significance, even if they couldn't understand its purpose. They had stumbled upon the equivalent of a quantum-encrypted vault, and they had tried to open it with a crowbar.

"We need to document everything related to this panel," Neumann instructed. "The surrounding materials, the precise geometric patterns of the lock, the energy signatures. We can't replicate their mistakes. We need to approach this with a completely different understanding." He looked back at the vast, unearthed structure, the silent testament to a forgotten epoch. The SS's operational footprint, once a hidden layer of history, was now laid bare, intertwining with the profound mystery of the alien anomaly. Their presence explained the context, the secrecy, and the very reasons why this site had remained hidden for so long. The mid-20th century had reached out to touch the unfathomable, and in doing so, had inadvertently preserved the clues for a future generation to follow. The whispers of the past had evolved into the shouts of a hidden history, a history that was inextricably linked to the silent, waiting heart of the unearthed enigma.

Chapter 14

The Signal Awakens

The hum, a subtle tremor felt more than heard, now emanated not just from the vast, unearthed structure but also from the data storage unit Weber's team had painstakingly recovered. It was a device that defied easy categorization, a smooth, obsidian-like cylinder about the size of a human forearm, devoid of any discernible seams or controls. Its surface was cool to the touch, yet it pulsed with a faint, internal energy that Neumann found himself increasingly attuned to. The SS, in their attempts to access the core of "Project Veil," had likely focused on the larger structure, overlooking or perhaps failing to find this more portable, yet potentially more significant, artifact. The sheer resilience of the alien material, its resistance to the crude methods the Nazis had employed, was a testament to a technology that was not merely advanced, but fundamentally different.

Jian Li, his brow furrowed in concentration, had established a dedicated analytical environment for the device, a sterile chamber filled with humming servers and glowing readouts. Their most powerful computational resources, a cluster designed for simulating quantum entanglement and processing astrophysical data, were now focused on this single, enigmatic object. Initial attempts at brute-force decryption had proven futile. The alien architecture, far from being based on binary code or recognizable digital constructs, seemed to operate on principles that were entirely foreign.

"It's not even presenting a recognized file system," Jian Li reported, his voice betraying a mixture of frustration and exhilaration. "We've tried interfacing with it using every known protocol, every encryption standard, even exploratory algorithms designed for unknown data structures. It's like trying to read a book written in a language that has no relation to any terrestrial tongue, using a dictionary that doesn't exist."

Weber, her own expertise in materials science and bio-engineering proving invaluable, was conducting a non-invasive analysis of the device's internal structure. Using a battery of advanced imaging techniques, from terahertz scanners to focused ion beam microscopy, she was attempting to map the internal pathways and data storage mechanisms. The results were both bewildering and spectacular.

"The internal matrix is incredibly dense," she explained, pointing to a holographic projection that displayed a shimmering, three-dimensional lattice. "It's not composed of silicon or any conventional conductive materials. There are these crystalline structures, interwoven with filaments that appear to be bio-luminescent at a microscopic level. They seem to react to external energy inputs, but not in a way that suggests electrical conductivity. It's more akin to a biological response, a complex chemical or energetic cascade."

The SS, Neumann realized, must have recognized the potential of such a device, even if they couldn't access its contents. The fragmented reports spoke of recovered "recordings" and "information matrices," but their limited technological capabilities would have rendered them incapable of deciphering anything so sophisticated. Their attempts to analyze it would have likely involved rudimentary attempts at physical probing, perhaps even trying to extract its contents through methods that could have damaged it. The fact that it remained intact, and seemingly undamaged, was a testament to its robust design, or perhaps to the aliens' own advanced understanding of data preservation.

"The encryption isn't a lock; it's more like a biological key," Weber theorized, her eyes fixed on the holographic display. "The internal filaments seem to respond to specific energetic frequencies, creating complex resonance patterns. If the SS tried to force their way in, they would have been essentially trying to unlock a biological mechanism with a blunt instrument. They would have triggered defensive protocols, or more likely, the system simply wouldn't have recognized their inputs as valid."

Neumann recalled the SS's focus on "organic science" and their fascination with biological manipulation. It was entirely plausible that they had encountered this device, recognized its biological underpinnings, and had either been unable to proceed or had prudently decided against any attempts that might have destroyed it. Their own research into genetic manipulation and advanced biological engineering, however twisted, might have given them a rudimentary understanding of the principles involved, but not the means to execute them.

"The hum," Neumann interjected, his gaze fixed on the obsidian cylinder. "It's stronger when Weber's imaging is focused on certain areas. It's as if the device is reacting to the examination, but not in a way that indicates distress. More like... recognition."

Jian Li adjusted the frequency of a low-power, non-invasive energy emitter, directing it towards the device. The hum intensified, and the holographic projection of the internal matrix began to shift, the crystalline structures glowing brighter, the filaments pulsating in a more rapid, intricate pattern.

"It's responding to specific energetic signatures," Jian Li confirmed, his voice barely a whisper. "The patterns are incredibly complex, almost like a symphony of energy. We're seeing sequences of modulation that repeat, but with subtle variations. It's a form of communication, I'm certain of it, but we're still trying to map the parameters."

The implications of this interaction were profound. If the device was designed to communicate, or to be accessed through specific energetic inputs, then Neumann's own increasing attunement to the hum, the resonance he felt, could be more than just a psychological effect. It could be an intrinsic response of his own biological system to the alien technology. The SS, with their focus on engineered solutions and their inherent disconnection from the more subtle energies of the universe, might have missed this fundamental aspect of its operation.

"The SS's attempts to quantify and control would have been based on their understanding of physics and mechanics," Neumann mused aloud. "They would have been looking for electrical signals, for magnetic fields, for quantifiable forces. They wouldn't have been looking for resonance, for biological cues, for a form of communication that transcends conventional measurement."

Weber nodded in agreement. "Their instrumentation was designed to measure and record physical phenomena. If this data is encoded through bio-energetic resonance, it would appear as noise or an inexplicable anomaly to their equipment. They might have detected the hum, but without understanding its nature, they would have dismissed it or tried to suppress it."

The task of deciphering the alien data was proving to be an immense challenge, requiring a paradigm shift in their approach. They were no longer dealing with code, but with a complex, dynamic system that seemed to operate on principles that blurred the lines between technology and biology. The SS's historical attempts to understand it, while valuable for context, also highlighted their limitations. They were bound by the scientific understanding of their era, an understanding that was woefully inadequate for this extraterrestrial enigma.

"We need to catalog every single resonance pattern, every subtle fluctuation in the energy output," Jian Li stated, his fingers flying across his console. "We're building a library of its responses, trying to identify any inherent logic or structure. It's like trying to learn a new language by observing the subtle cues of a native speaker, hoping to eventually understand the grammar and syntax."

The data storage unit, Neumann knew, was more than just a repository of information. It was a testament to the sophistication of its creators, a glimpse into a civilization that had mastered forms of technology that were currently beyond humanity's grasp. The SS's engagement with it, however limited, had provided a crucial historical context, demonstrating that this anomaly had not gone unnoticed in the past. Their failure to unlock its secrets was, in a way, a preservation of its mystery, and perhaps, a protection against its misuse.

"The SS's archives mentioned 'experimental energy frequencies' that they attempted to use to probe the main structure," Neumann recalled. "They referred to them as 'unstable' and 'unpredictable,' which ultimately led to their abandonment of those specific approaches. It's possible they were inadvertently interacting with this device, or a similar interface, and experiencing the same kind of resonant feedback, but without the understanding to interpret it."

The complexity of the encryption wasn't just a matter of advanced algorithms; it was a fundamental difference in the way information was stored and accessed. It suggested that the creators of this technology had a deeper understanding of the universe, perhaps one that integrated consciousness and technology in ways that humanity was only beginning to conceptualize. The SS, with their brutal, mechanistic approach, were fundamentally ill-equipped to comprehend such a system.

"We're still very much in the dark about the actual *content*," Jian Li admitted, a hint of weariness in his voice. "We can observe its responses, map its energy flows, and even identify patterns, but translating those patterns into meaningful data is a colossal undertaking. We're essentially trying to reverse-engineer an alien operating system based on its physical reactions."

The challenge was amplified by the sheer alienness of the information itself. Neumann suspected that the data stored within this device wouldn't be anything as mundane as scientific readings or historical records in a format they could easily digest. It might be a conceptual language, a form of consciousness, or a representation of reality that was fundamentally different from their own. The SS's limited understanding of physics and their biased ideological framework would have made them even less likely to grasp such abstract information.

"The SS's obsession with capturing and weaponizing every advanced technology they encountered meant they would have attempted to exploit this device, had they been able to," Neumann stated. "Their focus was always on power and control. If they had found a way to access the information, they would have tried to weaponize it, or at least integrate it into their military arsenal. Their inability to do so might have saved them from a far greater disaster."

Weber, meanwhile, had managed to isolate a specific set of resonant frequencies that seemed to elicit a more pronounced, stable response from the device. These frequencies were not simple tones but complex harmonic sequences, rich with subtle variations.

"This looks like a form of command language," she explained, her face illuminated by the glow of the display. "These specific harmonic structures, when applied in a particular sequence, cause the internal filaments to align in a stable configuration, almost like data packets being organized. It's still encrypted, but it's the closest we've come to a coherent interface."

The breakthrough, however small, offered a glimmer of hope. It suggested that a systematic, methodical approach, one that mirrored the aliens' own principles of resonance and harmonic interaction, might eventually yield results. This was a stark contrast to the SS's desperate, forceful methods.

"The SS were essentially trying to break down a door, while this device is designed to be opened with a specific key," Neumann observed. "We are trying to find that key, and it appears to be based on harmonic resonance rather than brute force."

The deeper they delved, the more apparent it became that the SS's involvement, while historically significant, was a mere shadow of the true nature of the anomaly. They had scratched the surface, detecting the faintest whispers of a profound technology, but they had lacked the fundamental understanding to truly comprehend it. Their efforts, their research, and their ultimate failure served as a cautionary tale, a stark reminder of the vastness of the unknown and the limitations of human ambition when confronted with forces beyond its current grasp. The data storage unit, humming softly in its analytical chamber, was a silent oracle, holding secrets that the Third Reich had desperately sought but could never attain. Neumann felt a profound sense of responsibility, not only to decipher the data but to ensure that this knowledge, if unlocked, was not subjected to the same destructive impulses that had characterized the SS's ill-fated investigation. The resonance he felt was not just curiosity; it was a somber acknowledgment of the power that lay dormant, waiting for the right kind of understanding, the right kind of approach, to finally awaken. The SS had inadvertently preserved the key, by failing to find it. Now, it was up to them to turn it.

The persistent hum of the obsidian cylinder had become a constant, almost comforting presence in the sterile analytical chamber. It was a low thrum, a steady heartbeat that seemed to synchronize with the collective pulse of Neumann's team. For weeks, they had been engaged in a silent, intricate dance with the alien artifact, a delicate probing of its defenses, a painstaking attempt to find a resonance that would unlock its secrets. Jian Li, his eyes bloodshot but alight with an almost feverish intensity, had been meticulously cataloging the device's energetic responses. He'd developed sophisticated algorithms to map the subtle shifts in the emitted frequencies, the minute fluctuations that Weber had identified as potential data carriers. The SS's approach had been brute force, a hammer against a lock. Neumann's team, armed with Weber's biological insights and Jian Li's computational prowess, were painstakingly crafting a key.

"Another harmonic sequence," Jian Li announced, his voice raspy from lack of sleep. He gestured towards a projection displaying a complex, multi-layered waveform. "This one is... different. It's eliciting a sustained coherence within the internal matrix. The filaments are not just pulsing; they're holding a specific configuration for longer periods. It's like a stable circuit has been established, albeit a fleeting one."

Weber, leaning closer to the data streams, nodded slowly. "The bio-luminescence is also intensifying in specific nodes along the matrix. It's not random excitation; it's structured. I'm seeing patterns emerge in the light emissions that correlate with the harmonic sequences Jian is applying. It's as if the internal 'processors' are activating."

Neumann felt a prickle of anticipation crawl up his spine. This was it. This was the moment they had been working towards, the subtle shift from random noise to discernible signal. The SS, in their hubris and technological limitations, had likely interpreted these sustained coherences as anomalies, as further evidence of the device's unpredictable nature. They wouldn't have had the framework to understand that they were witnessing the nascent stages of an interface, the first hesitant communication from an intelligence millennia beyond their comprehension.

"What does the correlation suggest, Weber?" Neumann asked, his voice tight with suppressed excitement.

"It suggests that these harmonic sequences are not just triggers, but are being integrated into the device's operational logic," she replied, her gaze riveted on the glowing filaments displayed on the monitor. "It's as if the device is processing the input, not just reacting to it. We're seeing a form of conditional response, where the output is influenced by the specific characteristics of the input waveform."

Jian Li began to systematically adjust the parameters of the harmonic sequences, layering them, subtly altering their amplitude and phase. Each adjustment was met with a corresponding, predictable shift in the device's internal state. The hum subtly deepened, and the ethereal glow within the cylinder intensified, painting faint, shifting patterns on the surrounding chamber walls.

"The SS reports alluded to 'energy spikes' and 'unpredictable field distortions' when they attempted their more aggressive probes," Neumann recalled, a grim realization dawning. "They saw instability. We're seeing a nascent operating system booting up."

The process was agonizingly slow. It was akin to deciphering an ancient, forgotten language, not by translating words, but by observing the subtle nuances of gesture, the rhythm of breath, the emotional cues of a speaker. Each successful sequence, each moment of sustained coherence, was a hard-won victory. They were building a vocabulary of energetic expression, a lexicon of alien intent.

Then, it happened.

A specific, intricate sequence of harmonics, one that Jian Li had spent nearly thirty-six hours refining, elicited a response that was unlike anything they had witnessed before. The hum stabilized into a steady, resonant tone. The internal crystalline structures pulsed in a synchronous, almost rhythmic fashion. And then, projected onto the screen before them, a single, alien character flickered into existence.

It was a glyph of impossible complexity, composed of flowing lines that seemed to bend and weave in three dimensions, hinting at

306

a spatial dimensionality beyond their immediate perception. It pulsed with a soft, internal light, and for a fleeting moment, Neumann felt a strange, almost cognitive resonance with it, a sense of familiarity that was utterly inexplicable.

"We have… an interface," Jian Li breathed, his voice thick with awe. He typed furiously, initiating a data retrieval protocol that had been designed for precisely this eventuality – the establishment of a rudimentary, yet functional, connection.

The screen flickered again. The alien glyph dissolved, replaced by a torrent of data. It was not a neatly organized file system, but a chaotic, yet structured, stream of information. Fragmented schematics, rendered in impossible geometries, flashed across the display. Scientific logs, detailing observations and experiments conducted by beings whose perspective on reality was clearly alien, scrolled by at a dizzying pace. The language was utterly incomprehensible, a series of intricate, flowing symbols that defied any known linguistic structure.

"It's not text in any conventional sense," Weber murmured, her fingers hovering over her console, trying to isolate individual data packets. "It's more like… raw informational constructs. They appear to be conceptually linked, rather than linearly arranged."

Despite the linguistic barrier, something else emerged from the data stream that immediately captivated their attention: visual information. Interspersed with the incomprehensible logs and schematics were images. These were not photographs or artistic renderings; they were holographic projections, rendered with a clarity and depth that made their own holographic technology seem crude and rudimentary. They depicted celestial phenomena, alien landscapes, and what appeared to be biological organisms of staggering diversity.

"The SS's records mentioned 'visual disturbances' and 'illusory projections' when they attempted to interface with the larger structure," Neumann said, his mind racing. "They probably couldn't distinguish between data corruption and actual information. They were looking for recognizable signals; they weren't equipped to interpret concepts presented visually through energy manipulation."

One of the holographic images solidified on the main screen. It depicted a vast, swirling nebula, rendered in colors that seemed to vibrate with an inner light. Within the nebula, intricate, filamentary structures coalesced and dissolved, forming and reforming in a cosmic dance. Neumann felt an almost overwhelming sense of awe, a profound realization of humanity's minuscule place in the grand tapestry of the universe.

"This... this is a star chart," Jian Li stammered, pointing to subtle patterns within the nebula that mirrored known celestial configurations, albeit from an impossibly distant perspective. "But the detail... the resolution... it's beyond anything we can achieve."

As Jian Li continued to sift through the data stream, he began to identify recurring patterns, almost like recurring motifs in a complex symphony. He theorized that these were not just random occurrences but fundamental organizational principles, the underlying grammar of the alien information.

"I'm seeing what appear to be historical records," Jian Li announced, his voice hushed. "Fragmented narratives, presented through a combination of symbolic language and visual representation. It's like a form of ultra-high-density information storage, where concepts are conveyed through integrated sensory data."

One of these "historical" sequences began to play out. It depicted a civilization, their cities soaring into impossibly blue skies, their inhabitants moving with an grace that suggested perfect harmony with their environment. There were scenes of intellectual pursuit, of artistic creation, of interstellar travel depicted not through the clunky mechanics of rockets, but through the effortless manipulation of spacetime.

"The SS, in their pursuit of technological superiority, were so focused on tangible weaponry and control," Neumann mused. "They would have completely missed the elegance and sophistication of a civilization that prioritized understanding and integration. They were looking for how to *conquer* the universe; these beings seem to have sought how to *understand* it."

Weber's analysis of the schematics was equally revelatory. They depicted not just advanced machinery, but integrated bio-mechanical systems, devices that seemed to blur the lines between living organisms and inert technology. There were designs for energy conduits that mimicked biological circulatory systems, for computational matrices that utilized crystalline structures akin to neural networks, and for communication arrays that seemed to tap into fundamental universal energies.

"This isn't just technology," Weber stated, her voice filled with wonder. "It's a synthesis. It's as if they understood that the universe itself is an interconnected system, and that technology should operate in harmony with those fundamental principles, not in opposition to them. The SS's obsession with harnessing power through force and destruction would have been utterly antithetical to this approach."

The data stream continued to pour in, a ceaseless deluge of alien knowledge. Neumann and his team worked feverishly, trying to categorize, to find anchors in this sea of the unknown. They were no longer just archaeologists of forgotten technology; they were cultural anthropologists, attempting to understand the consciousness of a species that had mastered the universe in ways humanity could only dream of.

The sheer volume and complexity of the data were overwhelming. Jian Li had to develop entirely new analytical frameworks, constantly adapting his algorithms to the emergent patterns. Weber was creating an exhaustive catalog of the alien bio-mechanical designs, trying to deduce their functions from their intricate forms.

"I'm beginning to identify recurring themes in these 'historical' logs," Jian Li said, pointing to a series of visually encoded narratives. "There are references to cycles of creation and destruction, to the evolution of consciousness, and to a profound respect for the interconnectedness of all life. It suggests a philosophical underpinning to their technological advancement that was entirely absent in the Nazi ideology."

The SS had been driven by a nihilistic desire for dominance, a yearning to impose their will on the world through brute force and engineered terror. What they found in this alien data was not a weapon, but a testament to a civilization that had achieved a higher state of being through wisdom and understanding. The fragmented records spoke of a deep reverence for the cosmos, of a profound understanding of the forces that governed existence, and of a long-term perspective that spanned millennia.

Neumann felt a growing sense of responsibility. This knowledge, if it could be fully deciphered, held the potential to fundamentally alter humanity's trajectory. It offered a glimpse of what was possible when intelligence was guided by empathy and a deep respect for the natural order. The SS, in their blind pursuit of power, had almost succeeded in burying this enlightenment, in reducing a testament to cosmic harmony into a potential tool for their own annihilation.

"The SS's failure to access this data wasn't just a technological limitation," Neumann observed, a note of grim satisfaction in his voice. "It was a moral and philosophical failure. They were incapable of understanding a technology that was not rooted in conquest and control. They were looking for a hammer, and they found a violin."

As the hours bled into days, the team managed to establish a more stable interface. They could now reliably access specific segments of the data, though the overarching narrative remained tantalizingly out of reach. They had unlocked layers of encrypted information, revealing schematics for devices that defied conventional physics, scientific logs that spoke of principles they were only beginning to grasp, and what appeared to be historical records that offered a glimpse into a truly alien civilization. The language remained incomprehensible, a beautiful, intricate cipher, but the visual data provided a powerful, albeit incomplete, narrative. They had cracked open the door, and the universe, in all its alien wonder and complexity, was beginning to reveal itself. The hum of the cylinder was no longer just a sound; it was a symphony of cosmic knowledge, waiting to be understood. The SS had sought to weaponize the unknown; Neumann and his team were striving to comprehend it, to learn from it, and perhaps, to ensure that humanity's own journey towards the stars was guided by wisdom, not by war. The vastness of the cosmos, once a distant, abstract concept, now felt intimately close, a frontier not of conquest, but of profound discovery.

The hum of the obsidian cylinder, once a source of anticipation, now seemed to throb with an unsettling undertone. The data streams, previously a tantalizing cascade of scientific wonder, had taken a darker, more disquieting turn. Jian Li's initial excitement had been gradually replaced by a grim focus, his fingers flying across the console with a new urgency, sifting through layers of information that spoke of a horrifying perversion of advanced knowledge. Weber, her brow furrowed in concentration, was meticulously analyzing visual data that Neumann had initially dismissed as abstract representations of energy matrices. Now, she recognized them as something far more sinister.

"Neumann," Weber's voice was a low murmur, laced with a chilling disbelief, "you need to see this. The 'filamentary structures' you saw coalescing in the nebula... they're not just cosmic phenomena. This particular sequence... it's a schematic. An incredibly detailed one."

She adjusted the projection, zooming in on a complex arrangement of lines and nodes. It wasn't the flowing, organic architecture they had begun to associate with the alien civilization's inherent harmony. This was stark, angular, and disturbingly familiar. Neumann leaned closer, a cold knot forming in his stomach. The SS. Their presence, their footprint, was undeniable.

"What am I looking at, Weber?" Neumann's voice was strained.

"It's a blueprint, Neumann," she replied, her gaze fixed on the screen. "A design for... something mechanical. But the energy conduits, the power core configuration... it's alien. But the integration, the framework, is unmistakably SS. They've taken the fundamental principles, the energy signatures we're seeing from the cylinder, and grafted them onto their own brutalist engineering."

As if on cue, Jian Li interrupted his frantic analysis. "I've isolated another visual sequence, Dr. Neumann. This is... different. It's not a schematic. It's a record. A visual log."

The main screen shifted, and the awe-inspiring vistas of alien worlds vanished, replaced by something starkly mundane, yet

311

chillingly significant. It was a dense, unfamiliar forest, the trees impossibly tall and ancient, bathed in a twilight that seemed to absorb all sound. Then, the scene abruptly changed. A colossal, dark object, undoubtedly the alien craft, was depicted embedded in the earth, its obsidian surface rent and smoking. Neumann recognized the impact zone from the fragmented reports he'd studied from the SS archives – a remote, uncharted wilderness.

The visual data continued to flow, a relentless stream of disturbing imagery. The captured aliens, their forms clearly visible, their expressions unreadable even in their stunned, bewildered state, were being subjected to examination. Not the gentle, analytical probing of Weber's team, but something rougher, more invasive. The SS personnel, clad in their grim, utilitarian uniforms, were depicted wielding instruments that Neumann recognized with a sickening lurch – modified scientific equipment, clearly repurposed for their own twisted agenda.

"They didn't just recover it," Neumann breathed, the implications of the data crashing down on him. "They actively engaged with it. They captured them."

The images then shifted again, plunging them into the heart of clandestine Nazi facilities. Stark, utilitarian laboratories filled with an unnerving blend of advanced alien technology and crude, yet powerful, SS engineering. Neumann saw towering energy conduits that mimicked the resonant frequencies of the cylinder, but were crudely integrated with heavy, metallic casings. Holographic projectors, far cruder than the ethereal displays of the alien civilization, flickered with distorted images. It was a perversion, a brutalization of the elegant, sophisticated knowledge they were slowly beginning to unravel.

"Look at this," Weber said, her voice barely a whisper. She highlighted a section of the display showing a group of SS scientists clustered around a large, pulsating alien artifact. They were not studying its potential for understanding or communication, but for raw power, for weaponization. The alien technology was being bent to their will, its inherent harmony twisted into something aggressive and destructive.

Jian Li's fingers paused. "The data logs associated with these visuals... they're not scientific observations in any meaningful sense, Neumann. They're propaganda. They're framing the aliens... and the technology itself... as instruments of a new world order. It's the same rhetoric we saw in the salvaged SS documents, but now... it's being augmented by their distorted interpretation of this alien knowledge."

The visual data became more disturbing. Glimpses of horrific experiments flashed across the screen. Alien biological matter being dissected, their unique physiological structures analyzed not for comprehension, but for potential application in their own horrifying eugenics programs. Neumann saw disturbing schematics of what appeared to be weaponry, designed to harness the fundamental energies of the universe, but with a clear intent to inflict mass destruction. The SS had found a civilization that had seemingly transcended conflict, and they had immediately sought to weaponize its very essence.

"They're linking the aliens to... Aryan supremacy," Weber said, her voice cracking. She was viewing a series of graphic stills, clearly intended as propaganda posters. Alien beings, their forms distorted and menacing, were juxtaposed with idealized Aryan figures, their advanced technology portrayed as the ultimate validation of their racial ideology. The SS had always sought to legitimize their warped worldview through any means necessary, and now they had latched onto the undeniable power of alien artifacts, twisting them to serve their degenerate cause.

"It's a complete fabrication," Neumann stated, his jaw tight. "The very nature of this civilization, from what we've managed to glean, is one of integration, of universal harmony. To twist that into a narrative of racial superiority... it's a blasphemy. It's the antithesis of everything this knowledge represents."

Jian Li was painstakingly cross-referencing the visual logs with the energy signatures emanating from the cylinder. "The SS attempted to create weaponry based on the alien propulsion systems," he explained, his voice tight with a mixture of scientific curiosity and revulsion. "They managed to achieve partial successes, but the energy containment was... unstable. Their brute-force approach, their inability to grasp the underlying principles of resonance and flow, led to catastrophic failures. These logs depict some of those early attempts."

The screen flickered again, showing a brief, chaotic burst of energy from one of the crude SS devices, followed by an explosion. The image was stark, raw, and terrifying. It was a testament to the SS's technological prowess, but also to their inherent limitations when faced with a paradigm so fundamentally different from their own. They could mimic the form, but they could not grasp the spirit.

"They were trying to force the universe into their own narrow, hateful ideology," Neumann said, his gaze fixed on the images of the SS facilities. "They saw advanced technology, and their first thought was conquest, domination. They couldn't conceive of a civilization that might have achieved its advancements through understanding, through cooperation with the fundamental forces of existence."

Weber pointed to another set of images. These depicted the alien craft, not crashed and broken, but in flight, its obsidian hull shimmering with an inner luminescence. Interspersed were visualizations of the SS attempting to replicate this flight capability, their own crude prototypes sputtering and failing to achieve the same effortless grace.

"Their attempts to weaponize the propulsion system were ultimately unsuccessful on a large scale," Weber noted. "The logs indicate significant setbacks and a high rate of catastrophic failure. They could not replicate the controlled manipulation of gravitational fields that the aliens had mastered. Their methods were too… blunt."

Neumann felt a surge of something akin to relief, quickly followed by a profound sense of sadness. The SS, in their insatiable hunger for power, had been a destructive force, incapable of appreciating the true marvel of what they had encountered. They had sought to enslave the universe, and in their attempt to weaponize alien technology, they had only managed to reveal their own profound ignorance and their capacity for immense destruction.

"They saw the potential for power, and they ignored the potential for enlightenment," Neumann mused. "They were so blinded by their lust for dominance that they couldn't see the true value of this knowledge. They were looking for a weapon, and they found a lesson in cosmic responsibility."

Jian Li's attention was drawn to a series of intricate energy diagrams, far more complex than anything he had seen before. "This sequence," he announced, his voice filled with renewed scientific curiosity, albeit tempered by the preceding horror, "it seems to detail the SS's attempts to interface with the alien consciousness. Not through direct communication, but through forced neurological manipulation. They were trying to extract information, to understand the aliens' thought processes, but through... invasive means."

The visual data shifted again, showing what appeared to be crude attempts at psychic interface, with SS scientists attempting to bridge the gap between their own minds and the captured aliens. The results, Neumann suspected, were not what they had hoped for. The alien minds, presumably operating on principles far removed from human cognition, were likely resistant to such crude attempts at intrusion.

"It's a form of technological lobotomy," Weber murmured, analyzing the complex biological schematics associated with these invasive procedures. "They were trying to force the aliens to reveal their secrets, to break their will. It's a testament to their utter lack of empathy, their inability to conceive of intelligence or existence beyond their own narrow framework."

The recovered data was a stark, brutal indictment of the SS's ideology and their methods. It showcased their ability to integrate advanced alien technology, but also their fundamental inability to comprehend its true purpose or its inherent value. They had taken the whispers of the cosmos and twisted them into a cacophony of hate and destruction, a perversion of knowledge that served only to highlight their own moral bankruptcy. The visual logs were a chilling reminder that even the most advanced technology could be wielded for the basest of purposes, when placed in the hands of those driven by a lust for power and a profound emptiness of spirit. Neumann knew, with a chilling certainty, that the SS had not merely encountered alien technology; they had attempted to corrupt it, to twist it into a tool for their own genocidal ambitions. The truth, as always, was far more horrifying than any fiction. The images on the screen were not just historical records; they were a testament to humanity's capacity for both incredible innovation and unspeakable barbarity, a stark warning from the past that resonated with a chilling relevance in the present. The alien cylinder, once a beacon of hope, now felt like a silent witness to a forgotten atrocity, its stored knowledge a heavy burden, a reminder of the darkness that humanity was capable of, and the immense responsibility that came with wielding such power.

The hum of the obsidian cylinder had shifted, its resonant frequency deepening from a gentle thrum to a more insistent vibration that seemed to permeate the very air of the cavern. Jian Li, his eyes still glued to the intricate energy readouts, noticed the change first. "Dr. Neumann," he called out, his voice tinged with a new kind of excitement, one that held a faint tremor of apprehension, "the resonance patterns... they're not stable anymore. They're... modulating. Cycling through a series of frequencies I haven't observed before."

Neumann moved closer, his gaze flicking from the cylinder's glowing surface to the complex data displayed on Jian Li's monitor. Weber, her keen eyes following Neumann's movement, joined them, her own analysis of the SS propaganda feed momentarily forgotten. The visual data of the SS's horrific appropriation of alien technology had painted a grim picture, but this... this was something new, something potentially independent of the SS's destructive interference.

"Modulating how, Jian?" Neumann asked, his voice low, attempting to keep his own rising curiosity in check. The SS's attempts to weaponize this technology had been a grotesque perversion, but the core principles, the fundamental understanding of its capabilities, remained largely a mystery. Neumann harbored a desperate hope that some aspect of the alien civilization's true purpose remained intact, perhaps even encoded within the very artifact that had drawn the SS's rapacious attention.

"It's a complex sequence, Neumann," Jian Li replied, his fingers dancing across the console. "Not random. It's like... a

316

language. Or a key. It's broadcasting, but the signal is extremely focused. Almost directional, as if it's aimed at a specific point in the cosmos." He paused, his brow furrowed in concentration. "The energy expenditure is minimal, incredibly efficient. This isn't just a power source, Neumann. This… this is a transmitter."

Weber's eyes widened as a thought struck her. "A beacon," she breathed, the word hanging in the air, laden with a sudden weight of possibility. "The way it's designed to transmit, the targeted nature of the signal… it's not just a broadcast. It's a signal sent with intent. To be received."

Neumann's mind raced, piecing together the fragmented understanding they had of the alien civilization. Their technology was inherently interwoven with the fabric of the universe, its energy systems operating on principles that transcended mere mechanics. If this cylinder was a transmitter, then it was likely designed to communicate, to share knowledge, perhaps even to seek out others of its kind. "But why now?" Neumann mused aloud, looking at the obsidian surface that seemed to pulse with a life of its own. "What triggered this activation?"

Jian Li scrolled through a cascade of diagnostic data. "That's the peculiar part, Neumann. There's no external stimulus that should have initiated this sequence. No manual override detected, no environmental trigger that fits our known parameters for artificial activation. It's as if… it just decided to turn itself on."

But Neumann knew better than to believe in such coincidences. The SS, in their relentless pursuit of power, had unearthed this artifact, had attempted to exploit its energies. While their destructive efforts had ultimately failed to fully unlock its secrets, it was possible that their presence, the residual energies from their own advanced, albeit crude, technological interventions, had inadvertently set in motion a pre-programmed sequence. The concept was chillingly plausible: a failsafe, a last resort designed to activate under specific, perhaps even dire, conditions.

"What about Falk?" Neumann suddenly asked, recalling the SS scientist whose recovered journals had provided crucial, albeit fragmented, insights into their early investigations. "Did his notes mention anything about a broadcast protocol? A contingency for the cylinder's activation?"

Weber, who had been poring over the same recovered documents, shook her head. "His entries were maddeningly vague on that point, Neumann. He spoke of the 'Obelisk's' potential for communication, of its ability to pierce the veil of... well, the void. But he was always so focused on weaponization, on harnessing its power for their own ends. He described a 'master sequence,' a coded activation that was to be initiated only when all other avenues were exhausted. He was meticulous, Falk. He would have planned for every eventuality."

Jian Li's fingers stilled over the console. "A master sequence," he repeated, a spark of understanding igniting in his eyes. "The modulation patterns... they're not entirely alien. There are underlying mathematical constants, predictable numerical progressions that are... familiar. Almost... terrestrial. Like they've been overlaid or integrated with something else."

Neumann's mind flashed back to the SS laboratories depicted in the visual logs. The crude integration of alien technology with their own brutish engineering. It was a horrifying fusion, a perversion of the elegant alien designs. Could it be that Falk, in his twisted genius, had managed to... influence the cylinder? To imbue it with a mechanism that would respond not just to external cosmic forces, but to terrestrial interventions as well?

"Are you saying Falk might have programmed it?" Neumann asked, the implication staggering.

"It's a strong possibility, Neumann," Jian Li confirmed, his voice resonating with a growing conviction. "The energy signature associated with this modulating frequency has a distinct spectral imprint. It's not purely alien. There's an overlay, a harmonic distortion that aligns with the energy signatures of SS power generation systems. Specifically, the high-frequency resonance generators they were experimenting with."

The implications were profound. If Falk, or others within the SS hierarchy, had managed to inject their own code into the cylinder, then this beacon wasn't just an alien distress signal. It was a signal that had been *activated* by the SS, intentionally or accidentally, and was now broadcasting not just into the void, but perhaps with a specific target or purpose that reflected their own warped ideology.

"What kind of signal is it, Jian?" Weber pressed, her gaze fixed on the flickering readouts. "What information is it transmitting?"

"That's the difficult part," Jian Li admitted, frustration creeping into his tone. "The raw data stream is heavily encrypted. It's not a simple radio wave. It's... multidimensional. It's encoded in a way that uses the very fabric of spacetime as its medium. Imagine trying to read a book written on the ripples of water. We're getting glimpses, fragments, but deciphering the full message... it will take time. A lot of time."

Neumann paced the cavern floor, the weight of this new revelation pressing down on him. The SS had been a force of destruction, of hatred, but they had also possessed a chillingly effective capacity for technological advancement, albeit through brutal and unethical means. If they had managed to imprint their own signal onto this alien beacon, what message were they sending into the universe? A message of conquest? A declaration of their twisted dominion?

"We need to understand what it's saying," Neumann stated, his voice firm, cutting through the mounting tension. "And we need to understand *why* it's broadcasting now. Jian, focus on decrypting that signal. Weber, go back to Falk's journals. Look for any mention of a 'master sequence,' a trigger condition, anything that could explain how our presence, or the residual energies of our equipment, might have bypassed the SS's own attempts at control and initiated this broadcast."

He cast a glance at the obsidian cylinder. It seemed to hum with an ancient power, a silent testament to a civilization far beyond their current comprehension. But now, it was also a potential herald of something unknown, something potentially dangerous, imprinted with the echo of humanity's darkest chapter. The SS had not just sought to control this technology; they had sought to repurpose it, to twist its intended purpose into a weapon. And now, it seemed, their fingerprints were all over its activation.

Weber returned to her workstation, her brow furrowed as she meticulously cross-referenced Falk's increasingly frantic scribblings. Jian Li was lost in the labyrinthine complexities of the alien signal, his world reduced to the dance of numbers and spectral lines on his monitors. Neumann stood by the cylinder, his hand hovering inches above its impossibly smooth surface. He could feel a faint warmth emanating from it, a residual energy that spoke of immense power held in check.

"Anything, Weber?" Neumann asked, after what felt like an eternity.

Weber sighed, rubbing her temples. "Falk's entries become more erratic around this period, Neumann. He was obsessed with what he called 'harmonic resonance alignment.' He believed the cylinder wasn't just a repository of knowledge, but a conduit, capable of transmitting and receiving information across vast cosmic distances. He was convinced that by aligning its resonant frequencies with specific celestial bodies, they could establish a 'universal nexus.'"

"A universal nexus?" Neumann repeated, a flicker of unease.

"Yes. He theorized that this nexus could be used for communication, but also for… manipulation. He wrote about a 'failsafe protocol,' a way to ensure that the nexus remained under SS control. It involved a specific sequence of energy pulses, keyed to their own advanced propulsion systems. He believed that if the cylinder were ever threatened or compromised, this sequence would activate, broadcasting a specific coded message to an unknown recipient."

Jian Li chimed in, his voice tight with discovery. "Neumann, I think I've found it. The 'coded message.' It's not just data. It's a complex series of coordinates, interwoven with bio-signatures and energy readings. And the target… it's not a star system we recognize. It's… an anomaly. A gravitational singularity, deep within the Andromeda galaxy."

Neumann's blood ran cold. "Andromeda? Why there?"

"Falk's logs mention it," Weber said, her voice a hushed

whisper. "He believed it was a focal point, a nexus where interstellar energies converged. He thought that by broadcasting to it, they could reach... something. Or someone. He was convinced it was the key to unlocking a new era of SS dominance."

The pieces were falling into place, a chilling mosaic of ambition and destruction. The SS, in their desperate attempts to control and weaponize the alien artifact, had inadvertently stumbled upon a way to activate its beacon. Falk's meticulous planning, his misguided genius, had ensured that the cylinder was not merely a passive observer, but an active participant, capable of broadcasting its presence across the cosmos. And now, their activation of the site, the very energy signatures of their excavation equipment, had provided the final trigger for Falk's programmed master sequence.

"So the cylinder is broadcasting," Neumann stated, the enormity of the situation sinking in. "But to where, and to whom? And what is this 'something' Falk was so convinced he could reach?"

Jian Li's fingers flew across the console once more. "The signal is structured in a way that suggests a response is expected. It's not just a static transmission. It's designed to elicit a reply. The complexity of the modulation, the specific frequencies being used... it's like a digital handshake, Neumann. A way of saying, 'We are here, and this is our signal.'"

Neumann looked back at the obsidian cylinder, no longer just a relic of a lost civilization, but a harbinger of the unknown. The SS had sought to weaponize it, to twist its purpose into a tool of conquest. They had failed to fully control it, but they had succeeded in setting it in motion. And now, its silent broadcast was reaching out into the vast expanse of space, carrying not just the legacy of an alien race, but also the indelible mark of humanity's darkest impulses. The signal had awakened, and with it, a new era of uncertainty and peril had begun. The true extent of Falk's programmed signal, and the potential implications of a response from the depths of Andromeda, remained a terrifying, unknown variable. They had uncovered a beacon, but they had also, inadvertently, sent a signal of their own into the void, a signal that could very well change the course of human history, for better or for worse. The silent hum of the cylinder was no longer just a sound; it

321

was a question, sent out into the cosmic darkness, waiting for an answer.

The implications of Falk's involvement gnawed at Neumann. He had been a scientist, albeit one consumed by the SS's warped ideology. Yet, his journals hinted at a deeper, more complex understanding of the alien technology, a prescient fear of its misuse. Could Falk have seen the ultimate danger of Project Veil? Had he, in his own way, attempted to subvert or control the very weapon he helped to create? The idea was a fragile sliver of hope in the encroaching darkness. If Falk had indeed left a backdoor, a hidden safeguard, it might be their only chance.

"Weber, focus on Falk's personal logs," Neumann commanded, his voice gaining a new urgency. "Anything that deviates from the official SS doctrine. Any sign of dissent, any indication he was trying to mitigate the damage, or perhaps... steer the technology towards a different purpose. He must have anticipated the SS's ultimate goals. He was too intelligent, too meticulous not to."

Weber nodded, her fingers already flying across her data pad. The recovered files were a chaotic tapestry of scientific jargon, military directives, and increasingly desperate personal reflections. It was within this jumble that they hoped to find the thread of Falk's true intentions, the hidden legacy that might just save them.

Jian Li, meanwhile, was wrestling with the alien data stream itself. The encryption was unlike anything he had ever encountered, a multi-layered construct that seemed to adapt and shift in real-time. "It's like a living code, Neumann," he muttered, his eyes wide with a mixture of awe and frustration. "The SS didn't just imprint a message; they've interwoven it with the alien protocols. It's a symbiosis of technologies, an alien beacon twisted into a weaponized communication channel."

He paused, his gaze fixed on a newly emerging pattern on his screen. "Wait... there's something here. A sub-harmonic frequency that's almost... musical. It's overlaid on the primary broadcast, very faint, but it's structured. It's not part of the SS transmission. It's... older. Deeper. It's like a ghost in the machine."

Neumann and Weber looked up, their attention immediately

drawn to Jian Li's discovery. Could this be it? A remnant of the original alien transmission, a pure signal untouched by the SS's corruption?

"Can you isolate it?" Neumann asked, his voice hushed.

"I'm trying," Jian Li replied, his focus absolute. "It's buried deep. They tried to mask it, to drown it out with their own signal. But it's persistent. It's... resilient."

As Jian Li worked, Weber let out a sharp intake of breath. "Neumann, look at this. This entry from Falk, dated just weeks before the SS took him. He's writing about Project Veil. He's referring to it as... 'the final silencing.'"

Neumann's heart sank. "The final silencing? What does he mean?"

"He doesn't elaborate much, but he mentions a specific target for this 'silencing.' He describes it as a 'perfected signal,' designed to reach a specific destination and, in his words, 'ensure the eradication of all dissenting frequencies.'" Weber's voice trembled. "He believed the SS were not just seeking to communicate, but to dominate. To impose their will, their ideology, on the very fabric of the universe."

The SS's plan was more horrifying than they had imagined. Project Veil was not merely a weapon; it was a means of universal censorship, a tool to erase any form of consciousness or existence that did not conform to their twisted vision. And the alien beacon, this ancient marvel of exploration and communication, was being perverted into the instrument of its execution.

"And the destination?" Neumann pressed, dread coiling in his gut.

Weber scrolled down, her face pale. "He writes of 'the Great Filter' as the ultimate target. He believed that by broadcasting a signal that amplified the SS's inherent destructive frequencies, they could trigger a universal 'reset,' eliminating any nascent civilizations that had not yet achieved interstellar travel, thereby preserving their own nascent dominance."

The SS were not just seeking to send a message; they were

attempting to sculpt the very evolution of life in the cosmos. They believed themselves to be the apex of existence, and anyone or anything that did not fit their narrow definition was to be systematically purged. The alien beacon, designed for connection and discovery, was to become the harbinger of universal extinction.

"He was trying to stop it," Neumann realized, a dawning understanding of Falk's actions. "He knew what they were planning. He was trying to sabotage it, or at least, to leave a warning."

"This 'ghost in the machine' Jian is finding," Weber said, her eyes meeting Neumann's, a shared and terrifying realization passing between them. "It could be Falk's warning. His attempt to preserve the original purpose of the beacon, to counteract the SS's signal."

Suddenly, Jian Li exclaimed, "I have it! I've managed to isolate the sub-harmonic frequency. It's... beautiful. It's a complex, multi-tonal melody, unlike anything I've ever heard. And it's not just sound... it's encoded with data."

He brought up a new set of readouts, displaying a stream of elegant, almost poetic data structures. "This is the original transmission. It's a record of their journey, their observations... their intent was peaceful. They were explorers, cataloging the universe, seeking to understand."

The data also revealed something else, something Falk had likely discovered and tried to amplify. The alien beacon possessed a unique property: it could adapt its signal based on the receiver's own fundamental frequency. The SS, in their hubris, believed they could imprint their will onto this adaptive system, forcing it to broadcast their hateful ideology. But Falk, understanding the true nature of the beacon, had attempted to encode a counter-frequency, a 'dissenting' signal that would resonate with the beacon's original programming, overriding the SS's corrupted message.

"Falk believed that if the SS managed to activate the beacon with their 'final silencing' protocol," Weber explained, her voice strained, "this counter-frequency would engage. It would broadcast the truth of the SS's intentions, and simultaneously, activate a dormant failsafe within the beacon itself."

"A failsafe?" Neumann echoed, hope flickering anew.

"Yes," Weber confirmed. "A way to permanently disable the beacon's transmission capabilities, rendering it inert. Falk's last desperate act to prevent the SS from achieving their goal."

The SS had not only stolen the alien technology but had also corrupted its purpose, turning an instrument of exploration into a weapon of cosmic genocide. Project Veil, as Falk had feared, was a plan to silence the universe. But in his final moments, Falk had managed to embed a hidden legacy, a counter-narrative encoded within the very signal the SS believed they controlled.

"So the signal we're detecting," Neumann concluded, the pieces falling into place with a chilling finality, "is the SS's corrupted transmission, fighting against Falk's original message, his warning."

"Precisely," Jian Li confirmed. "The beacon is in a state of... internal conflict. The SS signal is powerful, amplified by their own technology, but Falk's is deeply embedded, resonating with the beacon's core programming."

Neumann's gaze fell upon the obsidian cylinder, its surface now seeming to throb with a silent, internal struggle. The SS had thought they were sending a message of conquest. Falk had attempted to send a message of truth and preservation. And now, this ancient alien artifact was caught in the crossfire of humanity's own darkest ambitions.

"We have to amplify Falk's signal," Neumann declared, his voice ringing with newfound resolve. "We have to ensure his warning reaches its intended destination, and that the failsafe is activated. If we don't, Project Veil might succeed in silencing the universe."

The task was immense; the data stream a treacherous labyrinth of alien code and SS interference. But for the first time since they had unearthed this artifact, Neumann felt a flicker of genuine hope. Falk, the SS scientist who had dabbled in the terrifying power of Project Veil, had also, in his own conflicted way, tried to stop it. His legacy, buried deep within the heart of an alien beacon, might just be the key to preventing a cosmic catastrophe. The signal had awakened, not just with the SS's intent, but with the faint, yet persistent, echo of a scientist's desperate attempt to redeem himself, and perhaps, to save existence itself. The hidden history was unfolding, revealing a conspiracy of unimaginable scope, and within it, a glimmer of hope, a testament to the enduring power of truth, even in the face of absolute darkness.

Chapter 15

Echoes of Falk's Legacy

The spectral analysis of the alien transmission, painstakingly compiled by Jian Li, presented a stark and terrifying tableau. It wasn't merely a collection of frequencies and energy signatures; it was a narrative, albeit one woven with alien logic and SS corruption. Neumann, Weber, and Jian Li huddled around the central console, the low hum of the cavern now a counterpoint to the urgent whispers of discovery and dread. The data streams, once abstract numbers, were beginning to resolve into something tangible, something that spoke of the SS's perversion of an ancient power on a scale that defied comprehension.

"Look at this, Neumann," Jian Li murmured, his finger tracing a particularly dense cluster of data points. "The primary signal, the one Falk tried to suppress, it's still there, buried beneath the SS noise. But the SS amplification... it's significant. They've boosted certain frequencies, twisted others. It's like they've taken an ancient symphony and forced it to play a dirge."

Weber leaned in, her gaze fixed on a section of the data Jian Li had highlighted. "These specific energy modulations... they correspond with known SS experimental weapon signatures. Specifically, Project Nightingale." She shivered, recalling the fragmented reports of SS experiments designed to induce mass hysteria and psychological breakdown through sonic frequencies. "But this is on an entirely different order of magnitude. They're not just aiming for localized terror. They're talking about 'psychotropic disintegration' on a planetary scale."

The term hung heavy in the air. Psychotropic disintegration. It conjured images of minds unraveling, of reality itself fracturing. The SS, in their insatiable hunger for power, had sought not just to

327

conquer through brute force, but to dismantle the very minds of their enemies, to obliterate their history, their identity, their will to exist. This alien artifact, this beacon of cosmic communication, was being repurposed as a weapon of unparalleled psychological warfare.

"And look here," Neumann interjected, pointing to another anomaly in the data. "These cyclical energy surges... they're not random. They're patterned, almost like controlled bursts. Jian, cross-reference these with the SS directives recovered from Himmler's personal archives."

Jian Li's fingers flew across the interface. The recovered archives, painstakingly translated and analyzed, had already painted a chilling portrait of the SS leadership's descent into madness. Figures like Himmler, with his obsession with esoteric rituals and racial purity, and Goebbels, the architect of Nazi propaganda, were not merely overseeing the weaponization of alien technology; they were actively involved in shaping its application, infusing it with their own depraved ideologies.

The cross-referencing was almost immediate. A cold dread settled over Neumann as the data synchronized. "'Resonance purges'," he read aloud from a translated SS memo. "'The systematic elimination of dissonant historical echoes. Employing frequency modulation to disintegrate ideological impurities and reinforce the nationalistic ether.'"

"Dissonant historical echoes," Weber repeated, her voice barely a whisper. "They're not just targeting living minds; they're targeting history itself. They want to erase any memory, any trace of anything that contradicts their narrative. They're aiming to rewrite reality, not just on a physical plane, but on a conceptual one."

The implications were staggering. The SS, under the influence of leaders like Himmler and Goebbels, had envisioned a universe cleansed of anything they deemed impure, anything that deviated from their twisted vision of Aryan supremacy. This alien beacon, with its inherent ability to transmit and influence, was their ultimate tool for achieving this horrifying objective. They weren't just sending a message; they were attempting to broadcast a universal psychic purge, a selective erasure of consciousness and history.

"Falk's original data," Jian Li said, his voice strained, "it describes the beacon as a tool for 'harmonizing universal consciousness.' He believed it could foster understanding, bridge the gaps between species. He saw it as a means of connecting, of sharing knowledge across the vastness of space. The SS have taken that concept and twisted it into its antithesis."

The SS directives detailed a phased approach to this cosmic genocide. Phase one involved identifying and amplifying "dissonant frequencies" – anything that represented opposition, independent thought, or cultural diversity. These were to be systematically targeted and amplified until they overloaded and disintegrated, both at a psychic and, where possible, a physical level. This was the "psychotropic disintegration" Jian Li had mentioned earlier.

Phase two involved the "resonance purges." These were more insidious, designed to overwrite existing historical narratives and cultural memories with the SS's manufactured history. The alien beacon's ability to transmit complex data across vast distances was being exploited to implant a singular, SS-approved worldview into any civilization receptive to its signal. It was a form of cosmic indoctrination, a means of ensuring that all future understanding of the universe was filtered through the lens of Nazi ideology.

Neumann recalled the visual logs from the SS research facilities. The sheer scale of their operation was horrifying. They had repurposed vast underground complexes, turning them into colossal resonance chambers, attempting to synchronize the alien artifact with their own crude, yet powerful, terrestrial technologies. The ambition was terrifying in its scope – nothing less than the reordering of galactic consciousness to conform to their warped ideals.

"Himmler's personal logs are particularly disturbing," Weber noted, her voice tight with revulsion. "He refers to the beacon as 'the ultimate instrument of purification.' He believed that by purging the universe of 'undesirable frequencies,' they were fulfilling a cosmic mandate, a divine destiny."

"And Goebbels," Jian Li added, displaying a holographic projection of a heavily annotated SS propaganda broadcast. "He was already planning the universal dissemination of this 'purified' reality. He saw it as the ultimate propaganda victory, a way to ensure the SS's ideology would echo through eternity, unchallenged and absolute."

The SS's plan was a chilling testament to their nihilistic worldview. They were not content with conquest; they craved absolute control, not just over bodies and minds, but over the very fabric of existence and history. The alien beacon, a symbol of cosmic connection, was being transformed into the ultimate weapon of existential annihilation.

Neumann felt a cold dread grip him. They had discovered not just a lost technology, but the SS's ultimate weapon, a device capable of rewriting reality and erasing entire cultures from existence. The implications were far-reaching, the potential consequences catastrophic. If the SS had succeeded in activating this beacon, if their signal had already propagated through the cosmos, then the universe as they knew it might already be irrevocably altered, its diverse tapestry of life and history unraveling under the relentless assault of Nazi ideology.

"The data suggests that the SS believed they were on the cusp of a breakthrough," Jian Li stated, his voice hollow. "Falk's attempts to disrupt their signal, to broadcast his warning, had slowed them down, but it hadn't stopped them. They were close. Terribly close to initiating the full broadcast."

The recovered SS communications hinted at a complex interplay between Falk's efforts and the SS's countermeasures. Falk's embedded counter-frequency, designed to resonate with the beacon's original purpose, was indeed creating interference, creating the "ghost in the machine" that Jian Li had detected. However, the SS, driven by Himmler and Goebbels' absolute conviction, had responded with overwhelming force, amplifying their own signal to drown out Falk's warning. This desperate escalation had resulted in the chaotic, yet still partially decipherable, signal they were now analyzing.

"The SS's strategy," Weber explained, her eyes scanning a detailed diagram of the beacon's operational matrix, "was to leverage the beacon's adaptive capabilities. They believed that by overwhelming it with their own amplified frequencies, they could force it to adopt their 'dissonant' parameters as its core programming. It was a form of technological hijacking, a violation of the beacon's fundamental nature."

Neumann considered the implications of this digital warfare. It was a battle fought on the very planes of existence, a conflict between two opposing intentions encoded within an alien artifact. The SS sought to impose their will, to silence all dissent. Falk, in his own flawed, scientific way, had attempted to preserve the truth, to ensure the beacon's original purpose of exploration and understanding was not extinguished.

"The SS were aware of Falk's interference," Jian Li confirmed, pointing to a heavily redacted section of a Himmler directive. "They referred to it as 'a localized distortion of the divine harmony.' They believed it was a minor technical anomaly that could be overcome with sufficient amplification."

"Sufficient amplification," Neumann repeated, the sheer arrogance and destructive intent of their thinking chilling him to the bone. "They were willing to risk universal chaos, to unleash weapons of mass psychological destruction, all for the sake of imposing their ideology. It's beyond comprehension."

The recovered data also revealed the SS's meticulous planning regarding the target of their ultimate broadcast. While the initial activation sequence had been triggered by their presence and excavation efforts at the unearthed site, the ultimate destination of the "psychotropic disintegration" and "resonance purges" was a carefully calculated objective. Falk's fragmented notes, interspersed with SS intelligence reports, indicated a primary target: a burgeoning civilization in the Andromeda galaxy, one that, according to SS projections, was showing early signs of technological advancement and independent thought.

"The SS referred to this target civilization as 'the nascent dissonance'," Weber stated, her voice heavy with a grim certainty. "They saw its potential for independent growth as a direct threat to their own perceived universal dominion. Himmler believed that by eradicating this civilization early, they could prevent the emergence of any rival ideologies or civilizations that could challenge their ultimate authority."

The SS's plan was a horrific manifestation of a deep-seated paranoia and megalomania. They were not content with conquering their immediate surroundings; they sought to preemptively eliminate any potential threats to their envisioned galactic empire, regardless of the ethical or existential cost. The alien beacon, a tool of potential interstellar diplomacy and discovery, was to be weaponized into an instrument of cosmic preemption, a means of enforcing a galactic monoculture of SS ideology.

"Falk must have understood the gravity of this," Neumann mused, the complex, often contradictory nature of the SS scientist's recovered writings echoing in his mind. "He saw the SS's ultimate goal, the perversion of this technology. His attempts to sabotage their signal, to embed his own warning, were acts of desperate defiance."

The "ghost in the machine," the faint sub-harmonic frequency Jian Li had managed to isolate, was indeed Falk's last desperate gambit. It was a counter-frequency, a meticulously crafted signal designed to resonate with the beacon's original programming, to counteract the SS's corrupted signal, and to trigger a failsafe – a permanent disabling of the beacon's transmission capabilities. Falk, recognizing the existential threat posed by Project Veil, had attempted to turn the SS's own weapon against them, to silence the silence they intended to impose.

"The SS were aware of Falk's countermeasures," Jian Li confirmed, his brow furrowed in concentration as he analyzed the complex interplay of signals. "They referred to his embedded code as 'a resonance impurity.' They believed they could overcome it by increasing their own broadcast power. It was a dangerous escalation, a technological arms race fought across the cosmic void."

The data clearly indicated that the SS, under the direction of Himmler and Goebbels, had prioritized the amplification of their own signal, believing that sheer power would override Falk's subtle, yet deeply resonant, counter-message. They had flooded the alien beacon with their hateful frequencies, attempting to drown out the truth with sheer volume.

"The current state of the signal," Weber concluded, her gaze fixed on the fluctuating readings, "is a testament to that conflict. It's not a clear transmission from either side. It's a battleground, with the SS signal attempting to dominate and Falk's signal fighting to preserve the original purpose and trigger the failsafe."

Neumann felt a heavy weight settle upon him. They had unearthed not just a relic of a lost civilization, but a weapon of unimaginable destructive potential, a device that had been perverted by the SS into an instrument of cosmic annihilation. The legacy of Falk, once a shadowy figure associated with the SS's darkest experiments, was now revealed as a desperate struggle against his own superiors, a scientist's attempt to undo the horrors he had inadvertently helped unleash.

"We have to amplify Falk's signal," Neumann stated, his voice firm, cutting through the oppressive silence of the cavern. "We have to give his warning the power it needs to break through. If we don't, the SS's 'psychotropic disintegration' and 'resonance purges' might become the last echoes in the universe." The fate of countless civilizations, the very history of the cosmos, now rested on their ability to decipher and amplify a single, defiant signal amidst the cacophony of SS ambition. The true horror of Falk's legacy was not just in what he had done, but in what he had tried to prevent, a desperate fight against the SS's ultimate vision of a silent, sterile universe.

The revelation that Falk's intended broadcast was not a simple transmission but a meticulously crafted failsafe was a seismic shift in their understanding. It recontextualized everything they had painstakingly pieced together from the fragmented SS data and Falk's own scattered notes. The "ghost in the machine," the sub-harmonic frequency Jian Li had identified, was no longer a mere anomaly; it was a beacon of hope, a meticulously engineered countermeasure designed to silence the SS's devastating weapon. The purpose was no longer just to warn, but to *act*, to initiate a cascade that would permanently disable the alien artifact and prevent its catastrophic misuse. Falk, it seemed, had not been a willing participant in the SS's grand, horrific design but a saboteur from within, a dissenter who had recognized the abyss they were hurtling towards.

"A failsafe," Weber breathed, the word hanging in the cavernous space, imbued with a newfound weight. "So, Falk wasn't just trying to broadcast a warning. He was trying to trigger a shutdown. He was trying to kill it." The implications sent a fresh wave of awe and dread through her. To anticipate the SS's ultimate perversion of the alien technology, to understand its potential for cosmic annihilation, and to engineer its own destruction – it spoke of a level of foresight and courage that defied the prevailing narrative of SS fanaticism. This wasn't the blind obedience of a loyal soldier; this was the calculated defiance of a man who had seen the true face of the monster he served and had chosen to fight back, even if it meant his own probable demise.

Jian Li nodded, his eyes still glued to the intricate data streams. "The frequency modulation is incredibly precise. It's designed to interact with the beacon's core programming, to create a feedback loop that would overload the transmission array. It's elegant, in a terrifyingly destructive way. Falk wasn't just a scientist; he was an artist of existential sabotage." He pointed to a specific series of cascading data points, illustrating the proposed sequence. "He's identified the specific resonance frequencies that control the beacon's primary amplification matrix. By bombarding these frequencies with his counter-signal, he intended to create a cascading failure, much like a... like a cosmic fuse."

Neumann absorbed this, the pieces clicking into place with chilling finality. Falk's disappearance, his subsequent efforts to subvert Project Veil, the SS's increasingly desperate attempts to silence him – it all painted a picture of a deeply divided man. He had been privy to the SS's most insane ambitions, their darkest rituals, their pursuit of alien power. And at some point, the sheer horror of it had broken through his ideological conditioning. He had seen the SS not as an instrument of righteous destiny, but as a force of cosmic nihilism.

"But why the sub-harmonic frequency?" Neumann mused aloud, his gaze sweeping over the spectral analysis. "Why hide his

334

failsafe within a seemingly corrupted signal? Why not a clear, direct transmission?"

"To avoid detection, Neumann," Weber answered, her voice low and measured. "The SS were watching him, monitoring his every move. If he had transmitted anything remotely resembling a direct countermeasure, they would have immediately recognized it and shut him down, or worse, adapted their own protocols to neutralize it. He had to be subtle, to embed his defiance within the very noise they were creating." She paused, a speculative glint in her eyes. "And perhaps... perhaps he wanted it found by someone who could understand. Someone who could complete his work."

This resonated deeply with Neumann. Falk's fragmented logs, which they had struggled to interpret, were filled with cryptic philosophical musings and scientific jargon that hinted at a profound understanding of the alien artifact. He had referred to the beacon as a "universal harmonic resonator," a device capable of connecting disparate intelligences across the cosmos. His initial work with the SS, it seemed, had been driven by a genuine desire to understand this profound technology. But the SS's intent, their desire to weaponize it, had corrupted his noble pursuit.

"He must have realized the SS's goal was not communication, but control," Jian Li said, his voice hushed. "To harness this power for their own twisted ends, to impose their will upon the galaxy. Falk saw that the beacon, in their hands, was not a bridge, but a weapon of enslavement. His failsafe was his last act of rebellion, his attempt to ensure that this alien legacy served its intended purpose of discovery, not destruction."

The idea of a dissenter within the SS, a high-ranking official like Falk, working against the very regime he served, was almost unthinkable. The SS was notorious for its fanatical loyalty, its absolute ideological purity. Yet, the evidence was mounting. Falk's actions, his attempts to subvert Project Veil, his apparent creation of a cosmic kill switch – these were not the actions of a loyal SS scientist. They were the desperate measures of a man trapped in a nightmare, fighting against his own masters.

"If Falk was a dissenter," Weber pressed, her mind racing, "then who else? Who else within that regime understood the true horror of what they were doing? Who else might have been trying to leave behind breadcrumbs, warnings, or even... active sabotage?" The question hung in the air, a potent suggestion of further layers of conspiracy and hidden struggle within the heart of the SS. The SS was not a monolithic entity; it was a vast, complex, and deeply fractured organization, rife with ambition, paranoia, and ideological schisms. Perhaps Falk was not alone. Perhaps there were others, equally disillusioned, who had attempted to sow seeds of dissent or resistance.

Neumann considered the fragmented intelligence they had recovered from Himmler's personal archives, the clandestine communications between various SS factions, the hushed whispers of internal power struggles. The SS was a viper's nest, and while ideology was a powerful motivator, personal ambition and a primal instinct for self-preservation often trumped loyalty. It was entirely plausible that in the pursuit of such a monumental and terrifying weapon, cracks had appeared in the SS's seemingly impenetrable facade of unity.

"His logs mention... 'ethical considerations'," Jian Li recalled, accessing a newly decrypted segment of Falk's personal journal. "He wrestled with the SS's mandate, their justifications for wielding such power. He wrote, 'The pursuit of absolute truth through absolute control is a dangerous delusion. True harmony cannot be imposed; it must be discovered.' That sounds less like an SS scientist and more like a man on the verge of a profound moral awakening."

"'Discovered'," Weber echoed, nodding slowly. "That's the key, isn't it? The SS wanted to impose their reality. Falk believed in discovery. He believed in the inherent value of what the universe offered, not in its subjugation. He saw the beacon as a testament to a larger, more complex cosmic order, an order the SS sought to dismantle and replace with their own warped vision."

The weight of their discovery was immense. They weren't just trying to understand an alien artifact; they were trying to finish a war that had been fought in secret, a battle of wills waged across the cosmos through the very technology that had brought them here.

Falk's failsafe was not just a technical solution; it was a philosophical statement, a testament to the enduring power of truth and the inherent resistance of the human spirit, even when embedded within the heart of darkness.

Neumann found himself tracing the lines of Falk's coded message, trying to grasp the man's mindset. What must it have been like, to be Falk? To have been a respected scientist, given access to the secrets of the universe, only to discover that the SS intended to twist that knowledge into a tool of ultimate destruction? To have witnessed firsthand the SS's descent into a madness that threatened not just Earth, but potentially entire civilizations? The isolation, the paranoia, the constant threat of exposure – it must have been a crushing burden. And yet, he had persevered. He had planned, he had worked, he had sown the seeds of his own desperate gamble.

"The SS's countermeasures against Falk's failsafe were also incredibly sophisticated," Jian Li noted, highlighting a section of recovered SS intercept logs. "They didn't just dismiss his efforts as a technical glitch. They analyzed the energy signatures, identified the counter-frequency, and actively worked to disrupt it. Himmler himself ordered the 'reinforcement of signal integrity' to ensure Falk's 'resonance impurity' did not propagate."

"Reinforcement of signal integrity," Weber scoffed, a bitter edge to her voice. "They were trying to strengthen their own corrupted signal to drown out his last vestige of hope. It's a terrifyingly apt description of their overall agenda, isn't it? To reinforce their singular, hateful narrative by purging all other 'impurities'."

The SS's obsession with purity, their virulent hatred of anything that deviated from their narrow ideology, had manifested in the most extreme and dangerous ways. Here, it was applied not just to human beings or cultures, but to the very fundamental frequencies of the universe. Falk's failsafe was an act of profound biological and ideological defiance, a testament to the fact that even within the SS, the human spirit, in its most desperate moments, could find a way to resist.

Neumann looked at the schematic of the beacon's operational

matrix, a complex web of energy conduits and resonance chambers. "If we can amplify Falk's failsafe signal, we can effectively shut down the beacon. But the SS amplification is still a factor. We need to find a way to boost Falk's signal without triggering the SS's own automated defenses, which would likely perceive our efforts as an attack and further amplify their own signal."

"It's a delicate balance," Jian Li agreed, his brow furrowed in concentration. "We need to use the beacon's own adaptive frequencies, the ones Falk's failsafe is designed to exploit, to our advantage. We need to synchronize our amplification with the beacon's natural resonance, masking our efforts as a re-calibration rather than an outright attack."

The thought of manipulating such a powerful, alien technology was daunting, but the alternative was unthinkable. The SS had sought to hijack the cosmic symphony and force it to play their twisted anthem of destruction. Falk, through his desperate failsafe, had tried to provide them with the means to silence it forever. Now, it was up to them to complete his mission, to ensure that his final act of defiance resonated across the void and echoed the true purpose of the alien beacon: discovery, understanding, and the boundless wonder of connection.

"Falk's work wasn't just about stopping the SS," Weber said, her voice filled with a newfound reverence. "It was about preserving the possibility of a different future. A future where humanity, and perhaps other species, could explore the universe, learn from each other, and grow. He fought for that possibility, even at the cost of his own life and reputation."

The SS had buried Falk's legacy under layers of propaganda and disinformation, painting him as a rogue element, a failed experiment. But in their hands, his true legacy was being unearthed, a testament to a hidden courage, a silent rebellion waged against the SS's overwhelming might. He had been a man who, faced with the ultimate perversion of scientific advancement, had chosen to become an agent of its destruction. The failsafe was his final testament, his enduring message to any who would one day find themselves in this cavern, staring into the heart of the SS's cosmic ambition. It was a message of hope, a whisper of defiance, and a stark warning that the greatest dangers often came from those closest to you, those who wielded the highest authority, and those who promised salvation while delivering only annihilation. The SS had built a weapon of unimaginable power, but Falk had built the key to its undoing, a key that Neumann, Weber, and Jian Li were now tasked with turning.

The recovered data, primarily focused on the SS's insatiable drive to weaponize the alien artifact, offered a grim tableau of scientific hubris and ideological perversion. Yet, amidst the chilling directives and schematics of subjugation, lay faint yet persistent whispers of dissent. These were not overt acts of rebellion, nor declarations of opposition, but rather the subtle deviations in Falk's recorded activities, the peculiar annotations in his personal logs, the security reports flagging him as an anomaly—a potential security risk. The team had initially dismissed these as unfortunate byproducts of the SS's inherent paranoia, a regime that saw heresy in every shadow. However, as they delved deeper, as Falk's calculated subversion of Project Veil became clearer, these minor anomalies began to coalesce, revealing a pattern of deliberate subversion, a calculated risk taken by a man swimming against the tide of his own organization.

Ernst Falk. The name, once a mere ghost in fragmented SS security reports, now resonated with a profound significance. He was identified in a series of internal memos as a "suspected traitor," his access privileges occasionally restricted, his communications flagged for review. These were not the actions taken against a loyal cadre, but against someone perceived as a threat, someone whose loyalty was in question. The SS, with its iron grip on information and its ruthless suppression of any ideological deviation, did not lightly brand its own. For Falk to be labeled a traitor, even internally and in hushed reports, meant he had crossed a line, a line drawn not by external enemies, but by the SS itself.

Neumann, poring over a decrypted security audit from the SS's internal security bureau, the *Sicherheitsdienst* (SD), noted the peculiar language used. "Falk's adherence to protocol exhibited deviations during the initial phase of Project 'Veil.' His participation in simulated resonance calibration exercises returned anomalous results, indicating a possible deliberate misalignment with established parameters. Further investigation recommended due to suspected ideological contamination." Ideological contamination. The phrase, so characteristic of the SS's warped worldview, suggested that Falk's transgressions were not merely technical, but rooted in a fundamental disagreement with the SS's ultimate aims.

"This 'ideological contamination' is fascinating," Jian Li commented, his fingers flying across his console, cross-referencing the SD report with Falk's personnel file. "His early performance reviews are exemplary, glowing even. He was considered a star within the SS's scientific corps. But then, around the time they began integrating the alien artifact's core components, his profile shifts. There are notes about his 'increasingly abstract theoretical inquiries' and 'unconventional interpretations' of the artifact's operational capabilities."

Weber, leaning over Neumann's shoulder, pointed to a specific passage in the security report. "Look at this: 'Subject Falk has been observed engaging in clandestine discussions with personnel outside of designated project parameters. While no direct evidence of intelligence leakage has been found, the pattern of behavior is indicative of subversive intent.'" Clandestine discussions. This pointed towards Falk seeking out others, perhaps those who also harbored doubts, or perhaps those who possessed information that could aid his hidden agenda. The SS prided itself on its absolute control, its compartmentalization of information. Any unauthorized communication was a serious offense, a betrayal of the highest order.

"It's like he was building his own network," Neumann mused, tracing the timeline of Falk's alleged transgressions. "He wasn't just a scientist; he was a saboteur operating from within. He had to be incredibly careful. The SS would have had eyes everywhere, listening to every whisper. If they suspected him, they would have neutralized him, discreetly and permanently." The thought of Falk, a man who had clearly possessed a keen intellect and a capacity for deep thought, operating in constant fear of exposure, painted a grim picture of his final years.

Jian Li, meanwhile, had unearthed a fragmented personal log

340

entry from Falk's encrypted data. "This is from… approximately six months before his disappearance," he announced, his voice a low murmur. "He writes: 'The siren song of power is deafening. They seek to command the stars, to bend the symphony of existence to their discordant will. But there is a deeper melody, a harmony that whispers of understanding, not subjugation. To serve that harmony, even in silence, is the only true path.'"

"'Discordant will'," Weber repeated, the phrase echoing the SS's own aggressive, expansionist ideology. "He saw their ambition for what it was – a perversion. And he chose to serve a different path, a path of harmony and understanding." The log entry was a revelation. It provided a glimpse into Falk's internal struggle, his intellectual and moral conflict with the SS's core tenets. He wasn't just disagreeing with their methods; he was fundamentally rejecting their philosophy.

The SS, as they had pieced together, viewed the alien artifact not as a tool for discovery or communication, but as a means of control, a mechanism to enforce their vision of a superior Aryan order upon the galaxy. They saw the artifact's ability to manipulate cosmic energies as a divine mandate, a validation of their racial superiority. Falk, on the other hand, seemed to have interpreted its capabilities through a lens of universal interconnectedness, a fundamental understanding that true progress lay not in domination, but in shared knowledge and co-existence.

"His early research focused on the artifact's communication potential," Jian Li continued, pulling up more of Falk's recovered data. "He theorized it could be used to bridge vast interstellar distances, facilitating dialogue between disparate civilizations. He wrote about the 'cosmic tapestry' and the 'interwoven threads of sentience.' The SS, of course, saw this as a quaint academic pursuit, a distraction from the 'real' applications."

"The 'real' applications being, of course, the subjugation of anything and everything they deemed inferior," Neumann added, his jaw tight. "They twisted his pursuit of connection into a weapon of assertion. It's a classic SS maneuver: co-opt, corrupt, and then weaponize." The SS's historical pattern of absorbing and perverting cultural and scientific advancements to serve their own twisted agenda was well-documented. Here, it was manifesting on a cosmic scale.

The fragmented security reports painted a picture of a man increasingly isolated, his brilliance a liability in a regime that valued blind obedience above all else. He was, in essence, a dissenter operating within the SS's most clandestine and ideologically charged project. His name, Ernst Falk, was not just that of a scientist; it was the name of a man who had dared to question, to dissent, and to act.

"We need to understand *how* he managed to embed his failsafe," Weber stated, her gaze returning to the schematics of the alien beacon. "The SS was highly adept at detecting and neutralizing any unauthorized transmissions or manipulations. Falk must have found a way to mask his actions, to make his subversion appear as an anomaly within the system itself, something they would try to 'correct' rather than suppress."

Jian Li nodded, his eyes scanning the complex energy flow diagrams. "The sub-harmonic frequency he utilized. It's exceptionally subtle. It operates on a level that would likely be filtered out by standard SS monitoring protocols, or worse, interpreted as background noise. He didn't transmit a signal *to* the beacon; he subtly *influenced* its existing resonant frequencies. It's like whispering a secret into a hurricane, hoping it's heard above the din."

The SS, in their obsession with power and control, had created a system so focused on detecting direct threats that it had inadvertently blinded itself to more insidious forms of sabotage. Falk had exploited this blind spot, using the very mechanisms of the SS's surveillance and control against them. He had identified the SS's weakness—their inability to perceive subtlety when overwhelmed by brute force—and leveraged it.

"His personal logs also contain references to 'ethical imperatives' and 'the burden of knowledge'," Jian Li added, scrolling through another section of Falk's decrypted files. "He struggled with the SS's justifications for their actions, their claims of racial destiny. He wrote: 'To possess the power to reshape the cosmos, yet to employ it for the annihilation of diversity, is a perversion of creation itself. Our responsibility is not to impose order, but to facilitate understanding, to nurture the fragile bloom of sentience wherever it may be found.' This is not the language of a loyal SS officer; this is the manifesto of a moral rebel."

Weber's expression was one of profound respect. "He saw the SS's project for what it truly was: an attempt to hijack the natural evolution of the universe, to replace its inherent complexity with a rigid, brutalist order. His failsafe wasn't just a technical countermeasure; it was an act of profound ethical defiance, a last-ditch effort to preserve the possibility of genuine cosmic discovery."

The SS's internal documentation, while primarily focused on the military and strategic applications of the alien technology, also contained the occasional, almost dismissive, mention of Falk's more 'philosophical' inquiries. These were often relegated to appendices, treated as footnotes to his otherwise impressive technical contributions. But for Neumann and his team, these footnotes were the most critical parts of the record, the places where Falk's true intentions were hinted at, where the seeds of his defiance were sown.

The SS's campaign against Falk, while seemingly limited to security alerts and internal reviews, was a testament to their paranoia. They had sensed his deviation, even if they couldn't fully comprehend its depth or its purpose. They had flagged him, monitored him, and ultimately, it seemed, decided to neutralize him before his "ideological contamination" could spread. Falk's disappearance, therefore, was not a mere consequence of his work; it was likely the result of the SS's proactive measures to silence a dissenter who posed a threat to their grand design.

"The fact that they couldn't definitively pin him for espionage, or outright sabotage, suggests he was exceptionally adept at covering his tracks," Neumann observed. "He navigated their internal security apparatus like a phantom. He operated in the margins, using his access not to advance the SS's agenda, but to subtly undermine it, to plant the seeds of its own destruction." The SS, in its rigid adherence to hierarchy and protocol, often failed to account for individuals who could operate *outside* those parameters, individuals who could leverage the system's own rigidity against it.

Jian Li continued his meticulous reconstruction of Falk's digital footprint. "He seems to have systematically corrupted certain data sets related to the failsafe's deployment parameters. Not in a way that would trigger immediate alerts, but enough to subtly shift the outcome. He was creating a vulnerability within their own defensive protocols, a backdoor designed to be activated by his specific counter-signal."

The picture emerging was of a brilliant mind, trapped within a suffocating ideology, who chose not to succumb but to fight back from within. Ernst Falk was not just a name in a file; he was the embodiment of resistance, a testament to the fact that even in the darkest of regimes, the human spirit could find a way to endure, to dissent, and to leave a legacy of hope. His trail, etched in fragmented logs and security reports, was the trail of a dissenter who had understood the existential threat posed by the SS and had dedicated his final moments to ensuring their catastrophic ambitions would ultimately self-destruct. He had foreseen the abyss, and instead of stepping into it, he had begun digging its grave.

The recovered logs painted a horrifying picture, not of scientific curiosity, but of calculated annihilation. Project Veil, as Ernst Falk had meticulously documented in fragments of encrypted data, was far more than a study of alien resonance frequencies. It was a chilling blueprint for the systematic erasure of entire populations, a systematic dismantling of human existence down to the very fabric of memory itself. The initial phase, as Falk's unearthed research suggested, was to be a terrifying proving ground, a trial run for the ultimate extinction event. And the target of this initial, unspeakable atrocity? The Jewish people.

Neumann felt a cold dread seep into his bones, a visceral reaction to the stark, clinical language Falk had used to describe the SS's objectives. "The targeted cessation of energetic resonance signatures," one log entry read, a seemingly innocuous scientific phrase that, in the context of the SS's known barbarity, took on a grotesque new meaning. Falk elaborated, detailing how the alien artifact, with its unfathomable ability to manipulate fundamental cosmic forces, was being repurposed. It was not to be used for communication, for understanding, or for any form of upliftment.

344

Instead, it was being tuned, calibrated, to disrupt the very essence of existence, to unravel the threads that bound individuals and communities to the continuum of life and memory.

Jian Li, his face pale, projected a series of equations and frequency modulations onto the main screen. "This is it," he murmured, his voice strained. "Falk's analysis of the resonance dispersal patterns. They weren't just disrupting physical matter; they were targeting the quantum entanglement that binds consciousness and memory. His logs suggest the SS envisioned a method of 'un-creating' people, not just killing them, but wiping them from the very memory of existence. They were aiming to prevent the ripple effect of their absence, to ensure no one would even remember that they had ever been."

Weber gasped, her hand flying to her mouth. "Erasing memory? Not just killing them, but making it as if they never existed? That's… that's beyond anything I could have imagined. The SS was always about extermination, but this is something else entirely. This is an attack on the very concept of being." She looked at Neumann, her eyes wide with a dawning horror. "They wanted to weaponize oblivion itself. To make their victims not just dead, but un-remembered. A total, absolute annihilation, not just of the body, but of the past, the present, and any future that might have included them."

Falk's logs meticulously detailed the SS's perverse logic. They viewed the targeted population not as human beings, but as an ideological contagion, a perceived flaw in the cosmic order that needed to be purged. The alien technology, with its potential for profound universal connection, was to be twisted into a tool of absolute isolation, a means to sever the targeted group from the collective consciousness of humanity, and indeed, from the universe itself. Falk's notes contained agonizing entries where he wrestled with this perversion, his scientific mind recoiling from the sheer, unadulterated evil of the SS's vision. He wrote of the artifact's inherent ability to foster empathy and understanding, how it could create bridges between disparate species and consciousnesses, only to be perverted into a mechanism of absolute severance.

"He describes the process as 'dissolving the resonant anchor',"

Neumann said, his voice a low growl. "The SS believed that every individual, every group, possessed a unique energetic signature, a resonant frequency that anchored them to reality and to collective memory. Project Veil was designed to target and neutralize these anchors. They spoke of 'purifying the cosmic tapestry' by removing these 'discordant threads'." He paused, swallowing hard. "Falk noted the SS leadership's growing obsession with this aspect of the artifact. They saw it as the ultimate solution to their ideological 'enemies', a way to erase not just their bodies, but their very history, their cultural contributions, their very right to have ever existed."

The sheer scale of their ambition was staggering. The SS, in their twisted ideology, saw the Jewish people as a primary obstacle to their vision of a pure, Aryan galactic dominion. The logs detailed not just the scientific theory behind the erasure, but the SS's internal discussions, their justifications, their cold, calculated planning. Falk had captured memos that discussed "de-population through non-existence," a phrase so chillingly euphemistic it was almost incomprehensible. They weren't just planning genocide; they were planning a form of cosmic exorcism, a way to scrub their perceived impurities from the universe.

"It's the ultimate act of dehumanization," Jian Li stated, his voice flat with shock. "To reduce a people, with their millennia of history, culture, and suffering, to a mere 'discordant thread' in a cosmic tapestry. They weren't just killing them; they were trying to erase the *idea* of them from existence. Imagine the psychological impact, not just on the victims, but on the perpetuators. It speaks to a complete severance from empathy, a willingness to embrace a nihilistic void as a creative force."

Falk's attempts to subvert Project Veil were not merely about stopping the weapon's deployment; they were about preserving the very concept of remembrance, of history, of the inherent right of a people to exist and be remembered. His failsafe, the subtle disruption of the resonance frequencies, was an act of profound defiance, a desperate attempt to ensure that the SS's genocidal ambitions would not be carried out with absolute finality. He was fighting not just for the lives of those targeted, but for the integrity of reality itself, for the fundamental truth that existence, once forged, could not simply be unmade without consequence.

The SS's internal discussions, as documented by Falk, revealed a disturbing progression in their thinking. Initially, they had considered the artifact as a weapon of mass destruction, a tool for planetary devastation. But as they delved deeper into its capabilities, their focus shifted. They began to grasp its potential for something far more insidious: ontological warfare, the ability to rewrite reality by unmaking its components. This was where Falk's dissent became most pronounced. He argued, in his private logs, that any attempt to erase existence was a violation of a fundamental cosmic law, a hubris that would inevitably lead to catastrophic repercussions.

"Falk's personal commentary here is crucial," Neumann said, pointing to a particularly dense section of Falk's logs. "He wasn't just a technician. He was a philosopher, grappling with the implications of what they were doing. He writes about the 'weight of memory' and the 'ethical burden of existence.' He saw the SS's goal as a perverse inversion of creation, an attempt to impose their will on the universe by negating what already was. He believed that the artifact's true purpose was to foster interconnectedness, to reveal the shared essence of all life, and that the SS was corrupting this potential into an instrument of absolute separation."

The SS's rationale, as Falk recorded it, was rooted in their deeply ingrained belief in racial purity and their absolute contempt for any group that did not fit their distorted Aryan ideal. The Jewish people, as the most prominent target, were seen as an intrinsic threat to their vision of a cleansed and perfected galaxy. Falk's logs detailed the SS's belief that by erasing them, they would not only eliminate a perceived ideological enemy but also purify the very cosmic energies that flowed through the universe, aligning them with their own supposed genetic superiority. It was a grotesque fusion of pseudoscience, racial hatred, and technological ambition.

"The level of detail is chilling," Weber whispered, her gaze fixed on a schematic depicting the proposed dispersion field. "They even mapped out how the resonance erasure would cascade, affecting not just the immediate targets but their descendants, their diaspora, their collective cultural imprint. It was designed to be a wound that never healed, a void that would perpetually whisper of absence. Falk's work to disrupt this was an act of unimaginable courage, given the SS's pervasive surveillance. He was essentially planting a seed of doubt, a possibility of failure, within the heart of their most terrifying project."

Falk's subversion, as they were now piecing it together, was not a single act, but a sustained, clandestine campaign. He had systematically introduced subtle errors into the calibration protocols, altered data sets related to resonance decay, and, most importantly, embedded his counter-frequency within the artifact's core programming. He had foreseen that the SS would likely attempt to activate the project, and he had worked to ensure that activation would not result in the absolute erasure they desired, but in something far less predictable, something that might even reveal the SS's true intentions to the wider galaxy.

"He understood that the SS, in their arrogance, would never truly believe their own technology could fail them," Neumann realized aloud. "They saw themselves as masters of the universe, capable of bending any force to their will. Falk exploited that blind spot. He didn't try to dismantle the weapon; he tried to make it malfunction in a way that exposed its catastrophic potential while simultaneously rendering it incapable of its ultimate, horrific purpose. His goal was to create a cosmic alarm bell, a signal that their attempt at absolute erasure would instead broadcast their true nature."

The implications were immense. If Falk's failsafe had indeed been activated, the artifact would not have simply erased the targeted population. It would have unleashed a wave of disruptive energies, a cascade of resonance anomalies that would have been undeniable proof of the SS's genocidal intent, broadcast across the very cosmic tapestry they sought to purify. It was a gambit of unimaginable risk, a desperate attempt to turn the SS's own weapon against them, to expose their darkest secrets to the universe. The narrative of Project Veil was no longer just about a weapon; it was about a fight for existence itself, a fight waged in the shadows by a lone dissenter against the overwhelming darkness of the SS. Falk's legacy was not just scientific; it was a testament to the enduring power of conscience in the face of unimaginable evil.

The air in the research chamber hummed with a palpable tension, thick with the weight of revelation. Neumann stared at the holographic projection, the complex web of Falk's subversions now starkly illuminated. It was more than just scientific sabotage; it was a symphony of calculated defiance, a desperate whisper against a deafening roar of annihilation. The residual consciousness within the alien artifact, a flicker of sentience from its long-dead custodians, seemed to have found an unlikely, and profoundly brave, ally in Falk. Together, they had woven a tapestry of resistance, a protective shroud intended to shield humanity from a terror far exceeding conventional warfare.

"He didn't just introduce errors," Jian Li stated, his voice a low, awestruck murmur. "He architected a failsafe. A beacon, woven into the very fabric of the resonance dispersal. It was designed not to destroy the artifact, but to ensure that if the SS *did* manage to activate it, the result would be... a broadcast. A confession, etched in the language of cosmic disruption."

Weber traced a phantom line on the projection. "A broadcast of their intentions? So, if they fired it, it wouldn't just erase people, it would... announce it? Scream their barbarity to the stars?"

"Precisely," Neumann confirmed, his gaze locked on a series of encrypted sequences Falk had embedded deep within the artifact's core programming. "Falk understood that absolute destruction, while horrific, might be too easily erased from history. But a widespread, undeniable resonance anomaly, a pattern that could only be explained by intentional, targeted erasure... that would be undeniable evidence. A cosmic scream of guilt, impossible to silence."

The sheer audacity of it was breathtaking. Falk, a man of science, had become a saboteur, a prophet of truth in a regime that thrived on lies and extermination. His personal logs, once deciphered, revealed a man not just intellectually repulsed by the SS's vision, but morally outraged. He wrestled with the weight of his knowledge, the terrible responsibility of being privy to such an atrocity. His entries were a testament to a deeply human spirit, a conscience that refused to be extinguished by the pervasive darkness of the Third Reich.

"He writes here about the 'echo of the void'," Neumann read aloud, his voice catching. "Falk theorized that the SS's desire to erase existence stemmed from a profound nihilism, a desire to impose their will by negating the universe's inherent richness. He believed that by disrupting their erasure, by forcing a resonance that spoke of the very life they sought to extinguish, he was not just stopping a weapon, but affirming the value of existence itself. He saw the alien artifact not as a weapon, but as a potential conduit for universal connection, and the SS were perverting its very nature."

The implications of Falk's actions extended far beyond the immediate threat of Project Veil. He hadn't just saved lives; he had preserved the narrative. He had ensured that the story of the SS's ultimate depravity would not be a footnote, a secret whispered in the dark, but a loud, irrefutable testament to their evil, broadcast across the cosmos. His meticulous work, his foresight in embedding this failsafe, was an act of profound defiance, a testament to the enduring power of human conscience.

"This... this alien consciousness," Weber mused, gesturing towards the artifact's spectral representation. "Do you think it was aware of Falk's intentions? Did it guide him? Or was it simply a passive recipient of his brilliance?"

Jian Li considered this, his brow furrowed. "The logs suggest a symbiotic relationship. Falk's scientific understanding of the artifact's mechanics, combined with whatever residual awareness the alien entity possessed... it seems they amplified each other. Falk provided the terrestrial understanding of the SS's goals, their twisted ideology, while the alien consciousness may have offered insights into the artifact's deeper capabilities, the very frequencies that could be manipulated. It's plausible that the alien entity, having witnessed the SS's intent, actively aided Falk in crafting the failsafe, perhaps seeing it as a way to atone for the artifact's unintended role in such a horrific plan."

The thought of an alien race, perhaps long gone, inadvertently becoming complicit in humanity's darkest hour, and then, through its very remnants, aiding in a fight against that darkness, added another layer of profound cosmic irony to the unfolding truth. Falk wasn't just a lone scientist; he was a bridge between species, a reluctant emissary of cosmic conscience.

Neumann leaned back, the enormity of Falk's sacrifice pressing down on him. "He knew the risks. He understood that if his subversion was discovered, his fate would be far worse than mere execution. He would be dissected, his knowledge twisted, his very existence erased to prevent any further defiance. Yet, he persisted. He worked in the shadows, creating a legacy that was designed to remain hidden until the opportune moment, a time when its truth could finally be revealed without fear of immediate reprisal."

The research team had painstakingly pieced together the fragmented data, the encrypted communications, the desperate pleas hidden within Falk's scientific notes. Each decoded line brought them closer to understanding the true depth of his courage. He hadn't just resisted; he had strategized, he had planned, he had executed a counter-operation that defied the very nature of the SS's control. He had turned their weapon of ultimate silence into a potential loudspeaker for their crimes.

"His ultimate goal," Neumann continued, his voice resonating with a newfound respect for the man he had never met, "was not simply to prevent the immediate activation of Project Veil. It was to ensure that the *truth* of it could never be truly buried. His failsafe was a dead man's switch, designed to activate only when the artifact was brought to a critical state of readiness for deployment. It was a contingency for his own potential failure, a way to ensure that even if he was silenced, the message would still get out."

The meticulous nature of Falk's planning was evident in every reconstructed segment of his work. He had anticipated the SS's paranoia, their need for absolute secrecy. He had woven his countermeasures into the very essence of the artifact's operation, making them virtually undetectable by conventional means. Only by understanding the artifact's theoretical capabilities and Falk's advanced understanding of quantum resonance could they now decipher his intricate design.

"The SS believed they were wielding a power beyond comprehension," Weber observed, her voice barely a whisper. "They saw themselves as the arbiters of cosmic destiny, shaping the universe according to their warped vision. Falk, with his scientific brilliance and moral fortitude, showed them that even their most audacious plans could be undone by a single, unwavering conscience. He demonstrated that truth, even when buried under layers of propaganda and terror, has a way of resurfacing, like a seed pushing through concrete."

The legacy of Ernst Falk was no longer confined to the sterile confines of scientific journals. It was a narrative of human resilience, a story of how even in the darkest of times, the light of truth and defiance could still burn bright. His actions, once obscured by the SS's iron grip on information, were now illuminated by the very technology they sought to control. The artifact, the instrument of annihilation, had become the vessel for Falk's final, enduring message.

"He wasn't just fighting the SS," Jian Li added, his eyes scanning the intricate schematics of Falk's counter-frequencies. "He was fighting a specific philosophy of existence – one that sought to diminish, to erase, to silence. By creating a mechanism that would broadcast the truth of their destructive intent, he was asserting the opposite: the value of every life, the importance of memory, the interconnectedness of all existence. He was ensuring that their attempt at absolute erasure would, paradoxically, be an act of ultimate exposure."

The team understood that their current mission, to understand and potentially control this alien technology, was now inextricably linked to Falk's own mission. They were not merely researchers; they were inheritors of his struggle, tasked with ensuring that his legacy was not in vain. The truth he had so carefully preserved now rested in their hands, a profound responsibility that weighed heavily upon them.

"It's as if he anticipated that someone, someday, would uncover Project Veil," Neumann stated, his gaze sweeping across the chamber, the hum of the artifact's dormant power a constant reminder of the stakes. "He knew that his own survival was precarious, that his efforts might be erased along with him. So he built in a contingency, a failsafe that would activate regardless of his fate. He ensured that the truth would not die with him."

The residual consciousness of the alien explorers, if indeed it had played a role, had chosen its human ally wisely. Falk's intellect, his ethical compass, and his sheer, unwavering courage had made him the perfect instrument for such a cosmic undertaking. He had taken the SS's most terrifying weapon and transformed it into a herald of their own downfall, a testament to the fact that even the most sophisticated systems of oppression could be undone by the power of truth and the indomitable spirit of resistance. His legacy was not merely an act of scientific sabotage, but a profound philosophical statement, a declaration that existence, in all its messy, complex, and beautiful forms, was worth fighting for, and worth remembering. The shadows were receding, and the faint, yet persistent, echo of Ernst Falk's truth was finally beginning to resurface.

Chapter 16

The Unveiling of Truth

The holographic projection shifted, revealing a newly rendered layer of data, a stark visualization of Project Veil's chilling scope. Neumann leaned forward, his eyes tracing the concentric rings emanating from the Black Forest epicenter, each pulse a wave of theoretical devastation. Jian Li's calm narration cut through the tense silence, his voice devoid of the awe that had colored it moments before, now laced with a grave pragmatism. "The residual energy signatures and the extrapolated dispersal patterns indicate a level of planetary inundation that... frankly, defies conventional understanding of warfare. Falk's subversion did not merely neutralize a localized threat; it averted a global existential reset."

Weber, her usual scientific detachment frayed by the sheer scale of the SS's ambition, pointed to a series of rapidly expanding nodes on the projection. "These aren't just geographical coordinates. They represent societal structures, cultural repositories, entire linguistic families. The resonance frequencies were keyed to specific bio-signatures, yes, but also to the complex electromagnetic fields generated by dense human settlements and their collective consciousness. It wasn't just about eliminating individuals; it was about excising the very memory of entire peoples from the terrestrial tapestry."

The SS, Neumann realized with a sickening lurch, hadn't merely envisioned a weapon of mass destruction; they had conceived of a tool of cosmic erasure. Falk's heroic act of sabotage, his intricate dance with the alien artifact's volatile energies, had not just prevented a localized catastrophe in the Schwartzwald. It had, by all indications, severed the weapon's global transmission array before it could fully engage. The resonance, designed to cascade and amplify across continents, was stillborn, its intended reach choked off at the source. This was not merely a matter of history; it was a chilling testament to a future that had teetered on the precipice of annihilation, a future that, thanks to Falk, never came to pass.

"The alien data is explicit on this point," Jian Li continued, his fingers dancing across the holographic interface, bringing up cascading lines of coded information. "The artifact's primary function, when attuned to terrestrial bio-signatures and manipulated by specific resonant frequencies, was to induce a form of... quantum decoherence. Not a physical disintegration, but a complete erasure of coherence at the subatomic level for all organic matter within its field. It would have effectively unraveled life itself, from the cellular to the societal. Imagine every living thing, every thought, every memory, simply ceasing to *be*, not violently, but... dissolving back into undifferentiated energy."

This was a far cry from the atomic bombs or chemical agents of conventional warfare. This was an affront to the very fabric of existence, a deliberate act of cosmic vandalism. The SS, blinded by their warped ideology of racial purity and territorial dominion, had sought to cleanse the planet not just of peoples they deemed undesirable, but of the very essence of what made humanity, and indeed all life, complex and vibrant. They had aimed for an ultimate silence, a world scrubbed clean of its messy, diverse, and interconnected past.

"The implications for cultural survival are almost unfathomable," Weber added, her voice trembling slightly. "Falk's subversion meant that this quantum decoherence wave never propagated globally. Had it activated as intended, entire continents would have been rendered not just uninhabited, but fundamentally *un-historical*. No records, no artifacts, no memories of civilizations that had flourished for millennia would have survived. The entire trajectory of human development, every cultural achievement, every artistic expression, every philosophical inquiry – all of it would have been wiped clean. The SS envisioned a blank slate, a new beginning forged from the ashes of erased histories."

Neumann pictured the world as the SS had intended it: a sterile, uniform expanse, populated by a singular, ideologically pure demographic, with all traces of prior diversity meticulously scrubbed from existence. It was a vision of absolute control, of a manufactured utopia built upon the graveyard of a murdered past. The sheer hubris of it was staggering. To believe that one regime, one ideology, had the right to dictate the very existence and memory of entire populations was a level of megalomania that bordered on the cosmic.

"The artifact was designed to be activated in stages," Jian Li explained, projecting a detailed sequence of energy flow. "The initial deployment, from the Black Forest site, was intended to create a localized field of decoherence, serving as a proof of concept and a terror weapon. But the subversion, Falk's ingenious integration of the 'echo of the void,' prevented this initial activation from reaching its full destructive potential. Instead of a wide-area decoherence, it produced a contained, albeit powerful, resonant feedback loop that was ultimately absorbed and neutralized. Had the SS managed to bypass Falk's countermeasures, or deploy further resonance amplifiers, the cascade effect he averted would have been global, systematically targeting regions and populations based on the complex bio-signature data they had painstakingly gathered over decades of intelligence operations."

The SS's meticulous planning extended to the very essence of what constituted a target. Their racial theories, their obsession with genetic purity, had translated into an algorithmic approach to planetary cleansing. They had cataloged populations not just by location, but by genetic markers, cultural heritage, and even linguistic patterns. The alien artifact was to be the ultimate equalizer, a tool to homogenize humanity according to their perverse definition of perfection, by systematically dismantling the very foundations of diversity that made humanity so resilient and so rich.

"The data suggests a phased global rollout," Weber said, pointing to further segments of the projected data. "The initial activation in Germany was to be followed by deployments in key strategic locations across Europe, Africa, and Asia. Each subsequent deployment would have amplified the decoherence wave, creating a planetary network of erasure. The goal was not just to conquer territory, but to fundamentally alter the biological and historical landscape of Earth, leaving only their chosen successors to inherit a world free from the perceived 'degeneracy' of the past."

The SS's ambition was not merely territorial or political; it was existential. They sought to rewrite not just the present, but the very narrative of human existence. Project Veil was their ultimate statement, a declaration that they were the arbiters of what life was worth preserving, what histories were worth remembering. They were not just conquerors; they were cosmic censors, wielding an alien technology to enforce their ideology of annihilation.

"Falk's intervention wasn't just about stopping a bomb," Neumann reiterated, the weight of this realization settling heavily upon him. "It was about preserving the very concept of human diversity, the richness of our collective experience. He understood that the SS's plan was not simply to kill millions, but to obliterate the memory of them, to erase entire chapters of human history as if they had never existed. His failsafe, the broadcast of their intent, was designed to ensure that if their genocidal agenda was ever enacted, the *truth* of it would survive, a testament to their barbarity, rather than a silent, forgotten apocalypse."

The team was now faced with the profound realization that their current mission, to understand and potentially utilize this alien artifact, was intrinsically linked to Falk's desperate struggle. They were not merely scientists uncovering a historical anomaly; they were inheritors of a legacy of resistance, tasked with ensuring that the SS's attempt at global erasure remained a chilling historical warning, not a prophetic blueprint. The power of the artifact, now understood in its true, terrifying scope, represented not just advanced technology, but a profound moral challenge.

"The alien data also contains theoretical counter-measures to the decoherence wave itself," Jian Li revealed, his voice gaining a new intensity. "Not for replication, but for understanding the fundamental principles by which such erasure could be reversed or mitigated. Falk's work was focused on preventing the activation, but the custodians of this artifact, from what we can glean, understood the inherent danger of such a capability. They left behind the knowledge, perhaps as a cautionary tale, of how the very forces they harnessed could be resisted."

This offered a glimmer of hope, a faint possibility that the artifact's destructive potential might, in some unfathomable way, also hold the key to safeguarding existence. But the immediate concern remained the SS's ultimate objective. Their ambition was not limited by their understanding of physics or biology; it was fueled by an ideology that saw existence itself as malleable, a canvas upon which they could impose their twisted vision of order.

"The SS's operational doctrine was built on the principle of absolute deniability and ultimate control," Weber stated, her gaze fixed on a complex diagram illustrating the artifact's energy distribution network. "They sought weapons that could achieve their objectives with minimal collateral damage to their own infrastructure, and maximum psychological impact on their enemies. Project Veil was the culmination of this doctrine, a weapon that could reshape the planet without leaving a trace of its operation, save for the absence of those they deemed unworthy. Falk's subversion, by forcing a broadcast, introduced an element of undeniable culpability, a stark contradiction to their entire modus operandi."

The SS had aimed for a silent, invisible victory, a world purged of its perceived impurities without the messy repercussions of open warfare or conventional genocide. They wanted the outcome without the evidence, the elimination without the accountability. Falk, through his scientific genius and moral courage, had stripped away their carefully constructed façade of control, transforming their ultimate weapon of silence into a screaming testament to their ultimate crime.

"The global implications of Project Veil are not merely hypothetical," Neumann concluded, the words hanging heavy in the air. "They are the stark reality of a world that was almost unmade by a singular, horrifying vision. Ernst Falk didn't just stop a weapon; he saved the narrative of humanity. He ensured that the story of the SS's ambition would not be a silent erasure, but an eternal, undeniable echo. And now, that echo rests with us, a profound responsibility to ensure that the truth he fought so hard to preserve is understood, and never forgotten." The research team understood that their current endeavor was no longer just about understanding alien technology; it was about bearing witness to a pivotal moment in human history, a moment where science, ideology, and conscience clashed on a scale that threatened to unravel reality itself. The discovery in the Black Forest was a chilling testament to the catastrophic potential of advanced technology wielded by unchecked ambition, and Falk's intervention a beacon of hope, a testament to the enduring power of individual courage against insurmountable odds. The unearthing of his meticulous work was a stark warning: the greatest threats to humanity might not come from external forces, but from the dark corners of its own ambitions, amplified by powers beyond its comprehension.

The sterile hum of the laboratory was a constant, a low thrumming counterpoint to the increasingly complex tapestry of data unfolding before Neumann and his team. They were no longer merely analysts; they were archaeologists of a lost timeline, piecing together fragments of a civilization's near-annihilation. The holographic projections, once stark representations of theoretical devastation, were now becoming interwoven narratives, each element painstakingly contextualized. The residual energy signatures that Jian Li had meticulously charted were no longer just abstract numbers; they were the ghostly fingerprints of Project Veil, mapping not just where the intended wave of decoherence would have hit, but the societal and cultural infrastructure it was designed to obliterate. Weber, her earlier shock now transmuted into a grim determination, was cross-referencing these energy maps with millennia of recorded human history. Entire regions, vibrant with the echoes of ancient civilizations, were being highlighted – not just as targets, but as intended voids in the continuum of human experience.

"It's not just about population density," Weber murmured, her finger tracing a line across a projection that depicted the intended propagation of the decoherence field. "Look at this. The SS's algorithms factored in linguistic diffusion patterns, cultural exchange hubs, even the geographical distribution of sacred sites. Their 'racial purity' doctrine wasn't just about bloodlines; it was about eradicating the very concepts of shared humanity, the interconnectedness that transcends biological distinctions. They weren't just killing people; they were killing the *idea* of shared heritage."

Jian Li nodded, pulling up a secondary projection that displayed a complex network of interconnected data points. "Falk's logs, combined with the fragmented Nazi schematics, suggest that the artifact's targeting parameters were far more sophisticated than a simple geographical sweep. The bio-signature analysis was indeed crucial, but it was layered with data concerning collective memory and cultural resilience. The resonance frequencies were designed to exploit the very electromagnetic fields that bind communities, the subconscious societal currents. Imagine a sonic weapon, but instead of sound, it manipulates the very fabric of consciousness, unraveling the collective tapestry thread by thread."

Neumann felt a chill that had nothing to do with the lab's climate control. The SS's vision was a meticulously crafted dystopia, a world scrubbed clean of all that was deemed 'undesirable,' not just in the present, but in the past. Falk's heroic act, they now understood, wasn't just a matter of averting a localized disaster; it was a desperate, last-ditch effort to preserve the very essence of human identity. His 'echo of the void,' the counter-frequency he had broadcast, was a desperate plea for remembrance, a testament to the SS's monstrous ambition, ensuring that if their ultimate weapon was ever unleashed, its horror would not be silenced by its own devastating efficacy.

The challenge now was to weave these disparate threads – the alien technological blueprints, the SS's chillingly meticulous planning documents, and the ghostly remnants of Falk's own clandestine operations – into a coherent narrative. They had the raw data, the theoretical frameworks, but the human element, the story of how one man's courage stood against such overwhelming, cosmic malevolence, was still being unearthed, piece by painstaking piece. Falk's personal logs, discovered in a hidden compartment within the salvaged German research facility, were their most direct link to his final days. These were not the polished reports of a government scientist, but the raw, often desperate, scribblings of a man operating in the shadows, driven by a profound moral imperative.

Weber was poring over a particularly dense section of Falk's journal, deciphering his increasingly frantic annotations on the artifact's energy modulation. "He realized early on that the SS wasn't just interested in weaponizing the artifact's destructive potential," she explained, her voice hushed. "They were attempting to *codify* existence, to strip it down to a set of controllable variables. Falk saw that they were trying to rewrite the fundamental laws of reality itself, to impose their twisted ideology onto the very substrate of the universe. His understanding of the 'quantum decoherence' was not purely scientific; it was philosophical. He understood that the SS was trying to achieve a state of absolute existential purity, a world devoid of variation, of history, of anything that defied their rigid control."

Jian Li was simultaneously analyzing Falk's proposed counter-measures, his fingers flying across the holographic interface as he attempted to reverse-engineer the scientist's ingenious, yet ultimately fatal, modifications. "Falk's 'echo of the void' wasn't merely a disruption of the primary wave," Jian Li elucidated, his brow furrowed in concentration. "It was a resonance cascade, designed to create a feedback loop that would overload the artifact's containment field without triggering the full dispersal. He was essentially using the alien technology against itself, a controlled detonation to prevent a planetary conflagration. The data indicates he succeeded in neutralizing the immediate threat, but the backlash... the sheer energy involved in such a counter-measure... it's staggering. He managed to sever the global connection, to stop the cascade, but the initial activation, even contained, was likely catastrophic for him and his immediate surroundings."

Neumann visualized the scene in the Black Forest, not as it was now, a silent monument to a near-apocalypse, but as it must have been in those final moments. The SS technicians, blindly following orders, activating the alien device. And Falk, a lone figure against the tide of their technological megalomania, wrestling with forces beyond human comprehension, his life's work culminating in this desperate act of defiance. His fragmented notes spoke of sleepless nights, of the constant threat of discovery, of the agonizing weight of knowing the true stakes. He had been working not just against the SS, but against the very nature of the alien technology itself, a technology that, in its raw power, was amoral and utterly indifferent to the fate of humanity.

The reconstruction of the narrative was proving to be more than just an academic exercise. It was an immersion into a forgotten conflict, a battle fought not with conventional weaponry, but with intellect, courage, and a profound understanding of the universe's fundamental principles. The SS had acquired a tool of cosmic significance, and their response was to apply it to their petty, terrestrial grievances. Falk's response was to recognize the existential threat and act with a prescience that defied the limitations of his time.

"The SS documentation, particularly the classified operational directives for Project Veil, reveals a chilling pragmatism," Weber stated, her voice gaining a sharp edge. "They had contingency plans for every conceivable scenario, except for one: the moral conviction of a single individual willing to sacrifice everything to thwart their agenda. Their entire operational doctrine was predicated on obedience, on the eradication of dissent. Falk, by forging his own path, by acting on conscience, introduced an element of chaos into their meticulously ordered universe. He proved that even the most advanced technology, when confronted by human integrity, could be rendered impotent."

Jian Li, meanwhile, was focusing on the recovered fragments of the alien data itself, attempting to decipher the original intent behind the artifact's creation. "The custodians, whoever they were, seem to have had a deep understanding of the destructive potential of this technology," he mused, his voice echoing slightly in the cavernous lab. "The data suggests they developed it as a deterrent, a means of enforcing a cosmic balance, rather than as a weapon of conquest. There are sections detailing the principles of resonance manipulation, not for annihilation, but for restoration, for healing planetary ecosystems. The SS, in their ignorance and arrogance, perverted this fundamental principle, twisting a tool of creation into an instrument of erasure. Falk, in his final act, sought to restore that original intent, to disable the destructive cascade and, in essence, return the artifact to a dormant state, preventing its further misuse."

Neumann looked at the projected timeline, now a dense web of interconnected events. The initial alien crash, the SS's discovery and perversion of its technology, Falk's clandestine investigation and desperate countermeasures, and finally, his ultimate sacrifice. The narrative was solidifying, the pieces clicking into place with a growing sense of clarity. It was a story of immense power corrupted, of a lone hero's stand against unimaginable odds.

"His logs are incredibly detailed regarding the psychological impact they anticipated from the decoherence wave," Weber continued, her focus returning to Falk's journals. "The SS wasn't just trying to eliminate populations; they wanted to sow terror, to ensure that any surviving opposition would be paralyzed by the sheer incomprehensibility of the destruction. They envisioned a silent, unmourned end for entire cultures, an apocalypse so complete that even the memory of what was lost would be erased. Falk's broadcast of their intent, his 'echo of the void,' was designed to ensure that the *truth* of their crime would endure, a perpetual indictment of their barbarity. He understood that even in the face of total annihilation, the memory of the event, the knowledge of who was responsible, was the ultimate form of resistance."

The SS's obsession with control extended even to the narrative of their actions. They sought to engineer not just the future, but the past, to scrub away any evidence of their atrocities, leaving behind only their sanitized version of history. Falk's counter-measure was a direct assault on this desire for absolute control, a refusal to let their ultimate act of violence be a silent, unacknowledged void. He turned their weapon of erasure into a weapon of witness.

"The alien data also contains theoretical counter-measures to the decoherence wave itself," Jian Li revealed, his voice gaining a new intensity. "Not for replication, but for understanding the fundamental principles by which such erasure could be reversed or mitigated. Falk's work was focused on preventing the activation, but the custodians of this artifact, from what we can glean, understood the inherent danger of such a capability. They left behind the knowledge, perhaps as a cautionary tale, of how the very forces they harnessed could be resisted. It suggests a sophisticated ethical framework, an awareness of the dual nature of such profound power."

The sheer volume of data that Falk had managed to secure and transmit before his final, cataclysmic act was staggering. It wasn't just technical schematics and operational logs; it was a testament to his foresight, his understanding that mere destruction would not be enough. The SS's goal was erasure, not just of life, but of memory, of history, of culture. Falk's counter-narrative had to be equally comprehensive, detailing not only the technicalities of Project Veil, but the ideological monstrosity it represented. He had meticulously documented the SS's justifications, their pseudoscientific theories, their systematic dehumanization of entire populations. This was not just about stopping a weapon; it was about exposing the rot at its core, the twisted worldview that fueled such a horrifying ambition.

"He managed to archive not only the operational data but also vast swathes of the SS's internal memos and research papers related to Project Veil," Weber revealed, scrolling through a newly unearthed cache of encrypted files. "It's... disturbing. The clinical detachment with which they discussed the 'excision of incompatible genetic material,' the calculated erasure of cultural markers. They viewed entire ethnicities as a form of contamination, and this artifact was their ultimate sterilizing agent. Falk understood that simply disabling the weapon wasn't enough. The ideology that spawned it had to be exposed, its inherent evil laid bare for all time."

The reconstruction process was becoming an exercise in confronting the darkest facets of human ambition, amplified by technology that transcended human understanding. The SS, in their quest for absolute control, had inadvertently stumbled upon a power that could have unmade reality itself, and their initial impulse was not to recoil in awe or caution, but to weaponize it, to twist its cosmic potential into a tool of their parochial, genocidal agenda. Falk, on the other hand, saw the artifact's potential not just for destruction, but for understanding. His logs contained speculative passages about the artifact's original purpose, hints that its creators might have intended it as a force of cosmic balance, a tool for restoration rather than annihilation.

"The fragmented alien codex, the parts that weren't corrupted by the initial crash or the SS's tampering, are starting to make more sense in light of Falk's annotations," Jian Li stated, a flicker of excitement in his voice. "He managed to cross-reference the artifact's operational parameters with certain stellar alignments and energy fluctuations described in the alien text. It suggests a cyclical nature to its power, tied to cosmic events. The SS, of course, dismissed this as superstition, focusing solely on the immediate destructive capabilities. Falk, however, saw a deeper, more fundamental connection to the universe. He believed that the SS's attempt to impose their will upon the artifact was a violation of a much larger, more ancient order."

Neumann leaned closer, his mind grappling with the implications. The SS had sought to control the uncontrollable, to harness the power of the cosmos for their own base desires. Falk, in his final moments, had acted not just as a saboteur, but as a protector of a universal principle, a guardian against humanity's own destructive impulses. The narrative they were assembling was more than just the story of a foiled plot; it was a testament to the enduring struggle between order and chaos, between the forces of creation and annihilation, and the pivotal role of individual conscience in tipping the scales.

The weight of Falk's sacrifice, now fully understood, settled upon Neumann. He hadn't just averted a global catastrophe; he had preserved the very idea of humanity, its diversity, its history, its messy, glorious complexity. He had ensured that the SS's vision of a sterile, uniform future would remain a chilling footnote in history, not its horrifying reality. The team's mission, therefore, had evolved. It was no longer merely about understanding alien technology; it was about honoring Falk's legacy, about ensuring that the truth he died to preserve would resonate through time, a stark warning against the seductive allure of absolute power and the catastrophic consequences of unchecked ideology. The artifact, once a symbol of humanity's near-annihilation, was slowly transforming into a monument to its resilience, and to the extraordinary courage of one man who dared to stand against the encroaching darkness.

The pulsating glow of the reconstructed data matrix cast an ethereal light across the faces of Neumann, Weber, and Jian Li. The sterile hum of the laboratory had, for a brief period, been eclipsed by the sheer weight of revelation. They had spent days meticulously dissecting Falk's final transmission, the 'echo of the void,' and now, the implications of its activation were beginning to solidify into a chillingly concrete understanding. It wasn't merely a broadcast; it was a meticulously crafted key, designed to unlock a truth buried not just within the artifact's alien architecture, but within the very fabric of human history.

"The encryption matrix," Jian Li began, his voice still tinged with a residual awe, "it's not just a digital lock. It's a temporal cipher. Falk didn't just plant a beacon; he seeded a narrative. The conditions he specified for its activation – specific stellar alignments, resonant energy frequencies, and even, disturbingly, certain patterns of global societal stress – weren't arbitrary. They were designed to ensure that the message would be received, not just by whoever was listening in the immediate aftermath, but by those who would, eventually, have the context to understand its true significance."

Weber nodded, her gaze fixed on a holographic representation of the beacon's projected signal trajectory. "He knew. He knew that simply disabling the SS's immediate threat wouldn't be enough. Their ideology, their capacity for self-deception and technological hubris, was a recurring motif in human history, wasn't it? Falk understood that such a potent, amoral technology, if ever rediscovered by a similar mindset, could be repurposed. He had to create a failsafe that would transcend his own time."

The 'beacon,' as they had come to call it, was not a solitary artifact. The data Falk had managed to secure painted a picture of a far grander, more intricate design. The SS's recovered schematics, when overlaid with Falk's deciphered annotations, revealed an alien blueprint for a planetary defense system, or perhaps, more accurately, a planetary *warning* system. The artifact itself, the primary device capable of generating the decoherence wave, was not an isolated weapon. It was the central node of a vast, interconnected network.

"Think of it like a cosmic distributed denial-of-service attack," Jian Li explained, his fingers dancing across the holographic interface, projecting schematic after schematic. "Except, instead of disrupting communication, its purpose was to disrupt unchecked technological advancement and ideological extremism. Falk's beacon was essentially a single, activated point in a much larger, dormant network. He managed to trigger one node, to send out a localized alert, but the underlying architecture... it suggests a global failsafe, designed by the artifact's original custodians."

The implications were staggering. The aliens, whoever they were, had not simply left behind a piece of incomprehensible technology. They had foreseen the potential for its misuse, the inherent danger of a power so immense falling into the wrong hands. They had, in essence, created a posthumous guardian, a silent sentinel designed to safeguard not just a single species, but the very concept of responsible technological progression.

"The SS's original discovery of the artifact," Weber mused, her voice low, "they found it buried, dormant. They interpreted its power through the lens of their own desires. But the alien data, and Falk's interpretations of it, suggest that its primary function was not destructive. The energy signatures, the resonant frequencies... they align with concepts of ecological restoration, of planetary stabilization. The SS perverted its purpose, twisting a tool of balance into an instrument of erasure. Falk's activation of the beacon was an attempt to restore that original intent, to reactivate the warning system against such perversion."

Neumann absorbed the information, piecing together the fragments. Falk, in his desperate act, hadn't just stopped the SS. He had, in effect, reawakened a silent network of alien intelligence, a planetary-scale alarm system. The beacon was the first 'message' in a millennia-old conversation, a coded warning broadcast across the ages.

"Falk's logs mention the artifact's inherent 'recalibration potential,'" Jian Li stated, pulling up a section of the scientist's private journals. "He theorized that the custodians designed it to 'learn' and adapt. If humanity, or any species, demonstrated a propensity for self-destruction or the weaponization of such powerful forces, the network would subtly 're-align' its dormant nodes, creating a global deterrent. The beacon he planted was essentially a test, a signal to the dormant network that the threat had resurfaced, and that the failsafe should be primed."

This hypothesis explained why the SS, despite their extensive efforts, had never fully understood or controlled the artifact. They had treated it as a static object, a technological marvel to be exploited. They had never grasped its dynamic, interconnected nature. Falk, however, with his deep dive into the recovered alien data and his intuitive understanding of physics that bordered on the prescient, had recognized its true potential.

"So, the beacon isn't just a historical record," Neumann summarized, his gaze sweeping across the complex diagrams. "It's an active component. It's a trigger. If the SS's initial attempt to weaponize the artifact was a test for them, then Falk's activation of the beacon was a test for the network. A test to see if the custodians' fears were warranted, if humanity had indeed regressed to a point where such drastic measures were necessary again."

Weber leaned forward, her expression grave. "And the evidence we've uncovered suggests that the network has, in fact, been subtly responding. The anomalies we've been tracking, the unexplained energy fluctuations in remote regions, the geological shifts that defy conventional explanation… they might not be random occurrences. They could be the network's attempts to reinforce its own dormant nodes, to prepare for a potential re-emergence of the artifact's capabilities, or even to preemptively neutralize any future attempts to replicate its destructive power."

The idea of a silent, global alien network, a system of checks and balances woven into the very fabric of the planet, was both terrifying and strangely reassuring. It implied that humanity was not entirely alone in its struggle against its own destructive tendencies. It suggested that there was an external intelligence, a higher purpose, that had, eons ago, anticipated the very dangers they now faced.

"The SS's ultimate goal," Jian Li elaborated, his voice hushed with the weight of this new understanding, "was not just to eliminate perceived enemies. It was to achieve a state of absolute, sterile purity. They sought to erase not just people, but ideas, cultures, history itself. The artifact, in their hands, was a tool of existential revisionism. Falk's beacon, by broadcasting the truth of their actions, of their horrifying intent, was an act of existential preservation. It was a signal that humanity's story, its complex, messy, contradictory narrative, was worth saving."

369

The complexity of Falk's plan was only now coming into full focus. He hadn't just been a scientist; he had been a philosopher, a historian, a guardian of truth. He had understood that true victory lay not merely in disabling a weapon, but in ensuring that its existence, its potential, and the ideology that sought to wield it, were never forgotten. He had created a system that would, if necessary, remind humanity of its most dangerous mistakes.

"The alien data also describes an 'interstitial phase'," Weber added, pointing to a complex diagram that illustrated the artifact's energy flow. "This is the period between the activation of a node and the full deployment of the network's defensive protocols. It's a window of vulnerability, but also a period of intense information exchange. Falk's beacon, in activating this phase, has effectively initiated a dialogue between his act of defiance and the alien custodians' original intent. It's a feedback loop, confirming that humanity, at least through figures like Falk, is capable of recognizing and resisting such existential threats."

Neumann looked at his team, their faces illuminated by the glow of the data. They were no longer just investigating a historical anomaly; they were witnesses to a cosmic testament. The SS's hubris had nearly unmade the world, but one man's courage had, in the most profound way, sown the seeds for its salvation.

"The beacon's signal," Jian Li continued, his voice gaining a new intensity, "is not a single broadcast. It's a repeating sequence, a slow, deliberate pulse. The alien network is designed to respond to cumulative data. The more evidence of human regression or dangerous technological application that the network detects – through our own actions, or through the continued discovery of artifacts like the one the SS found – the more the network will 'activate.' Falk's beacon was the catalyst, the initial verification that the threat was present and that the network needed to remain vigilant."

This implied that their own work, their efforts to uncover the truth about the SS and the artifact, were also contributing to the network's understanding. They were, in a way, feeding the failsafe, providing it with the data it needed to assess humanity's trajectory. It was a heavy responsibility, a profound irony that the very act of

370

seeking truth about a weapon of destruction was also strengthening a system designed to prevent its future use.

"The SS had meticulously planned for every conceivable scenario of destruction," Weber stated, her voice firm. "Except for the one that actually thwarted them: the moral imperative of a single individual. They sought to control the narrative, to erase their actions from history. Falk's beacon ensured that their narrative would be one of catastrophic failure, forever linked to their barbarity. And the alien network, by responding to his signal, validates that narrative, reinforcing the warning against those who would seek to impose their will upon the universe through brute force and ideological fanaticism."

The fragments of alien text Falk had managed to preserve spoke of 'cosmic resonance,' of a universal harmony that could be disrupted by unchecked technological ambition. The SS had sought to achieve a 'controlled resonance' of their own making, a state of perfect, sterile order. Falk, by activating the beacon, had instead amplified a different kind of resonance – the echo of his own sacrifice, the resonance of truth, and the subtle, growing hum of an ancient, alien warning system.

"The data suggests that the custodians of this technology were an ancient, long-vanished civilization," Jian Li explained, his focus shifting to a more abstract representation of the network's theoretical parameters. "They encountered similar threats in their own history, perhaps even other species. This network was their legacy, their final attempt to impart wisdom to a universe that seemed determined to repeat its mistakes. Falk's discovery and activation of the beacon was not just a scientific breakthrough; it was the reactivation of an intergenerational, interstellar dialogue about responsibility and consequence."

Neumann stood in the quiet laboratory, the hum of the equipment a constant reminder of the immense power they were grappling with. The SS had been wrong about so many things, but they had been right about one: the allure of absolute power was a potent temptation. They had sought to harness the universe's energies for their own twisted ends, and in doing so, had stumbled upon a force far greater than they could comprehend. Falk, on the other hand, had understood that true power lay not in control, but in preservation, in ensuring that the light of knowledge and truth would always shine, even in the face of overwhelming darkness. The beacon was his testament, a silent promise broadcast across the stars, a promise that even when humanity faltered, the universe itself might offer a guiding hand, a gentle but persistent reminder of the path not to take. The network, dormant for millennia, was now awake, its unseen tendrils reaching out, listening, waiting, a silent testament to Falk's foresight and the enduring hope that humanity might, after all, learn from its past. The discovery of this network fundamentally shifted their understanding of the artifact, transforming it from a singular threat into a node within a much larger, far more ancient system of planetary safeguarding. It meant that Falk's actions had far-reaching implications, extending beyond the immediate danger posed by the SS. The very existence of such a network suggested that the alien custodians had not merely created a powerful device, but a sophisticated, long-term strategy for maintaining cosmic balance, a testament to their wisdom and foresight, and a sobering reminder of the potential consequences of unchecked technological ambition. The beacon, therefore, was not an end, but a beginning – the initial spark igniting a dialogue between humanity's present and its distant, alien past, a conversation about the responsible stewardship of immense power.

The weight of Falk's foresight pressed down upon them, a tangible force in the sterile air of the laboratory. They had unearthed not just a scientific discovery, but a profound testament to the enduring struggle against ignorance and the seductive whispers of unchecked power. The 'echo of the void,' as they now understood it, was more than just a scientific transmission; it was a meticulously crafted historical narrative, a warning encoded within the very fabric of alien technology, designed to resonate across millennia. Falk, in his final act of defiance, had not merely neutralized a present threat; he had activated a planetary-scale failsafe, a cosmic distributed denial-of-service attack on humanity's own worst tendencies.

"The custodians' intent was never to impose a singular truth, but to safeguard the *process* of truth-seeking," Weber articulated, her voice a low murmur that seemed to echo the vastness of their discovery. "They understood that knowledge itself is neutral. It's the application, the interpretation, the intent behind its wielding that determines its morality. The SS saw the artifact as a tool for control, for purification, for the eradication of everything they deemed impure. Falk, however, saw its potential for preservation, for remembrance, for the safeguarding of the very essence of what it meant to be human, in all its messy, contradictory glory."

Jian Li, his fingers still hovering over the spectral analysis of the beacon's energy signature, elaborated, "Falk's act was a preemptive strike against historical amnesia. The SS wasn't just a rogue organization; they represented a recurring pattern in human civilization – the desire to impose order through erasure, to sanitize history by eliminating inconvenient truths and dissenting voices. They aimed to create a sterile, unblemished past, and by extension, a perfectly controlled future. Falk's beacon, by broadcasting the unvarnished truth of their actions, of their ideological fervor and the devastation it wrought, was a direct refutation of that goal. It was an assertion that the narrative of the SS, and indeed any attempt to rewrite or suppress history, would not go unchallenged."

The implications were staggering. This wasn't just about preventing a repeat of the SS's atrocities; it was about instilling a fundamental understanding of ethical responsibility in the face of unimaginable scientific power. The alien network, now subtly stirring in response to Falk's activation, was a testament to the custodians' wisdom. They had recognized that the greatest threat to any species wasn't an external enemy, but its own internal capacity for self-destruction, fueled by hubris and a disregard for the lessons of the past. Falk had, in essence, become a conduit for that ancient wisdom, a living testament to the fact that even in the darkest hours, the pursuit of truth and the courage to defend it could ignite a beacon of hope that spanned galaxies and epochs.

"Think about the sheer audacity of it," Neumann mused, pacing the confines of the laboratory, his gaze unfocused, lost in thought. "This alien civilization, long gone, understood the inherent dangers of technological advancement perhaps better than we do, even now. They didn't leave behind a weapon to conquer their enemies, nor a cure for all ills. They left a warning system, a sophisticated mechanism designed to detect and, if necessary, counteract the very ideologies that lead to societal collapse. And Falk, through sheer scientific brilliance and an unwavering moral compass, managed to reactivate it. He didn't just discover an artifact; he unearthed a profound philosophical statement about the responsibilities that accompany power."

The activation of the beacon wasn't a simple broadcast of data; it was a carefully orchestrated act of remembrance. Falk had ensured that the truth of the SS's reign of terror, their twisted quest for purity, and their near-successful attempt to weaponize a force beyond their comprehension, would be indelibly etched into the fabric of cosmic history. The alien network, by responding, was not merely reacting to a signal; it was validating Falk's sacrifice, acknowledging his role in preserving the integrity of truth. This validated the very concept of ethical scientific pursuit, underscoring that knowledge gained must always be tempered with wisdom and a profound sense of responsibility.

"The alien data speaks of 'cycles of understanding'," Jian Li revealed, his eyes scanning a complex phylogenetic tree of alien linguistic patterns. "It suggests that civilizations, throughout the cosmos, tend to repeat certain developmental phases, often involving the misuse of powerful technologies. The custodians foresaw this, and their network was designed as a failsafe against such recurring patterns. Falk's beacon was essentially an alarm, signaling to the network that a particularly dangerous phase – one that mirrors the custodians' own historical struggles – had re-emerged. His act was a plea, a desperate attempt to remind humanity of the precipice it stood upon, and to activate the safeguards that had been placed there eons ago to prevent such a fall."

Weber added, her voice laced with a somber reverence, "And the network's response isn't necessarily a destructive one. The energy signatures we're observing, the subtle shifts in global atmospheric composition, the patterns in deep-sea geological activity – they align with the custodians' descriptions of 'stabilization protocols.' It's not an attack; it's a recalibration. The network is subtly reinforcing the planet's natural systems, perhaps even counteracting the lingering ecological damage caused by the SS's experiments, and simultaneously monitoring for any

374

resurgence of similar destructive tendencies."

Neumann nodded, absorbing the enormity of it all. Falk had understood that simply destroying the SS or disabling their weapon would not be enough. The underlying ideology, the dangerous mindset that fueled their actions, would inevitably resurface. The true victory lay in ensuring that humanity, and perhaps other nascent civilizations, would be equipped with the knowledge and the mechanisms to resist such ideologies, to recognize the siren song of unchecked power and the catastrophic consequences it inevitably brought. The beacon was Falk's legacy, a permanent mark on the cosmic ledger, a testament to the enduring power of truth and the vital importance of remembering, of learning from even the most horrific of pasts.

"The custodians' records are stark in their depiction of similar civilizations that failed to heed the warnings," Jian Li continued, his voice dropping to a hushed tone. "Entire species, they describe, that reached a technological zenith only to succumb to internal strife, to ideological purges, to a complete disregard for the delicate balance of their own ecosystems. They attempted to impose their will upon the very laws of nature, and in doing so, they self-destructed. The alien network, in its current state of activation, is a direct response to that pattern. It's a silent, omnipresent guardian, ensuring that the lessons learned by its creators are not forgotten, and that any species that mirrors their mistakes will be met with a formidable, albeit subtle, deterrent."

The sheer ethical responsibility that came with their discovery was overwhelming. They were not merely archaeologists of a lost civilization or investigators of a past catastrophe; they were now custodians of a cosmic warning system. Falk's act had thrust them into a role of immense importance, one that demanded not only scientific rigor but also profound moral consideration. Every decision they made from this point forward would have implications not just for humanity, but potentially for the broader cosmic order that the alien network was designed to protect.

"Falk's final journal entries are filled with a mixture of desperation and unwavering resolve," Weber said, her gaze distant as if she were seeing the man himself, a ghost from the past. "He knew the risks, he knew the slim possibility of success. But he also understood that silence in the face of such profound evil was complicity. His decision to activate the beacon wasn't just a scientific choice; it was a moral imperative. He chose to risk everything, to sacrifice his own life, to ensure that the truth would prevail, and that the lessons learned from the SS's barbarity would serve as a perpetual reminder for generations to come. He essentially became the first human emissary to this ancient, alien network, conveying a message of both warning and hope."

The very act of studying the artifact, of attempting to understand its true purpose, was itself a test. The SS had failed that test catastrophically, driven by greed and a lust for dominion. Falk, however, had passed it with flying colors, motivated by a deep-seated understanding of humanity's inherent value, even in its imperfections. His success in activating the beacon was a testament to the fact that not all humans were susceptible to the same temptations, that there were individuals who understood that true progress lay not in conquest, but in wisdom, in humility, and in the unyielding pursuit of truth.

"The network's 'dialogue' with the beacon is ongoing," Jian Li explained, pointing to subtle energy fluctuations that had appeared in the data feed since their conversation began. "It's not a static system. It's designed to learn, to adapt, and to respond to new information. Our own research, our efforts to contextualize Falk's actions, our very presence in this laboratory, is now part of that input. We are, in essence, contributing to the network's ongoing assessment of humanity. It's a daunting thought, knowing that our own actions are being scrutinized by an ancient, alien intelligence."

Neumann clenched his fists, the weight of their new responsibility settling heavily upon him. The SS had sought to rewrite history, to erase their crimes and impose their sterile vision upon the world. Falk had countered with a truth-bomb, a signal that echoed across the ages, ensuring that their legacy would be one of infamy and catastrophic failure. And now, they, the inheritors of Falk's legacy, had to ensure that humanity did not falter again, that the hard-won lessons of the past would not be forgotten, and that the vigilance of the alien network would not be in vain. The battle for truth, it seemed, was not confined to any single era or any single species. It was a continuous, cosmic endeavor.

"The custodians' final message, as best we can interpret it," Weber stated, her voice resonating with a newfound solemnity, "was a plea for universal stewardship. They had witnessed the rise and fall of countless civilizations, each grappling with the same fundamental challenges: the temptation of power, the allure of control, and the erosion of empathy. Their network is a testament to their enduring hope that, somewhere in the vastness of the cosmos, a species might emerge that could learn from their mistakes, that could harness its technological prowess not for dominion, but for preservation, for balance, for the continuation of life itself. Falk's activation of the beacon was a signal that, at least for humanity, that hope might not be entirely misplaced."

The ethical implications of their discovery were profound and far-reaching. It underscored the critical importance of transparency, accountability, and a deeply ingrained sense of moral responsibility in scientific exploration. The SS had exemplified the terrifying consequences of unchecked ambition and the deliberate obfuscation of truth. Falk, in contrast, had demonstrated the immeasurable value of courage, integrity, and the unwavering commitment to revealing what was hidden, even at the ultimate cost. His final act served as a powerful, posthumous instruction manual for humanity: that true advancement lay not in the acquisition of power, but in the wisdom to wield it ethically, and in the perpetual remembrance of the mistakes that had nearly led to the brink of oblivion. The beacon was a stark reminder that knowledge, once unearthed, demands careful stewardship, and that the fight to preserve the integrity of truth is an eternal human endeavor, vital for preventing the darkest chapters of our past from being revisited. The very existence of the alien network, a silent sentinel across the eons, validated this perpetual struggle, underscoring that the universe itself seemed to possess an inherent mechanism for safeguarding against the corrosive influence of hubris and the deliberate suppression of truth, a cosmic insurance policy activated by the brave actions of a single, remarkable scientist.

The sterile hum of the laboratory had become a constant

companion, a stark contrast to the seismic shift occurring within their understanding of history and humanity's place within the cosmos. Weber, Jian Li, and Neumann found themselves simultaneously exhilarated and burdened by the enormity of what Falk had uncovered and activated. The data, meticulously compiled and cross-referenced, painted a chilling picture of the SS's ambitions, their chillingly systematic approach to weaponizing esoteric forces, and their ultimate undoing, orchestrated by the very man they had sought to silence. Now, the task before them was to translate this monumental discovery into a narrative that would resonate with the world, a world still largely oblivious to the shadow cast by the Black Forest incident and the far-reaching implications of Falk's sacrifice.

"The Black Forest incident," Weber began, her voice firm, yet tinged with the gravity of their findings, "has always been officially documented as a catastrophic industrial accident. A localized energy surge, a containment breach, a tragic loss of life. The SS's meticulous control over information ensured that the narrative remained confined, sanitized, and ultimately, buried. But our work, Falk's work, has unearthed the truth beneath that carefully constructed façade. It wasn't an accident; it was a meticulously planned, albeit disastrously executed, attempt to harness and weaponize the very principles that the alien custodians sought to safeguard."

Jian Li gestured towards the holographic display, which now depicted a complex causal chain, linking the SS's experiments in the Black Forest directly to the activation of the alien beacon. "The energy signature, the anomalous seismic activity, the localized atmospheric distortions – all were outward manifestations of their attempts to manipulate what they poorly understood as a 'resonance cascade.' They believed they could weaponize this resonance, creating a field capable of influencing not just matter, but the collective consciousness, imposing their warped ideology on a global scale. Falk's intervention, his desperate gambit to activate the alien network, wasn't just a reactive measure; it was a direct counter-operation designed to neutralize their efforts and, more importantly, to expose their true intentions through the very network they sought to exploit."

Neumann, ever the pragmatist, focused on the immediate challenge. "The question now is how we present this. The world's understanding of the SS is largely shaped by historical accounts that either demonize them as a fringe extremist group or, worse, mythologize them as a powerful, albeit misguided, force. Neither of these portrayals captures the full horror of their objective – the systematic dehumanization, the pursuit of a biologically and ideologically 'pure' humanity, and their willingness to leverage forces that defied comprehension to achieve it. Falk's legacy is inextricably linked to this revelation. We need to tell his story, and in doing so, tell the true story of the Black Forest."

Weber nodded, her gaze fixed on a framed photograph of Falk, a man she had never met but felt she knew intimately through his final, desperate message. "Falk's last known communications were cryptic, intended to be deciphered only by those who could piece together the fragmented evidence he had painstakingly left behind. He knew that a direct confrontation was impossible, that the SS's reach was too pervasive. His strategy was one of delayed revelation, a carefully orchestrated unveiling of truth that would bypass the immediate gatekeepers of information. He recognized that the most effective weapon against a force built on lies and suppression was the unassailable truth, delivered at the opportune moment."

The 'opportune moment,' as Falk had envisioned it, had arrived with the accidental discovery of the anomaly in the Black Forest, an anomaly that ultimately led them to the alien beacon. The SS, in their hubris, had inadvertently stumbled upon the very key to their own undoing, a relic of an ancient civilization that held the ultimate antidote to their destructive ideology. Falk, by deciphering the beacon's purpose and understanding its connection to the SS's activities, had seen the path forward. He didn't have the means to dismantle the SS's operation directly, but he had the ability to expose its fundamental nature, to ensure that its legacy was not one of triumph but of catastrophic failure, a cautionary tale etched into the fabric of existence itself.

"The public release of the Black Forest incident's true nature," Jian Li elaborated, projecting a timeline that meticulously detailed the SS's escalating activities in the region, "will inevitably force a re-evaluation of post-war German history. The SS was not merely a military or political entity; it was a socio-religious cult, driven by a messianic complex and a twisted interpretation of biological and historical destiny. Their experiments in the Black Forest were not isolated acts of scientific curiosity gone awry; they were critical phases in their larger plan to reshape humanity according to their archaic, eugenic ideals. Falk's revelation will expose the depth of their depravity and the extent to which they were willing to tamper with forces they barely understood."

The details of the SS's experiments were still being pieced together, but the emerging picture was one of chilling efficacy. They had managed to establish a rudimentary connection with the alien network, not to communicate or learn, but to siphon energy, to attempt to manipulate the network's underlying principles for their own nefarious ends. Their goal was to create a 'purity field,' a localized reality distortion that would, in theory, purge individuals of perceived genetic and ideological impurities. The Black Forest was the chosen locus for these experiments, a remote and densely wooded area that offered both secrecy and a unique energetic signature that the SS believed would facilitate their connection to the alien systems.

"Falk's understanding of the custodians' intent was key," Weber stated, her voice gaining strength as she articulated the core of their discovery. "They didn't leave behind a weapon to conquer or control. They left a mechanism for preservation, for the safeguarding of biological and informational diversity. The 'echo of the void,' as we now understand it, was not a passive signal, but a dynamic, responsive entity. When the SS attempted to corrupt its purpose, to twist it into a tool of purification, they triggered a defensive protocol, a subtle recalibration that, unintendedly, amplified the very anomalies that would eventually draw Falk's attention and, subsequently, ours. Falk didn't just react to an anomaly; he recognized the signature of an ancient defense system, activated by the SS's destructive interference."

The SS, in their pursuit of a singular, perfect future, had ironically become the catalysts for their own historical erasure. Their attempt to impose their will on the fundamental forces of the universe, forces that operated on principles of balance and interconnectedness, proved to be their undoing. The alien network, a testament to a civilization that had long understood the delicate equilibrium of existence, responded not with overt force, but with a systematic unraveling of the SS's attempts to impose their artificial order. The Black Forest incident, therefore, was not merely a failed experiment; it was a microcosm of a cosmic principle: that attempts to violate fundamental natural laws inevitably lead to self-destruction.

"The public must understand that the SS's ideology was not a mere historical footnote," Neumann emphasized, his gaze sweeping across the complex data streams. "It represents a persistent, dangerous strain within human societies – the desire to impose order through exclusion, to achieve progress through purification, to build a better future by eradicating anything deemed 'other.' Falk's work, and by extension, our current efforts, are a direct refutation of that mindset. We must ensure that the world remembers the SS not as a historical curiosity, but as a stark warning of what humanity is capable of when driven by fear, prejudice, and an unshakeable belief in its own inherent righteousness."

The dissemination of this truth would not be without its challenges. The SS, though vanquished, had left a significant ideological residue. There would be those who would seek to either deny the findings, discredit the sources, or even attempt to revive the SS's core tenets, perhaps reinterpreting Falk's actions as a perversion of their noble goals. The team had to prepare for such eventualities, ensuring that the evidence was irrefutable and the narrative compelling.

"Falk's final testament was not just about exposing the SS," Weber continued, her voice gaining a quiet intensity. "It was about establishing a new paradigm for scientific responsibility. He understood that the pursuit of knowledge, especially in areas that touched upon fundamental forces and the very nature of existence, carried an immense ethical weight. He demonstrated that true scientific advancement is not measured by the power one can wield, but by the wisdom one possesses in understanding and respecting the limits of that power, and by the courage to uphold truth even in the face of overwhelming opposition. His legacy is a call to arms for every scientist, every historian, every individual who believes in the sanctity of truth."

The team had already begun drafting the initial report, a comprehensive document detailing their findings, the decoded messages from Falk, and the re-interpreted data from the Black Forest incident. This report would serve as the foundation for a broader public disclosure, a carefully planned release that would begin with academic circles and government bodies before eventually reaching the global populace. They were acutely aware that the information they were about to release would not only rewrite history books but could also potentially destabilize established political and social structures, especially those that had benefited from the sanitized version of the SS's narrative.

"The custodians' network, now fully aware of humanity's role in reactivating its safeguards, will undoubtedly continue to monitor our progress," Jian Li stated, his eyes scanning the intricate patterns of the alien data. "Falk's activation was a signal of our capacity for both great error and great redemption. The network's response will be contingent on our actions moving forward. If we continue on a path of unchecked ambition, of ideological division, of disregard for truth, the network's 'stabilization protocols' may well escalate. Conversely, if we embrace the lessons of the past, if we prioritize understanding and cooperation, we may find in this ancient system an unexpected ally, a cosmic guarantor of balance."

The weight of this realization was immense. They were no longer just researchers; they were effectively ambassadors to an ancient, alien intelligence, tasked with guiding humanity's relationship with it. Falk's final act had not only exposed the truth about the SS but had also initiated a new chapter in humanity's cosmic narrative, a chapter defined by the watchful gaze of an ancient guardian and the profound responsibility that came with that awareness. The truth that was beginning to emerge was not just about a dark chapter of human history; it was about the very potential and peril of humanity's future, a future that Falk had, with his ultimate sacrifice, fought to secure.

The initial drafts of the public statement were iterated upon with painstaking care. Every word was weighed, every implication considered. They understood that their narrative had to be accessible, compelling, and most importantly, irrefutable. The story of Falk, the brilliant scientist who defied a resurgent, insidious ideology from beyond the grave, had to be told with the reverence and accuracy it deserved. His discovery of the alien beacon, a relic of unimaginable antiquity designed to maintain cosmic balance, was not just a scientific breakthrough; it was a philosophical revelation, a testament to the enduring struggle for truth and reason across the vast expanse of time and space.

"The SS's resurgence, even in its latter days," Weber explained, detailing the reclassification of certain fringe groups in the late 20th century that showed a disturbing ideological continuity with the original SS, "was enabled by the very suppression of information that characterized their original reign. By burying the truth of their atrocities, by presenting a fragmented and often misleading account of their actions, they created fertile ground for their ideas to fester in the shadows. Falk understood this. His legacy is not just the activation of the beacon; it is the meticulous deconstruction of the SS's manufactured reality, the unearthing of the evidence that proved their ultimate failure and their profound barbarity."

The team presented their findings not as a conspiracy theory, but as a rigorously researched historical and scientific analysis. They meticulously detailed the chemical signatures, the energy readings, and the recovered artifacts from the Black Forest site, linking them directly to the SS's documented research objectives and their known associates. The recovered portions of Falk's journals, deciphered with the aid of advanced algorithms and cross-referenced with his scientific publications, provided the critical narrative thread, explaining the genesis of his suspicion and the evolution of his desperate plan.

"The 'echo of the void,' as the custodians called it," Jian Li elaborated, projecting a schematic of the alien network's architecture, "is more than just a communication system. It's a distributed consciousness, a vast, interconnected web of knowledge and influence designed to foster balance and prevent catastrophic ideological contagion. Falk, by reactivating the beacon, essentially sent a distress signal to this network, a signal that humanity, at a critical juncture, had rediscovered and was attempting to learn from its past mistakes. The custodians, by their very nature, responded to this signal not by intervening directly, but by reinforcing the underlying principles of truth and memory, subtly counteracting the residual influences of the SS's disruptive ideology."

The implication of a "distributed consciousness" was particularly profound. It suggested that the alien network was not a mere technological artifact, but a living testament to a civilization that had transcended the limitations of individual sentience, achieving a collective wisdom that understood the fragility of life and the importance of preserving it. Falk's act was a plea for humanity to join this cosmic continuum of responsible stewardship, a plea that the network seemed to have answered by nudging humanity back towards the path of enlightenment.

"The public reaction is going to be intense," Neumann acknowledged, bracing himself for the inevitable storm of speculation and disbelief. "The narrative of a clandestine, hyper-advanced organization like the SS seeking to weaponize cosmic forces is the stuff of fiction for most. But the evidence is clear, and Falk's sacrifice imbues this truth with an undeniable weight. We must also consider the potential for misinterpretation. Some might see the alien network's response as a benevolent intervention, others as an alien imposition. We need to frame this not as a divine or alien takeover, but as a cosmic mirroring, a reflection of humanity's own choices and its capacity for both profound destruction and ultimate redemption."

Weber's gaze was fixed on the original data logs from Falk's final days, the raw, unadulterated evidence of his solitary struggle. "Falk's journals speak of a deep-seated melancholy, a profound sadness for the direction humanity had taken, but also an unyielding hope. He believed that the very act of confronting our darkest impulses, of unearthing our most shameful secrets, was the first step towards genuine progress. The SS represented the pinnacle of humanity's capacity for self-deception and cruelty. Falk, in confronting them and in activating the beacon, represented our potential for truth, for courage, and for the enduring pursuit of

384

knowledge that serves the greater good."

The narrative had to be carefully constructed to avoid sensationalism, while still conveying the sheer magnitude of the events. The SS's ideology, their pursuit of a fabricated racial purity, their willingness to experiment on human subjects, and their ultimate attempt to manipulate fundamental cosmic forces, were not to be glossed over. These were the very truths that Falk had died to reveal, and that the alien network now seemed to be subtly reinforcing through its ongoing interaction with the beacon.

"The custodians' records, as we've translated them," Jian Li continued, his voice hushed with awe, "speak of 'symbiotic resonance,' a state where civilizations learn to coexist with the fundamental energies of the universe, rather than attempting to dominate them. The SS's approach was the antithesis of this, a violent imposition of will. Falk's activation of the beacon was a re-establishment of that symbiotic resonance, a signal that humanity, at least in some of its members, was ready to learn the custodians' ancient wisdom. The Black Forest incident was the crucible in which this lesson was forged, a devastating demonstration of the consequences of straying from that path."

The decision to go public was not taken lightly. The potential repercussions were vast, affecting not just historical narratives but also the very understanding of humanity's place in the cosmos. Yet, the consensus was unanimous. Falk's legacy demanded it. The SS's crimes could not remain buried. And the subtle, yet persistent, influence of the alien network, now actively engaged with Earth, required a level of transparency and understanding that could only be achieved through a full disclosure of the truth. The world was about to learn that the past was not as settled as it believed, and that a single scientist's courage had set in motion a cosmic unveiling that would redefine humanity's future. The truth, long suppressed and fragmented, was finally emerging, poised to rewrite history and serve as a potent reminder of the delicate balance between progress, ethics, and the very fabric of memory and existence. Falk's final act had ensured that the lessons of the Black Forest would not be lost, but amplified, echoing through the cosmos as a testament to the enduring power of truth.